ONE
TEXAS COWBOY
TOO MANY

CAROLYN
BROWN

sourcebooks
casablanca

Published by Sourcebooks Casablanca, an imprint of Sourcebooks, Inc.
P.O. Box 4410, Naperville, Illinois 60567-4410
(630) 961-3900
Fax: (630) 961-2168
www.sourcebooks.com

Printed and bound in Canada.
MBP 10 9 8 7 6 5 4 3 2 1

Chapter 1

THE RUMBLING NOISE OF A MOTORCYCLE TOOK LEAH Brennan's attention away from the produce in the Burnt Boot General Store. She pushed her cart up a few feet so she could see out the front window, expecting to see leather, chains, and shiny, black biker's helmets on maybe half a dozen cycles after all that noise. It had sounded like part of the Hell's Angels gang had come to town, so she was surprised when only one person removed his helmet and hung it on steer horns mounted on the front of the cycle. And she was even more surprised when a cowboy dismounted instead of a biker.

It was impolite to stare, but Leah couldn't tear her eyes away from the newcomer, especially when Sawyer O'Donnell shot out from behind the checkout counter and rushed outside. Horses and four-wheelers on the streets of the little town weren't unusual, but motorcycles were an altogether different matter, especially a big, tricked-out Harley with enough chrome on it to blind the angels. He met Sawyer in one of those fierce man hugs that involve a lot of slapping on the back and laughter.

She moved to a different vantage point so she could get a better look at the cowboy. His wavy, dark hair was wet with sweat and hung in ringlets to his shirt collar. He fetched a rubber band from the pocket of his tight jeans and whipped it back into a short, little ponytail. Green eyes sparkled beneath heavy brows, and a little soul patch of dark hair rested beneath lips that stretched out in a wide smile. A green-and-yellow plaid shirt hung open to reveal a damp, white T-shirt clinging to a perfect six-pack. He removed the overshirt and slung it over his shoulder, revealing a tat of longhorns on his right arm.

Her breath caught in her chest, and she forgot to exhale for several seconds. Her biggest fantasy, other than someday marrying Tanner Gallagher, was to ride on a cycle, holding on to a cowboy like the one talking to Sawyer O'Donnell. Neither one would ever happen, but it didn't hurt to dream.

They wasted no time getting out of the hot July sun and into the cool store, and Sawyer motioned to her as soon as he shut the door. "Hey, Leah, come on up here and meet my cousin Rhett O'Donnell. He's going to live on Fiddle Creek and help us out. We wanted him to join us last spring, but he had to fulfill another contract. But he's here now and believe me, we can sure use him. Rhett, this is Leah Brennan."

She pushed her cart to the checkout counter.

"Right pleased to meet you, ma'am." Rhett smiled and held out a hand.

She put her hand in his and his deep-green eyes bored into hers. She felt as if he could see all the visions in her head and hear her unspoken thoughts. Two spots of high color filled her cheeks and hot little vibes danced around the room. She quickly pulled her hand away from his and latched tightly on to the cart handle.

She could almost hear the gossip flying about Rhett O'Donnell and his tricked-out motorcycle, but that cowboy was way, way too wild and exciting for Leah

Brennan. She bit back a sigh as she said, "Welcome to Burnt Boot."

"Leah is a teacher over at the school on River Bend Ranch," Sawyer said.

"None of my teachers were ever so pretty," Rhett drawled.

Sawyer chuckled. "No, they weren't."

"Thank you." Leah smiled. "If you'll charge these things to River Bend, Sawyer, I'd appreciate it."

"Yes, ma'am," Sawyer said.

It was easy to see that Sawyer and Rhett were cousins. They had the same angles in their faces, and they were the same height. Sawyer's skin was the color of coffee with lots of pure cream and his eyes were brown, giving testimony that he had some Latino in his background. But while Rhett's skin was as brown, it looked more like a deep tan from working out in the sun all summer.

Rhett's green eyes were rimmed with dark eyelashes so thick that most women would commit homicide to have them. He'd better be able to run fast in those cowboy boots, because the women in Burnt Boot were probably already getting their jogging shoes out and cleaned up. A picture of her old, well-worn pink shoes with a white swoosh on the side came to mind. They were sitting beside the nightstand in her room. She'd worn them last Sunday when she went to the river to do some fishing.

Get ahold of yourself, Leah Brennan. Good God, girl! She scolded herself. *You don't get all woozy just lookin' at a new cowboy in town.*

She stole glances at that soul patch and the lip above it. What would it be like to kiss those lips? Or to wrap her arms around that broad chest with her breasts pressed against his back as she rode on the back of that cycle?

"That's an interesting motorcycle. Did you ride from very far away?" Her voice sounded a bit hollow in her own ears, but his eyes were locked on hers again and it flat-out made her antsy.

"I personalized it." He smiled. "I had a good long ride up across the state from down near Comfort, Texas. My sister and her husband are almost here too. They're bringing my truck and all my belongings with them, including Dammit. That would be my dog, not a cuss-word. Do you ride?"

Leah shook her head. "No, never have ridden on one. Is that really your dog's name?"

Rhett's head bobbed up and down. "It really is his name. Did you ever wonder what it would be like to have the wind blowing past you at seventy or more miles per hour?"

Could he read her mind? Surely he couldn't read minds. Holy Mother of God, what if he did and he knew what she was thinking when she looked at his lips?

"What makes you think that I ever even thought about riding?" she asked.

"The way you look at the cycle."

"Well, it's pretty unusual with those horns attached to the front."

"Just lettin' folks know that a cowboy rides that bike." He chuckled.

Sawyer finished sacking her groceries and shoved a ticket across the counter for her to sign. "There's a story about those horns, but he has to know you real well to tell you."

She initialed the receipt and asked, "Would it be the same story as the one about the tat on his arm?"

One of Rhett's eyelids slid shut in a slow, sexy wink. "It sure is, but it's not a first-date story. It could be a third-date story."

She was intrigued by the story, but she'd never see a third date with Rhett O'Donnell, because in order to get to that point, she'd have to have a first and second date. That would never happen no matter how many times he winked at her or how badly she wanted to ride the cycle or hear the story. Her grandmother hated motorcycles, and no one bucked up against Mavis Brennan.

Leah quickly changed the subject. "Dammit? Why would you give a dog such a name? Or is that a third-date story too?"

"No, it's only a dog story." Rhett smiled and the temperature in the store shot up several degrees. "I named him Lambert after Miranda Lambert, but I guess he didn't like bein' named after a girl, so he sat there like a knot on a log every time I called him. So I'd say, 'Dammit, come here.' And here he'd come runnin' hell-bent for leather. So I gave up and called him Dammit."

Leah reached to pick up two of the paper bags of groceries. "Smart dog. With a name like that, he sounds so mean that I bet all the other dogs leave him alone."

"You are so right. Here, let me carry those out to your truck for you." Rhett grabbed the two bags she had, and his fingertips brushed against her bare forearm. "They're way too heavy for a cute little woman like you."

Sawyer picked up the third bag. "What makes you think she drives a truck? Maybe she's in a van or a car."

"Leah is a truck kind of lady, and besides, there's only one other vehicle in the lot besides your truck, Sawyer." Rhett managed to open the door and stand to one side. "In the backseat or in the truck bed, ma'am?"

She had always imagined that Tanner's touch would set her hormones to spinning like Rhett's had just done. But she'd sure never thought a comment about what she drove would create a picture in her mind of making out in the backseat—or the bed—of her truck. Holy hell! Rhett had opened Pandora's box and Leah had no idea how to handle it.

"Backseat is fine, and thank you," she mumbled.

"Anytime. I understand there will be days I'll be helping out in the store and at the bar, so maybe I'll see you in one or either place this summer," he said.

She nodded. "Burnt Boot is a small town. I'm sure our paths will cross."

Rhett held the truck door open for her until she was settled into the driver's seat, and then he slammed it shut. She started the engine but sat there for a few minutes watching them go back inside the store. She took one more long, envious look at that motorcycle before she pulled out onto the road and headed toward River Bend Ranch. The air conditioner shot semi-cold air right into her face. It would cool down more as she drove down the paved road to the dirt one that turned in to the River Bend Ranch properties, but it wouldn't do a thing for the heat inside her body.

She slapped the steering wheel and inhaled deeply once she was out on the road. If she'd been a swearing woman, she would have turned loose every bad word in the dictionary. But Leah Brennan knew how to control her tongue and her thoughts. At least, she had until right at that moment.

"Dammit!" she said so loud that it bounced around in the truck and shot right back into her ears. "Damn cowboy has got me cussin' and I don't use that kind of language."

―――

"She's one of the Brennans. I told you about the feud," Sawyer said.

"Yep." Rhett nodded. "But I expected old people with shotguns and chaws of tobacco in their mouths, not knock-your-socks-off drop-dead-gorgeous women."

"Speakin' of which." Sawyer pointed.

"What?"

"More Brennans." Sawyer nodded toward another truck pulling up in front of the store. "I can give you directions to the bunkhouse if you want to get on down there. Jill is waiting on y'all. She's making one of her famous desserts."

"Hell no!" Rhett grinned. "I'm not going anywhere. Store closes in fifteen minutes and you can lead the way to the bunkhouse."

"And, besides, you do like to meet the pretty women, right?"

A burst of hot air followed two women into the general store. A tall, willowy blond with brown eyes stopped in her tracks not four feet from Rhett and slowly looked him up and down.

"You don't look like a biker," she said.

"Rhett, meet Kinsey and Honey Brennan," Sawyer said, introducing them.

"Pleased to meet you both," Rhett said. "Sisters?"

Honey, the dark-haired one with crystal-clear blue eyes shook her head. "Cousins."

"Kin to Leah, then?" Rhett asked.

Kinsey took a step forward, and he got a whiff of expensive perfume. With those velvety eyes, high cheekbones, and full lips that didn't ask but demanded a man to kiss her, she might have been considered down-right sexy in some men's eyes. Not Rhett's. He'd seen her kind at rodeos—their eyes always scanning for a cowboy looking for a good time.

"So you've met Leah?" Kinsey asked in a low, husky voice.

"There's lots of us Brennans over on River Bend." Honey smiled. "Would you like to come to Sunday dinner and meet all of us?"

Her dark hair floated down to her shoulders in big waves that begged a man to run his fingers through it. Eyes the color of a Texas summer sun floated behind black lashes and perfectly arched eyebrows. She wore a cute little sundress that hugged her curves, but both women made Rhett feel like they were studying a prize bull at an auction. In another place, like a rodeo, where they'd fit right in with the buckle bunnies, he might have been interested, but not in Burnt Boot.

"Well?" Honey asked.

"Not this week," Rhett said. "But thanks for the invitation."

Sawyer pointed at the clock above the register. "Ten minutes and we'll have to close, ladies. Y'all might want to get what you need so we can ring it up."

Kinsey ignored him and looked at Rhett. "Are you here for a visit? We heard that you were coming to help

Gladys and Sawyer, but no one could tell us how long you're staying."

Rhett propped a hip on the checkout counter. "I'm here for good or until Sawyer kicks me off Fiddle Creek."

Sawyer fixed his stare on the clock.

Honey's eyes kept running up and down Rhett's body from boots to ponytail. "It's hot enough to make a woman want to go skinny-dippin' in the Red River. You want to join me to cool off?"

Kinsey laid two candy bars and a couple cans of soda pop on the counter. "Don't give us the old stink eye, Sawyer. I know it's closing time and we won't be but a minute. We came in for an afternoon treat. Charge these to River Bend." Kinsey winked at Rhett. "FYI, darlin', River Bend is the Brennan ranch. I'll see you tonight, cowboy. You could be nice and save me a dance."

"I'll be the one behind the bar drawin' beer and makin' margaritas. Don't reckon I'll have time for dancin'," he said.

"I'll be the one wantin' a pitcher of those margaritas," Honey said. "If you asked real nice, I might let you take me home on that cycle out there, Rhett O'Donnell."

"How do you know that's my cycle?" he asked.

A throaty chuckle caused Rhett to shift his attention from Honey to Kinsey. Kinsey had a hand on a hip, a pose that should have made him drool and follow her around like a little hound dog puppy. "Everybody in town knew you were arriving today. But we didn't know you'd be so delicious. I've never ridden on a cycle with horns on the handlebar. It's a nice cowboy touch."

"I'll be driving my truck tonight, and I'll be going home all by myself when the bar closes," Rhett drawled.

"Oh, Kinsey, he's going to play hard to get. I do like a good chase," Honey said.

Kinsey slung a hip against her cousin. "I'll bet you a hundred dollars I can outrun you and get a ride on that cycle first."

"I'm standing right here, and I'll bet you both a hundred dollars that neither of you are going to ride on my cycle," Rhett said.

Honey reached up and touched the soul patch. "I do like a little facial hair, and that is so sexy. The Sadie Hawkins Festival is only two weeks away. If you're going to outrun me, darlin', you'd best start walkin' outside in your bare feet."

"Why would I do that?" Rhett asked.

"Because you'll want to toughen up those feet so that you can run faster through the grass and stickers when we are chasin' you...unless of course, you want to just sit down and let me catch you in the first two minutes of the race."

"And do the ladies run barefoot too?" he asked.

"Oh, yes," Kinsey said. "And we're already getting our feet ready for the race."

Kinsey picked up the brown paper bag with the soda pop and candy bars and motioned for Honey to follow her. They almost made it to the door when it opened wide and a redheaded woman with emerald-green eyes was right in front of them. Kinsey's nose curled and Honey rolled her eyes at the sight of the lady coming into the store.

Betsy moved from her place under the air-conditioning vent to stand so close to Kinsey that their shoulders almost touched. Kinsey moved away from her and held her nose.

"Are you another Brennan?" Rhett asked.

"Bite your tongue, cowboy. I'm a Gallagher. Don't you know you're in cowboy country? We ride horses and four-wheelers, not motorcycles. That's not cowboy, even if you do glue horns on the front of it," the woman answered.

Kinsey rolled her eyes toward the ceiling and sighed.

"What scorpion crawled up your prissy ass this morning, Kinsey Brennan?" Betsy asked.

"You smell like shit and don't look much better, Betsy Gallagher," Kinsey growled.

"Shit smells better than that perfume you took a bath in this morning."

"Ladies, remember where you are," Sawyer warned them. "You want to fight and argue, take it out in the middle of the road. Better hurry up and grab what you came in for, Betsy, because closing time is in five minutes," Sawyer said.

"What the hell is that out there?" Betsy pointed. "Is it a motorcycle or a bionic steer?"

Her jeans and boots testified that she'd been working in the hay fields all day. Sweat rimmed the misshapen straw hat shoved down on her red hair, and her knit shirt and tight jeans hugged her curvy body.

"Four minutes now," Sawyer said.

"Don't get your undershorts in a wad, Sawyer. I'm not here to buy anything. I stopped by to see what all the fuss is about. I see Honey and Kinsey did the same thing."

"What fuss?" Sawyer asked.

"This wild biker right here." Betsy's eyes did a sweeping scan of Rhett. "I do like the ponytail and the soul patch, and the tat is real nice." She traced it with her forefinger.

"Oh really?" Rhett grinned.

She was kind of cute, but she was another feuding woman. Too damn bad Leah had to be thrown in the basket with the likes of these hussies. Of all of them, she would have been his choice to get to know better.

Betsy gave him the once-over. "That's right. I happen to like trouble, so I came to see for myself. I think you might be a handful of fun."

"Three." Sawyer pointed toward the clock.

Betsy moved toward the door, brushing past Rhett. "I heard that you'll be working at the bar. See you there tonight. And leave that cycle at home. I like a truck bed to play around in under the moon and stars."

Kinsey smiled at Rhett. "You'll have to overlook Betsy. She's a Gallagher, and they are a coarse lot. They can't help it. All those people over at Wild Horse come from moonshiners and probably outlaws."

"And the Brennans"—Rhett raised an eyebrow— "what do they come from?"

"Preachers and God-fearin' folks," Honey said.

"That's interesting. Halos and horns both right here in a tiny little town like Burnt Boot," Rhett said.

"You got it." Kinsey nodded. "We'd best get on out to River Bend. Granny will be throwing a fit if we're late to supper. Don't suppose you'd want to join us for a good, hot meal tonight, would you, Rhett?"

"Not tonight. My sister and her husband will be along in a few minutes with the rest of my things."

Honey headed toward the door. "Will we meet them tonight at the bar?"

Rhett shook his head. "No, they're going to drop my truck and keep going."

"Too bad. I always like to meet the family," Honey said.

Sawyer followed them to the door and locked it behind them. "Well, now you've been formally welcomed to Burnt Boot. If I was you, I'd steer away from both of those families. They mean trouble and I mean serious shit, not little, piddlin' crap."

"I thought the two families lived in neighboring towns, not on neighboring ranches."

"River Bend and Wild Horse are ranches, but they're both bigger than the whole area that Burnt Boot takes up. Their feud might die down, but it's never ending. Everyone's been so busy with hay crops and getting summer ranchin' done that it's been fairly quiet in town. At least until now," Sawyer said.

"And what's that supposed to mean?" Rhett asked.

"New tomcat in town. They are already checking you out. So on first impression, are you going to change your name to Gallagher or to Brennan by Christmastime?" Sawyer teased.

Rhett put up both palms. "I'm an O'Donnell. Born one and plan to die one. None of those hussies appealed to me. Betsy didn't like my cycle. Honey and Kinsey were far too savage for my blood. The only one that caught my eye was Leah. Now that one, with those light green eyes and sweet disposition, that one I could go for."

Three lovely women, very different in size and looks, pretty equal in their come-on power, and he didn't feel the desire for a quick romp in the sheets with any of them. Hell, he didn't even want to flirt with any of them, only

Leah Brennan. That was not like an O'Donnell, especially Rhett, who had a definite way with the women.

Sawyer turned out the lights and headed toward the door. "Leah is the quiet one, and you know what they say about them."

"Oh, yeah, that underneath there is a tiger waiting if some old cowboy is man enough to unleash it," Rhett said, following him. "I'm starving. Take me home and feed me some of Jill's good food before we have to go to the bar."

"Jill can't cook."

"Well, shit. What are we having?"

"I made lasagna and she's heating it up. But believe me, you won't be disappointed in her abilities. Her baking is to die for. She can make cookies, cakes, and pies that taste better than Granny O'Donnell's, but don't tell Granny I said that." Sawyer turned off the lights and unlocked the door. "Follow me. I'll go slow so the dust don't blow back too bad."

"If she's that good at baking, why don't you tell her it's good as Granny's?" Rhett asked while Sawyer locked up.

"Keeps her trying." He laughed.

Rhett's sister, Katie, driving his truck, and his brother-in-law, Danny, pulling an empty cattle trailer, drove into the lot as Rhett climbed onto his cycle. "We're all following Sawyer down to the bunkhouse. Just pull in behind us. I understand Jill has supper ready."

Katie nodded and fell in behind the cycle. When they got to the bunkhouse, she parked beside Sawyer and bailed out of the truck before either of her relatives could open the door for her. She stretched and rolled her neck from side to side. "That was one long ride in a truck all by myself. I'll be glad to get in with Danny. I wish I'd have had Dammit in the truck with me to have someone to talk to."

Sawyer threw an arm around his cousin. "Welcome to Fiddle Creek, Katie. Supper is ready, so you can take time to eat with us and work out a few of the kinks before you get on up the road to Oklahoma City."

The hot summer wind blew her long, blond hair into her face. She tucked it behind her ears and said, "That sounds good. I'm hungry and Danny has called every thirty seconds for the last forty miles wanting to know if there was a McDonald's in Burnt Boot. I told him I'd rather eat at Olive Garden and almost had him convinced there was one here until he drove into town and saw all there is, is a school, a beer joint, and a general store."

"You are just plain mean," Sawyer said.

"Yes, she is. My mouth was watering for Italian food and she treats me like this. I think it might be time for the broom and the pen," Danny said. He wasn't any taller than Katie and had a round baby face and clear blue eyes.

Jill opened the door to welcome them inside the bunkhouse where she and Sawyer lived. "Broom and pen?"

"He's being a smart-ass," Katie said.

"I'm only returning your words back to you," Danny told her.

"And?"

Rhett hugged Jill. "She told him at the beginning of their relationship that if she caught him cheatin', she'd get out the broom and pen. She'll beat him all the way to the courthouse with the broom and then hand him a pen to sign the divorce papers."

"Sounds like a plan to me," Jill said. "But what's driving for hours got to do with cheating?"

Danny hung his hat on the rack inside the door and sniffed the air. "The way she had my mouth watering for Italian food and then I find out that Burnt Boot doesn't even have a burger joint is worse than cheating. But I swear I do smell oregano and chocolate."

Jill nodded. "Sawyer made a huge lasagna last night, and I made desserts this afternoon—tiramisu, brownies, and chocolate pie."

Danny smiled at Katie. "You've been saved from the broom and pen, woman."

Jill tucked her arm in Rhett's and led him to the kitchen. "So I hear you've already met some of the Brennan women and Betsy Gallagher."

"I did, but it was only five minutes ago," Rhett said.

"Honey called Mavis and told her that you were at the store. Mavis called Aunt Gladys, and she called me. Gossip travels fast in a small town. You going to hop the fence to the River Bend or the one to the Wild Horse?" Jill asked.

"Jump the fence?" Rhett asked.

"Fiddle Creek separates the two ranches. Wild Horse is on one side of us and River Bend is on the other. All you've got to do is climb over a barbed wire fence and you can be on either side of the feud," Jill explained.

"I'm not going anywhere, but I might get Leah to jump the fence to Fiddle Creek." He smiled.

"Aha, so it's Leah, the quiet one, that's took your fancy. Too bad, darlin'. She's had her eye on Tanner Gallagher for years."

"Mavis Brennan would string her up and see her die before she'd let her marry a Gallagher," Sawyer said.

"The heart will have what the heart wants," Jill said. "Now come on into the kitchen and let's eat. I know y'all want to make Oklahoma City by night, so we can visit while we have supper."

The Burnt Boot Bar and Grill was not exactly what Rhett expected. The parking lot was gravel, or at least it had been at one time. Now it was thinly distributed gravel on top of dirt with only one streetlamp to illuminate the whole place. The building was weathered wood that didn't look as if it had ever seen a drop of paint applied. Hell, it might have even been petrified, as old as that sign swinging above the entrance. The roof was rusty sheet metal, and the only window in the place was the one in the door.

"Not what you thought it would be?" Sawyer asked when Rhett got out of his truck.

"Looks more like a barn than a bar," he said.

"The inside is better—air-conditioning, jukebox, and even paint on the walls." Jill laughed.

"I like the air-conditioned part best of all." Rhett followed them inside.

The bar itself was only eight stools long and had a small area for grilling burgers and making fries behind it. There were no pool tables, which surprised Rhett. But not as much as the shelves holding loaves of bread, hot dog and hamburger buns, and a small assortment of prepackaged pastries, or the refrigerated section beside that, with milk, beer, wine, and soda pop behind sliding glass doors. The other end of the long, rectangular room sported a jukebox, a few mismatched tables with chairs around them, and a small area for dancing.

"After the store closes in the evening, folks can get milk and bread or beer in here," Sawyer answered the unasked question.

"And I thought Comfort was a small town. I'm not sure this qualifies as a town." Rhett chuckled.

Sawyer clamped a hand on his shoulder. "You'll get used to it. Besides, you know what Grandpa says: To be a town, the place has to have a church and a place to buy beer or get a shot of whiskey. So by the O'Donnell qualifications, Burnt Boot passes the test."

At nine o'clock, he'd filled a few pitchers of beer for folks who'd drifted in and out, and Sawyer had shown him the process of making burger baskets. Sparks danced around Jill and Sawyer every time they brushed against each other. It damn sure didn't take a rocket scientist to know that their honeymoon wasn't over.

Two lonesome old cowboys sat in a back corner drinking beer and telling tall tales. The jukebox had gone quiet and Rhett had wiped down the bar so often that it was shiny clean. If every night was like that, he'd have to bring some rope to make a bridle or something to keep himself from dying of complete boredom.

"Why don't y'all go on home? I can handle it for the next couple of hours," Rhett said.

"If you're sure, we won't argue." Jill removed her apron and hung it on a nail.

Sawyer didn't waste a bit of time hanging his apron right beside hers. "We damn sure won't. Can't remember the last time we got to go home before midnight.

Sweep up and put the chairs on the tables. We don't do mopping unless there's major spills. Here's the keys. Be sure to turn off the grill and the lights."

"Will do." Rhett rolled the sleeves of his white T-shirt and wiped down the bar one more time.

Jill and Sawyer were gone less than five minutes when the door flew open and suddenly the bar was crowded to capacity. Someone plugged money into the jukebox, and in seconds it was going full blast, playing "Boys 'Round Here" by Blake Shelton. Folks wasted no time getting out onto the dance floor and making a long line to do a line dance. The noise level went from zero to one hundred so quick that it took a while for Rhett's ears to adjust.

"Hey, Rhett, we need three pitchers of beer and about six red cups," Kinsey yelled from the end of the bar.

He quickly filled the pitchers, set them on the bar, and stacked up six plastic cups. Kinsey handed him a bill and he made change.

"And when you finish that, I need two longneck bottles of Coors," Betsy said from the other end of the bar.

It kept him hopping, keeping the beer orders filled, the money straight, and making a few pitchers of margaritas. Then there was a lull, and there she was, sitting on a bar stool, her light green eyes watching him. His heart threw in an extra beat and his chest tightened.

"Well, hello, did you just fall from heaven?" he asked.

"I'll have a double shot of Jack on the rocks, so the answer is no. I don't think angels drink whiskey, but it is a fine line," she answered.

"So you are a Tennessee whiskey lady?" he asked.

"Tonight I am," she said.

A tall, blond-haired cowboy with blue eyes propped a hip on the bar stool beside her and nodded. "Hello, Leah."

She nodded. "Tanner."

"I guess you're the new O'Donnell in Burnt Boot. Brett, is it?" Tanner eyed Rhett like he was trash left on the curb.

"Not Brett. My name is Rhett, after the hero in *Gone with the Wind*. My mama loves that book," Rhett corrected him.

"Well then, hero Rhett, we need two more pitchers of beer over at our table."

"Be right with you. And you'd be?"

"Tanner Gallagher of Wild Horse. Betsy's cousin. If you've got any notion of asking her out, don't. Granny wouldn't like that."

"And if I didn't have any thought of asking her out?" Rhett set Leah's whiskey in front of her on a white paper coaster.

"Then you're probably crazy or gay. Which one is it?" Tanner asked.

"I like women." Rhett grinned. "As for the crazy, that's debatable. Some folks would agree with you, but no one has been brave enough or big enough to have me committed yet."

"Smart-ass, are you?" Tanner asked.

Rhett filled two pitchers with beer and set them on the counter. Tanner handed him a bill and Rhett made change.

"You didn't answer me. Are you a smart-ass, or do you back up your words with actions?" Tanner pushed the issue.

"No, I didn't answer you."

Tanner picked up the pitchers. "Are you going to?"

"Not today."

"You don't like us Gallaghers?"

Rhett picked up a bar rag and wiped down the bar where the pitchers had been. "Don't know you Gallaghers."

Tanner raised his voice loud enough so that everyone in the area could hear him. "Well, we know your kind, and we'd be happy to see you ride that motorcycle on back to where you came from."

"What is my kind?" Rhett asked.

"Tanner, stop being a jackass and go talk to your little buddies," Leah said.

Tanner scowled. "So the Brennans are going to take in this stray coyote?"

"Whether we do or not is none of your business, but you don't have to be rude," Leah answered.

"I thought you were different from the rest of them," Tanner said.

"I thought you were different from the rest of the Gallaghers," she shot back.

"Guess you really can't change a leopard's spots," he said as he walked away.

"Or a skunk's stripes," she mumbled.

Rhett filled the beer pitchers, collected the money, and then moved down the bar to Leah again. "That line about the skunk's stripes was far better than mine. The way he looked at you when he sat down, I thought maybe y'all were a couple, but I guess you aren't?" Rhett asked.

"Tanner? He's a Gallagher," Leah said.

"And Gallaghers and Brennans don't play well together, right?"

Leah sipped her whiskey. "That would be an understatement."

"Then we won't talk about it. So, you are a school-teacher. What do you do in the summertime?"

"Help out on the Brennan ranch, River Bend. Not that I actually do much ranchin'. Mostly, I take care of the book work for Granny and help with the garden some. I like to cook, so I do some cannin' while the garden is producing and when the fruit ripens in the orchard."

"When does school start back?"

"Pretty soon. We don't have to adhere to the state-mandated rules, since we're a private school, so we usually start classes in August."

"Private school?"

"The Brennans have a school on River Bend. The Gallaghers have one on Wild Horse. Then there's the public school right here in Burnt Boot," she explained.

"Hey, Rhett, darlin'." Honey popped up on a bar stool at the other end and yelled over the loud music, "We need two more pitchers of beer."

Leah threw back the last of her whiskey and slid off the stool. "See you around. Maybe in church on Sunday?"

"You going to be there?"

She nodded.

"Then I'll be there."

Chapter 2

IT WAS DUSK ON SATURDAY NIGHT WHEN RHETT RUSHED back to the bunkhouse to clean up after he and the summer crew of high school boys had replaced fence all day. It involved getting the posts set, stringing barbed wire, then removing the old, rusty wire from the decaying wooden posts and pulling them out of the hard dirt. Lots of sweat, a fair amount of cussin', and a ton of energy went into the job, so he was already tired when he stepped into the shower. The cool water felt good on his body and he had to admit, he did smell a lot nicer afterward.

"Thank goodness," he murmured as he wrapped a towel around his body, "Jill and Sawyer are willing to share their bathroom with me. I sure wasn't in the mood to run a tub of water tonight in my bathroom."

He pulled his wet hair back into a ponytail and seriously considered getting it buzzed off the next week.

"What do you think, Dammit? Ponytail or buzz cut?" he asked his dog as he crossed the living room floor.

The old hound looked up from the sofa and yipped, his tail beating out a tune on the cushions and both cats crouching to spring on it.

"Ponytail it is, then. Are you sure?" Rhett stopped long enough to scratch his ears.

Another yip and both of Jill's cats jumped at the same time. Dammit growled at them, and they retreated to the corner of the sofa. There were some things that a dog did not tolerate, and clawing his tail was one of them.

"So you think Leah likes my ponytail, do you? You think maybe she's got a wild streak down under all that sweetness?" Rhett asked.

Dammit's tail did double time.

"The tail has spoken. I'll leave it alone. See you later tonight. Guard the place and don't let any varmints in the door." He scratched the dog's ears again and headed outside into the blistering-hot summer heat.

He made it to the bar a few minutes before six, parked his truck beside Sawyer's, and hated to step outside in the heat. The thermometer on the porch post had read 110 degrees when he left the bunkhouse. He inhaled deeply to get one more lungful of cool air and slung open the door. Music and smoke met him head-on when he entered the bar.

"I thought they outlawed smoking in public places," he said.

"Not in Burnt Boot, but I hear it might happen before the end of this year." Jill smiled. "It'll be busy tonight, so you man the drinks. I'll take care of money and Sawyer can cook."

"I'll help him when I'm not drawing beer or pouring whiskey." Rhett quickly scanned the few people already in the bar but didn't see Leah, or any Brennans for that matter.

"This is Saturday night. It's a hell of a lot different than any weeknight," Sawyer said. "And with this heat, there will be tempers flaring. Gladys said that she heard there's gossip about something going down with the feud, so that'll bring in more people."

Rhett rolled up his sleeves and slung a bar rag over his shoulder. "At least it's cool in here. I swear those boys and I were about to melt plumb away out there in the heat today. Now tell me why the feud has anything to do with the bar."

Jill removed pitchers from the dishwasher and refilled it. "Because this is more than a place to get a beer and dance. It's the local gossip place. Think of the church, the general store, and the bar as Switzerland. Those are the three places that the feud has to be left at the door."

Sawyer took three heads of lettuce from the small refrigerator in the corner. He plopped them down hard on a cutting board and pulled their cores out, filled them with water at the bar sink, and then turned them over to drain.

"What's that all about?" Rhett asked.

"I'll put them in plastic bags and back into the fridge. That keeps the lettuce crispy. This place has a reputation for the best bacon cheeseburgers in the whole state," Sawyer explained.

The sound of truck engines out in the parking lot and doors slamming preceded a dozen Brennan cowboys into the bar. One stopped at the bar and the rest went back to push two tables together to claim the far corner as Brennan territory.

"We need twenty cups and four pitchers of Coors," the cowboy said.

"Little thirsty, are you?" Rhett smiled.

"Whole lot thirsty and got a lot of talkin' to do. I'm Declan, and we're all from River Bend."

Rhett set two full pitchers on the bar and went back to fill two more. "Pleased to meet y'all. I'm Rhett from Fiddle Creek."

"We've heard about you. Leah says the Gallaghers don't like you too much," Declan said.

"Wouldn't know about that and could care less about it," Rhett said.

"Just so we're straight. The Brennans don't like you either. And this is your only warning to stay away from the Brennan women."

"Same answer. Don't care much if you do or don't like me," Rhett said.

"Why are you being so rude? And why does he have to stay away from the Brennan women?" Jill asked.

"He's not Burnt Boot material, much less River Bend material," Declan said.

"What kind of material is that? He's my cousin and no one ever told me I wasn't Burnt Boot material," Sawyer asked.

Hot air pushed Gallaghers into the bar before Declan could answer. He picked up two pitchers and headed to the back. When he returned for the rest of his order, he brought a couple of Brennans with him. Rhett wondered if it was for protection from the Gallaghers or to show him a force that said he should listen to their warnings about staying away from their womenfolk.

"Four pitchers of Coors." Tanner hiked a hip on a bar stool and ignored the Brennans. "And a dozen bacon cheeseburger baskets. Double meat and cheese. And two pitchers of margaritas and one of piña coladas."

"Yep." Rhett repeated back the order.

Jill made change for the bills Tanner handed her. "Remember to keep it civil, Tanner. Watch your mouth and don't start anything, or I'll take out the shotgun that's right here at my knees."

Tanner laughed out loud. "I do like a woman with spunk. See y'all later. And holler right loud when the burgers are done."

"What happened that they are all up in arms about you, Rhett?" Jill asked.

"Tanner Gallagher has a thing for Leah. It's in his eyes every time he looks at her. I expect that would really set off the feud, so he's not doing anything about the attraction. I'm damn sure not interested in being mixed up in their battles, so they don't have to worry about me."

"If you're talking to Leah, you're already mixed up in it." Sawyer set six red plastic baskets with burgers and fries in each on the bar and yelled, "Tanner Gallagher."

Leah slipped inside and Rhett's heart threw in an extra beat. She looked beautiful in those tight jeans, boots, and an orange tank top tucked down behind a belt with a big rhinestone buckle. Tanner gave her the once-over as he crossed the floor and stacked baskets of burgers up his arm like a seasoned waiter. Rhett almost felt sorry for the guy. There sat the woman he loved, and he couldn't do a damn thing about it because of the family feud.

"I'll be back for the rest," Tanner said.

"Bring someone with you. The others are almost finished," Sawyer said.

"What can I get you, Miz Leah?" Rhett's eyes were drawn to hers. His hands itched to run the back of his knuckles down her cheekbones before he kissed those full lips.

"I'd like a burger basket. No onions and double fries. A plain Coke this time around, but afterwards I'll want a double shot of Jack." Leah smiled.

"You got it," Rhett said as he filled a red plastic cup with ice and drew up a Coke. "Been busy today?"

She took a sip. "Yes, I have. I went to the school and took down all my old bulletin board stuff, put up new, arranged the seats, and got ready for the new school year."

"What grade do you teach?"

"Fourth," Leah said.

He shook his head. "Who'd have thought about a town this small having three schools?"

"Crazy, isn't it? But our private school has more kids than the Burnt Boot public school," Leah said.

"Tanner Gallagher, last three," Sawyer yelled above the jukebox.

Tanner came to the bar to claim them, and this time, he looked at Leah in the mirror above the grill and said, "Hot today, ain't it?"

"Sure is." Leah nodded at him, but neither of them ever looked directly at each other.

Was the man crazy or just plain stupid? Leah had been right there in front of him his whole life and the only thing holding them apart was a crazy feud? If that had been Rhett, he would have told the feud to go straight to hell and he'd have gone after the woman he loved.

The next time the door opened, several couples made their way to the bar stools. A woman hopped up on the one right next to Leah and asked, "You from around here?"

"Yes, ma'am."

"Burgers any good?"

"Best in Texas," Leah answered.

"Then give us a dozen of your biggest, best baskets," the woman told Jill. "We heard this was a good place to get some supper, dance awhile, and have a few beers."

"Where y'all from?"

"Up around Terral, Oklahoma. We're out ridin' our motorcycles for the weekend. We rode down to the Fort Worth Stockyards this morning and we're on our way home. Thought we'd stop by here and have some fun and then go on home when it gets a little cooler."

"Have fun?" Leah asked.

"Hell, yeah, but not as much fun as we'll have here. We love to dance," the woman said. "Hey, bartender, we'll have six pitchers of beer."

"Who's your designated driver?" Leah laughed.

"Honey, we don't need one. Ain't a one amongst us that can't hold their liquor. You here to flirt with the bartender?" the woman asked Leah.

Leah blushed. "No, ma'am."

"You crazy. I don't see a weddin' ring, and he's one hot-lookin' cowboy."

Rhett pulled up pitchers of beer and strained his ears to hear the conversation. It had been years since he'd seen a woman blush. He liked it—a lot.

The woman cackled. "Darlin', I'm over sixty, and once you hit that magical age, you can say anything you want and get into anyone's business, and everyone chalks it up to bein' old. You have a good time tonight. Tell that sexy cook to holler out 'Williams' when our burgers are done."

—∿∿—

Leah took her burger basket and Coke back to the Brennan table and sat down beside Honey, making sure her chair was in a position that allowed her to catch glimpses of both Tanner and Rhett.

Honey pilfered a French fry and popped it in her mouth. "You'd best stop flirting with Rhett. Granny says he's trouble. He's a sexy hunk, darlin' Cousin, but I wouldn't go against Granny for a night in a five-star hotel with Adam Levine."

"Why does Granny think he's trouble?" Leah asked.

"It's the motorcycle and the ponytail," Kinsey answered while Honey stole another fry.

"So? He's a rancher," Leah said.

"She's made her decision, Leah. Neither Kinsey nor I would take her on in a real battle, and you're not as tough as either one of us," Honey said.

"He's Sawyer's cousin and she didn't have a bit of problem with either of y'all tryin' to run him to ground," Leah argued.

"That had a purpose. If we took Sawyer out of the picture, then Jill might have hooked up with Quaid, and we would have inherited Fiddle Creek and all those wonderful water rights with her."

"Then maybe I'll go after Tanner Gallagher," Leah whispered.

"Good God almighty damn." Honey's eyes came close to popping out of her head and rolling across the dance floor like marbles. "She'll put your sorry ass in a convent. What's gotten into you, anyway? You've always been the good child."

"It's this hot Texas sun that's fryin' the good sense right out of her head, Honey. She needs a vacation to New York City to shop. It's a good thing we've got one planned here pretty soon," Kinsey said.

Honey sighed. "In some ways, I'm glad we're going to New York City. In other ways, I'm going to miss lying out there on all that pretty white sand at the beach."

Kinsey sipped at her beer. "Our sweet cousin needs to spend time in retail therapy, not frying more brain cells. Y'all can thank me later for choosing a spot for our annual girl's week away from Burnt Boot that has air-conditioned shopping on the agenda every single day."

"Maybe enough of my brain cells got fried that the good girl is about to go bad," Leah said.

"You can be as badass as you want, Cousin, but it had best not be with a Gallagher or with Rhett or with Granny. Rhett's not the settlin' type. Granny said so and she's never wrong."

"Granny hasn't even met him," Leah argued.

"Like Honey said, you don't argue with Granny," Kinsey said.

Leah pushed her burger toward Honey. "Help me eat this. I'm not as hungry as I thought I was. And why isn't Rhett the settlin' type?"

"If you hadn't had your head stuck in the classroom all these years, you'd know what to look for, trust me. That man is a player. He'll sweet-talk you into bed, and then you'll never hear from him again. It's a game with a cowboy like him." Honey picked up the burger and took a bite.

"What if I don't want to settle down? What if I only want a romp in the sheets with him or maybe with him and Tanner both? Not at the same time, but maybe a few times with Rhett and then a few times with Tanner, to see which one I like best?" Leah asked.

"How much Jack did you drink before you left home?" Honey gasped.

Leah motioned toward her lips. "You've got lettuce between your two front teeth."

Honey grabbed her purse from the floor beside her chair, found a small compact, and checked her reflection. Even in the dim light and the smoke-filled bar, she could easily see the bit of green stuck there. She flicked it out with a fingernail and ran her tongue over perfectly even teeth.

"All gone," Leah said. "Look who walked in the door. Isn't that the lawyer that you've been seeing, Kinsey? And who is that with him?"

"That would be my date for tonight." Honey blew her a kiss as she and Kinsey hurried across the floor, and Leah watched the four of them head on out of the bar.

Leah left the rest of her food on the table and claimed a bar stool as far away from the door as possible. Since Rhett had roared into town on that big cycle, she'd felt like a big storm was approaching. She'd even dreamed of a tornado the night before. It had come up from the southeast and the funnel cloud had set down right in Burnt Boot. When it moved across the river, it had taken the school where she taught with it, leaving nothing but the foundation of the frame building. Burnt Boot had seen some ice storms that broke down trees and power lines. It had lived though some ferocious wind, lightning, and thunderstorms, but in its history, not one tornado had touched down there.

Rhett moved from one end of the bar to the other and waited for the jukebox to go quiet before he spoke. His drawl created a stirring deep inside her that she'd never even felt when Tanner was around. She was almost thirty, had taught for six years, and had had two serious relationships in her life.

"What can I get you?" he asked.

"Double shot of whiskey," she answered.

He picked up the square Jack Daniel's bottle. "So you ready for a ride on my cycle?"

"I'm not so sure that's a smart thing for me to do," she answered.

"When you figure out whether it is or not, you give me a call." He reached across the bar and wrote his cell phone number on the palm of her hand. "Night or day, I'll take you for a ride."

The first guitar notes of Luke Bryun's "Drunk on You" rattled out of the jukebox and people filled the dance floor. Leah shut her eyes and imagined riding that motorcycle, her arms around Rhett, her blond hair blowing behind her, and that song playing in her ears. The ache to do it rather than dream about it was so real that it brought tears to her eyes. She didn't want to be the good child, but the mold had been set and she didn't have a clue how to break free from it.

———◆———

Luke's song was stuck in his head until the bar closed that night. On the way home, he slipped the CD into the player in his truck and listened to the song twice more. Dammit met him at the door, but the two cats weren't anywhere in sight. Jill and Sawyer's bedroom door was shut. The cats had most likely deserted poor old Dammit to sleep on the foot of their bed.

"Come on, boy. I'm going to have a bath and soak this cigarette smoke off my hide. You can sit beside the tub and talk to me," Rhett said.

Other than the fact that he didn't have a shower in

his bathroom, the setup in the house was perfect for privacy. A big center room with a kitchen toward the back took up more than half of the space. At one time, bunk beds had lined the walls and the place had probably been home to twenty men or more. Now, there was a big living area that was a perfect division between his part of the house and the newlyweds' room.

"They're not very good friends to desert you like this. But then they have to stay in the house all day and you get to go out and run around with me all day on the ranch." He grinned. "You're going to like Leah when you meet her. What's that? What if she doesn't like you?"

Dammit's tail set up a thumping noise on the bare bathroom floor.

"No such chance. She's going to fall in love with you before she ever even gives in and goes for a ride on my cycle. You are a real chick magnet." Rhett laughed.

Chapter 3

LEAH SAT BESIDE QUAID AND HONEY IN CHURCH THE NEXT morning, but she didn't hear a thing that the preacher said until he wound down his sermon and reminded them that the Sadie Hawkins Festival was on the calendar, like always, for the fourth Saturday in August.

"The festival will start with breakfast in the school cafeteria—all-you-can-eat pancakes and sausage for only four dollars each for adults and two dollars for the kids. The money goes to the public school library this year to buy books. We'll rope off two blocks of Main Street for the vendors and the carnival, and at three o'clock sharp, we'll have the Sadie Hawkins race. Y'all should be learning to walk around in your bare feet the next couple of weeks, because there are no shoes or boots allowed in this race. And the committee is working on a new rule to add to the race, so be sure to read the fine print when you sign up for it," he said.

Someone was staring at her, producing a crazy itchy feeling on her neck. The hair on her arms stood up, and she shivered so hard that Honey turned to look at her.

"Air-conditioning kicked on," Leah said.

She let her eyes slide over to the Gallagher side of the church. Tanner's eyes locked with hers, and she could feel the attraction drawing their souls together. It had been like that for years, but neither of them would ever take a step toward doing anything about it. He was a

Gallagher. She was a Brennan. Case closed. Besides, he had quite the reputation for being a womanizer, and even if they could date, she wasn't sure she would. And yet there was that thing that kept her wondering what it would be like.

Then she located Rhett, and his green eyes captured hers. He winked. Did that mean he was entering the Sadie Hawkins race? What would Granny Mavis say if Leah chased him down and brought him home?

She blinked and looked up at the preacher, who was telling them about the old-fashioned ice cream supper that would begin at five at the church and the fireworks that would end the day at dusk. Everyone was encouraged to bring a cake, a pie, or their favorite kind of homemade ice cream. She smiled as she imagined grabbing his ponytail to bring him down in the Sadie Hawkins race and then dragging him back to the ice cream social.

The race didn't mean that the guy she caught had to marry her like it did in the comic strip from the fifties. It did mean that she had to take him to dinner after church on Sunday. Her head started spinning, thinking about a date with Rhett O'Donnell.

I need to go fishing and clear my mind, she thought. *I've always been in love with Tanner, and now Rhett is in the picture. I had trouble handling one secret cowboy. Two is one cowboy too many.*

Mavis grabbed her arm on the way out of the church and said, "I hear you were flirting with that wild cowboy that Gladys hired down at the bar last night."

Leah set her mouth in a firm line. "Oh, really? Did the little bird that told you that also tell you that she got drunk and took a man home with her that she met last night?"

"I'm not talking to that little bird. I'm talking to you, Leah Brennan. I've got better things in mind for you than to get involved with a hired hand over on Fiddle Creek."

"And what is that, Granny?" They moved down the aisle toward the door to shake the preacher's hand before they went back to River Bend for a big family dinner.

"I'm grooming you to run River Bend," Mavis whispered. "You've always known that you're the kind of woman who will have to run the ranch when I'm gone."

Leah draped an arm around Mavis's shoulders. "Granny, darlin', you are going to live to be a hundred. Besides, you've always told us that Saint Peter doesn't want you and the devil is afraid of you, so there's no way either party is going to let you die."

Mavis laughed. "Don't try to change the subject, Leah. I may be old, but I'm not stupid. I won't have you ruining your life with that wild cowboy."

"But it's my life, Granny."

"Yes, it is, but you live in my house."

Leah bristled, "Is that an ultimatum?"

"It is what it is. I've never put any restrictions on you, but there's no place for that drifter on River Bend, and if you take up with him, there won't be a place for you either. So you better think long and hard about your decisions."

"I'm almost thirty," Leah said.

"And that's old enough to know better."

—~~—

Leah changed from her church dress into a pair of cutoff jeans and her lucky T-shirt that fell down over her hips. She pulled her honey-blond ponytail through the hole in the back of a River Bend ball cap and stomped her bare feet down into her oldest cowboy boots. Stopping by the kitchen, she loaded a small cooler with bottled water, sandwiches, one bright red apple, and a six-pack of beer. With the cooler and her fishing gear tied securely to the back of a four-wheeler, she headed out to the river for a long afternoon of watching a red-and-white bobber dance on the gentle waves of the Red River.

In places, the north edge of River Bend property was next to the Red River, so all she had to do was open a gate, drive through it, close it, and then drive right to her favorite spot. That's where the big weeping willow tree was close enough to the water that she could sit under the shade, toss her line out, and wait for a catfish or a bass to bite the bait. That day, she was fishing with chunks of fake crabmeat that Gladys sold down at the general store.

She parked a few feet away and carried her cooler in one hand and her rod and reel in the other. When she parted the limbs to slip into the shade, there was Rhett O'Donnell under her shade tree, wearing cutoff jeans with a ragged edge about knee level, old scuffed-up boots, and a tank top that should have been tossed in the ragbag a year ago. Several hooks and lures were stuck into a straw hat that covered his eyes and he was smiling up at her.

She dropped her things a few feet from him and said,

"This is my fishin' spot. You need to find another one." She'd go back to the four-wheeler for her tackle box and bait, but first she had to make him move either up or down the river. That shade tree belonged to her.

Rhett pushed his hat to the back of his head. "You're from River Bend, right?"

She nodded.

"If you will notice, ma'am, this willow tree is right below Fiddle Creek property and a good fifty yards from the River Bend property line. And I do not see a 'Do Not Trespass' sign hanging in this tree or a deed to it in your name either. Bein' as how I am a gentleman and I wouldn't mind havin' a fishin' partner this afternoon, I will share this tree with you, but I will not leave it."

God works in mysterious ways, she thought as she whipped around and went back for the rest of her gear.

"They ain't bitin' right now, but that's not to say they won't later on," he said when she set the tackle box down and opened it. "What are you usin' for bait?"

"Fake crabmeat from the general store," she said.

"I'm usin' grasshoppers. There's plenty of them in the jar over there. If you run out of bait, help yourself," he said. "I never pictured you for a fisherman or fisherwoman. Which one is it?"

"Fisher person, I suppose," she said.

She had intended to ignore him completely, not carry on a conversation with him.

"You do much fishin'?" he asked.

"If I don't have papers to grade on Sunday afternoon. There's not many more weekends between now and the time school starts back, so I won't get to fish much more this summer." She bit the inside of her lip to keep from asking him how often he went fishing.

He tipped his hat over his eyes and leaned back against a rock. After several minutes, she wished he'd say something else, anything but sit there with his eyes closed and the fishing rod in his hands. She baited her hook and threw out the line, letting it land downstream from his bobber. Could he really be sleeping? If that were the case, she sure didn't affect him like he did her, because there was no way she could sleep that close to him.

She glanced over at him, taking in his muscular calves and the fine, dark hair peeking out from the top of his shirt. If she were as brazen as Betsy Gallagher, she'd have reached across the distance and ran her hand up under his shirt to see if the hair was as soft as it looked.

And you'd bring back a wet hand from all the sweat. Take a look at his face, woman. That's not ice water dripping down his cheeks.

She wiped away the droplets under her nose on the tail of her shirt and braced her back against the trunk of the big willow tree. Was fate trying to tell her to let go of her childish crush on Tanner Gallagher by putting Rhett in her path? She mulled that over as she watched the bobber float down the Red River until her line was taut.

———∿∿∿———

Rhett was not asleep, and he could feel the moment her eyes settled on him and the very second that she shifted her gaze to the river. Evidently, she didn't want to talk because she didn't ask him any questions, so he'd made it easy for her by pretending to be asleep.

The fish were not biting that day. It was too damn

hot. The catfish were down on the bottom of the river, where it was a little cooler, and the bass where most likely keeping them company. Finally, thirst got the best of him, so he sat up, pulled a longneck bottle of beer from his cooler, and twisted the lid off. He touched her on the arm with it and she jumped like she'd been shot.

"Want one?" he asked.

She reached for it. "Thank you. It's too hot for them to bite, isn't it?"

"Yep," he said.

He took out another bottle, removed the lid, and turned it up, downing a third of it before he came up for air. A blur appeared to his right, and before he could turn his head, Dammit had licked him right up across the face. He chuckled and grabbed the dog by its big, floppy ears.

"How'd you find me, old boy? That was some fine tracking and you deserve a drink for it." He held the beer bottle up and the dog gulped several times, then burped loudly.

"There's a lady here," Rhett whispered.

The dog fell down at Leah's feet, rolled his big brown eyes up at her, and wagged his tail.

"He says he's sorry and to please excuse him," Rhett said.

She smiled and scratched his head. "Beer does that. You are forgiven. I guess this is Dammit?"

Leah was finally talking to him. The dog would get a beer of his own plus two treats when they got home that evening for making that happen.

"Yes, I'm sorry. I should have introduced y'all. Dammit, this is Leah. Leah, Dammit," he said.

"What about when the preacher comes to dinner? What's his name then?" Leah asked.

"Then his name is Holy Dammit."

She laughed.

Maybe the dog would even earn a spot at the foot of Rhett's bed that night.

Rhett stretched out his hand to pet the dog and deliberately let his knuckles make contact with hers. That little spark he'd felt in the store the first day and at the bar when he'd slid her drink to her was still there. It didn't matter if she was Brennan, Gallagher, or Jones, Rhett was damn sure interested in any woman who caused that kind of reaction.

He pulled his hand back and let her get to know Dammit while he finished his beer. "It gets hot in Comfort, Texas, but I don't think it gets this hot."

"It's the humidity coming off the river. So, did you and Sawyer grow up close together?" she asked.

"Not on the same ranch but in the same area. We went to school together, right along with Finn. You've met Finn, right? He bought a ranch here in Burnt Boot and wound up married to a lady he was in the service with."

"Of course, I know him, and I know he's Sawyer's cousin. I really like his wife, Callie." She hesitated. "And those kids of theirs are adorable."

"And Verdie?"

Leah smiled. "Everyone loves Verdie. I'm glad that she moved back to Burnt Boot and is living on the ranch with Finn and Callie. They need her and she sure needs them. Things tend to work on the right way and they sure did in that instance."

Dammit wiggled his way close enough that he could

lay his head on Leah's lap. He closed his eyes but his tail kept going, sweeping an arc in the sand that looked like half a set of angel wings. She jammed the handle of her fishing rod down into the sand and kept petting him while she fished around in her cooler for a sandwich.

She offered one to Rhett, and he took it without hesitation.

"Thank you. I didn't think to bring snacks."

"So, all three of you O'Donnells grew up in the same area?" Leah asked.

Rhett talked between bites. "Pretty much. We were usually together on Sundays after church. Probably not a lot different setup than you and your family."

Leah reached across Dammit and took the apple from the cooler. She'd only brought one, but he'd shared his beer with her, so she felt like she should at least offer. She bit off a hunk and handed it to him.

"This looks ominous, especially on a Sunday afternoon. Didn't Eve feed Adam an apple and then they had to make clothes out of fig leaves? These weeping willow leaves are pretty small." He grinned.

In a whoosh, her cheeks were on fire, but not as much as her fingertips when he held her hand in his and bit right next to where she had. She hoped he couldn't see the tremble in her hand as she finished the apple and threw the core out into the river. An instant splash said that a big fish had snagged it.

"They're too smart for me today," she said as she pulled her rod out of the sand. She reeled in the line, removed the soggy bait, and fed it to the dog. She carefully wound the hook and line around the rod and stuck the tip in the cork handle.

"You leaving?" Rhett asked.

"Not yet, but they aren't bitin' today. Did you come from a big family?"

Rhett followed her lead and brought his line in also. Dammit wasn't a bit interested in a soggy grasshopper, so Rhett tossed it back out on the water. Before he could get the line wound around the rod, a splash out in the river said that a fish had eaten the free food again.

"Dammit!" Rhett said.

The dog rose up and cocked his head to one side.

"Not you. That smart-ass fish," Rhett said.

The dog resumed his position and his tail started again, this time in a different spot in the sand.

"He knows his name and he understands you." Leah laughed.

"I raised him from a puppy. We're pretty good friends."

"You mentioned a sister in the store that first day. Is she your only sibling?"

Rhett shook his head. "No, but she's the baby of the family. I have three older brothers, then me, and then Katie. O'Donnells throw pretty good-sized families. You should see us when we all get together over in Ringgold, Texas, for a reunion."

"Why Ringgold?"

"My Uncle Cash has a horse ranch there, and it's kind of a central location. The reunion is the last Saturday in September. Maybe we'll be good enough friends by then that you'll go with me."

"Maybe. Or maybe we'll be Sunday afternoon fishing buddies," she said softly.

Dammit got mentally moved back to the rug beside

Rhett's bed. He had to earn that spot on the foot of the bed, and he hadn't done it that day.

"Time will tell," Rhett said.

"Guess I'd best get on back up to the ranch. Granny and I usually watch a movie together on Sunday night," Leah said.

"So you live with her?" Rhett shut the lid to his tackle box.

"Have all my life. My dad, Russell, was born in that house. He's the firstborn of five sons. The Brennans are a big family, but we all pretty much stayed on River Bend. Declan is my older brother, and both of us live with Granny and Daddy in the main ranch house."

"Your mother?"

"Left when I was a toddler and never came back. Granny and Daddy raised me."

"Maybe I'll see you at the bar tomorrow night?"

She shook her head. "I've got to go to the school again and do some work."

"Do you like teaching at a private school?"

"I never thought about whether I liked it or not. I got an education so I could teach at our school, but sometimes I wish all the kids in Burnt Boot went to the same school."

"Why?"

"It would better fit them for the world. They only see kids from River Bend and don't get as much outside contact as they need, and I'm tired of this feud."

"Did you go to the private school?"

"Yes, I did, and then to college, but I was not at all prepared for the world."

They bent to pick up their tackle boxes and her hair

brushed against the side of his face. He gently tucked it behind her ear, and the soft, dreamy look in her eyes drew him closer and closer until his lips found hers in a sweet kiss. It was impulse, spur of the moment, letting the heart lead the mind. And chaste as it was, it absolutely rocked Rhett's emotions to the core.

"Hey, can I have your phone number in case I need someone to talk to later tonight?" he asked.

Leah hesitated but then she rattled it off. "You won't remember it, but I don't have a thing to write with or anything to write it on."

"I'll remember," he said. "See you later, Leah Brennan."

———∿∿∿———

Leah mumbled something like, "See you later," before she turned abruptly and hurried to her four-wheeler. Her heart pounded like a bass drum in her chest all the way back to River Bend. She parked it beside the house, forgot all about her fishing equipment and cooler, and made her way through the kitchen and up the stairs without being seen.

One glance in the bathroom mirror said she was every bit as red as she felt. Her lips tingled and her hands trembled. She still couldn't believe that he'd kissed her or how one simple little kiss could stir such emotion.

"God Almighty, Leah Brennan, it was an impulsive thing out there on the riverbank. It probably didn't mean a thing to him, and it shouldn't mean anything to you, and what if someone saw him kissing you?" She fussed at her reflection.

She groaned when she checked the small clock on the bathroom vanity. She had exactly fifteen minutes to take a shower, wash the sweat from her hair, and get to the dining room for supper.

She made it on time, but supper was tense, with her grandmother glaring at her through most of it. Her father had left to go to Dallas for a tractor part of some kind.

Fine excuse, she thought as she chewed food that tasted like sawdust. If she'd thought ahead, she could have told her grandmother that she was going to Kinsey and Quaid's to play dominoes or watch a movie. But she'd been so bogged down trying to sort out her feelings for Rhett that she'd let the opportunity get past her. Now she was having supper with only her grandmother at the table. Declan had even begged off with some reason or other, leaving her to face the dragon alone.

"I meant what I said," Mavis finally said.

"I don't doubt it for a minute, but like I said, I'm old enough to make my own decisions," Leah said.

Supper seemed like it lasted an hour, when in reality it was barely thirty minutes. When Leah had swallowed her last bite of chocolate cake, she excused herself and went straight to her room. Throwing herself back on her bed, she stared at the ceiling. Things had sure gotten to be a tangled mess in a few short days.

Her phone rang at eight thirty. She figured it was Honey or Kinsey calling to quarrel with her for sitting on the riverbank with Rhett. As fast as rumors traveled, it surprised her that Mavis didn't mention it at the supper table.

"Hello, and if you called to fuss at me, then you can hang up now."

"Trust me. I'm not going to fight with you," Rhett chuckled.

His deep drawl sent a shiver down her spine. "Hello, Rhett."

"Hi, Leah. Want to go for a midnight ride on my cycle?"

Her breath caught in her chest. "Not tonight. Can I have a rain check?"

"Sure you can. Did you save my phone number?"

She nodded.

"Anytime you want to change your mind and go for a ride, you call me and I'll come and get you," he said.

"Where's Dammit?"

"Right here, but you don't get to talk to him tonight. This is my time. Where are you right now?"

"In my bedroom."

"Can you see the moon out the window?"

"Yes, I can."

"So we're lookin' at the moon and stars together?"

"I guess we are," she said.

"Tell me about your students," he said.

"They're fourth graders, which means that all bodily functions are funny to the boys, and the girls are at that age where there's lots of giggling and whining but not much in between. They aren't babies anymore, but they aren't to the puberty stage, so they're a lot of fun."

"Kind of like they're old enough to give up that teddy bear at night but not old enough to want to really put it in the closet?" he drawled.

"Exactly," she said.

"I like it when you smile."

"What makes you think I'm smiling?"

"Your voice changes when you smile, and I like that," he answered.

"Oh really?" she asked.

"And now you're really smiling big," he said.

"Is that one of your pickup lines?"

"No, ma'am. Just an observation."

"Tell me the story about those horns on your motor-cycle," she said.

"That's a third-date story, but I will tell you about the time I decided to go from Comfort, Texas, up to the Palo Duro Canyon for a long weekend ride."

She settled back against the pillows on her bed. "I'd love to hear that story."

"It was the weekend after Thanksgiving, and the weather was supposed to be cold but clear. A blizzard blew in about the time I dropped down into the canyon, and the trip down and out that should have taken two hours took about nine hours, and they were closing the roads behind me when I finally made it into Claude, Texas. There was one motel with one room left, and believe me, darlin', I didn't care how many stars it had as long as it had hot water and warm blankets."

Goose bumps popped up on her arms as she imagined how cold he must have been. "Holy smoke, Rhett! It's a wonder you didn't get frostbite. Was that two winters ago? I remember that storm. It was horrible. We got in on the tail end of it."

"I was pretty damned cold. I shed my clothes at the door, stood under a warm shower until I could feel my hands and feet again, and then dived under the covers on the bed and slept for twelve straight hours. I spent four days in that hotel and would have stayed longer, but Sawyer came to rescue me. We put my cycle in the bed of his truck and he drove me home. I haven't

done a lot of winter travel on the cycle since them."
He laughed.

She liked the way his deep Texas drawl was expressed
even in his laughter. It was like warm, silky lotion on her
skin after a long, lingering bath.

Three hours later, she looked at the clock and gasped.
"Rhett, it's eleven thirty."

"I don't turn into a pumpkin at midnight. Do you?"

She laughed. "No, but we should end this call now."

"Then good night, Leah. I loved talking to you."

"Me too," she said.

Chapter 4

SIRENS WOKE RHETT. HE SAT STRAIGHT UP IN BED AND glanced at the nightstand, thinking it was part of his dream and that the noise was really his phone or the alarm clock. The phone was dark; the clock said it was five minutes past midnight.

He bailed out of bed, pulled on his jeans, and stomped his feet down into his boots. The emergency vehicle had gone toward the general store and the bar, and they'd need all the help they could get.

He met Jill and Sawyer in the living room. Both fully dressed even if they were sleepy eyed. A lamp had been turned on, but there were still deep shadows and an eerie feeling about the room. Rhett could have sworn he smelled smoke, so that meant fire and that it wasn't far away. Jill had the phone to her ear and Sawyer paced.

"Is it the store or the bar?" Jill asked and paused slightly while she listened. "Well, thank God for that."

She hit a button and shoved the phone back into her pocket. "It's not our place. The Gallaghers' school is burning. Aunt Gladys says that the fire department isn't going to try to put it out because it's too far gone. They'll watch it all night and let it burn completely to the ground so the cleanup will be easier," Jill said.

"Couldn't they save any of it?" Rhett asked.

"Aunt Gladys said that by the time anyone knew there was a fire, it was completely engulfed in flames,

The Gallaghers are already blaming the Brennans, so I guess the feud is about to get hot and heavy again." Jill yawned.

"This may top the last battle that folks called the 'pig war,'" Sawyer said.

A heavy knock on the door startled all three of them.

"Aunt Gladys," Jill said and started that way.

"I don't really care about the fire. I'd rather go back to bed." Sawyer covered a yawn with the back of his hand.

"Is Rhett O'Donnell here?" a big, deep voice filtered through the shadows. The smell of smoke preceded the policeman into the room.

"I'm Rhett." He stepped forward.

The man wore a sheriff's patch on his uniform. Shorter than both Rhett and Sawyer, he had broad shoulders and a spare tire that said he enjoyed his meals. His eyes were serious and his mouth set in a firm line.

"I'm Sheriff Orville Dawson and I have a few questions for you."

"Yes, sir," Rhett said.

"Where were you all evening?"

"Right here on Fiddle Creek."

"And this afternoon?" Sheriff Orville asked.

"Fishing in the river until chore time."

"Did you set that fire that burned down the Gallagher school?"

Jill raised her voice. "Hell no, he did not!"

"I'm askin' him, Jill." Sheriff Orville frowned.

Rhett locked eyes with the sheriff and said, "I did not."

"Well, you were fishing with Leah Brennan. Who's

to say that you weren't conspiring to burn down the school in retaliation for the last thing that happened in the feud?" the sheriff asked.

"I can vouch for my cousin. He's been right here all evening," Sawyer said.

"When was the last time you actually laid eyes on him? It's only about three miles to the school. He could have crawled out a bedroom window and jogged that far, set the fire, and been back in bed when the sirens started," Sheriff Orville said.

"I could have. I could have done lots of things, but I did not leave Fiddle Creek from the time that I stopped fishing and came back here to do the evening chores. I'm not an arsonist, Sheriff, and I've been right here in this bunkhouse since about eight o'clock. That's when Dammit, my dog, wanted to go outside and I stood on the porch while he watered down a couple of trees. And, yes, I was fishing this afternoon. Leah Brennan was fishing too, but it was a coincidence that we both showed up there, and I assure you, sir, we were not conspiring to do anything other than catch a few fish."

"And I stood on the porch with him when he let the dog out to go take a piss," Sawyer said.

"There's a lot of time between eight and midnight," Orville said.

"Yes, there is," Rhett said.

"Don't leave town. I'm going to talk to Leah Brennan right now. If there are holes in your story—"

"Sheriff, I was on the phone with Leah until eleven thirty tonight," Rhett said. "I don't think she could have jogged to the Gallagher school and set fire to it either."

Orville crossed his arms over a belly that hung out

over his belt. "So that's the way it is. Y'all are going to be each other's alibi. That looks damn suspicious to me."

"It's the truth. We were talking until almost midnight. You can ask her if you want, but she'll tell you the same thing," Rhett said.

"I'm sure she will. Like I said, don't leave town." He turned and slammed the door behind him as he left.

"Wouldn't dream of it," Rhett mumbled.

"You're wadin' into some mighty deep water," Sawyer said when the sheriff had left.

"I can swim," Rhett said. "Is there any of that chocolate cake left, Jill? I'm hungry, and it'll take the taste of the smoke out of my mouth."

"Yes, half the cake is left, in the kitchen. Rhett, were you really talking to Leah that long?" Jill asked.

"Yes, I was, and, yes, we did wind up at the same spot and went fishing together, and, no, we were not making out but we did share one very brief and very sweet kiss. We didn't mention it when we were talking though, and I'm afraid it was too soon and spooked her more than a little bit so I will go slower from now on," Rhett answered on the way to the kitchen.

———◆———

Mavis Brennan was sitting at the dining room table with Sheriff Orville Dawson when Leah made it downstairs to breakfast the next morning. She caught the faint whiff of smoke and frowned.

"Orville, what brings you out this early?" She headed toward the buffet where breakfast had been set up and kept warm.

"The Gallaghers' school burned last night. Didn't you hear the sirens?" he asked.

"No, I was on the phone with a friend until late, and then I took a long shower and had music playing. I guess it muffled the sounds," she said.

"Who was the friend?" Orville asked.

Leah smeared cream cheese over a bagel and laid it on a plate along with a piece of sausage and two strips of bacon. "Why?" she asked.

Orville picked up his coffee and sipped it. "Rumor has it that you were down at the river all afternoon yesterday with Rhett O'Donnell. I reckon the Gallaghers think you done went into cahoots with that wild cowboy and y'all conspired together to burn down their school."

Leah didn't flinch. "Yes, we did wind up at the same fishing hole and we did talk last night, but we did not burn down anything."

Her grandmother's eyes flashed with anger, and Leah expected a tongue-lashing right there before she could even eat her breakfast. But Mavis turned her gaze to Orville.

"Anything else, Sheriff?" Mavis asked.

"Yes, ma'am. I want to know what you were doing between eight and midnight last night."

"Me or Leah?"

"Both," he answered.

"I was right here in this house. My door was open and Russell was in the office until midnight. I was in and out of that room until maybe eleven, when I went to bed. That enough of an alibi for you?"

Orville leaned across the table as far as his gut would allow. "I know the Brennans did this. Maybe it wasn't

Rhett O'Donnell and Leah. Maybe you didn't do it yourself, Mavis, but you sanctioned it, and some of your other relatives did the dirty deed."

"Prove it," Mavis said.

"What will the Gallaghers do about their kids and school?" Leah asked.

"They're going to send them to public school this year and decide later what to do about putting up a new building," he answered. "If I ever find enough proof, Mavis Brennan, to justify a warrant or an arrest, your family is going to spend some time behind bars."

Mavis pointed a long finger at Orville. "Find the proof before you come back here accusing my family of anything."

The minute he was outside the house, she turned to Leah. "I meant what I said yesterday. This is your last warning, Leah."

"I'm almost thirty, Granny. I reckon I can make my own decisions about who I talk to and who I go fishin' with," Leah said.

"And I will judge who lives in this house and on River Bend," Mavis shot right back at her.

"Guess we'll have to abide by each other's right to do that, won't we?" Leah said.

"What happened to you this week, Leah? You've always been the good granddaughter, the one with her head set solidly on her shoulders. Don't let some wild cowboy ride into Burnt Boot on a damn motorcycle and turn your thinking into mush," Mavis said.

"Maybe the good granddaughter is tired of being good," Leah whispered.

"Well, she'd best learn that her granny has spoken,

and when I speak, it's the law on River Bend. You cut that cowboy loose, or you're going to be finding another place to live and another job too."

"You'd fire me from the school as well as kick me out?" Leah asked.

"Now you're finally beginning to understand," Mavis told her.

"I can't believe you're threatening me, Granny. Rhett is a good man and he's a rancher. Kinsey is dating a lawyer and Honey has dated all kinds of men. You haven't acted like this with them," Leah argued.

"I'm still mad that Sawyer O'Donnell swept in and took Jill away from us. We could have had Fiddle Creek if he'd kept his sorry ass in Comfort, Texas. Or better yet, if his cousin, Finn, hadn't come to Burnt Boot. That's what started all this, anyway. Now there's a third one of them O'Donnells in town and I'm not havin' one of them in the Brennan family. And that's not a threat, Leah. It's a promise. You either back away, or I'll make good my word."

Mavis Brennan's round face was stone cold. Her blue eyes, set in a bed of wrinkles, did not leave room for argument. She reached up and patted her stovepipe-black hair into place.

"I guess we've both laid our cards out on the table," Leah said.

"Yes, we have. The difference is I'm holding the winning hand. Right now I've got a meeting with my grandsons. You think about what I said."

"Oh, I will, Granny. I certainly will."

"Good. I trust that your good judgment will override your hormones."

Mavis left the table and Leah fished her phone from the back pocket of her pair of designer jeans. She flipped through several windows before she found the right one and dialed the superintendent/principal of the Burnt Boot public school.

"Hello, Wanda, this is Leah Brennan. I heard that the Gallagher school burned and that the public school is going to take in the students that had been going there. Y'all are going to need more teachers," she said.

Leah had been in charge of the eight- to ten-year-old Sunday school class for years and Wanda helped her out almost every Sunday. They weren't best friends, but like most folks in Burnt Boot, they knew each other well.

"Yes," the woman said quickly. "I don't even need to interview you. There have already been more than a dozen Gallaghers in here this morning, and more have called to get their kids enrolled. I'm surprised that you called, Leah, but the answer is yes. I know you're a good teacher and I'll gladly hire you right now. We've only got three weeks until school starts, and we're going to be scrambling for extra teachers. But why do you want to leave the Brennan school?" Wanda asked.

"Thought I might like a change," Leah said.

"Well, I'm glad you want a change. I'd like to put you down to teach fourth grade. Let me know by noon, and I'll get the contract ready for you to sign," Wanda said.

Leah inhaled deeply and let it out slowly. "I've thought about it long enough. I'll take the job. Thank you for offering it to me. You reckon the Gallaghers will have a fit about a Brennan teachin' their kids?"

"I'll put those kids in with the other fourth-grade

teacher and give you the ones who aren't Gallaghers. Hey, I heard that you and that cowboy who's gone to work for Gladys at Fiddle Creek are an item now. That got anything to do with this decision?"

"Rumors can sure stretch things out of proportion, can't they?" Leah chuckled.

"You didn't answer me, but it doesn't matter. I'm glad to have someone like you on our staff," Wanda said.

"Think you can keep this under your hat for a few hours?" Leah asked.

"I can until noon. We've got an emergency school board meeting then," Wanda answered.

The next call Leah made was to her own principal, Matthew Brennan. "Hey, Matt. How are things at the school?"

"Wouldn't know. I'm on my way to a meeting with Granny. She's afraid the Gallaghers are going to retaliate for the burning."

"Did we do it?" Leah asked.

"Doesn't matter. We got the blame for it," Matthew said.

"I didn't ask that. I asked if we did it."

"You know the family creed, Leah. When Granny says do something, we do it and we don't talk about it, or else the law would come down on us. I can tell you that I did not do it, but I can't tell you the Brennans didn't do it," Matthew said. "What can I do for you?"

"I'm handing in my resignation today. The public school has offered me a job and I'm taking it," she said.

He gasped. "You can't do that."

"I just did. Amanda has finished her degree and is looking for a job. Give her my classroom. I'll be

in this morning to clear it out and hand in my keys,"
she said.

"Does Granny know?"

"No, sir, and I'd appreciate it if you kept quiet about
it until I can tell her myself."

"She's going to raise hell."

"Yep."

"I wouldn't want to be you."

The line went dead before she could say anything
else.

Chapter 5

MAVIS DIDN'T FIND OUT ABOUT THE NEW JOB UNTIL MONDAY evening, and she was furious when Leah sat down at the supper table that evening. Honey and Kinsey sat on one side of the table, with Declan, Russell, and Leah on the other side.

Granny had brought reinforcements, no doubt to either toss Leah off River Bend or to talk her out of her decision. Her blue eyes were barely visible she was squinting so much, and her lips almost disappeared when she set them in a hard line. Leah's stomach twisted up into a pretzel and she sighed. It was going to be one long night and she'd told Rhett that she would be at the bar by eight.

Too late to change my mind, Granny, she thought.

She'd already handed in her resignation. Her second cousin, Amanda, now had the job, and Leah had signed the contract for a year at the Burnt Boot Independent School District. She'd cleaned out her schoolroom, the boxes still in the back of her truck. Tomorrow or Wednesday, she'd take them to the new school and start getting her new classroom ready.

Mavis picked up a platter of steaks and passed it down the table. "I understand that you've got something to tell us."

"Not me." Honey took the sirloin from the top and slid it onto her plate. "Other than that Leah, Kinsey, and

I are sure looking forward to our little vacation to New York City. That's still on, isn't it?"

"I expect she's talking to me," Leah said. "I resigned my position at the school and I'll be teaching at the public school this year. My room has been cleaned out and Amanda has been given my job. And, yes, our vacation is still on, Honey, no matter where I'm teaching."

"Why would you do that without even talking to me about it?" her father asked.

He and Declan were definitely father and son: both six feet tall with sandy-brown hair, dark blue eyes, chins with dimples in the middle, and broad shoulders.

"Granny gave me an ultimatum," she said.

"I'm going to shoot Rhett O'Donnell," Declan said.

"Why? He didn't tell me to make this decision."

"He's got you bewitched."

"Maybe I changed jobs so that I can see more of Tanner Gallagher. He might be bringing his sister's kids to school some of the time and I can flirt with him. Now that we burned their school, the Gallagher kids will be attending public school, and they need more teachers."

"Good God almighty damn." Mavis slapped the table so hard that the silver and crystal rattled. "Declan won't have to shoot that sumbitch Tanner. I'll string him up with a length of barbed wire in the nearest scrub oak tree if he even looks at you sideways. I won't have it, Leah. I swear to God I will not. The Brennans and the Gallaghers will never, ever get involved with each other. Not while I'm alive."

Honey inhaled so sharply that for a second, Leah thought she was choking. Kinsey's eyes came nigh to popping right out of her head. They both looked like they were going to break and run any minute. So much for them being the strong cousins. They couldn't hold their own at the supper table when the Gallagher name came up.

Mavis shrugged. "I'll call Matt and straighten this out. Leah isn't going to any public school, especially in Burnt Boot."

"Yes, I am and I'd rather have a hamburger from the bar tonight instead of a steak. I'll see y'all tomorrow. If my clothes are thrown out in the yard, then I'll see if Gladys Cleary will take me in," she said.

"Why are you acting like this?" Mavis asked through clenched teeth.

"It's not even three weeks until school starts. I had to find a job in case you made good on your threat, Granny. If you toss me out, I'll have to have a place to live, which means rent, which means I have to have an income."

"What are you talking about?" Russell asked.

"Granny gave me an ultimatum this morning. She can tell you all about it." As Leah marched out of the house, she threw over her shoulder, "I'm going to the bar."

"What in God's name happened to her?" Honey whispered.

"I heard she was making out with Rhett O'Donnell," Kinsey said.

"And we will break that little affair up before it goes one step further," Mavis said. "You are in charge, Honey. Do whatever it takes."

"Yes, ma'am. I'll take care of it right now, Granny. You go on and call Matt." Honey sighed at the beautiful sirloin in her plate, pushed back her chair, and followed her cousin out into the night.

—⟨⟩—

"Hey, I was hoping you'd be here this evening." Rhett smiled when Leah slid onto a bar stool. "What can I get for you tonight? A double shot?"

"I'd like a double cheeseburger basket and a beer," she said.

"Sure thing." He slapped two meat patties on the grill and sunk a double portion of fries into the hot grease. "Did the sheriff come see you today?"

"He was there at breakfast." She smiled.

"Did he tell you not to leave town? He sure gave me orders to stick close to Burnt Boot," Rhett said.

"No, but then where would I go?"

"We could run away to a faraway island where there are no other people. Of course, we'd have to live on coconuts and fish until the first crops came in. But I like to fish, and I know how to grill them over an open fire, so we wouldn't starve." He grinned.

"Sounds wonderful, but I've signed a contract to teach at the Burnt Boot school for the next year. Think you might hold on to that thought for a year and check out some remote islands during that time?"

"That is one fine pickup line," Honey said from the shadows.

"What are you doing here?" Leah asked.

Honey wiggled her eyebrows across the bar at Rhett. "Thought I'd like to have a burger too. Fix me up my favorite, like you did this afternoon at the bunkhouse."

"I sure will," he said.

Leah frowned.

"You sure you want one exactly like I made you at the bunkhouse?" he asked.

Leah's eyebrows became one solid line.

"Yes, darlin', like the one right after we came out of your bedroom after...well, you know." Honey giggled like a little girl.

Rhett picked up a red plastic basket, lined it with a white paper, and set it along with an empty cup in front of Honey.

"Where's my burger?" she asked.

"You said you wanted one like the one I made you at the bunkhouse this afternoon. Since I spent the whole day out driving a tractor, plowing up about forty acres to put in winter wheat, you must have eaten an invisible one with an imaginary Rhett O'Donnell. And here it is. It's free, by the way, so keep your money in your purse," Rhett said.

Leah's smile warmed his heart.

"And now I'll get your burger ready, Miz Leah. What made you decide to change schools?"

"Job security," Leah said and then turned toward Honey. "So Granny sent you to take care of the problem, did she?"

Honey glared at her. "You are a fool. All of us would love to have the chance you've got at River Bend, but you've been the chosen one since you were a little girl. There's not a man on the face of the earth worth messing up that kind of sweet deal for."

Rhett set the basket in front of Leah. "Want to explain what she said?"

"It's like this," Honey said. "Leah has been groomed from the time she could walk to take over Granny's job someday. That means running the whole ranch. Granny let her have her way when she wanted to teach rather than learn the ranchin' business, but she knows ranchin' upside down and backwards, even if she doesn't get her hands dirty real often. Her daddy made her learn all the ranch stuff when she was a kid. Granny made her learn the financial part, and she's supposed to get the River Bend crown when Granny gets ready to pass it down."

"That is enough, Honey." Leah could feel the burn starting at the base of her neck and traveling around to her cheeks. Honey had no business airing the Brennan laundry in the bar, not one damn bit. Especially not to Rhett.

"She's throwing it all away because Granny confronted her this morning," Honey went on.

"About the school burning? Neither of us had anything to do with that," Rhett said.

"Not about the burning. Hell, if Granny didn't have a hand in it, I'd be disappointed. About you, Rhett O'Donnell," Honey said. "Now I'd like a double cheeseburger basket and a pitcher of beer. Real ones."

"Yes, ma'am."

Rhett filled her order and set four red plastic cups on the bar with the beer when it was done. She stacked the cups on top of the burger and carried it all to a corner table. She'd barely sat down when several other Brennans joined her. They'd just gotten their red plastic cups filled when six Gallaghers made their way into the bar. Tanner stopped long enough to order two pitchers of beer, and the whole bunch of them went to a table on the other side of the bar.

"Think we'll have a bar left after tonight?" Rhett asked Leah.

"It's a tough old bar that's withstood a lot more than you can imagine," Leah said. "And, Rhett, let's get something straight right now. I don't know how I feel about you, but it's my business to figure that out. Nobody needs to throw ultimatums at me and expect me to heel like a huntin' hound that they can pen up until they're ready to let me loose for a few hours—not even Granny, as much as I love her. I'll be thirty years old this fall, and I can make my own decisions."

"Yes, ma'am." He grinned.

"What's so funny?"

"We're probably about the same age. My birthday is in November. When's yours?"

"October," she answered.

"I always did like older women."

Things got so busy that Rhett had to call Sawyer and Jill to come help him at nine o'clock. The bar was full. Tension was even thicker than the smoke. The noise level—from the jukebox to the sounds of noisy dancing boot heels—was so loud that behind the bar, they had to use hand signals to communicate.

Around nine thirty, Rhett looked back at Leah to find her bar stool had been claimed by a big, husky man with a beard and long hair. He had a tattoo of a parrot on his right arm and he motioned for a beer in a bottle.

Rhett twisted the top off and set it in front of him. "Pay the lady at the end of the bar," he said.

The man nodded and handed Jill a bill. "Jumpin' joint tonight. What's the occasion?"

"School burned last night," Jill said.

The man threw back his head and laughed. "I guess that the feud is fired up?"

"Kinda looks that way. You a Brennan or a Gallagher?" Jill answered.

"Neither one. I'm from the other side of the river. I was passin' by and decided to stop for a beer. Who's the pretty girl who left this bar stool?"

"That would be Leah Brennan," Jill yelled.

"Mavis Brennan's kin?"

Jill nodded.

"Man would be crazy to mess with that. I'll be on my way."

Rhett spotted Leah at the Brennan table, with Kinsey on one side and Honey on the other. He wondered what in the hell they were trying to talk her out of or into, but he could not read lips.

At eleven, he sent Sawyer and Jill home and unplugged the jukebox. "Last call. Closing time," he yelled, and the last three customers left.

He was busy sweeping the floors when Leah poked her head back inside the bar. "I hate to bother you, Rhett, but my truck won't start. I think I left the lights on and ran the battery down."

"Give me a minute to finish picking up this trash, and I'll come out and jump-start it for you. We keep a set of cables under the bar for times like this," he said.

"I'll wait right here," she said as she hiked a hip on the first bar stool.

Rhett had barely finished his job when Betsy Gallagher poked her head in the door. "Rhett? Well, look at this. So it's true about you two, is it?"

Leah's chin raised an inch. "I'm too tired to argue or to fight with you, Betsy."

"I'm sure you are, screwing around with Rhett all afternoon yesterday down at the river and then burning down our school."

Rhett stopped what he was doing and moved across the floor toward the bar. "What do you need, Betsy?" he asked.

"I've got a flat tire. My spare is flat too, and my phone is dead. I need a lift home when you get done."

"Soon as I give Leah a jump start, I'll be glad to take you home."

"Thanks."

He picked up the orange jumper cables and motioned for the women to follow him. Leah led him straight to her truck while Betsy waited in the shadows. It only took a couple of tries to realize that the batter was completely dead in Leah's truck and there was no way it was going to start.

"I'll take you both home," he said. "But my truck is like the bar, the church, and the store in that it is neutral territory."

"It doesn't look that way to me," Betsy said coldly. "Kind of hard to deny the rumors when here y'all are together after-hours."

"Don't be sarcastic," Leah said.

"Hey, you don't have any right to tell me how to be," Betsy smarted off.

"I told you this is neutral territory," Rhett said in

exasperation. "I think you live closest, Leah, so you're going first," Rhett said.

Betsy smiled. "Does that mean I get to sit in the middle?"

"No, it means Leah does. I like her better than you," Rhett said.

All he wanted to do was go home, wash away the smoke in a cool bath, and fall into bed. But they were both damsels in distress and he didn't have a choice but to take them home.

"You ain't no fun at all." Betsy pouted.

Rhett didn't give a damn right then if Betsy pouted until Judgment Day. Six o'clock came early, and there was ranch work to do. Maybe, if he was lucky, he'd dream about Leah without being awakened by Sheriff Orville.

Leah put the console down and slid into place between him and Betsy. A Brennan and a Gallagher that close together. Lord love a duck, as Granny O'Donnell used to say. There would be a brand-new war come morning when folks found out they'd ridden in the same truck together.

Chapter 6

RIVER BEND RANCH WAS A CONGLOMERATION OF SEVERAL ranches. The main ranch had started off with a couple of sections of land more than a hundred years before, but as the family grew and children moved out, they'd acquired more land until it stretched twenty miles west from the original house. They'd built their school when indoor plumbing was still a luxury that was unheard of, and in the beginning, there had been two little white-washed buildings on the back side of the school property, one with a star on the door for the boys and one with a quarter moon for the girls.

Sometime in the late forties, after the war was over, the Brennans outgrew their little two-room school, so they added several classrooms onto it, and while they were building, they added a couple of bathrooms—one for the boys, with two stalls, two sinks, and three urinals, and one for the girls, with four stalls and two sinks.

To save the money to put in a proper septic system, the head of the school of the time, Miss Elizabeth Brennan, came up with the idea of using the old cistern for a septic tank. With the new well they'd had put in, they had running water inside the school. The big under-ground cistern would be totally useless, and what was a septic system anyway but a holding tank in the ground? So they routed all the new plumbing into the cistern. For the past sixty years, the school had paid a company to

pump it out twice a year. They had a permanent sched-
ule: pump the cistern during Christmas break and in late
summer, before school started.

—⁓—

"Why do we have to go inside their school?" Eli
Gallagher asked.

A tall, lanky cowboy with a mop of blond hair and
brown eyes, he and his cousins Randy and Hart had been
chosen to do Naomi Gallagher's bidding on this job.
They'd managed the last assignment, which involved
stealing Mavis Brennan's entire pig stock and selling
it off, so they were now in Granny Gallagher's good
graces. That, according to Hart, was a damn fine place
to be.

Randy, who was as tall as Eli but outweighed him
by thirty pounds, took off his cowboy hat and mopped
his sweaty face with a red bandanna. When he finished,
he shoved his bandanna back into his hip pocket. "It's
damn hot in here, but we promised nobody would get
hurt, so we got to make sure nobody is hiding out in
the school."

"Why would anybody be in here at midnight?" Hart
asked.

Shorter by a few inches than the other two, he was
the pretty cowboy that all the girls flocked to in the bar
or at a rodeo. He oozed charm and had a swagger that
drew female eyes to his tight-fitting jeans. And he knew
his way around dynamite and any other kind of explo-
sive, which was a good thing when it came to blowing
up tree stumps or taking care of a rock in the middle of
a pasture.

"Why can't we burn the place down like they did ours?" Randy asked as the three of them made their way down the halls, opening doors and checking closets.

"If I were a teenager, lookin' for a hidey-hole to make out in with my girlfriend, it wouldn't be in a schoolhouse in August It's like a furnace in here," Hart whispered.

"If things work like they should, then I don't reckon it matters if it's hot as hell or if the air conditioners are runnin' full force, does it?" Eli said.

"Looks like it's empty as a tomb," Randy said when they'd checked the whole place. "Did you check the girls' bathroom, Hart?"

"Yes, I did, and if y'all go tellin' anyone I was snoopin' in a girls' restroom, well, remember I know shit on you too." Hart smiled.

"We're ghosts. We were never here." Eli opened the back door, and they looked around before trooping out across the yard to the implement shed, which they'd parked the truck in.

"I guess it's a go, then?" Eli asked.

"Did you poke that dynamite down in the hole like I told you?" Hart asked.

"I did. You run the wire to the truck, Randy?"

"I did, but Hart has to hook it up to the battery. Ain't no way I'm touching that shit. It scares me worse than rattlesnakes. I'll be sittin' inside the truck. Soon as it blows, we'll back out of the shed and be halfway to Dallas by the time Orville gets here," Randy answered.

"Y'all get on in the truck. Granny is a genius. Blow up their septic tank and there won't be no school here next month either. It'll take weeks for them to clean up the mess and decide what to do. If they can set fire to our school, we can blow up their shit," Hart laughed.

"Wait!" Randy yelled from the truck bed. "I'm back here shutting the toolbox, and there's no dynamite left."

The smile left Hart's face. "What did you say?"

"I said there was five sticks and now it's all gone. That shit is hard to get."

"Eli, how many sticks were left when you shoved one down the cistern opening?" Hart asked.

"None. I used all five of them," Eli said. "I figured as thick as that concrete is down there, it might take more than one to blow it up good enough they couldn't use it no more."

"Holy shit!" Hart said.

"Nope, just plain shit."

"One would have done the job," Hart said.

"Then five will be fantastic." Eli grinned. "Blow the damn thing and let's go home."

Rhett turned off the main road onto River Bend land at a few minutes before midnight. Leah's shoulder and hip were scrunched against his and she was as stiff as a board. Hopefully, it was because Betsy Gallagher's was smashed against her other side. He wondered if a member of each of the feuding families had ever been that close to each other without involving hair pulling or fists.

The same moon he and Leah had talked about the night before still hung in the sky, throwing off enough light to silhouette the playground equipment in the school yard. The movement of the swings powered by the night breeze made it look like the children of the past had come to play after the sun had gone down.

"Never been on River Bend property before. Is that the school over there?" Rhett asked.

"Yes, it is. Started off as a two-room school and then the Brennans built onto it," Leah answered.

"Wouldn't be more than half a mile as the crow flies to Fiddle Creek, then, would it?"

Leah shook her head. "It was built on the original ranch. We grew to the west as the family expanded."

"And we grew that much to the east," Betsy said.

"So Fiddle Creek is the only thing separating y'all? I can't for the life of me see why either of you would want it, then. If either of you got control of it, that would mean you'd butt right up to each other. You can't get along with land separating you now. You should be giving Gladys and Jill protection money to never sell that land, so there will always be space between you," Rhett said.

Suddenly, the ground rumbled and the truck shook. Rhett held on to the steering wheel and jammed his foot against the brake, throwing gravel and dust every which way. He'd never heard of an earthquake hitting in northern Texas, but they were sure enough experiencing one right then.

"Sweet Jesus, I promise I won't ever step foot on River Bend again," Betsy squealed.

It only lasted a couple of seconds, but it seemed like eternity. Rhett got control of the truck, stopped it right in the middle of the road beside the school, and threw his arm around Leah, drawing her closer to his side as the truck rocked from side to side.

Then a shaft of black shot up from the ground and Rhett's first impression was that the Brennans had been drilling for oil and had hit an old-time gusher. It went straight up in the sky, past the top of the school and the huge old oak trees surrounding it, before it mushroomed and started back down.

All the windows in the school exploded outward and debris flew through the air as the black cloud fell to earth. Betsy screamed and covered her head when something bounced off the truck's hood. Then something else hit a truck tire and the explosion sounded like a shotgun blast at close range. In no time, the truck was sitting at an angle, sliding all three of them against the driver's side and plastering Leah even tighter against Rhett.

Then another heavy object landed in the truck bed, raising the front end up until the passengers were practically looking at the ceiling before it finally popped back down. It slowly settled back down and what was in the mushroom cloud started raining down on the truck.

Rhett took a deep breath then grabbed his nose. "That's not oil."

"Hell, no, that's shit!" Betsy screamed.

Leah gasped. "I thought it was a tornado."

Rhett saw a couple of headlights through the fog of the stuff falling all around them as it blew in the same breeze that made the swings move. He squinted to see if it was help or the culprits, but then they were gone. He took out his cell phone and punched in the number to the bunkhouse, but nothing happened. When he looked down, his phone was registering no service.

"Looks like we're stuck, ladies," he said.

"Granny is going to kill me," Betsy said.

"If my Granny don't get to you first," Leah told her. "Y'all Gallaghers just blew up our school."

"Not the school, the septic tank. That is not mud covering my truck," Rhett said.

They sat there in stunned silence, their noses twitching and eyes so wide that the whites showed all around the edges. Rhett turned on the windshield wipers and hit the button for water to wash the crap away. Long before he had a clean glass, the reservoir ran out of water.

Leah moaned when she saw what was left of the school. It had no windows, no doors, and what had been painted white was now dripping with brown liquid. The walls still stood upright but the roof had big holes in it. A toilet sat upright on the roof, and one had landed upside down on the lawn.

"Were there only four toilets?" Betsy asked.

"I can't remember," Leah answered.

"Lord help us all. They'll dub this one the shit war," Betsy said.

"And it's your fault, like the pig war was your fault," Leah said.

"You started it when you burned down our school."

"It might be covered in crap, but this truck is still neutral. What y'all should be worried about is how in the hell we're getting out of here. We've got a flat tire and a toilet blocking our way if we could go forward. Plus, there's another one in the bed of the truck that could possibly have knocked a hole through the metal and damaged everything underneath it, in which case, even if the tire wasn't blown, we can't go backwards," Rhett said.

Betsy threw the back of her hand onto her forehead.

"We couldn't drive in this slime even with four wheels that worked perfectly. I'm a dead woman."

"You got any cell service, Leah?" Rhett asked.

She shook her head. "If I had power left in my phone, I would have loaned it to Betsy back at the bar, so I wouldn't have had to ride with her."

Betsy whipped around as much as she could and glared at Rhett. "Why didn't you think of that?"

"Because I was tired and trying to get Leah's truck started. This is not my fault, ladies," he protested.

A truck drove up beside them and honked. Betsy rolled the window down and Declan yelled across the distance, "What the hell happened? We heard a... Good Lord, what are you doing here? I thought the smell was from all this crap and now I find out it's from a Gallagher."

Betsy shot him a dirty look. "I was sitting beside your sister when this happened, so don't go blaming it on me."

Declan's phone rang and he hit a button. "Granny, the Gallaghers have blown up our school. Looks like they did it through the old cistern we use as a septic tank. Everything is dripping with crap. Stay in the house. The breeze is coming from the north tonight, and you do not want to smell this. We should have posted guards." There was a long pause as he kept nodding. "Leah is sitting in Rhett O'Donnell's truck with him on one side and Betsy Gallagher on the other side, so I don't think it was Rhett that did it."

"Give me that phone," Leah said tersely as she carefully reached through the window to take it from Declan's outstretched hand.

"You drop it. You retrieve it," he said.

She hung on like a bulldog with a ham bone. "Granny, my truck battery went dead at the bar and Betsy had a flat tire and no spare, so Rhett was taking both of us home when all this rained down on us. His truck is ruined." There was another long pause, and then she said, "Yes, ma'am, I understand."

"So?" Betsy asked.

"Declan, you are supposed to take Betsy to the back side of our property and turn her loose. You can let her use your phone if you want to, so she can call for someone to come get her, or she can follow the river until she's past Fiddle Creek and to Wild Horse. Rhett, you are to sit right here with me until more help comes," Leah said. "Granny says we're not even calling the sheriff because the damn Gallaghers own him. She wants you to deliver a message, Betsy. You are to tell Naomi that hell is going to rain down on the Gallagher family."

"Hell won't be as bad as what's just rained down on y'all," Betsy said, smarting off at her.

"Then you're admitting that you did it?" Declan asked.

"I did not admit anything, and I do not know anything, so torturing me won't do a bit of good," Betsy said.

"Oh, I'm going to torture you all right, Betsy Gallagher. You are going to walk through this shit to the bed of my truck, where you will ride in the back of it because I don't want a Gallagher inside it."

She opened the door and set her fancy boots down in two inches of brown matter that made her snarl. "I hate you, Declan. I hope when you come back that you fall in this and it gets all inside your truck."

"Feelin' is mutual," Declan said.

Betsy stepped on the running board of the truck, slung a leg over the side of the bed, and settled in with her back propped right under the window. Declan's tires slipped when he first tried to drive away, but he eased off the gas and finally got enough traction to disappear into the darkness.

"Now what?" Rhett asked.

"When Declan gets back, he'll take you home to Fiddle Creek and then me to the house. We can't clean this up until morning," Leah said. "Your truck is probably totaled. I'll have the guys haul it to a barn and spray it off. You can send your insurance people here to assess the damage."

"No good deed goes unpunished."

"I'm sorry, Rhett, but it's the Gallaghers' fault, not mine."

"Who burned down their school?" he asked.

She raised her right hand. "Probably the Brennans, but honest to God, I did not know anything about it."

"Someone is going to get hurt before this is over."

She nodded in agreement. "They have in the past. Back when it first started, there were actual killings and hangings. Nowadays, there might be property damage, but no one has been killed since Rayford Brennan died back in 1900."

"What was his great sin?"

"He fell in love with a Gallagher, and when she wound up pregnant, the Gallaghers hanged him and sent her to California. She died giving birth to the baby and it died with her."

Rhett draped an arm around her shoulders. "And the Brennans retaliated?"

"We always do."

"That mean this isn't the end of this?" he asked.

"That's what it means. Granny will literally rain down hell upon Naomi Gallagher. And then she'll do something back and it'll go on for months. The dust from the last battle has barely settled. Betsy is right—this will be known as the shit war."

"Even in polite company?" he asked.

"Then it will be the toilet war." She sighed. "I didn't think anything could be worse than the pig war, but this will top it for sure."

He drew her even closer. "Or maybe the Holy Shit War."

She chuckled. "It's not funny."

"Got to laugh or you'll cry."

"I can hear the jokes now, and they are going to fuel Granny's anger." She sighed.

"I'm sorry, Leah. You don't seem to be the feudin' type to me. Now, Betsy is another story, and so are Honey and Kinsey. But you have an old soul that likes peace and order, not chaos and craziness."

She looked up into his eyes. "What makes you say that?"

"It's the way I see it."

"Don't know about an old soul, but I do like peace. I don't want to be the next Brennan queen. I want to teach school and enjoy the kids. I want to settle down sometime in the not-to-distant future with a man who loves me like I am and who doesn't want to change me. I want to grow a vegetable garden and roses, and read books in the summer while my kids romp around in the yard with a water hose and spray each other. I want peace and order in my life, and as long as this feud is going, I'll never have it because I'm a Brennan. But I hate this feud."

He kissed her on the forehead. "Maybe someday you won't be a Brennan anymore."

"Might as well wish for the moon and all the stars," she mumbled.

Their noses twitched less as they grew accustomed to the horrible aroma. With the windows rolled up and the engine turned off, they were in their own little cocoon, even if it wasn't a pleasant one. Rhett liked the way that Leah fit in his arms, especially when he sunk his nose into her hair and got a whiff of coconut shampoo, barroom smoke, and the faint scent of beer.

With his fist, he tipped her chin up, and then he lowered his lips until they covered hers in a passionate kiss that fogged the windows of the truck. That lead to another long, lingering kiss with the fingers of his right hand tangling into her hair to hold her head steady for more leverage. His left hand splayed out on her back, and he could feel the strap of her bra. He found himself hoping for a time when they could shed the confinement of clothing and he could feel her bare skin against his.

Her arms snaked up around his neck, her hand undoing the rubber band holding the ponytail in place.

"I love your dark hair. Don't ever cut it off," she said.

"I love your blond hair. I won't get a buzz cut if you leave yours long." He strung kisses from her forehead to her eyelids, to the tip of her nose, and down the sensitive skin on the side of her neck.

—⁓—

Drawing even closer to him, she shifted her weight until she was sitting in his lap with the steering wheel against her back. She traced the tat on his arm with her forefinger and asked. "Want to tell me about this while we wait?"

"It's not a third date yet." He grinned and then kissed her again.

It felt oh so right for her to be there in his truck with him—even covered in crap.

"Dammit!" he said.

"Where? Is he getting that mess on him?" Leah asked.

"No, look." Rhett pointed toward two headlights coming at them "Not dammit, as in my dog, but dammit, as in I wanted to make out with you some more."

The headlights of a truck approached slowly, and she quickly moved to the far side of the seat; it wouldn't do for her brother to catch them making out like a couple of teenagers. The truck carefully backed up beside Rhett's poor, crippled vehicle, and Declan honked. Leah took a deep breath and rolled down the window.

"I want you to open the door and very carefully step from that truck to this one. I swear to God, Leah, if you make a mistake and step wrong, you will ride in the back just like Betsy," Declan said. "And once you are inside, then Rhett can come across and get in the back. I'll take him home first. Granny will have a shotgun loaded by now and you sure don't want to take him to the house."

"Pull up a little more," Leah said.

"Why?"

"Because if Rhett can't ride in the cab, neither will I," she said.

"What in the hell has gotten into you?"

"I mean it. We are all three going to ride in the front seat, because if any of this splatters up on me in the back, Granny will have your hide, not mine, for bringing the smell in the house."

"Then you'd both better be careful. Granny's anger won't be nothing compared to mine if you get that crap inside my truck. I can hose off the back where Betsy was, but the inside is a different matter," Declan said.

She eased out carefully and slid across the seat and into the other truck. Rhett did the same, going slow so that he didn't touch anything. Even though Declan was behaving like a jackass, she couldn't blame him a bit for not wanting that stuff inside the cab of his truck. Thank goodness Rhett hadn't been driving with the windows down, or the story would have had a whole new ending to it.

"Thank you for taking me home," Rhett said after they were both in Declan's truck.

"You were trying to help my sister. It's the least I can do."

Leah poked Declan in the ribs with her elbow. "And his truck is ruined because of our feud that he didn't have a thing to do with."

Declan's truck tires spun, and Leah inhaled deeply, getting a nose full of the horrible smell again. She said a silent prayer that they wouldn't get stuck and need another truck to come pull them out of the slime. He gunned it, and they were on the way, leaving a four-foot splash of crap in their wake.

"Dammit," Declan groaned and slowed down.

"Just be damn glad I wasn't back there," Leah told him.

"I believe that's the first time I've ever heard you cuss," Declan said.

"Well, it might not be the last time after this. You know they're going to dub it the shit war now," she said.

"I'd already thought of that, but if you're smart, you won't be using words like that in front of Granny." Declan drove slowly until they were out on the paved road, and then he floored it, going ninety miles per hour down the winding road toward Fiddle Creek. He barely slowed down to turn onto the gravel road beside the store.

Leah slapped his arm so hard that the noise echoed in the truck cab. "Slow down. You're going to knock your alignment out, driving like this. Just because you're angry with me, you don't have to drive like a maniac."

"I hate this feud," he mumbled.

Leah raised her voice an octave. "You think I don't? Maybe when our generation has a turn at running things, we can make some changes, but right now Granny and Naomi aren't going to budge."

"Not after this stunt tonight."

He came to a halt in front of the bunkhouse and Rhett opened the door. "Thanks for the ride home. I'll call my insurance company as soon as it opens tomorrow morning."

Leah laid a hand on his thigh, and when he turned, she pulled his face down to hers for a quick kiss. "Thank you, Rhett, for trying to take me home. I'm sorry about your truck and I'll make it up to you one way or the other."

Declan set his mouth in a firm line and glared at her. "Granny is serious about this, Sis."

"I know she is. I'll talk to you tomorrow, Rhett."

Rhett closed the door and waved. "I'll look forward to it."

"Why?" Declan asked.

Leah shrugged. "Because I'm a big girl and I should get to make my own decisions."

He put the truck in gear and drove away from the bunkhouse. They were all the way out on the road and headed back to River Bend when he finally said, "I respect your right to make your own decisions, but remember, you'll have to sleep in the bed you make so be very careful."

"I will," she answered.

———

Rhett took several long gulps of fairly fresh air while he tried to sort out the evening. Had those kisses made Leah's toes curl like they had his? The answer didn't fall down from the starlit sky, so he sucked in one more lungful of air and went inside the lit-up bunkhouse. Jill and Sawyer were sitting at the kitchen table, sharing a cup of hot chocolate, and they both looked up at the same time.

"Why did Declan bring you home? Did you feel that earthquake?" Jill asked.

"Good God! What is that smell? Have you been in a hog house or did you step in something on your way home from the bar?" Sawyer asked.

Rhett took a beer from the refrigerator and twisted the top off. "It's a long story, but that was not an earthquake. It was the beginning of a new level of the feud that goes on around here."

"Well, shit!" Sawyer said.

Rhett pulled out a chair and sat down. "Quite

literally. And I would advise you both to pray that the wind doesn't blow tomorrow, as close as the bunkhouse is to the Brennan school."

"Why?" Jill asked.

Rhett told the story.

"Whew! The shit war has begun." Jill chuckled.

"That's what Leah said it would be called. She said it would be even bigger than the pig war. I guess now all the kids on both sides will be enrolled in public school." Rhett finished off his beer.

"I wonder what they used on that septic tank," Sawyer said.

"Dynamite would be my guess and entirely too much of it if they were just trying to blow up the sewer system so the Brennans couldn't have school. That poor school won't be good for nothing but bulldozing," Rhett said.

"Did you see any of them?" Jill asked.

"I saw the faint blur of headlights through a shit-covered windshield. If either of those toilets had fallen differently, they could have come down through the roof and killed all three of us right there on the spot."

It started as a chuckle in Sawyer's chest and developed into a masculine roar that bounced of the walls and sent both cats scurrying for cover. Poor old Dammit came out of the bedroom, dropped to lie on the ground, and put his paws over his ears.

"And that is funny, why?" Rhett asked.

"Because I can see the headlines." Sawyer made a sweeping motion in the air with his hand. "Deadly Toilet in Shit War Kills Three."

Jill giggled so hard that she got the hiccups. "Feud takes three out in initial battle of the shit war."

"I'm going to take a bath and go to bed. You two ain't funny."

His phone rang while he was digging through a drawer in search of his favorite well-worn T-shirt that he liked to sleep in.

"Hello, Leah. Are you still alive?" he answered when he saw her name on the ID.

"For tonight," she said. "After I took a shower and got the Gallagher germs off me, Granny wasn't nearly as mad. She's got a war to plan, so I'm not in the limelight anymore. Do you work at the bar every night this week?"

"Not Wednesday. Jill and Sawyer are taking that night to give me a rest," he said.

"I'd like to take you up on that motorcycle ride you offered," she said.

"Shall I pick you up about six?"

"No, would you please meet me in the school parking lot?" she asked.

"I hope you aren't talking about the Brennan school," Rhett said.

"No, the public school. It'll be empty except for my truck."

"What time?"

"To meet or going to the bar?"

"To meet at the parking lot." He grinned.

"Six o'clock."

"I'll be there."

Chapter 7

Sweat poured from Leah's forehead down into her eyes that afternoon. Finally, she got tired of the sting and wrapped a bandanna around her forehead and tied it in the back. The public school wasn't so different than the private one in that they did not turn on the air-conditioning in the summer months. That meant she was setting up her classroom with the windows open, praying for a breeze to flow through.

Her tank top was glued to her with sweat. The waist-band of her cutoff jean shorts was wet. She'd long since kicked off her shoes and had been running around barefoot for the past hour. Now she was putting up the last of the bulletin board welcoming the kids to the fourth grade when the door opened.

She turned to find Tanner Gallagher standing there with his arms crossed over his chest. "So it's true. You're going to be teaching here."

"It's true. What can I help you with?"

"I'm waiting on Wanda. She was supposed to meet me here. I'm bringing some of the Gallagher kids' shot records and birth certificates for her to copy." He crossed the room and sat down behind her desk. "You ever get tired of all this feudin' shit?"

She stood on tiptoe to put a butterfly on the *W* in *Welcome*. "I do, but it seems to get worse instead of better. How about you?"

Tanner pulled out a chair and sat down. "It gets in the way of lots of things. Did you know I had a big crush on you when we were teenagers?"

"I had one on you when we were kids too," she said.

"If it hadn't been for the feud, we might have…" He let the sentence hang.

"But it was, and you're a Gallagher and I'm a Brennan," she said.

"I've always liked you, Leah. You are so sweet and kind, not like those other Brennans," he whispered.

Leah didn't know what to say or if she should say anything. Tanner was a Gallagher. There was a feud, and this could easily be a ploy of some kind to get back at the Brennans.

"And how are the other Brennans?" she finally asked.

"I don't have to spell it out to you. I'd ask you to dinner, but…" He let another sentence hang.

"But Naomi would disown you like Granny would me if I even entertained notions of going with you." She sat down in one of the children's desks.

"We could keep it a secret until we see if we really do like each other," he suggested.

A year ago, she would have said yes without blinking. Two weeks ago, she might have hesitated, but today, she shook her head slowly. She still had feelings for Tanner. Maybe she always would—but she couldn't trust him. He was not only a Gallagher but he was the resident bad boy in Burnt Boot, the womanizer who chased anything in tight jeans and boots and who had a reputation for one-night stands.

"You like me. I like you. Why not? We're grown

adults, Leah." He pushed the chair back and kneeled in front of her, wrapping his arms around her waist.

Too fast, the voice in her head yelled. *Something isn't right here.*

There was no pizzazz, not a single solitary spark dancing around her. It was nothing like what happened when Rhett looked out over the bar at her. And Tanner's touch absolutely didn't have a bit of the fizz that one of Rhett's kisses created.

"Tanner, I can't."

He grabbed her hand and kissed the palm before he stood up. "I won't give up. You've shown me a side of you that makes me like you even more these past few days and, Leah, I get what I want, one way or the other. Wanda just drove up. I'll see you at the bar or at church, or I'll call you. Number please?" He picked up a pen from her desk and held out his hand.

"I can't. What if Granny answered the phone?"

"Your cell number, darlin'." Tanner smiled.

"It wouldn't be wise."

"To hell with wise. But if you want to play it safe and let this be a big secret, I'll go along with you. Tonight at the bar, I'll slip you another phone, a private one for us to use." He waved over his shoulder as he left the classroom. In a few minutes, she heard him talking to Wanda in the hallway.

Leah sat in stunned silence until her thighs were sticking to the wooden desk with sweat. What in the hell should she do now?

Yes, Declan, I used another swear word, but it is warranted. I've had such a big crush on Tanner for so long, but can I trust him? Rhett is a good man and I do trust

him. However, I can't have anything with either of them
and continue to live at River Bend.

"Hey, it's hot in here, girl. You should go home and
come back in the morning when it's cooler, and by the
way, your room is looking great." Wanda broke through
her circling thoughts.

Leah smiled but it felt fake. "I was about to call it a
day and go home."

Home was the last place she wanted to be right then,
but she didn't know where else to go.

Later that night, she was standing in the middle of her
bedroom with a phone in each hand. To her, it was symbolic of each cowboy that had come into her life. In
her left hand was the one that she'd found in her purse
when she'd left the bar that night. Tanner must have
had an accomplice because he hadn't been in the bar
all evening.

"Which means I was right in thinking that there is
something going on," she whispered. "The whole family
is using me as a means to get back at Granny."

In her right hand was the phone she used every day.
Granny didn't like it when she called Rhett, when they
were thrown together, or anything about him, but Leah
had no doubts that he was honest.

She looked from the phone in her right hand to the
one in her left and back again. "Last month, I didn't
even have the prospect of a relationship. Now I've got
one cowboy too many," she said.

She contemplated throwing the one in her left hand
in the trash but she couldn't. She'd liked Tanner for so

long, and now there was a possibility. Then the damn thing rang, and it startled her so badly that she threw it against the wall. Her heart thumped and her stomach tightened up.

It was lying in pieces on the floor, and yet the blasted thing rang again. Maybe it would never be dead, like the feud—if she threw it in the river, maybe it would crawl back up on the bank and ring again.

Then she realized that it was the phone in her right hand ringing, and she quickly answered it, breathlessly and cautiously, "Hello?"

"Hey, you sound like you've been running. Did you go to the bar tonight?" Rhett asked.

"Only for a few minutes," she said. "Long enough to drink half a bottle of beer before I got bored and came home."

"Sorry I wasn't there. Sawyer and Jill decided to manage it tonight and let me and the guys finish up hauling in one more load of hay. They're calling for rain tomorrow night, but it's for after midnight, so we don't have to cancel the motorcycle ride," he said.

"I'm still looking forward to it. Where are we riding to?" she asked.

"It's a surprise, but don't get all dressed up. Jeans and a long-sleeved shirt will do fine."

"Long sleeves in this weather?" she asked.

"Bugs hurt pretty bad when they hit your bare flesh." He chuckled.

"And I sure don't want bug splatter on me when we get to wherever we're going," she said.

"Bring another shirt with you and you can change when we get there or wear one underneath and you can take off the long-sleeved one," he said. "I missed seeing you tonight, Leah."

She liked the way he said her name—she also liked the way he looked at her and the honesty in his smile when they were together. They didn't have to talk over a secret phone even if her Granny disapproved, and she didn't have to worry about whether she was a pawn in a Gallagher game.

"Me too," she said. "See you tomorrow night then."

"Six at the schoolhouse. It's written on my heart."

"That's a pretty good pickup line." She laughed.

"It's not a line, Miz Brennan. It's the truth. Can't wait to see you."

The call ended on that note. She slipped her phone back into her purse and picked up the one she'd thrown across the room. It was in two pieces with the battery pack and SIM card showing. She removed the card and tossed it in the trash can, then ripped the phone apart and threw it in behind it.

Tanner might always have a little corner of her heart, but she couldn't make herself start something that she couldn't finish.

Leah was super nervous the next night. She liked the reflection in the mirror a lot better with her hair down than she did with it slicked back. "But if it's down, it'll blow in my face and I'll spend the whole ride trying to keep it out of my mouth."

She twisted it up one more time and flipped an elastic holder around it before she slipped her feet down into a pair of cowboy boots and picked up her purse. The

clock in the foyer rang out one time, which meant it
was five thirty. As usual, she was ready fifteen minutes
early, and she would have spent it in her room pacing
if she'd known that her grandmother was sitting on the
porch swing.

"Granny, it's awful hot for you to be out here," Leah
said.

"Little hot weather is good for the heart. Come on
over here and sit beside me. You don't have to be at
the school yard for another thirty minutes, which means
you've got fifteen or twenty to spare right now," Mavis
said. "You think those jeans and shirt are tight enough?"

Leah sighed. Nothing was a secret in Burnt Boot. She
might as well have crawled up on top of the bar with a
megaphone and shouted that she was going for a ride on
the back of Rhett O'Donnell's motorcycle that evening.
She crossed the porch in a few long strides, dropped her
purse beside the swing, and sat down beside Mavis.

"I'm not going to change my mind about that man,"
Mavis said.

Leah nodded. "Neither am I."

"You're leaving tomorrow for a week. Have you
told him? And I do insist that you go on this trip, Leah!
Honey and Kinsey have planned it for weeks."

"I'm not changing my mind about going. I have not
told Rhett, but I will before the evening is over."

"I wish you would've had a rebellious streak when
you were sixteen, like Honey and Kinsey did."

"So do I," Leah said.

"I stand by my word. This is the final night you get to
see him and still live in my house."

"Why? What's the matter with Rhett?" Leah asked.

"I don't like him. That's reason enough," Mavis said.

"No, Granny, it isn't."

"Child, sometimes an older person can see things clearer than a younger one. Why won't you listen to me? You've always been so obedient and easy to get along with."

Her words grated against Leah's nerves. Good old, obedient Leah who did what she was told without any sass. Nice, easy Leah who never veered off the pathway that had been laid out for her. Sweet, little Leah who paid attention and made good grades. Smart Leah who had graduated valedictorian of both her high school class and her college class.

Maybe if she was a good girl, Granny wouldn't see signs of Leah's mother in her. That had been the ultimate goal her whole life: keeping Mavis from seeing Eden every time she looked at Leah. There were no pictures in the house, but from what Leah could remember of her mother, she'd been a short blond with light green eyes. In Leah's mind, Eden had smelled good, looked pretty, and always read to her before she tucked her in with a kiss at night. Leah'd been four when Eden had left and never returned. She'd cried for her mother for weeks but her father, Russell, had read to her and tucked her in at night and kept saying that everything would be all right. And eventually, she'd stopped crying and life had gone on without her mother.

A faint memory surfaced as Leah sat on the swing with her grandmother that evening. It had to have been from right before her mother left River Bend, because it was on Leah's fourth birthday. She was hiding under the dining room table with a piece of cake, licking the icing off her fingers. Mavis and Eden were only a few feet away, and they were arguing—again. Leah hated it when they yelled at each other, and she usually put her hands over her ears, but that evening, she had icing on her hands and it would get in her hair.

"I'm not leaving without my kids," Eden said.

"You don't have a choice. Russell should have never married you in the first place, but your children are Brennans, and they'll stay on River Bend. You will be gone by morning."

As hard as she tried, she couldn't hold on to the memory to find out why her mother had had to leave the ranch.

"Why did my mama leave?" she asked.

Mavis blanched and locked her hands together in her lap so tightly that her knuckles turned white. The veins in the top of her hands looked like they might explode before she finally relaxed enough to unclasp her fingers.

"Why are you asking?" Mavis whispered.

"I was thinking about her and a memory popped up. I look like her, don't I? What is your problem with her anyway?"

"You're old enough to know, Leah. I've kept you and Declan protected from the whole sordid story, but before I open this can of worms, why don't you leave well enough alone and trust me?"

"Open the can," Leah said.

Mavis frowned. "Remember you asked for it."

"Yes, I did," Leah said.

"Your mother was the resident bad girl of Burnt Boot. They moved here when she was seventeen and your dad was eighteen. We hired her father to help on River Bend, not knowing that her mother was a drunk who flirted with every hired hand on the place." Mavis paused.

"Go on," Leah said.

"Her dad wasn't much better, but he did stay sober through the week and was a good hand. Because Eden lived on the ranch, she attended our school, and your dad fell under her spell. Lord only knows how hard I tried to break it up. I sent him to college here in Texas and gave her money to go to school in California. She got on a bus in Gainesville and followed him to his college, and they lived together for a year before they went to the courthouse and got married."

"Maybe I got the rebellion from him instead of my mama," Leah said.

"I don't want to talk about this anymore." Mavis took a deep breath and hesitated before she said, "It's time for you to go."

Leah's phone rang before she could stand up. She smiled when she saw that it was Rhett and nodded as he told her that he'd be a little bit late.

She slipped the phone back into her purse and told her grandmother, "You might as well get the whole story out right now. My date is going to be at six thirty instead of six."

"Eden slept with several of the boys before she settled on your father. Of course, she would want the best, and by that I mean the one with the most money," Mavis said.

"You know for a fact that she slept around?"

Mavis nodded. "Your dad told me he didn't care if he wasn't first with her because she damn sure wasn't his first. What mattered was that they were last with each other. They didn't have kids until your dad finished college, and then they moved back to River Bend and she had Declan the next year and two years after that you were born."

"And?" Leah asked.

"Her mother died from too much whiskey and her dad left River Bend. She got in touch with an old boyfriend and had an affair. Didn't even deny it when your dad confronted her. So I calculated how much money she'd get in child support until you and Declan were eighteen and gave it to her in a lump sum to leave River Bend."

Leah checked her watch. "Go on."

"I don't give second chances. Neither does your dad. She yelled and screamed that she wouldn't leave her precious children behind, but she crawled on that cycle with that hippie and took the check I'd written with her. We never heard from her again," Mavis said. "Since Rhett O'Donnell moved in next door, I've seen that same look in your eye that she had in hers that morning she left."

"I'm not my mother," Leah said.

"Prove it." Mavis stood up and headed for the door. "You are right; it's hot out here. I'm going in for some iced sweet tea. Join me and tell that hippie cowboy that you aren't interested in him?"

"I've got a date."

"Remember what I said, child. Either this is the last one, or you'll leave. Only you don't get a check."

How in the hell had something that big never been talked about all over Burnt Boot? Surely everyone knew about it at the time and even twenty-five years wouldn't have covered up that story. Not when folks still talked about Rayford Brennan's hanging and that was a hundred years ago.

The story about her mother was slowly settling into her heart. None of it surprised her. Her grandmother had always had the last word. Someday in the near future, she intended to corner her father and get his version of the story of Eden and the man she left River Bend with that day.

What if I can't be true to the man I fall in love with? The question was like a hard punch to her gut.

She turned on the air conditioner in her truck and let it blow on her face for a full minute before she put the truck in reverse and backed out of the driveway. Could she walk away and leave two precious children? Was she hardwired with that kind of DNA? Did her mother ever truly love her father? Was Eden even capable of love? If not, did she pass on that inability to Leah?

Leah put the vehicle in gear and drove to the school lot reserved for teacher parking. She was determined to put it all out of her mind and think about it tomorrow. Like little orphan Annie sang in the childhood movie she liked so well, tomorrow was only a day away, and tonight might be the last time she ever got to see Rhett O'Donnell other than in passing.

She truly wanted it to be a night to remember, even if it was only a fifteen-minute ride down through Burnt Boot toward the river and back to town for a beer at the bar. Tomorrow, she'd leave with Honey and Kinsey, like she did every summer. They'd stay at a fancy hotel in Times Square and shop, party, shop, and party some more until they were sick of the big-city life and ready to come home to Burnt Boot. Honey and Kinsey had been researching spas and nightspots. In the past, Leah had gone along with whatever they'd wanted, but not this year. She was spending her days taking long walks in Central Park and her nights in the hotel room making a lot of decisions.

The DJ on the radio said something about the heat and then Trent Tomlinson started singing "One Wing in the Fire." She turned off the highway and nodded in agreement with the lyrics that said his daddy was an angel with no halo and one wing in the fire. Was that the story of her mama? Was she a woman with no halo and one wing in the fire?

The temperature was hovering in the high nineties, and the sun was hanging on the western horizon, still a big, yellow ball fighting against going to bed for the night, when she heard the roar of the cycle. Her heart tossed in a couple of extra beats when she caught sight of Rhett with a red bandanna do-rag on his head. The sleeves of his chambray shirt had been cut off, leaving frayed edges around his big biceps, which sported a farmer's tan. The tight-fitting jeans, big silver belt buckle with steer horns on it, and boots said that he was a cowboy, not a motorcycle hippie.

She got out of her car and leaned against the fender.

He stopped the cycle a few feet from her, kicked the stand down, and slung his leg over the side. "Hey, don't you look gorgeous tonight. Does Cinderella have to be home at midnight?"

"Only if that thing turns into a pumpkin then. In that case, I'd like to be home. I don't think I'd fit too well inside a pumpkin," she answered.

"Ain't never happened before. I reckon if it turned

into anything, it might be a rangy old bull." Rhett took a couple of long strides and held out his hand.

She put her hand in his and the heat that passed between them had nothing to do with the thermometer or the hot wind sweeping up from the south.

"First, we put this on you." He let go of her hand, whipped out a do-rag from his hip pocket, and deftly tied it over her head.

His touch sent delicious shivers down her spine, and she forgot all about anything but spending time with him.

"And then this." He opened up the saddlebags and pulled out a fancy helmet that he settled onto her head. "Fits fine. Touch this button and you can talk to me. Touch this one and listen to the radio station of your choice. Please tell me that you like country music."

"I do." She nodded.

"Then sit back and enjoy the trip."

"Where are we going?" she asked.

"To a country music concert." He smiled.

Chapter 8

FREEDOM.

Pure, unadulterated freedom.

That's what Leah felt as the wind whipped past her body at more than seventy miles per hour with Miranda Lambert singing "Mama's Broken Heart" in her ears. The lyrics said that she was breaking up with her feller and her mother was telling her what she had to do to keep face. The line that kept going through Leah's mind was something about how her mama raised her better, but it wasn't her mama's broken heart.

"And now let's go back twenty-five years and listen to Garth. The seventh listener to call me with the exact year and name of this song this will win a signed CD with this song on it," the DJ said.

"'The Dance,'" she said.

Rhett's deep drawl came right inside the helmet with her. "Nineteen ninety. My cousin still sings this when we get together. Mama played it a lot when it first came out. I was a little kid, but I remember her dancing with Daddy."

Suddenly, the song meant much more as Leah remembered her mama swaying in front of the window in the heat of that summer that she left. Could she have been thinking about leaving her children and wondering why she gave birth to them in the first place if she was going to suffer the pain of leaving them?

"You're awfully quiet back there," Rhett said.

"I'm lovin' this country music concert," she answered.

"Oh, honey, this is only the opening show. The real concert is at the end of the journey."

"That sounds like a country song." She laughed.

"Maybe someday we'll go into the songwriting business in addition to managing a bar and running a ranch and teaching school."

"I'm not sure I'm that good at multitasking," she said.

At seven thirty on the button, he made a left-hand turn and slowed the cycle. They'd come to the end of their journey, and Leah was sure they were about to turn around because there was no way on God's green earth there was a country music concert going on in Ringgold, Texas. It had less than a hundred people in it and only a handful of houses lined the intersection where Highway 82 and Highway 81 met.

A mile down the road, he made another left and pulled up into the yard of the O'Donnell Ranch, according to the swinging sign above the arch they'd passed under a couple hundred yards back. He parked the cycle beside a long row of trucks and swung off, shook the legs of his jeans down over his boots, and removed his helmet and hung it on the bull horns. Then his hands circled her waist and he lifted her off the cycle like she was no more than a sack full of chicken feathers. He carefully removed her helmet, hung it on the other side of the horns, and helped her remove the do-rag and the long-sleeved shirt, which did, indeed, have some dead bugs on it.

"Where are we?" she asked.

"At the concert," he answered. "That would be my family over there, under the shade tree, doin' the concert."

"This is your family?" Her eyes widened.

"Yep, they said they were playin' tonight, so I thought we'd ride over and listen to them and…" He slipped an arm around her waist.

"Hey, Rhett, bring your lady friend on over here and make her acquainted with some of us. I need a rest from the drums, so make it fast. You can take over after this one," a dark-haired man yelled.

"You play?" Leah asked.

"Little bit."

"And sing?"

"Little bit." He crossed the green grass and the whole place went quiet. "Hey, everyone. This is Leah Brennan from over at Burnt Boot. She tells me she likes country music, so I brought her along. Don't know if she sings or plays, but she's so damn pretty, she can sit out here on a quilt, and I can watch the sun set behind her."

Leah blushed. "My God, Rhett."

"It's the truth, darlin'," he whispered and then raised his voice. "Now, y'all make yourself known to her. One at a time, please, and no stories tonight. I don't want to scare her away."

"Well, boy, you might have already done that when you brought her here. I'm Cash O'Donnell, this ornery boy's uncle. And this is my wife, Maddie. The rest of them you can get to know better each time Rhett brings you to visit. Rhett, you go on and give Raylen a rest. We've had him singin' for half an hour," Cash said.

"Yes, sir." Rhett grinned.

Maddie stepped up and threw an arm around Leah's shoulders. She was a tall woman, big boned, and with dark hair sprinkled with a touch of gray. "You come on with me, honey, and we'll tell you tales that might make you change your mind about that cowboy. I swear his mama nearly died when he brought that cycle home."

—∿∿—

"Hey, Rhett. Glad to see you again. Leah sure is sure pretty. How'd you snag a woman like that?" Gemma teased. "I'm his cousin, darlin'. We were the wild ones in the family. I rode bareback broncs and he rode a cycle."

"Miracles do still happen." Rhett smiled. "And don't listen to her, Leah. She's married and has a beautiful daughter these days." Rhett settled in behind the big set of drums.

"I'm sittin' this one out," Rye said. "And I'm Gemma's brother, Rye." He introduced himself. "That would be my wife, Austin, and our two kids over there on the quilt."

"Let's do an Alan Jackson number," Granny said.

Cash pulled Maddie to her feet, and they started two-stepping as Rhett leaned into the microphone beside the drums sang about walking through fire without blinking. Leah's eyes locked on his and she smiled.

She mouthed the words at the end of the song, and he motioned for her to join him. At first she shook her head, but his eyes drew her to him a step at a time until she was behind the microphone.

"Do you know 'Heaven's Just a Sin Away' by the Kendalls?" he asked.

She nodded. "I do."

He handed the drumsticks to a cousin and led her to the microphone in front of the band. The two of them leaned forward, their eyes still locked together as she sang the lyrics about how his eyes kept tempting her. When she harmonized with him on the part about heaven being a sin away, the whole crowd whooped and yelled.

They sang two more songs together, and then Rhett handed the microphone to his grandmother. "It's time for someone else to take the stage. Honest, folks, I didn't even know this woman could sing, but now that I do, I'm going to hold on real tight."

"One more, darlin'," his granny said to Leah. "I want to hear that sweet voice of yours do 'Amazing Grace.' I bet you sing in church, don't you?"

"Yes, ma'am," Leah said. "But only if Rhett will sing with me."

"I could sing that one in my sleep." He smiled.

Chills danced up and down his back and the hair on his arms stood straight up when she hit the high notes in the old hymn. When they finished, the whole yard was quiet for several seconds before the applause started.

Granny hugged Rhett and whispered, "She's a keeper."

"Here's your guitar back, Rye. I've got something better to hold for the rest of the evening," Rhett said.

—⁓—

Leah was amazed that she'd been so comfortable up there in front of complete strangers, singing with a man she'd only met a week ago.

"Let's go inside and get a beer or a glass of sweet tea. Singing is hard work," Rhett said.

"Speakin' of hard work, that reminds me. They've bulldozed our school and our kids will be going to public school this year. I'm not sure how it's going to work, having Gallaghers and Brennans in the same school, but I guess we'll see," she said.

Rhett opened the door to a huge kitchen and went straight for the refrigerator. "My insurance agent said my truck is totaled and they'll send me a check next week. Y'all want to haul it to the junkyard for me?"

"I'll see to it that Declan does that." She nodded.

"Beer?"

"Please."

He twisted the tops off two bottles and handed one to her. "You surprised me out there, Leah. I thought you'd be shy."

"I am most of the time. Don't know what got into me. Guess it's hidden genes popping out."

"Well, I sure like 'em, so turn 'em loose and let it rip." He grinned.

"Seems like I don't have much control over that." She smiled back at him.

Music came through the open screen door, and she swayed to it as she tipped her beer up. When she set it down, Rhett wrapped his arms around her waist and drew her close to him. Suddenly, they were doing a country waltz around the kitchen to a George Strait song.

Leah looked up and didn't even have time to moisten her lips before Rhett's eyes shut and his mouth was on hers. It had the sweetness of ice cream, the fire of a double shot of Jack Daniel's, and the steam of a hot Texas summer night all rolled into one.

When he ended it, she remembered what she needed to tell him. "Hey, I'm leaving tomorrow."

"How long will you be gone?"

"A week. We'll be back the day before the Sadie Hawkins Festival," she said.

He toyed with a strand of her hair. "I'll miss you, Leah. We can talk and text, right?"

"Of course we can. We're going to New York City, not the moon. This year, Kinsey got to choose the place and make the plans. I got to do it last year, and we spent a week on the beach in Florida," she said.

He took her hand in his and led her back to the table where they'd set their beers. "You're probably going to find some rich entrepreneur and forget all about this old dirt-poor cowboy you left behind in Texas."

"No I won't," she protested, then blinked up at him several times. "And if I did, we'd always have Ringgold."

"You, Leah Brennan, are wicked. You come off as a shy schoolteacher, but underneath that homespun is someone else."

"I don't let my alter ego come out and play very often. Matter of fact, I only discovered this past week that she lives inside of me," Leah said.

"So I'm the first one to meet her?" Rhett moved close enough to push her blond hair over her shoulder and plant a kiss on her neck.

"I do believe you are. She's so new that she hasn't been named yet, but I'm thinking about calling her Eve."

"Sounds like a fine name to me. Does she carry apples in her purse?" he drawled softly, moving from her neck to her earlobe.

Leah shivered. "You might be the only one who'll ever meet her, Rhett. She doesn't play by the rules and her apples grow all yearlong on a special tree."

"Oh, really? I think I like Miz Eve."

"She likes you too. She says that you're charming."

"I'd rather be sexy, but I'll take charming if that's what she likes."

"I'd probably give you half-and-half," she whispered when his lips kissed her eyelids shut.

"I don't take cream in my coffee."

"Half sexy, half charming, half wild."

"That's a lot of halves for one old dirt rancher."

Leah looped both arms around his neck. "I do believe the rancher is strong enough to handle an extra helping of half-and-half. But, Rhett, please be patient with me and Eve. She and I are getting to know each other, and I have a feeling that we will definitely argue at times."

"Oh, honey, I intend to be very nice to both of you, and I am a very patient man," he whispered.

It was nearing midnight when he walked her to her truck and penned her against the door with an arm on each side. "Don't forget me up there in that big old city," he said in a low voice.

"As if that could happen." She smiled.

His lips lowered to hers, and she rolled up onto her toes to meet him. One kiss led to another until Leah had to break away or else clear out a spot in the bed of her truck to satisfy the cravings in her body.

"Good night, Rhett. Thanks for the most wonderful evening I've ever spent," she said.

"Of all time?" he asked.

She nodded. "Of all time."

He kissed her again, passionately, lingering, making her wish she weren't leaving Burnt Boot for even a minute.

"You will think about me once in a while, won't you?" he asked.

"Every day, probably several times a day," she answered.

"Will you call me before and after you get on the plane?"

Another nod. "Why?"

"I want to know that you and Eve are safe. I've just now found you both. I don't want to lose you." He planted a soft, sweet kiss on her forehead and opened the truck door for her.

She started the engine and watched the taillights of his cycle get smaller and smaller as cold air filled the truck. It helped cool her body, but it did very little for her insides that were close to melting. She put it in reverse and had her foot on the gas pedal when a truck pulled in right behind her blocking her way. She stomped the brake and wondered if Honey or Kinsey had been sent to spy on her.

"Well, shit fire!" she swore when she realized it was Tanner Gallagher getting out of the vehicle.

He tapped on the window, and she hit the button to roll it down. "What are you doing out this late, Tanner?"

He leaned his elbows on the window and propped his chin on his fists. "I might ask you the same thing. Everyone knows Mavis gave you strict orders about that motorcycle cowboy."

"I'm a grown woman. I told you before, I can make up my own mind about who I see or don't."

He leaned in farther, and she caught a whiff of whiskey and expensive shaving lotion mixed together. "Tanner, I'm flattered that you're paying attention to me, but this isn't going to work."

"I thought we had an understanding and you'd call me on the phone I gave you," he said.

"I can't, Tanner. I can't start something that has no future," she answered.

"And there's one with Rhett? If you're going to get kicked out for seeing him, why not get kicked out for seeing me?" he argued.

"Are you ready to face Naomi for talking to me? Rhett took me to an O'Donnell family gathering. Can you do that?" she asked.

"Darlin', I will escort you to Sunday dinner on Wild Horse if you say the word," he whispered seductively and brushed a kiss across her cheek.

Not his low drawl, his handsome looks, nor his kiss did one thing to excite her. All she felt was fear that someone might see them even talking and the news would make the feud even worse.

"My God, Tanner. This is a Gallagher game. The only way you'd be so brazen is if Naomi was plotting to tear apart the Brennan family from the inside. Admit it. You are using me," she said.

"I'm not admitting anything, and I'm not giving up on us." Tanner grinned.

"There is no us. There never was an us. It was only an attraction between a couple of kids."

"I'm still not giving up, and I get what I want," he said. "I hear you're leaving tomorrow for your annual trip with Honey and Kinsey. What if I show up in New York City?"

"Don't, Tanner. Just flat out don't."

"Don't tell me not to do something. It makes me determined to do it," he said softly. "Have a good time,

Leah, and remember, darlin', you never get over your first love, and I was yours." He blew a kiss her way as he backed away from the truck.

Chapter 9

FROM THE WINDOW OF THE THIRTIETH FLOOR OF THEIR hotel overlooking Times Square, Leah watched the sun slowly sink. The bright orange, purple, pink, yellow, and lilac hues were so surreal as the New York skyline settled into dusk that she sighed and wished for the thousandth time that she'd been given the talent of art rather than singing. Honey could pick up a watercolor pad and make that sunset come to life with a few strokes, but Honey couldn't carry a tune in a milk bucket with a lid on the top. Right then, Leah would have gladly traded with her.

The sight calmed her as much as was possible since the very thought of talking to Rhett via Skype in a few minutes made her pulse race.

Honey came out of the bathroom, dressed and with her makeup all perfect. "Hey, girl, you'd better put that laptop away and get dressed. We've got a taxi ordered. It'll be here in ten minutes, and our reservations at the restaurant are in half an hour."

"I'm not going. I'll order up room service. I'm going to sit right here in front of this window and watch the different views of the city as the light changes," Leah said.

"We didn't come all this way to sit in a hotel room," Honey said.

Honey had inherited her dark hair from Mavis and her blue eyes from her mother, which was another thing that

Leah had always envied her for having. Leah had always felt downright dowdy next to Honey, with her exotic looks, and Kinsey, with her height and sassy attitude.

Kinsey came out of the bathroom, sat down on the sofa, and gazed out at the view. "I love this place. We should come here every single year instead of just when it's my turn to choose. And, Leah, poutin' does not look good on you. Get dressed and brush your hair. God, I wish I had your complexion. You can go without a drop of makeup and look stunning."

"I'm not pouting," Leah protested.

"Yes, you are. I heard that Granny waited up for you last night and she says you can't have that new cowboy toy over on Fiddle Creek. Don't get your under-britches in a wad over it. She's put him off-limits for all of us," Honey said.

"Even me," Kinsey said. The total opposite of Honey, she had long, blond hair flowing down over her well-tanned shoulders, compliments of her own private tanning bed. Her brown eyes danced with excitement, but then, Kinsey loved to party and they were so far from Burnt Boot that whatever happened in New York City stayed there.

"She said you can't chase him either? I figured she would put both of you out there to seduce him, to prove to me that she was right about him being a horrible person," Leah said.

"Yes, even me, and Granny has never told me I couldn't see someone. She practically threw me in bed with Sawyer when she was trying to break him and Jill up last spring," Kinsey said.

"Well, that was the famous pig war era and now we're

in the shit war battles. God I hate that name," Honey said. "This time around, it's more serious. Granny don't like Rhett O'Donnell and, by damn, she's not having him in the family."

"I didn't say anything about marrying the man," Leah said.

"Kissin' leads to sex and y'all were goin' at it hot and heavy in the school yard last night, from what I heard this morning before we left town. Sex has the possibility of leading to marriage. Come on, Honey, they won't hold our reservations. Want us to bring you something back to the hotel? Maybe something fancy?" Kinsey asked.

"No, I can order room service," Leah answered.

"And talk to Rhett while you eat it, right? Darlin' Cousin, you are about to get into more shit than you did when the Gallaghers blew up the school." Honey laughed.

Kinsey opened the door. "Did y'all know there's a meeting tonight at River Bend? What do you bet something happens while we're gone?"

"I'm not losing my money. I won't wait up for either of you," Leah answered.

She heard them laughing as they left. She'd already sent a text telling Rhett that they had arrived and settled in for the week. He'd replied that he'd be at the bar until closing but maybe they could Skype after he got home that evening.

Leah opened her email account to find one from Wanda at the Burnt Boot school informing her of the newest development. With the Brennans and the Gallaghers both entering the school, they'd decided to make it as fair as possible; they would put all the fourth-grade students' names in a jar, shake it up, and draw out a child for each of the three teachers, repeating the process until all the names were gone. That way there could be no screaming from either feuding family that there had been discrimination.

She groaned when she got that news. "So I'll be teaching both—probably doing less teaching than settling arguments among the boys and listening to the girls whine. I might need some of your sass, Eve."

There was a message from her dad, telling her to have a good time and to be sure and take in at least one play, and more than a dozen emails from various sites where she'd bought school supplies. They were offering all kinds of discounts on bulletin board art, stickers, and crayons.

She deleted most of them and clicked over to her Facebook page. It was then that she got the bright idea of finding her mother. Lots of people did it that way. They made a sign and held it in front of them, and two weeks later, they posted that they'd found their sibling, their birth mother, their long-lost cousin, or sometimes even their cat.

Since she didn't have a sign, she opted to type in "Eden Wright Brennan," but nothing came up that resembled her mother, so she dropped the last name. An Eden Wright Massey flashed on the screen the minute she hit the button, and there was no denying that was her mother. Right there in front of her eyes—older but still with thick, blond hair and green eyes—was a picture of what Leah would look like when she was in her mid-fifties. On the left side, it said that she lived in Abilene, Texas, and that she was a high school English teacher. According to the profile, she was married, and from the pictures, Leah figured out that her mother must have lived on a ranch in some capacity, that she wore reading glasses, and that her husband still owned a motorcycle. There were no pictures of children or grandchildren. Did that mean Leah and Declan were her only kids?

"Wow! I wonder why I never even thought about searching for her before now," Leah whispered. But she couldn't make herself hit the message button—not yet, not until she had time to think about it.

An ill wind had blown in Burnt Boot all week, and when rumors spread like a Texas wildfire, the folks flocked to the bar. The parking lot was already half-full when Rhett opened the doors. It was well after nine when things slowed down enough that he could step outside for a minute and call Leah.

"I'm so sorry that I'm just now calling," he said. "But it's crazy here. The Gallaghers are guarding Wild Horse twenty-four hours a day and plotting about something. The same with the Brennans. Something is about to blow even worse than the school did."

"Good for business, isn't it?" Leah said. "So no Skype tonight?"

"I don't think so, but it's sure good to hear your voice. Am I talking to Leah or Eve?" He chuckled.

"This would be Leah, but Eve did come out to play a while ago. I found my mother with a couple of clicks on the Internet," she said.

"You didn't know where she was?" Rhett asked.

"She left when I was four. I wondered about her a few

times but knew better than to go investigating. Granny would have had a heart attack," Leah said.

"She didn't like her?" Rhett asked.

"That would be the understatement of the century," Leah said.

"So what are you going to do about it now that you're a grown woman?"

"Eve wants me to send her a private message, but I'm scared," she answered.

Hearing her voice created delicious little quivers down in his insides, "Are you and Eve arguing? Who's winning?"

"I'm not sure."

"Tell me about your mama. How old were you when she left?"

"I've only got a few clear memories. One is of her and Granny fighting, but the others are good ones I think I loved her very much. I asked Granny about her yesterday, and she told me her side of the story— Mama cheated on Daddy, and Granny paid her to leave without me and Declan. That's the short story, anyway."

"What's your mama's name?"

"Eden."

He laughed out loud. "So that's where you got the Eve. Very good choice of a name for this new woman you've found living in your body."

"Thank you. I thought so," she said.

"I could listen to your voice all night, darlin'. I love the softness of it, but I'd better get back inside. What's on your agenda for tomorrow?" he asked.

"We're doing a bus tour of the city, going downtown to do some serious shopping in the afternoon, and then tomorrow evening, we're taking in a Broadway play. Call me when you have a chance. It doesn't matter where I am, I'll answer," she said.

"I miss you," he whispered.

"Me too, Rhett."

He took one more big gulp of fresh air before he went back into the smoky bar. Leah was two people in one. She was a fragile teacup made of the best china, filled to the brim with Jack Daniel's whiskey. He could easily fall in love with both Leah and Eve.

Mavis Brennan passed the pitcher of sweet tea around the table, so her son and two grandsons could refill their glasses. She'd heard that Naomi had a fear that Mavis would retaliate by blowing up her septic tank to the main house on Wild Horse, so she was having it pumped out as soon as possible.

Mavis had considered it, but if a Brennan did that, there could be dead bodies when the shit settled. Mavis didn't want Naomi dead; she wanted her to suffer humiliation.

"The wheels are set in motion, and it cost me a pretty penny to get it done. Y'all don't need to know how or who, but I will tell you this much." Mavis went on to tell them that, when morning came, the main house on Wild Horse would be surrounded with what came out of the septic tank.

"I'll show her that two can play in this shit war," Mavis said.

"Granny," Quaid said seriously, "you're not thinking about technology—cell phones, laptops, for that matter, the computer that they use in their office. They can call out for help the minute the smell hits their noses."

"I didn't think of that!" Mavis groaned. "What are we going to do? I want her to be imprisoned until after church on Sunday, so everyone will know that she has been served justice."

"I'll take care of it," Quaid said. "Leave that part in my hands. Her electricity, Internet, and phones will be out of order from midnight until noon on Sunday."

"How can you do that?" Russell asked.

"Like Granny said, I can tell you what, but not the how. And since it's only twelve hours, it's not likely they can trace it or throw me in jail." Quaid smiled.

"And the whole time it's going down, we'll be at the bar, right?" Declan said

"I'll be playing canasta with Polly and Gladys that night, right here at my kitchen table," Mavis smiled.

"And I'll have an ironclad alibi." Russell nodded.

"Then it's a go," Quaid said.

"If it's all in place, I'm going down to the bar and seeing if that pretty girl from across the river wants to dance," Declan said.

Quaid stood up. "Me too. I reckon the front Gallagher pew in church will be empty come Sunday morning."

"Let's hope to hell it is," Mavis said.

She couldn't tell a soul what was about to happen, but she wanted to talk to someone. She'd tried Leah earlier but she wasn't answering her phone. Mavis picked up the house phone and called Gladys.

"Out of sight, out of mind," she quipped.

"What?" Gladys said.

"I was talking to myself. Remember what we used

to hear when we were kids about out of sight, out of mind?"

"Of course I do," Gladys said.

"Well, it works. A week in the big city and that cowboy you've got on Fiddle Creek will be out of Leah's mind."

"But will she be out of his mind? Seems like I heard something about absence makes the heart grow fonder too. And that wild cowboy is one hardworking rancher. You'd do well to look past his hair and motorcycle. If I were sixty years younger, I'd be chasin' him," Gladys fussed at her.

"Dammit, woman! You are supposed to be on my side. Your kin married into the Brennans. That makes you shirttail kin."

"I might be inclined to lean more toward you than the Gallaghers, but I'm not in anybody's pocket," Gladys declared. "Not even in the shit war."

"I hate that name. If I'd known—" She stopped dead before revealing anything else.

"Hey, y'all started all this by burning down the Gallaghers' school."

Mavis giggled like a little girl. "I'm not saying another word without my lawyer."

"That means we don't talk about my hired hand, who is a damn fine man, or the shit war, right? Does that mean you've got something up your sleeve to get back at Naomi?"

"It means that she shouldn't have done what she did," Mavis answered. "We still on for a game of canasta Saturday night?"

"Yes, we are."

Chapter 10

"GOOD MORNIN'," LEAH ANSWERED HER PHONE. "I HEAR AN engine. Did you get another truck?"

"No, thought I'd wait a while to do that. Gladys says I can use the work truck to go back and forth to the bar. I can't risk getting my cycle messed up, so I've been leaving it locked up in one of the barns."

"If it's your only way to get around, I sure understand, especially with the Gallaghers and Brennans both up in arms."

"Feud doesn't have a lot to do with it. There's this gorgeous woman who likes to go for rides on it. I hear a lot of noise and people in the background. Where are you?" Rhett asked.

So he thought she was gorgeous, did he? "On the ferry going out to Ellis Island. You must be in a tractor with the radio playing, right?" she asked.

"First part, yes. Second part, no. That would be George Strait on CD."

"No MP3 player?"

"Tried that and didn't like it. Guess I'm gettin' old. I like plain old CDs turned down low so I can hear the words," he answered.

"Then you wouldn't be much for a real loud concert?" Leah asked.

"No, ma'am. I prefer listenin' to the music on a quilt under a shade tree with a beautiful woman beside me and the stars and moon above," he drawled. "Where are Honey and Kinsey?"

"Honey is flirting with some fellow she met last night in a bar, and Kinsey is in the corner with a bottle of wine, whispering to some guy she met last night while she and Honey were out partying."

"Are the men in that state all blind?" Rhett asked.

"I don't think so."

"Then they're stupid."

"Why?" she asked.

"Because if I were on a ferry with you, I damn sure wouldn't be drinking wine with Kinsey or flirting with Honey. They wouldn't even be dots in the rearview mirror with you in the picture," he answered. "Where would you be if I were there?"

She blushed and be damned if Honey didn't look back over her shoulder and start in her direction. Kinsey did the same thing, both of them leaving their fellers behind.

"Well, you can damn sure bet I wouldn't be on this boat, with my two cousins coming to see why my face is so red," she answered. "Got to go so I can think up a plausible lie."

"Sunburn." He chuckled.

"I don't think that one will fly. Talk to you later," she said and hit the end button.

Honey flipped her dark hair back over a shoulder that only had a thin strap holding up her flowing, floral top. It barely reached the top of her white shorts that looked like she'd been melted down and poured into. "Are you okay? Was that Granny on the phone, telling you that you can't even talk to Rhett while we're away?"

Kinsey patted her on the shoulder. "Don't pay any attention to her."

"It wasn't Granny. It was Rhett," Leah said.

"Oh, then we interrupted phone sex. Forgive us." Honey laughed.

"Only phone foreplay. Y'all don't have to babysit me." Leah smiled.

Honey leaned forward and whispered, "Tell him thank you. I decided that guy I was talking to isn't worth even a day of my vacation and taking care of you was a perfect excuse to get away from him."

Kinsey nodded. "Me too. After a couple of strong drinks last night, I thought that guy was Mr. Right. But now that I'm sober, he's gone from a nine and a half to a zero. I really have to stick close to you because you might faint. You are the delicate cousin."

"Crap! I'm the designated driver all over again," Leah said.

Honey and Kinsey sat down on either side of Leah and let the breeze blow their hair back away from their faces.

"Do you ever wish this damn feud would be done with?" Leah asked.

"Hell yes," Kinsey said.

Honey nodded. "Only before it ends, I want to knock Betsy Gallagher on her ass one time. What do you think Granny is planning? She called a meeting with Uncle Russell and two of the cousins."

"Which two?" Leah asked.

"I heard it was Declan and Quaid," Kinsey answered. "They're the heavy lifters when it comes to the feud, so I know she's got something up her sleeve."

Leah shook her head slowly. "When the older generation is gone, I hope we can start to tear down the whole feud."

"It'll take two generations, and we'll be old as dirt by then. Uncle Russell is as solidly into the feud as Granny."

Leah flicked a bug off her khaki shorts. "Do either of you remember my mama?"

"Wow, that was an abrupt topic change," Kinsey said.

"I know, but she's been on my mind. I asked Granny about her the day before we left, and she said that they threw her out because she was cheating on Daddy. I found her on the Internet last night. Do you think I should reach out?" Leah's voice sounded hollow and unsure in her own ears.

"I remember Aunt Eden playing with us out on the lawn. She was always smiling and laughing from what I remember. I asked my mama about her when I was a teenager, and she said that she and Uncle Russell never were meant to be together. That they got caught up in a rebellion and wound up married to the wrong people," Kinsey said.

Honey took a ponytail holder from her pocket and whipped it around her hair, pulling it to the side in a messy ponytail. "My mama told me that you look like her and Granny has always been scared that you'll go huntin' for her."

"Was she scared Declan would too?" Leah asked.

"He did, but don't tell anyone I told you. He was about sixteen when he found her. I walked in on him sitting in a horse stall, and he was crying so hard I thought you or Granny had died," Honey whispered.

Leah had never seen her big, strong brother cry before, not once in her whole life, and the picture in her mind brought tears that hung on her long lashes.

Honey patted her on the leg, "That was years ago. Don't get all misty-eyed about it now."

"What did Declan say?"

"He said that he called her and she told him there were two sides to every story and that she'd given her word she wouldn't talk to or see him again as long as he was living on River Bend Ranch. When he asked her why, she told him to ask his grandmother and hung up the phone," Honey answered.

"Did he talk to Daddy?" Leah asked.

"I asked Declan about it a few days later, and he said that all he got out of his dad or Granny was that his momma was gone and it was best to let sleeping dogs lie."

"So the Brennans have secrets," Kinsey said. "I wonder if the feud figures into it and that's why they don't want anyone to know. It'd be a trick to keep gossip from spreading in Burnt Boot, so whatever it is must be buried real deep. So are you going to contact your mama?"

"Maybe I'll talk to my dad first," she said.

Kinsey raised an eyebrow. "You think he'll tell you anything more than he did Declan?"

Leah shrugged. "Won't know until I try. And I'm not sixteen. That could make a difference."

"Girl, underneath that sweet little facade, you've got some nerve. I wouldn't go askin' Granny or Uncle Russell anything," Honey said. "But we're not here to worry about the past or the future. We're here for the present and to have a good time."

—∿∿—

Rhett had baled hay until five thirty, parked the tractor in front of the bunkhouse, and made a mad dash for the bathroom to clean up for bar duty that Saturday night. He felt like he washed a bushel of dirt and sweat down the drain before he got out of the tub and stood, dripping on the bath mat.

"Hey, we're going to go on and open up for business," Sawyer yelled at the door. "I quit a little before you did, and business was slow at the store, so Jill closed ten minutes early."

"Sure thing, but if you wait five minutes, I'll ride with y'all and leave the old truck here," Rhett hollered back.

He wrapped the towel around his waist, checked to be sure Jill wasn't in the living area, and hurried into his room. The ringtone that he'd set up for Leah's calls sounded out loud and clear from his dresser. He picked up the phone with one hand and deodorant with the other.

"Hey, are you finished with your tour?" he asked.

"We're about to go out for supper. How are things in Burnt Boot? Never thought I'd think this, much less say it out loud, but I wish I'd stayed home," she said.

"Me too. Do I hear water running? I'm picturing you in the shower." He drawled seductively.

"I just got out of the shower and forgot to turn off the water."

He groaned at the visual. "I wish I was there beside you right now."

"Why don't you run away from Burnt Boot? You could be here by morning if you grabbed a red-eye flight," she said.

"Sounds tempting, but who would take care of the chores? I was hired on to do a job, so I guess I'd best stick around and make good on my word."

"A woman can dream." She sighed.

"Will you dream about me tonight?" he asked.

"I'd love it if I did."

"Then I hope you have sweet dreams."

"I'm sure they will be," she whispered. "Good night, Rhett."

He dressed in record time, throwing on the first T-shirt he dug out of a dresser drawer and a pair of jeans. He flipped his hair back into a ponytail and immediately the curls started working their way out. A fast look in the mirror showed that he should have shaved, but he hadn't had time for that. Tonight he'd rock the scruffy look, but it didn't matter. The only woman who had caught his eye in Burnt Boot was over a thousand miles away.

Chapter 11

LEAH ESCAPED OUT ONTO THE PATIO AT THE RESTAURANT while Honey and Kinsey were in the gift shop, buying souvenir T-shirts for their friends and some of the favorite cousins. She found a table in the corner, under the awning, and ordered a shot of Jack with a back of Coke and watched the people still out and about after eleven o'clock. Back in Burnt Boot, even the bar closed at eleven and then the whole town was totally dead. A couple sets of lovers walked past Leah, and two became one in silhouette in the distance as they hugged up close to each other.

She sipped the whiskey, letting the warmth slide down her throat as the taste took her back to the Burnt Boot Bar and Grill. Even without closing her eyes, she could see Rhett with that little soul patch below those lips that felt like pure, white-hot coals when he kissed her.

"I bet she's dreaming about Rhett O'Donnell," Honey said as she and Kinsey joined her at the table.

"Why on earth would you think that?" Leah asked.

Kinsey raised her hand to get the waiter's attention. "There's a look in your eyes when you think about him, something that I've never seen there before."

"Oh, really? Maybe your vision is blurry from three margaritas and mine are twinkling from this Jack Daniel's," Leah said.

"I'm glad we're only a block from the hotel, since I might have to carry both of you home," Honey said.

"I'm only having one drink and I'm chasing it with a Coke, but I'm ready to go back to the hotel," Leah said.

"Then you go right on, darlin'. We're not through partying or drinking either one. Don't wait up for us," Honey said.

"I can stay." Leah sighed.

Kinsey shook her head. "No, ma'am, you can't."

"Why?"

"Be honest with yourself, Cousin. Do you really want to be on this vacation? Where would you rather be?"

Leah nodded. "I'm going to sit here awhile and finish my Coke, go back to the hotel, and do some thinking about where I really want to be now that you've brought up the question."

"Think real hard about Rhett and the ultimatum Granny gave you."

"And about my mother," Leah said.

"Girl, you'd best let that one go. Granny won't go back on her word when it comes to Rhett, but she'll disown you if you talk to your mother," Honey said.

"Doesn't seem quite fair for you to be in such a dilemma when we're out having a good time," Kinsey said. "We should be there supporting you."

Leah's smile was almost shy. "This is my burden, not yours, and there's not a better place to figure it all out than right here. At least I'm not in the middle of the forest, where I can't see the trees."

"Leave it to you to find a silver lining in a jet-black cloud," Honey said.

I wonder if Eve can do the same, Leah thought.

"I hope there's one to find when I rip open the black clouds. Y'all get on out of here and have fun. I'll be up before you two, so I'll order waffles from room service for breakfast."

Honey pushed her chair back and patted her on the shoulder. "And tell them to send up some scrambled eggs and bananas. They're great for hangovers, and I've got a feeling Kinsey might have one."

Kinsey popped her on the shoulder. "Speak for yourself, girl. The way you've been knocking them back, it'll be you who's whining in the morning."

"You got it," Leah said.

She waited until they were gone and then held up her hand to get the waiter's attention. When he came to her table, she asked him to put her Coke in a to-go cup.

He lingered beside her table. "I'll be glad to do that for a beautiful woman like you, ma'am. You here on vacation or did you move to the area?"

"Vacation."

"And you're all alone?" He wiggled his eyebrows.

It came off more sinister than sexy. How could she have felt so comfortable with Rhett from the beginning and yet so uneasy around this man? It didn't make sense unless her inner voice, the one that she had dubbed Eve, was telling her not to be so trusting.

"Not for long. I'm meeting someone as soon as I leave." She smiled.

"Lucky man," he said with a long, sly wink.

She nodded but didn't answer and left before the waiter returned. She walked back to her hotel, and fifteen minutes later, she'd changed into a long, flowing caftan and was sitting on the sofa. It was so late that there was no way her mother would answer her if she did send a message.

She opened her laptop and went straight to the Internet and her mother's Facebook page. She felt like she was making the right decision—right up until she looked at her mother's face again, and then an icy chill shot down her spine.

"Well, no freakin' wonder," she mumbled as she scrolled down and noticed her mother's favorite music. "Lady Gaga and Jason Mraz. It's a wonder Granny didn't string her up for that alone. Anyone who doesn't listen to country music on River Bend might get beheaded."

She looked up the songs mentioned. Lady Gaga came first because she liked the title of the song, "The Edge of Glory." She flipped over to YouTube and found the song. The first time she listened to it, she had to remind herself to breathe. The second time, tears rolled down her face, bathing it salt water.

The lyrics said she was on the edge of glory and she was hanging on the moment with her love. She played it through a third time, reading the lyrics as Lady Gaga hit all the high notes. It was exactly where she was right then—hanging on the moment on the edge of glory, and Rhett O'Donnell was the cowboy holding her hand as they climbed up the cliff together. But was it her alter ego, Eve, or Leah that he was with when they were together?

Her phone rang, so she hit the pause button and dried her eyes with the sleeve of her caftan.

"Hello, Granny," she said.

"I don't hear music or dancing," Mavis said.

"I'm in the hotel," Leah said.

"Honey and Kinsey?"

"Probably dancing the leather off their sandals."

"Have you gotten over your folly?"

"No, ma'am."

Leah heard a muffled cussword. "Well, work harder at it. You know the Sadie Hawkins Festival is the day after you make it back home, and I damn well do not expect you to catch Rhett O'Donnell," Mavis told her.

"I don't want to talk about this right now."

"Well, we will talk when you get home, and that's a promise," Mavis said, and the phone went dead.

That's when the Leah's new alter ego surfaced, and she hit the message button on her mother's Facebook page and wrote, "Hello, this is your daughter, Leah. I've got questions. Got time to give me answers?"

The three little dots at the end of her note said that it had been seen, and then a line appeared, saying that Eden was typing.

The two minutes that it took for a reply lasted three days past eternity, but it finally flashed on her screen. "Are you still living on River Bend?"

Leah wrote, "For the time being, but the future is getting shaky."

The next one read, "When you divorce River Bend, get back with me. Until then, I signed a paper and gave my word."

Evidently, Eden did not go back on their word either. Now her curiosity was piqued. There were skeletons hiding, and they were rattling loud enough that Leah wanted to open the door.

Her phone rang again. She hoped it wasn't Granny for the second time that night, but the picture that came up was one of Rhett at the bar.

"Hey, what's happening? Talk to me. I'm homesick," she said.

"After only two days?" Even his deep drawl was sexy.

She closed her eyes and pretended that he was sitting beside her. "I sent my mother a Facebook message."

"Wow! That was a change in subject."

"I'm sorry," she said.

"Don't be. What did she say?"

"To get back to her if I divorced River Bend," she answered.

Rhett chuckled. "And have you even talked to a lawyer?"

She eased back in the sand and opened one eye to see the big lover's moon hanging out there above the sky-scrapers. "No, but I looked one up in the yellow pages."

"Why? Are you teasing me, Leah?"

She took a deep breath. "Yes, I was teasing. But it would be like a divorce, because Granny told me I had to make a choice."

"Between?"

"The ranch and you."

The silence was so long that she held the phone out and glanced at it to be sure the connection hadn't broken. "Rhett?"

"Sorry, that took me by surprise. We've only known each other a week and, Leah, I would never come between family. You've seen how close the O'Donnells are and—"

"I'm not proposing to you," she said.

"Well, thank God for that. I'm not sure what Eve would do, but you seem like the type of woman to let a man have his moment and do that job," Rhett said.

"Even Eve isn't that brazen," she said. "Do you have an alter ego, Rhett?"

"We all do. Some of us call it a conscience."

Leah sat up and shut her laptop. "What if you have both?"

"Unless there's a psychological problem, it's called a conscience. You can name it if you want. I call mine Scorpion."

The giggle came from her chest. "Like the bug."

"That's right. Because, more often than not, it stings me, it's not pretty, and it's sneaky."

"Mine is sneaky too, but it doesn't sting me. It tells me to not be so trusting and laid-back, to make up my own mind and not let others do it for me," she said.

"It sounds like you're becoming friends with yours," he said.

"Do I hear you filling beer pitchers? Please tell me you don't have this on speakerphone."

"No, ma'am, I've got you wired up to my ear. Bought this thing to use when I'm driving and it works very well in the bar when I want to talk to you," he said. "But"—his voice dropped to a whisper—"I'd rather be close enough to whisper in your ear in person."

"Me too, Rhett. Why don't you fly up here for the weekend?"

"Hey, Jill, I'm stepping outside for some fresh air," Rhett said, his voice coming through loud and clear.

"When you get back, I'll take a turn outside. Polly should have made it a nonsmoking place years ago. I'll be glad if the law is passed that declares we don't have a choice in the matter and all public places are non-smoking," Jill hollered back.

"Might as well shut it down," Rhett said. Polly was Gladys's sister-in-law and she still owned the bar. She'd broken her ankle in a fall a while back and it was taking longer to heal than she'd have liked. Nowadays she was even talking about selling the place, but so far it was just talk.

And then the noise softened.

"Pardon that interruption. Are you still there?" he asked.

"Yes, I'm still here. Are you on the way to New York to take me up on my offer?"

"I wish I could, but the bar stools are all lined up with Gallaghers, and the Brennans have three tables at the back instead of their usual one or two, and there's something in the air, Leah. It's heavy and thick, worse than the tension in church when everyone is leaving and some of the Brennans get tangled up next to the Gallaghers."

"Granny is going to get revenge, and then in a few days or weeks, the Gallaghers will do something right back at us. I've lived with that tension my whole life." Leah sighed.

"No wonder you want to divorce the ranch. I couldn't live six weeks under a roof like that. Come home and let's go skinny-dippin' in the river," he said.

"Can I have a rain check? I don't expect that the Red River would be a good place to partake in such an adventure, but I know where there is a wonderful waterfall less than two hours north of us that would be perfect for a midnight swim in the nude," she said.

"Really?" He sounded surprised.

"Eve came out to play. We could ride up there late one evening on the cycle, spend some time at the falls, and be back by morning. Or if it's a Saturday night, we could rent a cabin close by."

"It could be your divorce celebration," he said. "Are you smiling? I could swear I heard a smile."

"How can you tell when I'm smiling?" she asked.

"When you're happy, your voice has a lilt to it. Remember, I told you that the first time we talked on the phone? When you're sad, it's deeper and you talk slower."

"You figured all that out in such a short time?"

"Darlin', I figured all that out in the first few minutes."

A smile spread across her face. "Next you'll be tellin' me you can read my mind."

"I'm not that good yet." His laughter had a twang to it that sent shivers down her backbone. "Leah, all kiddin' aside, I can't make decisions for you, but I can listen anytime you want to talk."

"That means a lot," she said.

A man who listened? Had she found the eighth wonder of the world?

"Got to get back inside or Sawyer will send Jill outside to get me. I'm not afraid of Sawyer, but Jill is a different matter. She might stop making cakes and pies." He laughed. "Good night, love. Sleep tight and call me tomorrow. We've got church tomorrow, but I'll be doing chores before that, and afterwards, Dammit and I are going to the river to see if the fish are biting. Think about me if you don't call."

"I will. Good night, Rhett."

He'd called her love. Yes, he'd definitely called her love—not darlin', not sweetheart, not even honey, but love. A man who listened and wasn't afraid to let that word slip out of his mouth was truly a treasure. She flipped through the dozens of pictures she'd snapped of him in secret. She imagined the two of them standing behind a waterfall, tangled up in each other's arms with the water flowing down over their naked bodies. A slow heat started in the pit of her gut and traveled with the speed of light through her body.

She wanted Rhett O'Donnell to make love to her. Slow, sweet love. Wild, passionate love. It didn't matter as long as she was in his arms.

To have that, she'd have to give up River Bend. To talk to her mother, she had to give up River Bend. She sighed as she shut her laptop and pinched the bridge of her nose with her thumb and forefinger to ward off the threatening headache.

She'd barely shut her eyes when someone knocked on the door. Supposing that either Honey or Kinsey had forgotten their key or they were too drunk to figure out which way to slide the key down the slot, she slung it open without even looking through the peephole.

"Are you Leah Brennan?" a man, holding a long, skinny box tied with a bright red ribbon, asked.

"I am," she said.

"This came to the front desk for you. We don't give out room numbers, so I told the fellow I would bring them up." He handed them off to her. "You have a nice evening."

She closed the door, set the box on the coffee table, and opened the card to find nothing but a phone number.

Icy chills chased down her spine when she realized that it wasn't Rhett's phone number.

"Stop letting Tanner get under your skin. This is probably the number to the bar," she said aloud. "But if it's Tanner and I call with my cell phone, he'll have my number."

She finally decided to call on the room phone. It rang several times before a man answered. "Hello, Leah. So you got the roses. They are to let you know I'm serious about seeing you."

"Where are you?" she asked bluntly.

"I'm in Burnt Boot, but I can be in New York by dawn. Just say the word," Tanner said.

"This is beginning to feel like stalking," she said.

"Darlin', there's no such thing when two people have been in love as long as we have," he told her.

When Rhett said "love," she wanted to run into his arms. When Tanner said the same word, she wanted to run away from him. Yes, sir, there was definitely one cowboy too many in her life right then, and she had no idea what to do about it.

"Are you there?" Tanner asked.

"I am, but please, Tanner, let this go. I should have never told you that I had a crush on you when we were teenagers."

"But you did, and now I'm ready to tell the whole world about it," he said. "I miss seeing you at the bar. I can't wait for you to come home. Just call, and I'll be there in person as soon as I can get a flight out of Dallas."

She was sitting on the sofa with a beer in her hands when Honey and Kinsey came in together. The roses were on the table, still in the box, and Kinsey homed in on them like a hound dog after a coyote.

"From Rhett? I swear, girl, you are going to be in big trouble," she said.

"From Tanner Gallagher," Leah said. "And what are y'all doin' home this early?"

Honey gasped, "We got bored. You know Granny will strangle you herself for even saying that Tanner is in your sights."

Leah's head went slowly from side to side. "He's not even a dot on the horizon. Not anymore." She went on to tell them the whole story.

"That's stalking," Honey said.

"That's the Gallaghers trying to tear up the Brennan family from the inside. Naomi has sanctioned it if he offered to take you to Sunday dinner. She's a sly old bitch," Kinsey said.

Leah motioned toward the flowers. "What do I do with them?"

"I'll set them outside the door and the cleaning lady can throw them away," Kinsey said.

"That sounds like a wonderful idea to me," Leah said.

"Want to keep the card?"

"Hell no!" Leah said quickly.

"You cussed again. You might be right about not being the good girl anymore."

"I hope so. Thanks for listening to me and for taking care of those things for me," Leah said.

"Hey, we're blood kin. We might fight and we might bitch, but it's our fight and our argument, so everyone else best leave us alone." Kinsey gathered up the dozen red roses and carried them out of the room.

Chapter 12

THE GALLAGHER SIDE OF THE CHURCH WAS MISSING Naomi, Betsy, Tyrell, and Tanner the next morning. All during the sermon, members of their family kept their cell phones on their laps and their eyes glued to them, hoping for a text.

On the Brennan side, the pews were full, with only Honey, Leah, and Kinsey missing, and everyone knew they were on vacation.

The middle section was about half-full. Rhett sat with his family and friends: Sawyer, Jill, Polly, and Gladys. His cousin Finn and Finn's family were lined up in the oak pew in front of him.

Rhett spent most of the time during the opening hymns and the sermon thinking about Leah rather than listening. He did come on back down to earth when the preacher finally wound down his sermon. He glanced over his shoulder at the clock on the back wall of the church and wondered if Leah was having a late breakfast or if she'd been up for hours and was maybe having a hot dog from a cart on the street right about then.

Expecting the preacher to ask someone to give the benediction, Rhett had already bowed his head when the preacher said, "Zachary, would you please stand up, so everyone can see who you are?"

A young man over on the Gallagher side rose to his feet and turned around to face the congregation. He smiled and waved as the preacher went on to say, "I'd like to introduce you to Zachary Milton, who is engaged to our own Burnt Boot girl Angelina Gallagher. He and Angelina will be living on Wild Horse Ranch after their wedding in October. He's a horse breeder in addition to helping with the Lord's work in the youth program. Y'all, make Zachary welcome here in Burnt Boot. He'll be sending out emails about his new youth programs. And thank you to the Gallaghers for the fine donation to the church that has allowed us to offer him a three-year contract. Now, Zachary, will you please deliver the benediction?"

Rhett looked over at Mavis, and from the way her face was turning from red to crimson, he'd have been willing to bet her blood pressure had jacked up to stroke level. Evidently she wasn't too happy about the new youth director or the fact that the Gallaghers had donated the money for his salary. He'd have to ask Leah about it when he talked to her later. He was thinking about that when he realized that he and Verdie were walking out right behind Mavis and several members of her family. Verdie was the elderly lady who'd sold her ranch to his cousin, Finn, and then wound up returning to Burnt Boot to live with Callie and Finn. She was the same age as Mavis and Naomi, and was Gladys and Polly's dear friend.

"Granny, why would they do that to Quaid? He's worked with the church youth for years, and he deserves that title. Besides, he's been doing the job for free. This is a slap in the face," Declan whispered on the way out of the church. "Do you think they know about last night?"

She shot him a dirty look. "Shhh! This didn't happen

in ten hours. It's been coming. Naomi has been going around all smug for weeks, and I'll bet you a million dollars this isn't the only thing she's got up her sleeve. That bitch is about to pay for this."

"Now they've got the sheriff's department and God both on their side. Everyone knows that Orville is nicer to them than he is to us, and now the youth director? They'll be running the church in no time," Declan said.

Rhett flashed his most brilliant smile. "Hello, Miz Mavis. I missed seeing Leah in church this morning."

"You stay away from my granddaughter," she hissed.

"Which one?" Rhett asked.

"Every damn one of them."

"Why?"

"Because I don't like you."

"Because I'm not a youth director?" Rhett smiled. "I used to be one, down at my church in Comfort, Texas. You can call for references if you want."

"Did you Brennans kidnap Naomi?" Gladys touched Mavis on the shoulder. "I figured she'd want to be here for the announcement this morning."

Mavis's smile was pure evil. "Not me. I was playing cards with my friends, and you were one of them, Gladys Cleary."

Verdie ignored Mavis and whispered to Rhett, "Finn and Callie are having a baby in about six months over on their ranch, Salt Draw. But don't let the cat out of the bag. They're telling everyone else at lunch."

"Well, how about that?" Rhett said.

"Shhh. Finn wants to spring the news on everyone at the dinner table. Not even the kids know yet."

"I heard you, Verdie. You never could whisper worth

a damn. Dear Lord, don't Finn and Callie already have four kids?" Mavis gasped.

Leah had already decided what she was going to do when the phone call from Rhett came in right after noon. Her suitcase was on the bed, and Honey hadn't even put up too much of an argument. Kinsey had told her to do what she had to do.

She answered the phone with, "Hello, Rhett. I've got a big favor to ask."

"Name it," he said.

"I'm flying home. Can you pick me up at DFW at four?"

"I'll be there. What airline?"

"American."

"I called to bring you up-to-date on the feud, but I'll tell you the story on the way home. I'm afraid this one is going to blow Burnt Boot off the map. Naomi Gallagher might even put a hit out on your grandmother," he said.

"You can tell me all about it when I get there. I've got to get to the airport in record time. Talk to you when I get there and believe me when I say it can't be worse than the pig war."

Leah zipped her suitcase and wheeled it to the door.

"You sure about this?" Honey asked. "You're going home to an argument with Granny, and that never goes well. You might as well put it off as long as you can."

"I've thought about it, worried about it, and now it's time to face it head-on and get it over with before it gives me ulcers," Leah said.

"I can't talk you into staying?" Honey asked.

"There aren't enough words in an unabridged dictionary to do that." Leah opened the door and walked out with Honey right behind her. "You don't have to go with me. I'm perfectly able to catch a cab by myself."

"I'll walk with you down to the lobby. I wonder what Granny would do if I told her I was in love with a Gallagher?" Honey asked as she opened the door for Leah.

"Are you?"

"Hell no, but you should tell her about Tanner and that we all think it's one of Naomi's tricks," Honey said. "That'll take some of the heat off you and Rhett. I still can't figure out why she hates him so bad. I bet it's the ponytail and the cycle."

"Why?" Leah asked.

"I was flirting with a guy at Germanfest down in Muenster last year that looked a little like him, only his ponytail was longer and his cycle didn't have horns on the front. Granny called me into her bedroom later that evening and put the fear of God into me. No Brennan was ever bringing home a man like that, so I could damn well watch who I was hangin' all over—her words not mine," Honey answered.

"You're probably right." Leah explained the ordeal with her mother leaving with the guy on the cycle.

"Well, I'll be damned," Honey said. "I always figured it was Uncle Russell who did the cheatin'."

"Why would you say that?"

"Just something I overheard him sayin' one time. I was hiding in the living room up under a desk when us kids were playin' hide-and-go-seek. He came in and shut the doors, looked out the window, and then made a phone call. I was a kid, but it sure sounded like he was talkin' to another woman to me. His voice went all soft and he said he'd meet her later," Honey said.

"And you never told anyone?" Leah gasped.

"Lord, no! They already said that I exaggerated and even accused me of lying. I wasn't about to get myself sent to my room for a week with nothing but crayons and a coloring book. I wasn't old enough to read, and I sure didn't have a television in my room back then."

"How old were we?" Leah asked.

"It was before either of us were in school."

"Then it was at the same time Mama had her affair with the old boyfriend," Leah whispered.

"I don't know about all that. I only remember it because he shut the door and no one found me, so I won the game."

She was the last one to board the plane taking her back to Burnt Boot. She had a window seat beside a small guy wearing a three-piece suit and a hundred-dollar haircut. He nodded and she did the same, and then she spent the rest of the flight looking at the clouds and thinking about Rhett. Something deep inside her said she was doing the right thing. That same feeling told her that even if she had to live in a tent on the banks of the Red River and eat nothing but catfish and bologna sandwiches, she'd be happier than living in the house on River Bend and wondering what life would have been like with Rhett.

He hasn't proposed, and you're fantasizing about living with him, her new alter ego asked.

I'm not giving him up, she answered.

There's no going back.

That's what makes this such a difficult thing, Leah argued. *But it's the right thing. I don't want to run River Bend. I don't want to be a part of this feud anymore. I want to live a peaceful, happy life without all the tension. I want what I saw when Rhett took me over to Ringgold to meet part of his family.*

When the plane descended onto the DFW runway, her chest tightened and her hands went clammy. Rhett was waiting. He'd said he would be there, and she could trust him with her life. That tingle inside her said that he was already there. Everything was going to work out exactly like it was supposed to because Rhett had come to take her home.

Chapter 13

SHE TURNED ON HER PHONE AS SHE HEADED FOR THE baggage claim area and found that she had three missed calls from Rhett. She quickly hit the button to call him, hoping he wasn't stuck in Dallas traffic.

"Are you on the ground?" he asked.

"I'm in baggage claim."

"I'll be sitting on the bench in front of the doors when you come outside," he said.

"Thank you, Rhett."

"No thanks necessary. I'm glad you are home."

As luck would have it, her suitcase was the last one to appear on the conveyor belt. She quickly grabbed it before she had to wait another five minutes for it to roll around again. She stopped a few feet back from the door and scanned the area. There he was, waiting patiently and staring at the doors. Her pulse raced and she forgot to exhale for so long that she got a little dizzy.

He looked up and saw her, waved, and stood up, shaking the legs of his jeans down over his boot tops. Today he was dressed up, wearing his best boots, jeans that had been starched and creased, and a green-and-yellow plaid Western shirt with the sleeves rolled up right above his elbows.

Sex on a stick, Eve's voice inside her head said with a giggle.

You got that right. Leah smiled.

She pushed her way through the revolving doors, out of the cool air and into the sweltering hot Texas summer heat. Rhett met her, hugged her, and kissed her on the forehead.

"Welcome home to Texas, Leah. Ain't nothin' like it at this time of year." He laced his fingers with hers. "I borrowed Sawyer's truck. Didn't think we could manage luggage on the cycle." He opened the truck door for her and then shoved her suitcase into the backseat.

"I appreciate this, Rhett," she said and then noticed a bouquet of pink mimosa blooms mixed with greenery and baby's breath. It happened to be her all-time favorite flower, and one that nobody had ever given her. As a child, she'd told herself that when her true prince came along, she would know he was the one because he would give her a bouquet of mimosas like the ones from the tree below her bedroom window on River Bend.

She picked up the bouquet and slid into the passenger's seat, not even minding the heat. Rhett hurried around the back of the truck and quickly got inside, turning the air conditioner on high right after he started the engine.

"It's lovely. How did you know I liked mimosas?" she asked.

"You are a mimosa, Leah. You are delicate, but inside you are wild and free. You are sunshine to everyone around you, and there are many layers to you as a woman, like there are many little petals on the mimosa bloom. I expect it will take a lifetime to see all the layers," he said.

Her eyes misted. "That's pretty romantic for a biker cowboy."

"I was speakin' from my own heart and tellin' it the way I see it." He opened a small cooler, brought out a plastic container with a cupcake inside, and handed it to her. "It's your welcome-home cake. I had to keep it on ice so it wouldn't melt."

She put the bouquet in her lap and took the chocolate cupcake. When she popped the top off, the smell of chocolate filled the cab of the truck.

"I hope I'm right and you aren't a red rose lady," he said.

"Mimosas and chocolate cake—my two secret delights. How on earth did you find mimosas at this time of year?" she asked.

"I went into a flower shop and asked for them. The lady said they only used them as fillers for wedding bouquets and she had a few left. Must have been an omen. I'm glad you like them," he answered. "So the mimosas and chocolates are secrets?"

"Most folks have figured out the chocolate, but no one knows about the mimosas," she said.

"Then that can be our secret."

She stuck her finger in the icing and held it out toward him. "You should have the first bite for giving up your fishing to come down here to get me."

He gripped her wrist, and his mouth closed around her forefinger. His tongue licked away every bit of the icing, and all the air left her lungs. Heat shot through her like she had a full-out drip of pure Tennessee whiskey flowing through her body.

Then he popped her finger from his mouth and returned the favor, scooping up an inch of frosting on his finger and offering it to her. She took a deep breath and grabbed his wrist. His eyes went wide as she cleaned every bit of that chocolate from his finger, working her tongue around to make sure nothing was left behind.

"Sweet Jesus," he mumbled.

She opened her lips enough to slide his finger out and then kissed his wrist before she let it go. "That is some fine chocolate, and I do know good chocolate."

"You are not a sweet little angel, Leah Brennan. You might come off as a pampered rose, but, darlin', you are a wild and free mimosa bloom for sure."

"I'd say that we match pretty good then, wouldn't you?"

"I never was accused of being an angel." He laughed as he backed the truck out of the parking spot.

—⁂—

Rhett's finger burned and then it tingled. Hell, it might never be the same.

"Share this with me. I didn't even realize I was hungry until I smelled the chocolate." She pinched off a bite and held it close to his mouth. "And speaking of sharing, tell me the story of the horns on the cycle and the tat while we drive."

"No, ma'am. This is our second date. That's a third-date story, remember?" He opened up wide enough that she had no excuse to put her fingers in his mouth again. "Good," he said, chewing.

"It's not good. It's excellent. It will hold me until we get out of the traffic, but then I'm buying supper for us to repay you for all this," she said.

"No, ma'am, you are not. I'd love to take you to

supper at the restaurant of your choice, but my mama would come after me with a switch if I let a lady pay on a date," he said.

"You're afraid of your mama? I wouldn't think you'd be afraid of a hungry grizzly bear." She polished off the last of the cupcake.

"Honey, my mama puts fear in the hungry grizzly bear," he told her.

"No wonder you're still single at nearly thirty."

"You got it." He grinned. "So what do you have a hankering for?"

"Are we still talking about food?"

He slid a long look toward her, and their eyes locked. "That's up to you, Leah."

She sighed. "I want a big, fat hamburger with double meat, an order of fries to dip in ketchup, and a tall glass of sweet tea."

"Then I know the place to go." He blinked and looked back at the highway stretching ahead of him.

"You said you had something to tell me about Burnt Boot or the feud when we talked this morning." She looked out the side window.

He nodded. "It can't be proven, but last night, for the sake of the story we'll say the Brennans intercepted a bit of information saying that Naomi Gallagher was afraid the Brennans might blow up the septic tank to her house, so she'd called a company to have it pumped. I'm thinking she let the news out on purpose, so that Mavis would know it was empty, and therefore, she wouldn't blow it up in retaliation."

"That sounds like the two of them," Leah said.

"Your family must have paid someone to do the

dirty—and I do mean dirty—deed. Instead of putting what was in the septic tank into the truck's holding tank, they let it flow out all around the main house, trapping Naomi, Betsy, Tanner, and Tyrell in the house. Story has it that the company called Naomi and said they'd had some kind of trouble, and it would be real late when they got there. So it was after everyone had gone to bed when it all happened."

"Why didn't they call out for help?"

"I guess their computers, cell phones, and even the landline was down until right after church."

"Quaid." She smiled.

"What about Quaid?"

"He's a computer genius. When he finished college, he was recruited to work for one of those alphabet sections of the government, but he turned them down. This serves them right for blowing up our school the way they did. It's a stroke of genius. I'm glad Betsy was stuck in there. She's such a bitch."

"The claws have come out," Rhett said.

"When it comes to Betsy, they stay out."

"Oh, and the Gallaghers made a donation to the church sizable enough that they've hired Angelina's fiancé as the new youth director. They gave him a three-year contract. Mavis looked pretty upset about it when we were leaving church this morning," Rhett said.

"Granny will be so worked up, she won't even know I'm home for a week. My cousin Quaid should have been given that position years ago," she said.

"That's what I heard from Sawyer and Jill. I overheard one of the Brennan cowboys saying that now the Gallaghers have the law and God both in their pockets." Rhett chuckled.

Leah's eyes widened as big as silver dollars. "Granny is meaner than the law or God."

"And yet you've cut your vacation short to come home to face off with her when she's in this mood. You sure you don't want to come live in the bunkhouse on Fiddle Creek until she gets in a better mood?" Rhett asked.

"I don't move in with a man after only knowing him eleven days and before I've been on a third date with him," she said.

He tapped the clock on the dash. "Eleven days, one hour, and eleven minutes. That extra time should make a difference."

The glorious beauty of her laughter filled the truck and put a smile on his face.

"So you think that's funny?"

"You make me laugh, Rhett. I like that."

"And no one else makes you laugh?"

"Not like you do. Why do things have to be so complicated when it comes to families?" She wiped her eyes with the napkin that had come with the cupcake.

He turned off an exit ramp into Gainesville. "Some things can't be explained. Ever eaten at Five Guys?"

She clapped her hands together. "I love their burgers. There's one not far from the condo in Florida where I stayed with Honey and Kinsey last year. This is perfect, Rhett." A frown suddenly covered her face.

"What's wrong?"

"You know me so well after only eleven days, it's scary," she answered.

"I told you it's that extra hour and minutes that make the difference." He covered her hand with his. "Leah, all love and relationships are dangerous. That's what makes them exciting, but it also teaches both parties that they can trust each other in times of danger."

"The path ahead of me looks pretty dangerous, all right." She nodded.

"Sometimes you've got to get a machete and hack your way through the kudzu to make your own path in life."

"You ever do that?"

He leaned across the console and kissed her on the cheek. "Yes, I have. Now let's go get a burger."

She left her mimosas on the seat and hoped the heat didn't wilt them. She looked at them one last time and smiled. In her imagination, the bouquet morphed into a machete, ready to hack down the kudzu and create a path for her.

Chapter 14

THE BURGER SHOP WAS BOOMING, WITH ONLY ONE table left, and it was at the back, close to the soda pop dispenser. While they stood in line, someone claimed that spot too, leaving Leah and Rhett with two choices — wait for a table or take it to go.

"What do you think?" Rhett asked.

"We're parked under a shade tree and the whole bed is empty," she said.

"Brazen lady, aren't you?" Rhett grinned.

She raised an eyebrow.

"You offered to share supper with me in a bed, and it's only our second date."

Her green eyes twinkled long before the smile materialized. "I guess I did. Are you going to take me up on it, or are we going to wait for a table in here?"

"Oh, honey, I'd never refuse the offer of going to bed with you."

"Rhett O'Donnell, you are the devil reincarnated," she whispered.

They moved up in line. "I never have been accused of havin' a halo or wings."

She started to ask him if anyone had ever accused him of being sexy but clamped her mouth shut when Tanner and Betsy Gallagher pushed through the doors and lined up right behind them.

"What are you doing back in Texas? I thought you were on vacation in the big city," Tanner said.

"I was." She nodded.

He took a step forward and whispered, "Did you like the roses I sent? I've missed you so much, and I'm glad you are back home."

Betsy slapped him on the shoulder. "Speak up and stop whispering. Anyone sees you making eyes at a Brennan, they'll tell Granny. What are you saying to her?"

"That I wouldn't have liked spending a whole week in a big city either," Tanner answered.

Rhett turned around and said, "What brings y'all out of Burnt Boot today?"

"Granny sent us on a mission," Tanner answered. "And y'all?"

"Rhett was kind enough to pick me up at the airport," Leah said. She hoped their mission didn't have anything to do with blowing up septic tanks or spreading any more shit in Burnt Boot.

"I thought you went with Honey and Kinsey," Betsy said.

"I did, but I decided to come home early."

"Are you crazy? If I had a week in New York City, you can damn sure bet I wouldn't come home early," Betsy said. "You hear about what your Granny did?"

"I heard that your septic company made a big mistake," Leah said.

"Mistake, my ass. When we got ahold of them, they told us this big story about how we'd rescheduled, but we didn't. You Brennans did this and you can bet your sorry ass we will get even," Betsy said.

"If you had a scrap of evidence that my family had anything to do with that mistake, you'd already have Orville out on River Bend flashing his gun and cuffs," Leah said.

"We don't have to prove jack shit. We know, and you will pay for it," Betsy said.

"And then you will after that," Leah said. "Don't you ever get tired of this feuding?"

"Not when I've had to smell shit for half a day, until the family came home from church and shoveled us out and fixed the electricity. I won't be tired of it until I get even, so watch your back, Leah Brennan."

"Is that a threat?" Rhett asked.

"I'd call it a promise," Betsy said.

"Next," the cashier said as she looked up at Rhett and Leah.

"I'll have a burger with lettuce, tomatoes, jalapeño peppers, dill pickles, and mustard, and I want a big order of fries and a large drink," Leah said.

"Double that and add cheese to mine," Rhett said as he turned to face Tanner and Betsy. "It's your turn. I'd say it was nice seein' y'all, but I'd be lyin'."

"Same here," Betsy growled.

Rhett and Leah moved down the pathway made by stacked bags of potatoes to the drink machine and filled their cups. Then they went back to stand beside the door until their number was called.

Leah was sipping on a diet cola when Rhett nudged her shoulder and said, "I bet you're ready to get away from the Gallaghers. Want to wait in the bed of the truck while I pick it up?"

"I'd love to," she answered.

She glanced over her shoulder before she walked out the door and Tanner blew her a kiss. Once outside, she crawled over the side, into the truck bed, and braced her back under the rear window. Her stomach growled, but she wasn't sure if it was real hunger or maybe just pure, old anxiety. There was no way that Tanner and Betsy could have known they were in the burger joint, so that was coincidence, but was Tanner crazy, flirting with her like that? Naomi would kill him for that after what had happened, unless she really was in on the whole thing.

Rhett picked up the brown paper sacks, and carried the whole load out to the truck. He handed it over the side to Leah and let down the tailgate to make getting up in the back a whole lot easier.

She opened a bag and blew on the hot fries before she popped one into her mouth. She chewed while she removed the paper from her hamburger and bit into it, making appreciative noises like she'd done with the cupcake.

"Pretty good, huh?" he said.

"Fantastic," she answered.

"Imagine running into Gallaghers in there."

She nodded. "They're like cockroaches. They're everywhere."

"So what are you going to do when you get home?" Rhett asked.

"I've got some things to work out from the past, some things to get straighten up about the future, and…"

"Why did you stop?"

"I forgot about the present. That's right now. I should be enjoying it instead of worrying about the past and future," she answered.

"What does your heart tell you about the past and future?"

"To get all my ducks in a row, so I can enjoy every minute of the present," she answered.

"And what do you have to do for that to happen?" Rhett asked.

She took a long drink of her soda. "Get things straightened out with my family, and that's not going to be easy."

"You're a strong woman. I've got faith that you can do whatever you set your mind to," he said.

She set her drink down and laid a hand on his thigh. "That's a lot of faith."

He smiled, and she noticed that the soul patch was gone.

"When did you shave?"

"I shave every morning," he answered.

She touched her bottom lip.

"Oh, that. I got tired of messing with it," he said. "Do you miss it?"

"No, you're handsome with or without it," she said.

"Does your Granny know you're on the way home?"

She shook her head.

Rhett finished his burger and stuffed the paper down into the empty bag. "I won't come between you and family. I couldn't do it and live with myself."

"That's not your decision to make or your burden to bear," she said softly. "I sent my mother a message. She said she wouldn't talk to me until I was away from the ranch. I told you that already. It's time I knew what happened, so I'm going to start by talking to my dad."

He slid down to the end of the tailgate and took the food bags to the can outside the restaurant's door. She'd made her way to the passenger side of the truck while he was gone and waited for him to unlock the door. She'd cupped her hands over her eyes and was looking inside when he hit the right button on his key fob to open the door.

"Look, Rhett. It didn't wilt. My bouquet is still pretty."

She took a step back, and he opened the door for her. "The stems are in little vials of water, and besides, mimosas can take the heat. A rose or an orchid would wither up and die, but those things can withstand a lot."

She pulled the seat belt across her chest and fastened it. "And I'm like that bouquet, right?"

He kissed her on the cheek and hoped to hell it wasn't the last time his lips had the chance to touch her. "Yes, darlin', you definitely are."

"Then take me home. I can withstand whatever heat gets thrown at me."

He whistled as he rounded the back of the truck. He'd started the engine before he remembered the serious conversation they'd had before she saw her mimosas again.

"Leah, there are some things better left in the past. Maybe what happened is best left in the closet," he said.

She shook her head. "I want to know. I feel like they owe me that much. I bet it has something to do with this damn feud. I hate it. I wish it would end and we could live normal lives."

"What's normal?" Rhett asked.

"Good question. I bet a million dollars couldn't buy the answer."

Thirty minutes later, he pulled into the Brennans' driveway, set her suitcase on the concrete, and opened the door for her. She stepped out, holding her purse in one hand and the bouquet in the other. The front door flew open, and Mavis Brennan filled it, hands on her hips, bigger than life, glaring at Leah.

"I talked to your cousins, but they couldn't tell me what kind of bee got in your under-britches," Mavis said.

"Well, maybe you can tell me, Granny. I think it's time we air out the dirty laundry from years ago. Thanks, Rhett, for taking your only day off to come to the airport for me." She stood on tiptoe and planted a kiss on his cheek. "I can get it from here."

"You are very welcome. That's what friends are for," he said. "Good day, Miz Mavis. See y'all at the Sadie Hawkins Festival next weekend."

"I hope to hell you are long gone from Burnt Boot by then," Mavis said.

"That isn't likely. See you later, Leah." He whistled a country music tune as he rounded the front end of his truck and got inside.

"Tell Sawyer thanks for letting you borrow his truck," Leah yelled and waved.

Anything worth having or loving is worth fightin' for, so put on your fightin' gloves, man. That inner voice kept on repeating it until he finally nodded.

"Yes, sir! Leah is worth fighting for."

Mavis reminded Leah of a drum major as she marched into the house ahead of her, not offering to carry the little bouquet, much less roll her suitcase into the house. Stopping in the middle of the foyer, her grandmother spun around and set her mouth in a firm line. Her hands went to her hips. "I'm mad at you for calling that cowboy to come get you. You've got dozens of cousins, and your Daddy could have made the trip to Dallas. Why are you home, anyway?"

"Answers," Leah said simply.

"To what?" Mavis dropped her chin, frowned, and glared through eyes that were little more than slits.

"Questions, but I'm not having this conversation tonight, Granny. I want to take a long shower, sit on the porch with a glass of sweet tea, watch the sun go down, and think."

"Fair enough. When you get done figuring it out, I know you'll do the right thing. I can always depend on you to have a level head on your shoulders. You are a Brennan, and you'll see right quick when you think about it that wild cowboys aren't for you." Mavis patted her hair. "You hear what happened out at Wild Horse? I swear to God, Naomi blames me if she eats cabbage and farts."

"Did you make it happen?" Leah asked. "Tell me the truth. Is this the work of Brennans, or are we taking credit to keep the feud going?"

"Hell yes, we did it. Cost me a ton of money, but it made me happier than anything we've ever done. They shouldn't have blown up our school the way they did. If they want a shit war, by damn, I'll deliver them a shit war."

"Granny!"

Mavis shook her finger at Leah. "Don't you take that tone with me, young lady. I'm old, but I still know how to fight. If Naomi wants to meet me in the middle of the road in front of the bar, I'll wipe up the street with her ass and enjoy doin' it. Crazy old broad never has forgiven me for takin' her feller."

Leah had started up the stairs, but she stopped midway. "Oh? I've never heard this before."

"She was dating your grandpa and he broke it off with her to ask me to go to a street dance. She had to settle for Jimmy Gallagher, who wasn't nearly as good-lookin'."

"And the feud took on a whole new life, right?"

Mavis grinned. "Oh, yes, it did. And it ain't never ending, long as either one of us has got breath in our lungs."

"I believe you," Leah said.

Mavis nodded and headed to her quarters at the back of the house.

Leah pulled her suitcase into her bedroom and fell into a rocking chair beside the window. Granny was right when she'd said that Leah had always done the right thing, but Leah wasn't so sure what that was anymore. Did she do the right thing for her, for River Bend, or what?

She dug her phone from her purse and dialed Rhett's number.

"Did you forget something? I can bring it to you," he said.

"No, I need something though. Which heart do I follow, the one that makes me happy or the one that makes me responsible?" she asked.

"I heard a story once that says that we all have three hearts. There's one that we let our family inside to see, one that we let our friends see, and one that we keep all to ourselves that no one ever gets to see except maybe a soul mate. It would be wonderful to make a decision that can make them all happy, but if you can't, then you make the third heart happy because it's the one that you keep all for yourself," he said.

"Are you back at Fiddle Creek?"

"I'm here all alone. There's a note on the table that says Sawyer and Jill went to a movie down in Gainesville," he said.

"Do you think they're soul mates, and they get to see each other's third heart?"

"I really do," he answered.

"They are some lucky people. Good night. And thanks, Rhett."

"I'll be fixin' fence with a crew of high school boys all day tomorrow and working the bar alone tomorrow night. It'd sure make the day go better if you called or sent me a text. And the evening would definitely be nicer if you spent a little time nursin' a Jack Daniel's on the end stool."

"I'll see if I can make that happen."

Chapter 15

RHETT WAS HOT, SWEATY, AND LOOKING FORWARD TO a cool bath that evening. It was the middle of August, so a person could not beg, borrow, buy, or steal a breeze. At the beginning of the day, the boys had told jokes and ribbed each other about having farmer's tans when they started back to school, but now nothing was funny.

The phone buzzed in Rhett's pocket near quitting time, and he hoped it was Leah, calling for the second time that day. She'd called early that morning, and they'd shared a sunrise over the phone, and she'd sent two text messages during the day.

Sawyer's picture came up on the phone instead of Leah's. "Where're y'all at with the new fence?" he asked.

"More than halfway across the back side of the ranch, up next to the river," Rhett said.

"Ask the guys if they'd mind staying with it until it's done. There's a big moon, and y'all could probably do the work with your eyes closed," Sawyer said. "Jill and I will take care of the bar tonight."

"Why the hurry?" Rhett asked.

"The weatherman says we've got a ninety percent chance of rain tomorrow. You might be able to build fence in the dark, but I don't think you can do it underwater. If we can get that done, then we can start clearing mesquite off another forty acres while the ground is soft from the rain."

Rhett turned around and yelled, "Hey, it's going to rain tomorrow. Who wants to make up the hours you're going to lose by working until this job is done tonight?"

Five hands shot up.

"The vote is in, and I guess we'll keep working," Rhett told Sawyer.

"That's good. I know the boys are tired, but let them know how much I appreciate it. Make a run down to the store and get sandwich makings and whatever else you want so they can have some supper. Can't expect them to work on empty stomachs," Sawyer said.

"Will do." He hit the end button and called Leah, but it went to voice mail, so he sent a text saying that he would be building fence instead of bartending that night.

She didn't text right back, so he checked the time and yelled at the guys that he was going to the store to get some supper for them. The air conditioner had long since gone out on the ranch's old work truck, so Rhett drove with an arm propped on the open window. Since the radio didn't work either, he hummed one of Blake Shelton's older tunes, "Sure Be Cool If You Did," with Dammit howling in the seat beside him.

He let go of the steering wheel with his right hand and rubbed the dog's ears. "I bet if they let dogs sing in karaoke bars, I could make a mint with you. But what would be really cool is if I got to see Leah today. I wouldn't even care if it was a glimpse and a wave from a truck going down the road," he said as he parked in front of the store. Dammit bounded out of the truck right behind him and beat him to the porch, where he sprawled out in the shade.

"You stay right here. I won't be long."

Dammit yipped and wagged his tail.

"Hey." Jill waved from behind the counter. She looked like a teenager with her hair pulled up in a ponytail and the freckles shining on her nose. "I'll trade places with you anytime you want an afternoon in the store. This is so damn boring I could scream."

"No thanks. I'd rather be outside putting up barbed wire than sitting in here, even if the cool does feel wonderful. I need about three pounds of lunch meat. Just mix it up—ham, turkey, bologna, salami."

"Hungry, are you?" Jill asked.

"No, but there's a bunch of boys out there who could eat a whole hog. We're going to work until the job is done because Sawyer says it's going to rain tomorrow. Y'all will be running the bar by yourselves tonight," Rhett said.

Jill headed toward the back of the store. "I'll take care of the meat. You go on and get the bread and a sack of ice and a case of soda pop. I'm glad they're willin' to stay with it. Oh, Rhett, pick up a couple packages of cookies for them too, and a bag of those apples."

He was pushing a half-full cart to the front of the store when the little bell at the top of the door rang. He looked up into the eyes of Betsy Gallagher who was right behind her grandmother, Naomi.

"Well, hello, Rhett. Seems like we run into each other pretty often. Think it's an omen?" Betsy asked.

Naomi stopped in front of the counter and eyed him from boots to ponytail. Her hair had probably been as vibrantly red as Betsy's when she was younger, but it had a few gray streaks in it these days. She wore it short, in a no-nonsense cut that feathered back, away from her green eyes. That afternoon, she was dressed in jeans, a hot-pink Western shirt with pearl snaps, and black, shiny boots.

"So, you're the one who's turning Leah Brennan into a bad girl," Naomi said.

"I'm Rhett O'Donnell, ma'am. I've seen you in church, but we've not been formally introduced. About Leah, has she always been a good girl?" Rhett asked.

"Yes, she has," Betsy answered.

"I might even like her if she wasn't a Brennan," Naomi said. "But I'm glad you're giving Mavis some grief. After what she did to me this week, she deserves it."

"Did I hear my name?" Mavis pushed her way into the store with Leah right behind her, letting cold air out the door and making no attempt to shut it.

Leah caught Rhett's eye and smiled at him.

"My prayers have been answered," he said.

"Well, mine haven't," Mavis snarled.

Instant tension sucked all the air out of the store. Mavis and Naomi locked eyes, their brows drawing together and their mouths pursed up like they'd eaten green persimmons.

Jill jogged from the back of the store, three packages of lunch meat wrapped in white butcher paper in her hands. "You'd do well to remember, folks, that this is neutral territory."

"Then, by damn, we'll take it outside." Naomi grabbed Mavis by the arm and shoved her out the still-open door. Mavis came back with a right hook and got Naomi on the upper arm, knocking her backwards off the porch. Naomi reached up from the ground and got a firm hold on Mavis's ankle and brought her to her knees on the porch. Then she gave a jerk and Mavis bounced down the steps on her butt and landed on the ground, sending red dust up in a cloud above them.

Mavis snatched at Naomi's hair and Naomi did the same, pulling Mavis's hairpiece off like she was scalping her and slinging it behind her. It flew across the gravel parking lot and Dammit caught it midair, but he spit it out quickly when he got a taste of the hair spray. It looked like a roadkill skunk without the white stripe, lying there on the ground beside the truck tire. Dammit wouldn't stop growling at it.

"Stop it!" Betsy screamed as she pulled Naomi off Mavis. "Dammit!"

The dog jumped at the sound of his name, ran over to get a firm hold on Naomi's jean leg, and pulled as hard as he could.

Betsy slapped the dog on the flank. "Dammit, dog, don't you dare bite her or I'll shoot you between the eyes."

Leah locked her arms around Mavis's waist and pulled her away from Naomi. To Rhett, it looked like a Chihuahua trying to control a pit bull, and he started to give her a hand but changed his mind and whistled shrilly. Dammit let go of Naomi's jeans and trotted up to the porch where he sat down beside Rhett.

"Do something, Rhett!" Jill yelled.

"Why? If they kill each other, maybe this feud will end."

Naomi made another dive at Mavis. Betsy managed to get in front of her and push her backwards with a hand on each shoulder, but Naomi slapped the shit out of

Betsy's cheek. "Get the hell away from me. I'm going to kill that bitch for what she did to my house."

Mavis broke free of Leah, and the two old women met each other with such force that it would have put the Texas Longhorn football team to shame. Hell, if Rhett could have talked either one or both of them into trying out for the team, he might have left ranchin' and gone into the sport's agent business.

"Rhett!" Jill stomped her foot.

Since she did make a killer apple pie, he pointed at Dammit and said, "Stay." Then he forced the old gals apart, a hand on each of their heads like they were a couple of grade-school kids who'd gotten into a battle over a game of marbles.

"Get your damn hands off me, you hippie!" Mavis screamed.

"I'll put you down like a rabid dog if you don't turn me loose," Naomi yelled.

"You are both getting the hell out of here. You have to fight, you take it somewhere else. We don't need it on Fiddle Creek. Leah, get in your truck and get it started. Open the passenger door. Betsy, you do the same."

Fists and swear words swung, with most landing on him. Their punches stung, but he doubted if they'd even leave a bruise because the old gals were wearing out. Their breath came in gasps, and even a cussword took lots more air than they had in their lungs. Finally, he motioned for Jill.

"You hold Naomi right here and don't let her take a step. Knock her flat on her ass if she even picks up a foot," he said.

Jill nodded and put a hand on each of Naomi's

shoulders. "I've never hit an old lady before, but you can bet your sweet ass I will. What in the hell is the matter with you two?"

"I'm not old," Naomi hissed.

"Yes, you are," Mavis said. "You're an old bitch." That's all she got out because Rhett tossed her over his shoulder like a bag of chicken feed and carried her to Leah's truck. He deposited her in the passenger seat and said, "Take her home."

"You take me to Gainesville right now. I need a beauty shop," Mavis panted.

Naomi broke free from Jill, trotted across the gravel parking lot, and grabbed up Mavis's hairpiece. "I scalped a rotten, damned, old Brennan. I'm going to put this in a frame and hang it above my fireplace, Mavis, to show the whole world that I scalped you." She shook it at the truck as Leah pulled out on the highway.

"Granny!" Betsy said.

"Don't you say a word to me. You should have killed Leah and helped me stomp Mavis to death instead of pulling us apart. Some granddaughter you are," Naomi said. "Take me home and call a taxidermist. I want this pelt cleaned and fixed up to look like a skunk hide. That's what those Brennans are—roadkill skunks."

"Now, am I going to carry you over my shoulder to the truck, or will you get out of here peacefully?" Rhett asked.

"You touch me and I'll see to it you're dead by morning," Naomi said.

"Come on, Granny. Let's go home." Betsy helped Naomi limp over to the truck and then drove away.

Jill sat down beside Dammit and exhaled loudly.

"You are a good boy. You tried to stop that mayhem. I'm proud of you."

Rhett plopped down on the other side of the dog. "After that, it's going to be a busy night at the bar. If y'all get too busy, call me and I'll put an end to the fencing."

"I keep hoping this shit will end, but today proves it ain't about to happen," she said. "You sure fried your ass with Mavis today. She won't ever let Leah date you now, for sure."

"Leah is a grown woman. She can make up her own mind about who she dates," Rhett said.

"I like her better than any of the Brennans or the Gallaghers but, Rhett, don't get your hopes up. She's never gone against her family."

"Not until recently." He grinned.

"She has had a little independent streak in her these past few weeks, but it won't last. Let's go get the stuff ready for you to take out to the field to those boys. I bet they've starved plumb to death. You can take the ice out and dump it in your cooler while I charge the food to Fiddle Creek." Jill stood up and headed inside.

Rhett followed her. "You really think Leah will forfeit what she wants to toe the line for her grandmother?"

"Depends." Jill grinned.

"On what?"

"On whether a cowboy with a big motorcycle can sweep her off her feet and take her away to the promised land, where there are no feuds and only beautiful sunsets and mimosas that bloom all year long."

Chapter 16

THE GUYS WERE STILL BUILDING SANDWICHES AND eating supper when Rhett got the first text message: At the beauty shop. Thank God it stays open late and takes walk-ins. Won't be at the bar tonight. I had no idea Granny wore a hairpiece. This is worse than the school getting blown up.

Rhett quickly wrote back, Me either. I'll be building fence until midnight. Is Mavis buying another wig?

The answer, No, she's getting her long hair cut really short and a new color put on. She doesn't look like Granny with thin, short hair.

Rhett's answer was, Time for a lot of changes.

He got back one word: Amen!

Hoping she'd found a way to call rather than text when his phone rang, he snatched it from his pocket so fast that it slipped out of his hands and went skittering under a big bull's hoof.

"Better grab that in a hurry. If he takes one step forward and lets go, it'll be covered in shit!" one of the boys yelled.

"Yeah, but that's okay. There's a shit war going on in Burnt Boot, so it would fit right in. I heard you already got in the middle of one storm when it rained shit," another one shouted.

Their laughter rang through the rolling hills and echoed off the mesquite trees. Rhett chuckled and very carefully reached under the bull, picked up the phone, and said, "Hello."

"What took you so long? I was about to hang up," Gladys said. "I heard that Naomi scalped Mavis and she's got the pelt to prove it."

"It's not Mavis's real hair, but that's the truth." He went on to explain what had happened, including the part about Dammit trying to stop the fight by hanging on to Naomi's jeans.

"Good dog you got there. When Mavis thinks about it, she'll spread the news that Naomi might have scalped her but that Dammit bit Naomi's leg and now gangrene has set it. I know those two old farts."

"Do you think my dog going for Naomi will buy me any points on the Brennan side?"

"Don't get your hopes up. She might try to buy Dammit, but your fate was set in stone the day she heard about that motorcycle," Gladys answered.

"Dammit isn't for sale." He chuckled.

"Keep him close by your side. She might steal him. Or then again, Naomi might have him shot for ruining a pair of jeans."

"Holy shit!"

"That's the Sunday term for this new phase of the war. I'm glad I hired you, Rhett, and I hope you make a lifelong home here in Burnt Boot, but it won't be with Leah. If you'd set your sights on Betsy, you might have had a chance. She's wild and independent. Leah is the sweet girl who does what's expected of her. Bye now. I'll drive down and look at that fence tomorrow."

The hired hands took another break at ten o'clock and polished off the last of the sandwich makings, then went back to work. Dark clouds had begun to drift over the moon when they tightened the last strings of barbed wire and called it the longest day of their lives. They rode in the back of the old truck back to the bunkhouse, where they moaned and groaned all the way to their own vehicles and drove away in a cloud of dust.

Dammit hopped out of the passenger seat when Rhett opened the door, bounded up the steps, and came to a halt on the bottom step. The hair on his back stood up like a punk rocker's, and then it flattened as he wagged his tail. He tucked his chin down shyly and walked into the shadows, where he could now make out Leah's outline in the rocking chair on his porch. He approached her slowly and rested his head on her lap.

"Tired?" Leah scratched Dammit's ears and looked up at Rhett.

Rhett pulled a rocking chair close to hers and sat down. "Tired and sweaty but glad to see you."

She reached across the distance and laid her hand on his. "I wanted to see you too."

"How long have you been here?"

"An hour at the most, but the night breeze is nice, and this is a perfect place to think," she answered.

"Is Mavis still fuming?"

"Smoke will be coming out her ears until way past Christmas. There was a meeting tonight of the boy cousins to talk about revenge. I'm so sick of this feud that sometimes I dream of running away."

"Give me time to get a quick shower and we can be two hundred miles down the road in any direction you want to go by the time the sun comes up."

She smiled, and he held his breath.

"I can't do that. Burnt Boot is my home, but I wish I'd been born a Cleary instead of a Brennan."

"Then you would have grown up in a bar or a general store." Rhett pulled his hand free from under hers and laced their fingers together. Her hand was so small and delicate that his dwarfed it, but her fingers felt so right curled between his.

"Either one would have been better than River Bend with all the secrecy and plotting and feuding."

"Did you get anything settled about your mother?" he asked.

She shook her head slowly. "I'm planning to talk to my dad about that tomorrow."

"Is Leah or Eve going to talk to him?"

Leah squeezed his hand. "Both."

"Then I'm glad I'm not your dad. You and Eve together will be a formidable force."

"You think?"

"No, ma'am. I know." He smiled. "Underneath all that sweet is a core of steel."

"You keep telling me that, I might start believing you." She squeezed his hand.

"You don't have to do what everyone expects of you. You can get out the machete and make a path right off of River Bend if you want to," Rhett whispered.

Her laughter was as soft as butterfly wings. "You are the only person on the face of this great green earth who believes that."

"Then everyone else on this great green earth is crazy." He laughed with her.

"I should go. You are tired and morning comes early for ranchers."

"Where's your truck?"

"At the store parking lot. I walked from there."

"I'll drive you if you don't mind dog hair on the seat. I'd offer to take you on the motorcycle, but it's so noisy, it would wake up Sawyer and Jill."

She stood up. "I don't mind dog hair and I'd love a ride."

When they walked off the porch, hand in hand, he noticed that she was wearing cutoff jean shorts, cowboy boots, and a Western shirt that hung over her shorts. She looked like she was about to stroll onto a country music video set.

"You take my breath away," he mumbled.

"Ditto."

"But I'm dirty and sweaty and…"

"Sexy as hell," she finished for him.

"In that case," he said as he settled her into the passenger seat of the old truck. He tipped her chin up with his knuckles and ran the palm of his other hand from her jawbone to her neck, where he splayed out his fingers in her blond hair. When his lips met hers in a searing kiss that sent all his senses spiraling up toward the moon, he knew he was falling for Leah. Tanner Gallagher could damn well step down, step aside, and get the hell out of Dodge, because Rhett O'Donnell would fight to the death for Leah Brennan.

"Don't get out," she said when they reached the store.

"I'm tired. I'm not dead."

She scooted across the seat and cupped his face in her hands. "Rhett O'Donnell, one more kiss and Eve is going to take over my body forever. I have to be Leah for a little while longer to get things sorted out. Thank you for the ride, for being you, and for having faith in me." She gently touched her lips to his and then quickly left the truck.

—∿∿—

Leah awoke the next morning with a smile on her face. She reached for her phone and there were six messages from Rhett—short, sweet notes that she read through at least a dozen times before she slung her legs over the side of the bed, kissed the mimosas in the bud vase on her bedside table, and headed toward her bathroom.

Noises in the kitchen and dining room told her that dinner was being prepared when she started down the stairs at eleven thirty. Her father shot her a look and a quick nod toward the kitchen when she passed through the dining room.

"It'll take some getting used to. I didn't even know she wore fake hair," Leah said quietly.

"No one did. She's kept her hair fixed like that since I was a kid," Russell whispered. "What's got her in a stew is what Naomi has done with it."

"Leah, you can set the table for eight, not six. Honey and Kinsey are still where they're supposed to be." Mavis's voice carried into the dining room. "If you'd been with them, this would have never happened."

"Now it's my fault?" Leah raised her voice.

Mavis appeared in the doorway, eyes flashing and new, short haircut making her look like a different woman. "Yes, it's your fault. If you hadn't wanted to go to the store for a pound of bologna, it wouldn't have happened. Now I'm humiliated, and Naomi has the upper hand, but not for long. I swear to God, she'll regret saying that she scalped me."

"I'm not even going to ask what you're going to set in motion," Leah said.

"Good. You've caused enough trouble. Ever since that damned Rhett O'Donnell showed up in town, you've been a different woman—defiant and willful."

"And that's bad? I guess I could start hanging out with Tanner Gallagher. He's interested in me," Leah said.

"You're acting like your mother," Mavis said, smarting off.

Russell raised a palm. "That's enough. Don't lay everything that's happened in this feud on Leah's shoulders."

Mavis glared at him for a few seconds, then whipped around and went back to the kitchen, where they could hear her barking orders at the ranch cooks.

"We've got half an hour. Let's go to my office," Russell said.

"I should set the table."

Russell looped his arm through hers and led her out of the dining room. "She pays people to do that. I think it's time we had that talk you've been asking for."

He closed the door to his office and sat down on the edge of his desk, motioning for her to take one of the leather chairs facing him. "You've contacted or at least tried to contact your mother, haven't you?"

"How did you know?"

"Honey told Declan and he came straight to me. He did the same thing when he was a teenager."

"Does that make you sad, Daddy?"

Russell touched her cheek like he had when she was a little girl. "No, it makes me sad that you never knew her. She was quite a woman, but things got twisted up when we came back to Burnt Boot after we finished college."

"She had an affair with her old boyfriend. Granny told me."

Russell's smile looked tired. "It's a deeper story than that. I told Declan last night, and now he can make up his own mind about getting in touch with her."

He circled around behind his desk and sat down. "It all started when we were kids. I was about seven, and she was six and I think we fell in love that summer at Bible school."

"But my mother didn't come to Burnt Boot…oh!" She slapped a hand over her mouth. "It wasn't her that you fell in love with, was it?"

"No, her name is Joyce. She's a cousin to the Gallaghers on the maternal side, but that was enough that your grandmother threw a fit and forbid me to bring her on the ranch."

"Oh. My. Lord."

Russell pinched his nose between his fingers. "Now you are beginning to understand. We snuck around and saw each other when we could, but I knew it could never work. Then your mother moved to town and we started dating. I picked your mother in a fit of rebellion because I couldn't have the woman I really loved. It was complicated, as you kids say today."

"You married Mama, but you still loved Joyce, right?"

Russell dropped his hand. "I tried to forget her, but then we moved back here, and those were hard times for me and Eden both. Our marriage suffered and so did you kids. Mama hated Eden and made life miserable. Eden wanted us to build our own house. Mama said if we did, she'd disown me."

"Granny ruled the roost like she still does today," Leah said.

"Yes, she did. Joyce had never left the area. She worked at a bank over the line in Oklahoma and spent a lot of time at Wild Horse. She was at church, at the bar when I'd drop in for a beer, at the store when I went in for supplies. Hell, she was even down at the river on Sunday afternoons when I went fishing."

"And you started the affair?" Leah asked.

Russell nodded. "We did, and Eden found out. To retaliate, she got in touch with her old boyfriend. Mama found out, and you probably know the rest."

"What happened to Joyce?" Leah asked.

"She never married, and we've been seeing each other for more than twenty-five years now. She works in a bank over in Saint Jo these days, and I see her as often as I can."

"And you never married her?"

Russell shook his head. "Not because I didn't ask. She refuses. I don't blame her. She knows Mama. Someday, when I'm in full charge there, maybe she'll say yes. But we have a good thing, Leah. Neither of us is unhappy with our arrangement. Like I said, it's complicated, but it works for us."

"I can't believe you kept this a secret," Leah said.

"I didn't. Mama knows. Naomi knows. Joyce isn't welcome on Wild Horse anymore, even if she is shirttail kin. But there's been a lot of battles since that one, and no one cares about it anymore."

"I'm sorry, Daddy. I wish this damn feud had never gotten started, and I wish it would end."

"So you could fall in love with Tanner?"

"So I could fall in love with whomever I please."

"Leah, don't follow in my footsteps. Let your heart guide you, not your head."

She leaned across the desk and hugged her father. "Thank you, Daddy. That couldn't have been easy to tell me all that."

"You should have been told years ago, but days run into years and years into decades, and suddenly my little girl was all grown up. Speaking of being grown and standing your ground for what you believe in, I don't think it was Tanner that you were out with until the wee hours of this morning, was it?"

She shook her head. "No, it was Rhett O'Donnell. I used to have a crush on Tanner, and we talked about it when he showed up at the school a few days ago. Now he's flirting and trying to get me to go out with him. I think Naomi is behind it, thinking that if she can tear down the Brennan family through me that it would be a feather in her cap."

"And do you still like Tanner?" Russell asked.

She shook her head. "I don't. I thought he'd always have a little place in my heart since he was my first crush, but even that's gone."

"Whoever you fall for, I will go to war for you, darlin'. Not even this feud is going to stand in the way of your happiness."

"If you hate the feud, then why do you keep doin' whatever Granny demands?" Leah asked.

"Because that damned Naomi was really ugly to Joyce when she found out about the affair. You know nothing stays a secret very long in Burnt Boot. Naomi created a problem for Joyce. I'll do whatever I can to bring the Gallaghers down for that alone."

Chapter 17

BETSY GALLAGHER PULLED UP A STOOL AT THE FAR end of the bar, raised her beer toward Leah, and smiled as if she knew something that Leah didn't. Leah ignored her and polished off her shot of Jack on the rocks.

"Hey," Jill yelled above the noise of a line dance on the wooden floor and the jukebox turned up to the max. "You want another one?"

She shook her head. "Not tonight. I can't stay long."

Jill moved out from behind the bar and cupped her hand over Leah's ear. "Rhett won't be in tonight."

Leah nodded and mouthed, "He called me already."

Betsy shot a dirty look her way as Leah left, but she ignored it, a blast of smoke and noise following her as she stepped out into the darkness. The moon and stars were covered by dark clouds.

Half expecting Betsy to come storming out of the bar to argue, she didn't hurry to her bright red truck sitting at the back of the lot. Instead, she took her time, because if she couldn't see Rhett, then a good old catfight might be the next best thing. She'd never been in a hair-pulling fight like Mavis and Naomi had gotten into at the store a few days before, but it might be fun to knock Betsy square on her ass.

Why can't you see, Rhett? Nothing is keeping you from going to the Fiddle Creek bunkhouse to see him.

A broad smile covered her face and suddenly all

thoughts of Betsy sitting on her stool and trying to rile her up disappeared. With a little extra bounce in her step, she quickly climbed into her truck. She started the engine and looked up to see a sheet of copy paper taped to her windshield. A big heart, drawn with a red crayon, covered the entire paper. "TG + LR" was written in the middle with a smaller heart drawn around each set of initials. The plus sign was in the middle, where the two hearts connected.

She got out of the truck and tore the paper off, but peeling the tape off was another matter. He must've used a steamroller to make sure the wind didn't blow it away. She gave up trying to remove it and carried the paper over to Tanner's truck. She ripped it into tiny little pieces and tossed it onto his windshield. The slope carried it down into the valley that kept the wipers out of sight. Hopefully, it would be raining when he came out and they would be smeared into his sight when he flipped on the wipers.

"That is stalking," she mumbled.

That is doing what Naomi told him, the voice inside her head said loudly. *This is a war, a stinky war, Leah. No one is nice, and every trick in the book is fair.*

She got back into her truck and drove straight to Fiddle Creek, throwing up a cloud of dust behind her all the way to the bunkhouse. Dammit met her on the steps and walked beside her until she settled into a rocking chair. Then he put his head in her lap and rolled his eyes up at her.

"You are spoiled," she said.

His tail wagged in agreement.

"Hey." Rhett opened the door and stepped out onto

the porch. His hair was wet and hung almost to his shoulders. A white tank top hugged his body like a glove and baggy pajama pants rode low on his hips.

"Am I seeing things? Is this a mirage?" He crossed the porch in his bare feet and sat down beside her in the other rocking chair.

"It's not a mirage," Leah answered.

Dammit moved from her over to Rhett.

"Fickle, isn't he?" Leah said. "Did he learn that from you?"

"No, ma'am."

She changed the subject. "Looks like rain."

He reached across the distance and covered her hand with his. "I was about to call you, and yes, it feels like rain. I'm glad you came by."

"Rhett..." she started.

"Leah..." he said at the same time.

"You go first," he said.

"I feel awkward coming here uninvited."

"You have a standing invitation, twenty-four hours a day, seven days a week," he said. "I was going to call you to ask you out on a real date, maybe dinner and a movie. I get my new truck next Monday. We could celebrate that and you finishing your first day of school."

"I'd like that." She smiled.

"Then I'll pick you up at seven? And that will be our third date, right?"

She nodded. "I'll be ready."

"Your grandmother?"

"Will pitch a hissy, but I'm not going to think about that tonight."

A clap of thunder sent Dammit whining to the door.

A streak of lightning too close for comfort brought Rhett to his feet. Keeping her hand tightly in his, he led her inside the bunkhouse.

The minute the door was open, Dammit raced inside, curled up on the sofa with the two cats, and put his paw over his eyes.

"I'd like to do that too," Leah whispered.

"Don't worry, darlin'. I'll protect you," he said.

Lightning split the clouds and the rain started—not a few sprinkles that increased to an intense rain in a few minutes, but a downpour that started with enough power to create a solid sheet, blocking out everything.

Rhett drew her closer and led her to the other end of the sofa. "Meet Jill's two cats. That one is Chick and the one closest to Dammit's face is Piggy. Now we're all acquainted, let's sit down and visit."

He pulled her onto the sofa beside him, sitting so close that she could feel the heat coming off his body. She wanted more than conversation, more than kisses, and lots more than making out. She was ready to take the next step, and she wasn't real sure how to tell him.

"Hungry? There's a chocolate pie in the fridge."

She shook her head. Food wasn't what she was hungry for that night.

"Something to drink?"

She nodded. "Sweet tea would be nice."

"Got a pitcher full. Bless Jill's heart, she keeps one in the fridge all the time," Rhett said. "Give me a minute."

Another clap of thunder made Dammit whine and both cats sat up and looked at him as if he'd caused the noise. They'd barely settled back down, their legs wound around each other in sleep, when Rhett carried two glasses into the living room and handed one to Leah. She drank deeply, downing a fourth of it before she put it on the coffee table.

Rhett laid a hand on her shoulder. "Leah, what are you nervous about? I've never seen you like this. Is it Eve or me?"

"It's me. I'm not real aggressive, Rhett, but I…"

He gently ran a hand down her cheekbone and stared into her eyes. "But what, Leah?" he whispered.

"But, oh, hell." She shifted her weight until she was sitting in his lap and pulled his face to hers in a passionate, lingering kiss that left her wanting more than his hands splayed out across her back.

"I like that *but* very well," he drawled. "You got any more of them hiding?"

The desire running through her body, melting her into a hormonal puddle, scared the shit out her. She should tell him how she felt, but she wasn't sure how to do it. She wanted tell him about the thing going on with Tanner, but the very idea of him knowing terrified her.

She shut her eyes and laid her head on his shoulder. "No more buts," she said.

"Sleepy?" he asked.

She shook her head. "I couldn't sleep if I were lying on a big, white cloud."

"Something is on your mind. Just spit it out, Leah."

"I want you," she said. "I'm not like Honey or Kinsey. I'm not used to making the first move or stating what's on my mind, so I'm new at this, but I want you, Rhett."

"Hang on," he said as he stood up slowly, his hands cupping her bottom.

With her legs wrapped around her waist, he carried

her to a bedroom, with Dammit right behind them. "Not tonight, old boy. You go let the cats protect you from the storm," he said as he kicked the door shut with his foot.

"He sleeps in here?"

"Oh, yeah, that would be his rug beside the bed."

"Lucky dog," she said.

It had to be Eve surfacing, because Leah had never been so bold in her whole life. In both of her semi-serious relationships, she'd waited for the fellow to kiss her first, and she would have damn sure never said those three words—*I want you*—not even after they'd been to bed together.

Instead of dropping her on the bed and diving right into the sex business, he sat down in a recliner and read-justed her legs until he was holding her like a groom carrying her over a threshold. It was dark and there was no moon, so she could only see him in silhouette when the lightning shot through the sky outside the window.

"Do you know that when someone is blind, their other senses are heightened?" he asked.

What the devil did that have to do with sex?

"We can't see too well, so this should be an experi-ence," he said.

By his tone, she could tell that he was smiling. She reached up and traced his jawline with her fingertips and be damned if he wasn't right. Her fingers were on fire. She circled his eyelids and then drew a line down his nose.

"Sweet Jesus," he moaned. His mouth covered hers, first in a sweet kiss and then in a hungry one. "It's true. Every touch, every kiss is so much more."

"When the lightning flashes, I see you in

silhouette, Rhett, and you are one damn sexy cowboy," she whispered.

"Lord, even your breath against my skin makes me… well…" He took her hand and pressed it to the front of his pajama pants.

There was no doubt that he was ready, and she had been since he'd appeared on the porch with his hair wet and his muscles stretching that tank top. She reached down and tugged the shirt up over his head and then laid her face on his chest.

"Darlin', you aren't one bit hotter than I am right now," she said.

And that's when Eve did a 180-degree turnaround. *Good God, Leah, is instant gratification worth getting thrown off River Bend? You'd better think, girl, before you dive into this water. It's pretty damn deep.*

Leah listened to Rhett's heart doing double time and wondered when she'd started using swear words even in her thoughts. Not even her alter ego was going to keep her from what she wanted that night. Not Eve. Not River Bend. And for damn sure not Granny Mavis.

She pushed back a little and raised her chin. Lightning lit up the room for a split second, and in that time, she could see the desire in his eyes. He wanted her as much as she did him, and that fueled the fire raging in her gut.

"Leah, if you're going to push a button and a red light is going to flash to stop, please do it right now," he whispered.

"I'm not," she said.

She'd started it, and she was going to finish it. Maybe when they finished tonight, it would be over. Maybe it would be the beginning of something wonderful. The future was never clear, but the present, the right now, was, and she wanted Rhett more than she'd ever wanted anything in the whole world.

She sunk her hands down into just the right amount of hair on his chest and said, "I never knew that my fingertips could feel so fiery hot and yet be so cool."

"Guess it all depends on what you're touching."

His lips found hers before she could say anything else and he slowly unfastened every single one of the twenty small buttons up the front of her shirt. He laid it open like he'd unwrapped a present and kissed her between her breasts. His warm breath and lips on that part of her skin made her squirm. She yearned for him to get on with it and yet she wanted this new experience to last forever. Was this what they talked about in the romance books? Foreplay? Did that also mean there would be afterglow?

He stood her up and led her to his room. Somehow, her shirt was gone and then her bra, and her bare breasts were against his chest, the soft hair teasing them until they ached. His hands brought about sizzling heat as they pulled off her boots, peeled her jeans down to her knees, and then laid her on the bed.

Naked. She was naked and it didn't feel wrong. Instead, it felt right. Then he was beside her, minus pajama pants. Wrapping his arms around her, he drew her to his side and brushed her hair back from her face. "I don't have to be next to you to know how beautiful you are, Leah. Just thinking about you makes me hot. I've wanted you since the first time I laid eyes on you."

She pressed closer to him, feeling his erection against her. She was ready for the foreplay to be over, ready to feel him inside her, ready for that magic thing called afterglow. She'd never had sex or made love with a man who talked during it. Mostly, it was a few fumbling kisses and then the act itself followed by snores and boredom. This was a whole new ball game for her, and she liked it a lot.

She slid her body over until she was on top of him, one leg on each side of his waist. Leaning forward and pressing her breasts against his chest, she bookended his cheeks with her cool hands and brought his lips to hers again. His hands moved from her back to her breasts and she moaned out loud.

The combination of his touch in the darkness and the sensations in every part of her body as it touched him fueled a fire that grew hotter and hotter until she thought she'd explode before they ever got around to having sex.

"My God, this feels good. Your skin is like cool water on a hot summer day," he whispered.

She inched her fingers down. "And this?" She teased the already hard erection.

"That is going to get you in big trouble."

"What kind?" she whispered.

He kissed her hard and rolled on top of her.

Her hands automatically went around his neck. She readied herself for the first thrust, but it didn't happen.

"What do you want, Leah? Talk to me."

She wrapped her legs around him. "I want you to make love to me. I don't want sex, Rhett. This is so much more, and I like it."

With a firm thrust, he started a rocking rhythm that had her panting in less than a minute. "Like this, darlin'?"

"Just like that. Don't stop." Her voice was ragged, and she was frantic in her desire for release within ten minutes.

"Oh. My. God," she mumbled.

"Now," he said. "I want this to be good for you."

"I feel like I'm somewhere in the clouds, looking down, and my body is on fire," she said.

Then his mouth covered hers. They moved in unison until he growled her name hoarsely. She dug her nails into his back and tried to melt her body into his.

"Rhett," she wailed.

"Leah, darlin'," he said.

Her breath came in quick, short gasps, and then the whole room exploded in a bright array of sparkling colors visible only behind her eyelids. A bit of lightning suddenly gave her a moment's light, and she could see his face, inches away, staring right at her.

"It's true. It really happens," she said.

"What's that?"

"Afterglow."

"Your first time to experience it?" He cupped her chin in his big hand and kissed her lips, rekindling the fire in her gut.

"Yes, it is."

"I'm glad it was with me."

"Me too," she said.

Leah Brennan had never spent the entire night with a man in her life. When she'd had sex, she'd left long before daylight. So when she awoke at daybreak with the first morning light peeking through the window and

Dammit scratching at the door, it took a few seconds to get her bearings.

"Good mornin'. You look pretty damn sexy lyin' there with the first sunrays of the day in your hair." Rhett was propped up on an elbow, looking right into her eyes.

"Is it morning? Oh my Lord, Rhett. What have we done? Do you think Sawyer and Jill are up?"

"We had an amazing night, darlin'. Don't worry about Jill and Sawyer. They'll sleep for another hour. I do early morning chores when they work the bar." He tucked her hair behind her ear and kissed the lobe, sending hot little waves down her naked body. "But I do have to let my dog outside. Don't go away. I'll be right back."

He reminded her of a body builder, standing there all naked, his wide shoulders narrowing down to a slim waist and narrow hips.

"How about waffles for breakfast?" he asked.

"I can't stay for breakfast. I've got to get dressed and get home." She pushed the covers back and started picking up her clothing. High color filled her cheeks.

"Is that a blush I see?" he asked.

"I don't… I haven't… I mean…" she stammered.

"I know, Leah. I never thought you were." He chuckled.

Their eyes met and held. He crossed the room, picked up her bra, and helped her put it on, then kissed her on the forehead. "I could take today off since the ground is wet, but I really do have to do maintenance on the tractor."

"I'm from a ranchin' family, Rhett. I know what happens on days when you can't be in the fields. I'll see you tonight at the bar and tomorrow at the festival."

"And then Monday we have a date, right?"

The dog scratched on the door and whined pitifully.

"Nothing can change any of that." She smiled, "Dammit sounds pretty desperate. You should go."

He eased the door shut behind him, and she finished dressing. When he returned, she was sitting in the recliner, putting on her last boot. He bent at the waist and cupped her cheeks in his palms. The kiss they shared then was one of those hungry ones that made her forget about breathing.

"Take that home with you and think about me today, because I won't be able to get you out of my mind," he said.

"Me either." She stood up, rolled up onto her toes, and kissed him.

If she hadn't stopped to pet the two cats, she might have gotten out of the bunkhouse without being seen, but they looked so cute sitting on the coffee table. And their little eyes looked up at her and begged for a moment of attention.

She heard a door squeak and looked toward Rhett's bedroom, but it was closed. Every hair on her arms stood up and her neck itched as a scorching-hot blush made its way from her toenails to her scalp.

"Good mornin', Leah." Jill yawned. "You arrivin' or leavin'?"

"Leavin'," she said.

"Got time for a piece of pie? I woke up early and hungry. I could make coffee to go with it."

"I'd better not," Leah said.

"Well then, I'll see you at the bar or at this big festival thing tomorrow. I'm glad I'm already married, so I don't have to run in the race. You and Rhett have a plan?"

Leah shook her head.

"You'd best make one and get it settled tonight. I'll tell him that you'll be waiting for him outside the bar when we close up. Have you told him about this shit with Tanner?"

"No. I should, but the time hasn't been right."

"Promise me you won't hurt Rhett. He's a good man, Leah."

"I couldn't hurt Rhett. Not for the world," Leah said as she hurried out the door. Did folks think that she had a thing for Tanner and for Rhett? She'd talk to Rhett soon, but she could care less what the rest of the people in Burnt Boot thought.

She parked in her usual spot under the carport and eased the front door open. She could hear Mavis in the kitchen, rattling pots and pans and talking to the ranch cook. Then her voice got louder and louder as she made her way from the kitchen to the foyer. Leah's feet were glued to the floor. She couldn't make them move, no matter how badly she hated facing off with her grandmother.

Russell came in right behind her and quickly put a bag in her hands. "Good mornin', Mama," he said when Mavis reached the foyer. "Leah and I got up early and ran in to Gainesville to put a bank deposit in the night deposit slot. We stopped by the doughnut shop."

Leah held out the bag. "I know how you like maple long johns, Granny."

"Well, bless your heart, but don't think for one minute that butterin' me up is going to make me change my mind about that hippie biker that Gladys hired. No, sir. When I speak, it's the law. Now y'all come on in the kitchen. We've made bacon and eggs and hot biscuits. We'll have the doughnuts for our breakfast dessert," she said.

Russell draped an arm around Leah. "Rhett?" he whispered.

She nodded. "Muenster or St. Jo?"

"She works in St. Jo but lives a few miles away in Muenster, so both."

"I owe you one."

"I will collect it."

"Anytime." She smiled. "A bank deposit? For real?"

"Put it in this morning on my way back home. I did not lie."

"What are you two talking about?" Mavis asked.

"Whether or not we should have bought a dozen doughnuts for later," Leah answered.

"Of course not. Do you know how fattening those things are? I won't eat but one, and there's a dozen in this bag," Mavis declared.

Chapter 18

MAIN STREET IN BURNT BOOT STOPPED A FEW HUNDRED yards from the turnoff to the bar, and from there, it was nothing but a rutted path that went on down to the Red River. Two blocks before the big yellow dead-end sign, the street had been roped off for the carnival. Leah sat in the back of her truck in the bar parking lot and listened to the noise of the carnies setting up the rides and the stands. The Ferris wheel had always fascinated her, but with her fear of heights, she'd never been brave enough to ride one before. Not even with her father protecting her from falling, or with Honey and Kinsey promising they would sit right beside her.

People were starting to leave the bar, so she slipped back inside the truck cab and slid down in the seat. Tanner and Betsy walked right past her, and she caught remnants of something about the race and Sunday dinner, but she couldn't make out the rest with all the other noise. The parking lot cleared out pretty quickly, and she straightened up in the seat. Evidently, Rhett had ridden to the bar with Sawyer and Jill because only one truck remained in the parking lot.

Leah felt more and more like the stalker she'd accused Tanner of being as she waited for Rhett. But then she'd rationalized on her way to her vehicle that evening, he couldn't very well show up at River Bend, could he?

She leaned back against the headrest and shut her

eyes. She must have dozed, because a touch on her arm startled her, and she sat up with a jerk. When she focused, she was looking at Rhett, not a foot from her face.

"What a wonderful surprise," he said. "Are you here to give me a ride home?"

"I thought we could talk about our plan for tomorrow," she said.

"Hey, Leah, are you going to see to it this tired old bartender cowboy gets home tonight?" Jill yelled.

"Do my best. Does he have a curfew?" Leah asked.

"Chore time in the morning," Sawyer answered.

"I think we can manage that," she said.

"See you tomorrow morning at the festival?" Sawyer asked.

"I'm helping serve breakfast. Come on out and have pancakes with us," she answered.

"Jill and I were plannin' on it," Sawyer said.

"See you there." Jill waved out the window.

Sawyer's black truck faded into the darkness, leaving Rhett and Leah alone in an empty parking lot. He opened the truck door and leaned in and kissed her with so much raw passion that it took her breath away. She tasted smoky bar, beer, and a hint of hamburger as she wrapped her arms around his neck.

He pulled away. "You smell like heaven, and I'm all sweaty."

She hopped out of the truck and handed him the keys. "You drive and we'll talk about our plan for tomorrow. You got anything in mind?"

"I do and I was hoping you'd show up tonight so I could walk you through it rather than discussing it over the phone." He circled her waist with his arm and walked with her around the back side of the truck. "We can park at the store and do a practice run."

He settled her into the seat and quickly made his way back to the driver's side. "I figure we'll go hide out in the hay barn on Fiddle Creek until about ten minutes before time for checkin' in at the station, and then you can drag me back in handcuffs."

"I get to spend two whole hours with you in a hay barn. I wonder if we'll get bored," she teased.

"I'll do my best to see to it that you're entertained." He parked in front of the store building and leaned across the console. Their lips met in a fiery kiss that left them both panting.

"We have to talk," she said.

"Oh no. I hate those words," he said.

"It's not a breakup talk."

"Then is it about the race or about Tanner Gallagher? If it's about the race, then I think I've got a pretty good plan already. But if it's about Tanner Gallagher trying to get you to go out with him, I know all about that, so there's nothing to talk about it."

"How do you know?" she asked.

"Polly told me. I was the third in a game of canasta one of the evenings while you were gone, when they didn't need my help at the bar. She said that Naomi had decided to destroy Mavis through you and she's using Tanner to do it. This is Burnt Boot, town of a feud so old that y'all should have a Feud Festival instead of a Sadie Hawkins Festival, and it is also the town where the gossip is hot—and one lady I know is even hotter."

"Okay, then let's talk about the race." She smiled.

"All the guys I've talked to say that it starts at the store and we get a ten- or fifteen-minute head start to run and hide. That about right?" he asked.

"That's the rules," she answered.

He kissed her and she completely forgot about everything and everyone but Rhett. She was somewhere between earth and heaven, floating on a lovely cloud where nothing—feuds, Sadie Hawkin's festivals, or anything else—even mattered.

The kiss ended, but he kept an arm around her. "The preacher will fire the shot for the guys to take off."

"That's right," she said.

"I understand that the guys take off seven ways to Sunday, running through the carnival, around trucks and cars, and leaving nothing but a ghost of where they have been. Then they all meet up under the weeping willow tree on the banks of the river. At least those who don't want to get caught do. The others stay out of sight until the woman of their dreams comes along. They put up a fight, but they usually get caught by the right woman."

"So my willow tree has been their hiding place all these years. What are you going to do?" she asked.

"I'm going to run like the wind through the carnival. Then I'm going to circle around the fence line at the back side of Fiddle Creek and make my way to the hay barn. We'll walk from here to there right now, so you'll know the path I'll take. It's not hard to follow, and I'll be waiting for you."

"Which barn? There are two or three back behind the bunkhouse."

"I'll show you," he said as he opened the truck door and got out.

Together, they followed a cattle path from the back of the store, through the rolling land, toward the bunkhouse. When they were about halfway there, the path veered off to the right, and in a few minutes, she recognized the oldest barn on Fiddle Creek.

"I'll be waiting in the hayloft," he said. "You go on up first, and I'll follow you." He pointed toward the ladder leading up through a hole in the barn roof floor. She scrambled up the ladder, very well aware of his eyes on her butt.

"I'm close enough I could kiss your ass," he laughed as he started up right behind her.

"I might enjoy it," she said, flirting back.

The loft had some loose hay scattered around on the floor, a few small, rectangular bales stacked along one side, and the big double doors were thrown wide-open. From that vantage point, she could see the empty Ferris wheel slowly making its rounds as they carnie folks tested it.

"Tomorrow I want to ride that thing," she said.

Rhett wrapped his arms around her and snuggled his face down into the hollow of her neck. "All day long if you want to."

"And you'll ride beside me as long as I want to stay on it?" she asked.

"Of course I will. But remember it would be real easy for one of your cousins or your brother or even Mavis to shoot me dead. I'd be a sitting duck," he joked.

"I'll protect you." She turned around and rolled up onto her toes for a kiss.

He removed his phone, touched a few buttons, and put it back.

"Turning it off for a reason?" she asked.

He pulled her close to his chest and started swaying to music coming from his pocket. The lyrics from "Don't Close Your Eyes," an old tune by Keith Whitley, played softly as he two stepped with her in the hayloft.

The words begging her to let yesterday go and not to close her eyes and pretend it's someone else brought tears to her eyes.

"I don't think about Tanner when I'm with you," she said.

He held her chin in his hand and gazed down into her eyes. "I can never hope to give you what he can offer. All I've got is my heart and soul, and you deserve so much more than that."

A solitary tear escaped and traveled slowly down her cheekbone. He wiped it away with his finger and kissed her eyelid. Heat, passion, understanding, and friendship all combined into a big ball of desire deep inside of her body.

"Let's don't let a silly teenage crush ruin what we have. It's gone and forgotten, and what my heart and soul deserves is a life of happiness and trust," she said softly.

He stopped dancing and combed through her long, blond hair with his fingers. "I don't ever want to look into your eyes and see regrets." He sunk his face into her hair. "Your hair is like silk. I love the way it smells. It reminds me of apples."

"Like Eve's apple?" She leaned back and smiled up at him, glad that he'd changed the subject.

"Exactly. Dangerous and sweet and everything in between."

"Then I'll never change my shampoo." She cupped

his cheeks in her hands and kissed him hard. When she opened her eyes, she caught sight of a horse blanket flapping in the night breeze from a nail beside the loft doors.

She backed him up two steps and reached for it. "Hay sticks to naked bodies."

"Oh, are we about to get naked?" he asked.

"Yes, sir, we sure are."

Life was perfect and complete. They had a horse blanket, the stars and the moon shining down on them, and the promise of a Ferris wheel ride the next day. The road ahead was clear of all rocks and obstacles.

She spread the blanket out in the hay and pulled him down beside her. He pushed her back gently, and starting with her boots, he slowly undressed her, taking off her socks, then massaging her feet before he kissed each toe.

She was glad that she'd worn a sundress, a bra, and panties, or she couldn't have withstood the excitement as each piece of clothing came off her body. Tight-fitting jeans, underwear, and a button-up shirt would have taken too damn long. As it was, he took his own sweet, precious time untying the straps of the brightly colored sundress and easing it down over her hips.

"God, you are gorgeous," he said.

"My turn," she said when she was totally naked.

She pulled his knit shirt up over his head and kissed the hollow of his neck, his ears, and his eyelids before settling her lips on his.

"I love the way you look at me, Rhett. I love that we talk before, during, and after sex. I love your slow drawl when you say sweet things to me," she murmured when the kiss ended.

"Then we make a good pair because I could look at you every hour of every day and never get tired and, darlin', I love everything about every moment when I'm with you," he said.

"Do you believe that things happen for a reason?"

"Tonight, I believe in miracles because you are in my life."

He took charge at that point and quickly undressed, throwing all his clothing and boots into a pile beside the hay bales. He stretched out beside her, and she snuggled up close to his side.

"When you're in my arms, my life is complete and time means nothing," he whispered softly.

His warm breath sent shivers down her spine to her knees. She rolled to one side and pulled him on top of her. He entered her in one fluid motion, and they rocked together, lost in their own world where only two people existed. Neither of them closed their eyes that night.

He took her to the brink of climax, then everything began to swirl and whoosh in her ears as she let go at the same time he did. His breath was ragged, and she had to remember to inhale. It was even more spectacular than bedroom sex, even though they were both drenched in sweat.

He rolled off her to one side. "My God, Leah! That was…was… Words can't describe it."

"I know," she said, gasping. "Since we're already sweaty…" Her eyes twinkled as she moved closer and kissed him hard and passionately.

———

"You comin' in from doin' chores or from a night with Leah?" Sawyer asked Rhett the next morning.

"Both," Rhett said. "Feeding is done. All right if I traipse through your room and take a shower?"

Jill poked her head around the kitchen. "Coffee is ready. When you get done, grab a cup to wake up, and we'll go down to the school for their pancake breakfast. We're supposed to pick up Aunt Polly and Aunt Gladys on the way, so you'll have to drive the work truck."

"No problem. I'll be out in ten minutes." He yawned.

Jill sipped at a cup of coffee. "Not smart."

Rhett stopped on the way across the living room to pet Dammit and the cats. "What's not smart?"

"Layin' out all night and having to outrun those women this afternoon."

"Leah and I have a foolproof plan." He grinned.

"Shhh," Sawyer said. "If Madam Fate hears you say that, she'll toss a monkey wrench into the works and spoil your plans."

Rhett laughed. "We even practiced our plan. We're going to meet in the hay barn where she will cuff me and drag me back to the finish line."

"Good luck," Jill said. "But remember, the Gallaghers and the Brennans might have booby traps laid, so be careful."

———

Honey grabbed Leah by the arm when she got out of her truck and led her around the house to the patio. "Sit," she said.

Leah plopped down in a chair across the table from Honey and picked up the glass of orange juice in front of her. "I can't talk right now. I've got to take a shower and get ready to go serve pancakes."

"You've got to sit right here for ten minutes and pick that damned hay out of your hair," Honey said.

"Why?"

"Because Granny is already watchin' you like a hawk. She almost put me and Kinsey in a torture chamber last night when we got home. I've never answered so many questions in one night," Honey said.

"And what does orange juice have to do with anything?"

"I told her that I would wake you up and we'd be waiting for her on the patio. I was trying to figure out a plausible lie to cover for you when you came in the door. I've brought out orange juice, and she's bringing some leftover doughnuts to hold us over until we get to the pancake breakfast. I wish it were the Gallaghers year to cook breakfast and not ours. I bet next year they'll expect us to work together, since all our kids will be in public school starting Monday," Honey answered.

"Maybe that's what it'll take to end this feud," Leah said.

"Here she comes. There's one more piece of hay in the top of your dress. Where did you spend the night? In a hayloft?"

Leah grinned.

Honey clapped a hand over her mouth. "You really have gone bad."

"Good morning, granddaughters," Mavis singsonged. "Are you ready to chase down a good-lookin' cowboy?

One that's not a Gallagher and for damn sure not one who rides a cycle and has a ponytail?"

"Rhett's hair isn't much longer than Declan's, and you don't fuss at him," Leah said.

Mavis's chin popped up two inches. "Declan doesn't have one of them motorcycles."

Leah countered with, "Rhett is getting a new truck tomorrow."

"Y'all must talk a hell of a lot down at that bar," Mavis said.

"We do," Leah said. "Pass those doughnuts. Are these the ones Daddy and I brought in?"

"Yes. I heated them in the microwave, and they're good as new. Don't eat too many. Save some room for the pancakes and sausage. Too bad the sausage is that old, store-bought stuff. If Naomi hadn't stolen my pigs back in the spring, I would have donated all the sausage like I do every year. Well, her punishment is that she'll have to eat sorry sausage," Mavis said.

Leah's phone buzzed in her pocket, and she removed it to find a text message from Rhett that said, I miss you already.

"Put that phone away. I swear to God's angels that technology is going to be the death of this great nation. It starts with manners and who knows where the hell it will end. Kids these days ain't got a bit of respect. Can't even put those phones away while they have breakfast," Mavis fussed.

"Granny, I'm not a kid. I'll be thirty this fall, and I didn't answer it. I checked it to make sure it wasn't an emergency and put it back in my pocket," Leah said.

"See what those things cause? You are sassin' me.

What's the world comin' to? I swear it's on a downhill slide right into hell." Mavis threw her hand over her forehead in a dramatic gesture.

"Granny, I'm having trouble getting used to your hair," Honey said, trying to get her off the rampage, but all she got was the old Brennan stink eye.

Leah mouthed, "Thank you."

Honey's brief tilt of the head said that she'd seen it.

"Should have had it fixed like this years ago, before that rotten Naomi got her hands on my hairpiece. I swear if she hangs that in her house and says that it's a Brennan's scalp, I will burn her house to the ground and then do a jig on Main Street in a pig trough to celebrate," Mavis said.

Leah polished off a doughnut, drank all of her juice, and said, "Hate to leave good company, but I need to make a dash through the bathroom and then get my purse. Have to be at the cafeteria in"—she looked at the time on her cell phone—"thirty minutes."

Mavis's lips puckered up like she'd been sucking on a lollipop made with alum. "Can't wear that nice watch I gave you for your college graduation, but you depend on the cell phone for time as well as getting mail."

"Tell me, Granny, which one of the beauticians did your hair?" Honey asked. "I'd like to give her a try."

While Mavis was trying to remember the woman's name, Leah escaped through the sliding glass doors into the house. She ran up the stairs, shucked off all her clothing, and took the fastest shower she'd ever had in her life. She donned a pair of cutoff jean shorts with a ragged hem, flip-flops, and a sage-green T-shirt that she knotted at the waist, and then grabbed her purse.

As luck would have it, Mavis was in the foyer when she started down the steps and there was no getting out the door without another confrontation.

"See you at the breakfast," Leah said.

"Dressed like that? Good God Almighty, Leah."

"I won't be back home until after the race, so I'm dressed for Sadie Hawkins." She smiled sweetly.

"Like I said, the world is going to hell in a handbasket." Mavis clucked like an old hen all the way to her bedroom suite at the end of the foyer. "But I'd rather see you dressed like that than see you fully clothed on the back of a motorcycle with that hippie cowboy."

What about clothed like this on the motorcycle? Leah thought as she hurried out to her truck. Then she looked around to make sure she hadn't said the words out loud.

Four Brennan daughters-in-law had taken over the school kitchen and organized the cooking process. Kinsey and Honey had been given the job of serving, and when Leah arrived, she was told to take the money at the door. She was set up with a gray metal box with dividers for the bills, a small desk, and a folding chair.

As luck would have it, Tanner Gallagher was the first person to walk into the cafeteria, with Betsy and Naomi right behind him. He flashed his most brilliant smile at her and laid a twenty-dollar bill on the desk. When she reached for it, he covered her hand with his.

"Don't make change. Just put it all toward the library for the kids, since our kids will be here too," he said.

She pulled her hand free. "Thank you for your generous donation, Tanner."

"I'll be hanging back waiting for you at the race. Don't run past me," he whispered.

"Don't hold up the line," the person behind him said with a raised voice. "You can run in the race and let her catch you later this afternoon. We're all hungry."

"From his lips to God's ears," Tanner said.

"Good morning, Leah." Betsy nodded.

"Hello," Leah said. "Enjoy your pancake breakfast."

"Oh, we will." Naomi smiled, but it did not reach her eyes.

Leah scarcely looked up for the next half hour. The cafeteria quickly filled with Brennans, Gallaghers, and neutral folks coming and going. She had about two minutes to catch her breath, and then Rhett, Sawyer, and Jill stepped up to her table. Jill shoved a bill at her and said, "Three adults, and I don't care if these two cowboys think it's a sin for a woman to pay for breakfast."

"Reckon you could take a break and eat with us?" Rhett asked Leah.

"No, but I would like a funnel cake afterwards," she answered.

"Consider it a date," he said.

She handed Jill the change. When she looked up at the next person, she saw her grandmother scowling at her. "Two adults. One for me and one for your dad here. Just remember this: when you play with fire, you will get burned."

Rhett turned around, bent low, picked up Mavis's hand, and kissed her knuckles. "Hello, Miz Mavis. Don't you look lovely this morning? Are you going to be entering the race this afternoon? I swear if you are, I might let you catch me."

Mavis jerked her hand free and glared at him. "I'd catch a Gallagher before I would you."

"Ouch!" He threw a hand over his heart. "Does that mean if Leah catches Tanner, you won't throw her out in the yard?"

"It means that you should mind your own damn business."

Russell winked at Leah.

Chapter 19

RHETT PUT THE TAILGATE OF HIS TRUCK DOWN AND scooted to the back of the bed, using the cab for a leaning post and stretching out his long legs. The sounds of the carnival filled the air, along with the laughter of kids and people talking, but he didn't hear much of it. Mostly what he heard was the Keith Whitley song playing in his ears from the night before. She'd assured him that Tanner was no longer in her heart, and she'd kept her eyes open while they made love, but still there was a small voice in the back of his head saying that first loves were hard to forget.

"I forgot Mary Lynn Walden," he muttered.

You were eight years old, the voice argued.

"I forgot Lisa Lawson," he said.

You were twelve. You want to talk about Anita Green?

He closed his eyes, and there was a vision of the first girl who he'd kissed, with her long, dark hair and big, brown eyes. Another picture appeared of her in a yellow formal dress at their junior prom, and a red formal dress lying in the corner after their senior prom. It had been the first time for them both, and he'd fumbled his way through it. She'd cried afterward, and he'd promised that they would be together forever.

You didn't forget her, did you?

"But I'm not still in love with her. She broke it off with me and married someone else two years later. I moved past it."

He quickly opened his eyes and looked around to make sure no one had heard him talking to himself. Leah was the only one around, and she was coming out of the school cafeteria, so she couldn't have heard him. She smiled when she saw him and he waved. All thoughts of that first love were erased immediately when she started toward him.

"I hoped you'd be somewhere close by," she said.

"Want to take in the carnival?" Rhett asked.

Leah hopped up on the tailgate. "I'd love to. I believe you owe me a ride on the Ferris wheel."

"Yes, I do, and you sure look cute in that outfit. If you braid that blond hair, you'll be set to catch me," he teased.

She slipped her hand into his. "I can catch you fine with my hair down. I look like Pollyanna with my hair in braids. I have about an hour before I have to be at the bicycle judging, so let's go check out the fun."

"Finn and Callie's kids have spent a week working on their bicycles for the parade. It should be cute." Rhett took her hand in his.

"It starts at eleven at the school yard and goes to the bar, where Polly always gives the kids cookies and juice packs. Jill and Tanner are the other two judges. To make it fair, the committee chooses a judge from each family and one who's not a Brennan or a Gallagher."

"Finn couldn't judge because his four kids will be riding, right?" Rhett asked.

Leah nodded. "That's right. Judges can't have kids in the parade."

"I'll wait for you at the bar and watch it at the finish line. Polly is still having trouble standing very long on that ankle she broke last winter. She might need some help." Rhett let go of her hand and slung a leg over the side of the truck bed.

When his feet were firmly on the ground, he held out his hands and said, "Jump."

She smiled and fell forward into his arms. Nothing she'd ever experienced prepared her for the feeling that shot through her body in the split second between when she left the solid truck and trusted Rhett to catch her. Without even bending his knees or making any kind of noise indicating that she was too heavy, he caught her and held her like a bride as he carried her to the passenger side of the truck.

"We don't have to drive," she said. "It's not that far, and we may not find a parking spot any closer anyway, so let's walk."

"I could carry you. If we had those cuffs, we could take care of everything right now," he said.

She wiggled until he finally set her on the ground. "Why didn't I think of that? I could have bought a pair of cuffs, and we wouldn't have even needed a plan."

He tucked her hand inside his. "Hindsight is twenty-twenty."

When they got close to the carnival, Rhett caught several stares and noticed a few women talking with their hands held over their mouths. The feud might have to take a backseat to the new gossip about the battle at River Bend.

"What?" she asked.

"I didn't say anything," he answered.

"Yes, you did. Not out loud, but your body went all stiff. I could feel it."

"I can see the way folks are reacting to us being together, and I hate that," he said.

"It's worth it." She smiled. "You are worth it."

"Just know that if you need me for anything when she comes at you with those long, red fingernails, I'm only a phone call and five minutes away."

"You can't get from the bunkhouse to River Bend in five minutes."

He squeezed her hand gently. "I can if I make a hole through the fence separating us and goose my motorcycle a little."

Her smile turned to laughter. "My knight in shining motorcycle."

"I'll have to practice my war maneuvers. I can see Mavis standing on the porch, swearing at me as she fires a shotgun toward the cycle as I haul you off on the back of it," he said.

"Who says I'm going to be on the back? I might be riding on front, holding on to the horns." She dropped his hand and pointed at the shooting gallery. "Look, there's a stuffed bull. You think it's an omen?"

"I'm a fair shot. Want me to win it for you?"

"Maybe later. I'd rather go for my Ferris wheel ride."

"I thought we were going for funnel cakes," he said.

"After we ride the Ferris wheel. So if I get sick, I don't hate them forever," she said.

"Have you ever gotten sick on one before?"

"I've never been on one."

He came to a halt right there in the middle of a crowd pushing their way to the Ferris wheel line. "Never?" he asked.

"I've never trusted anyone to keep me safe before," she said.

"Darlin', I promise I will keep you safe."

"Want to seal the deal with a kiss? I like the way we do that." Her eyes sparkled.

"You sure?" His eyes darted around to see who might be watching them.

She raised up on tiptoe and wrapped her arms around his neck. He could almost hear the phone lines buzzing as he bent his head and her lips touched his. It was a sweet kiss that only lasted a few seconds, but while her lips were on his, the whole world disappeared. For that short span of time, they were the only two people left in the universe.

"Now you have to hold me tight and not laugh at me if I get scared when we get to the top," she said.

"I give you my promise, but we could seal it with another kiss."

She rolled up on her toes and brushed a quick kiss across his lips. "There, now you have to take care of me, because the deal is sealed."

They were the last ones that the attendant allowed on the wheel for that ride. When he pulled the bar down, Leah slid over close enough to Rhett that she could lay her head on his shoulder. One of his arms was around her; the other was crossed over in front of his body to hold her hand.

"Want me to stop it at the top for you two lovebirds?" the attendant asked.

"Yes," Leah answered. "He's going to keep me safe because we sealed the deal with a kiss."

"I'd keep you safe if you'd kiss me," the elderly, gray-haired man teased. "But like usual, I'm a day late for the pretty girls."

"I bet you've known lots of pretty girls." Leah smiled.

"Oh, yes, I have, but when the carnival moved, I left them behind."

"A handsome but fickle fellow," she teased.

"You better hold on to her, cowboy, or I'll sweet-talk her into leaving with me when we tear this place down tonight."

"I plan on it," Rhett said.

The old guy flipped a switch, and the swing moved up. "Next," he called out.

They moved a few feet at a time as he filled the wheel with more passengers. As the buckets went higher and higher, Rhett could feel the fear tensing Leah's muscles, so he drew her even closer to his side, his arm tight around her shoulders.

"I'm afraid of heights," she whispered.

"Don't look down. Just look into my eyes," Rhett said. "Think about last night and the stars outside the hayloft."

"I didn't look down from the doors," she admitted.

He kissed her on the nose and kept his eyes locked on hers. "Right now, it's me and you, and I'll tell you when you can look down."

When they made the first round and were on the way up again he said, "Now look to your right. There's your dad and Mavis over there at the funnel cake wagon."

"She's pissed," Leah said and then turned to lock her eyes with his again.

"Oh, yeah, but she'll get over it. Next time we go around, I'll tell you to look when we're a little bit higher up."

She kissed him on the cheek, and he turned so that their lips met in a sweet, quick kiss. "And then the next time a little more, until we are on top, right?"

"You've got me figured out," Rhett said.

"Have you ever made love on one of these?" she asked.

He chuckled. "No, ma'am, but I'm willing, even if it means a night in jail, if you are."

"Tell me when to look. I like the feeling of knowing that we're going up and you're right here. Hey, you think if we did have sex on this thing that Orville would let us share a cell?"

"It's our story, Leah. We can tell it any way we want, and in this story, they'd put us in the same cell where there is a king-size bed strewn with mimosa petals," he answered. "Okay, now look to your right again. There's Finn and Callie at the fried pickle wagon. I guess it's true about pregnant women."

When the ride stopped at the top, she peeked over the edge. "It's a long way down there."

"Look at those big, white, puffy clouds up in the sky, not at the ground," he said.

"Oh, Rhett. They're beautiful."

He kissed her on the forehead when the ride started again. "Now we're going down again, so keep looking at the clouds and not at the ground."

"Look!" Her eyes widened as the wheel started descending. "I can see the quilts on the school yard."

"Is that something to do with the festival?"

"Not really, but kind of. Everyone brings a quilt for their family, spreads it out in the school yard, and has a picnic. I looked forward to that all year when I was a little girl," Leah answered. "We could go visit Finn and Callie before the race starts. I always thought it was so much fun to go visit other people on their quilts."

"Did you ever visit a Gallagher, like Betsy?" Rhett

asked, thrilled that she was loosening up and starting to enjoy the ride.

She shook her head. "If I had, I wouldn't be here today. Granny would have sent me away to a convent."

"You're not Catholic."

"She would have converted if she'd caught me with a Gallagher."

The ride stopped, and the attendant blew a kiss to Leah as he unfastened the bar holding them inside the bucket.

"So how was your first time?" Rhett asked.

"Amazing but I don't want to do it again for a while," she said.

"You don't have to ever do anything you don't want to do, Leah. What now?"

"It's time for the parade," she answered.

Rhett walked with her down to the school, where dozens of bicycles, decorated in all kinds of ways, were lined up with numbers fixed to the back of their seats. Orville stood beside the sheriff's car, waiting to lead the parade down the street. He glanced at Rhett and Leah but didn't wave.

"He still thinks we burned down the Gallaghers' schoolhouse, doesn't he?" Rhett asked.

She nodded. "And he probably thinks that they blew our school up, but he can't prove anything on either side."

Tyrell Gallagher held up a hand and waved when they got close to the congested area, where parents and kids both were milling around like ants around a honey jar.

Leah waved back and explained, "He's in charge, getting everything in order this year. The Brennans and the Gallaghers alternate everything. I hate this feud. I know I've said it before, but I do."

Tyrell jogged over to her and Rhett and handed her a pen and clipboard: "Your chairs are in front of the store. Tanner is up there setting them up. Judge only by number, even if you know the kids. And you have to agree on the three winners without bloodshed."

Rhett kept hold of her hand as they headed back toward the store.

"What do the winners get?" he asked. "I don't think Finn's kids even knew they would win anything other than a ribbon."

"They'll be giving away a coupon to each kid that enters for five free rides or visits to a food vendor, so they get to call the shots on the when, where, and how. And then there are three big prizes," Leah said.

"More tickets?" he asked.

"First prize is a hundred dollars, second is fifty, and third is twenty," she answered. "It's been that way ever since I was a kid, but I understand that years ago, the two feuding families tried to outdo each other every year with prizes, giving away bicycles and even prize steers for the livestock show. It got to be a mess, so Verdie, Polly, and Gladys made it a rule that the prize would be monetary and could only go up in value if the committee agreed on it. I think the first year it was fifty, twenty, and ten, but it's climbed up through the years."

"What if the vote goes to all Brennan kids?"

"Then the Gallaghers will be pissed off even more than Granny is right now."

"Dammit!" Leah swore when she saw the three lawn chairs waiting for the judges. Tanner had put her in the middle, so she'd have to sit beside him.

Rhett let go of her hand and quickly changed the name cards on the back of the chairs, so that Jill sat between Tanner and Leah. "There, darlin'. Things like that can be fixed. Now sit down before Tanner comes back, and I'll see you at the bar when this is over. Unless you want me to stay here with you."

"I conquered the Ferris wheel with your help, but it made me stronger. I can take on Tanner if he says a word about the change. You can come and bail me out of jail if I have to hurt him though." She smiled up at him.

He dropped another sweet kiss on her forehead and waved as he joined Finn, who was a few steps ahead of him. Yes, sir, she'd gotten a jewel when Rhett O'Donnell had roared into town. She picked up her clipboard and noted that there were fifty-six entries in the parade. There was a place for her to choose three for first place and the same for second and third. After it was over and while the kids had cookies and juice, the judges would confer.

Jill plopped down in the chair beside her. "I wish they'd have this thing in the spring rather than at the end of August. My legs are going to stick to this webbing."

"Plastic does that. Where's Sawyer?" Leah asked.

"Catching up to Rhett and Finn so they can go to the bar together. I saw y'all on the Ferris wheel. The way Mavis was lookin' up there, I figured it would put a chill on the whole town. To tell the truth, I was hoping it would." Jill fanned herself with the clipboard.

Leah did the same thing. "No such luck. I know her

glares, and those were not cold looks. They were full
of fire and anger. They probably raised the temperature
twenty degrees rather than lowering it."

Tanner startled both of them when he sat down in
his chair. He wore a ball cap, sunglasses, khaki shorts,
and an orange tank top with the Wild Horse Ranch logo
on the front. "What if Leah catches me? Think Mavis
will be mad enough to raise the temperature twenty
degrees then?"

"More like to the degree of hell's furnace," Jill said.

Leah turned to look at him, and her neck popped.

Tanner wiggled his fingers toward her. "I will gladly
massage that kink out when you catch me. Did you read
the new rules?"

"Same as the old ones, right? Handcuff your catch,
haul him to the finish line, and have Sunday dinner with
him the next day."

"The committee added one this year. Handcuff your
man to you, and the handcuffs don't come off until after
the ice cream supper at the church. The preacher will
fire the shots to set the race off, and he'll have the keys
to the cuffs."

Leah and Rhett would be handcuffed together for at
least two hours. Maybe longer if they made sure they
were the last people in line to get them removed. Now
that was something to look forward to.

*Wonder what kind of wild sex you could have if you
were handcuffed together.* Eve's voice sounded so loud
in her head that Leah glanced at Jill to be sure she hadn't
heard the comment too.

Maybe it would be misconstrued as favoritism
when she marked down Martin O'Donnell's bike as

her number one choice, but those horns wired up to his handlebars and the spurs attached to his boots were priceless. Of course, Tanner's first choice was not Martin's bike, and Jill had chosen a cute, little pink bike all done up with pink satin streamers.

They talked about it when the parade had finished, finally made their decisions, and handed in the list to the judge.

Tanner bumped her with a shoulder. "I'll look forward to having ice cream with you this evening."

"Don't count your chickens before they're hatched," she said.

Rhett's hand was suddenly in hers and those old familiar sparks danced around the parking lot, wiping out everything but the two of them.

"Good job to all three of you judges," he said.

"Thanks," Tanner said and then turned his eyes toward Leah. "See you later. I told Granny to bring banana nut ice cream. A little birdie told me it was your favorite. I'll feed it to you."

"Like I said. Don't be countin' chickens," she said.

He moved on toward a group of Gallaghers, and Rhett squeezed her hand. "Ready to go get some tacos and funnel cakes, or maybe some of those cinnamon rolls?"

She looped her arm through his. "Rhett, about Tanner."

"There's nothing to explain. Let's go find some food."

She nodded. "I am so hungry. Pancakes are failing me. And I want a beer too."

"Hey, where are y'all going?" Jill hollered.

"To the taco wagon," Rhett said.

"Wait up and we'll go with you. I could eat half a dozen tacos." Jill grabbed Sawyer's hand.

"I thought you were going home," Leah said.

"Food changes my mind real easy." Jill laughed.

"Did y'all hear about the new kink in the race?" Jill asked.

"I didn't, but then I'm not running, so I didn't pay any attention to it," Sawyer answered.

She told them about the handcuffs staying on until after the ice cream supper.

"I like the new rule. Reckon we could keep them on until after Sunday dinner." Rhett wiggled his dark eyebrows at Leah.

"Damn!" Sawyer exclaimed and pulled Jill closer to his side. "Now I wish I were in the race so you could catch me. I wouldn't mind being handcuffed to you for a couple of hours."

"I'm looking forward to the race. Never did before. Usually I took off with the ladies when the gun went off and hid on the back porch of the church until the next shot signaled it was time for the girls to bring their catches back to the line," Leah said.

"You mean I'll be your first catch?" Rhett asked.

"Yes, you will be."

Jill sighed. "That is so romantic. If I'd known about this, we might have put off our wedding until after it was over. Now I'll never know the joy of catching you."

"We could play chase around the bunkhouse and you could handcuff me." Sawyer grinned.

"We could do that," Jill agreed. "But right now, I want tacos more than handcuffs."

"What about you?" Rhett whispered in Leah's ear.

"Can I have both?"

Chapter 20

THE PREACHER CLIMBED UP ON THE FLATBED TRUCK beside the store and picked up a microphone. "Gather 'round, folks. It's time for all y'all fellers to check your boots in with Miz Gladys. She will tie them together and give you one end of a ticket that you'll bring back to her to reclaim them once you get the cuffs off. However, if you have the good luck to outrun all these lovely ladies, then when you hear the all-clear shot at five o'clock, you can come on to the school cafeteria when the ice cream supper starts and reclaim them. I want to wish you all good luck and may the girl of your dreams catch you."

The preacher reminded Rhett of an old-time snake oil salesman as he held the microphone close to his mouth and motioned to the young men with his hand. If he'd been selling a healing elixir, he could have probably made millions from the crowd, who was hanging on every word.

"That's my cue. Remember the way?" Rhett asked Leah.

She kissed him on the cheek. "If you get there before I do, don't give up on me."

"I'll hear that song playing in my head the whole time I'm dodgin' and duckin'." He laughed.

The country music tune played through his mind as he sat down on the edge of the trailer and handed his boots to Gladys. She tied them together with a zip tie and handed him a ticket stub. "Put this in your pocket and don't lose it."

"Yes, ma'am." Rhett grinned.

She patted him on the shoulder. "Good luck, Rhett. I already heard several women sayin' as how they've memorized that shirt you're wearing, and they're going to be after you. You better have some fancy moves."

"I've got something better. I've got a plan."

Tanner stepped up beside Gladys and handed his boots over to her. "Here you go, Miz Gladys."

"Thank you. You know the rules, right?" Gladys asked.

"I do. I'll get my boots back as soon as I get the cuffs off."

"Line 'em up, boys!" the preacher yelled into the microphone. "See the line made out of duct tape right there under the banner? Put your toes on the tape and get ready to run. You'll have fifteen minutes, but if a pretty girl winks at me, I might get trigger-happy and you'll only have five minutes, so you better run fast, boys. When you hear the second shot, you'll know the ladies are on the run. The third shot is the all-clear shot."

Tanner lined up beside Rhett and said, "I hope you aren't a poor loser."

"I don't intend to lose," Rhett said.

"Okay, ladies, here's this year's pickin's," Emory said. "Take a long look at them and get a picture of what they're wearing in your mind so you don't go tackling the wrong cowboy. We've got three whole minutes for you to walk up and down the line to talk to them. No touching, but you can ask whatever questions you want."

What happened next reminded Rhett of speed dating. Half a dozen women gathered in front of him, asking him what his favorite foods were, and if he liked picnics or restaurants best. Thank goodness Betsy Gallagher wasn't one of them.

"Time's up, ladies. Back to the sides, so these guys can get their proper head start," Emory said. "On your mark."

Rhett bent like a track runner.

"May the best man win," Tanner said.

Rhett didn't answer but kept his mind and eyes set on the goal.

"Get set," Emory yelled.

The gunshot startled some of the guys so badly that they looked back at the preacher, who shooed them on with a wave of his hand. Soon, guys were tearing down the road like football players on their way to the goal line. Rhett stuck to the plan and was already on the path headed for the barn when he stepped on one of those Texas grass burrs called a goat head. He plopped down on the path and pulled the sorry sucker out of his heel and stood up to run again, only to feel half a dozen more poking into the ball of his foot.

"Dammit!" He swore and sat back down to pull them out. He didn't remember those rotten things sticking to his jeans when he and Leah had made the practice run. He thought back to the night before and frowned.

"There weren't any. I'd swear on a Bible that there weren't, and now Leah is going to get them in her feet too," he said. "I've got to go back and warn her."

Leah handed her flip-flops off to Gladys and tucked her ticket into her hip pocket before lining up with Honey on one side and Betsy on the other.

Betsy cut her eyes at Leah and winked. "I'm planning on having dinner at Wild Horse with Rhett tomorrow."

"I wouldn't bet on it," Leah said.

"I would put five hundred dollars on it if you want to put your money where you mouth is," Betsy said.

"Okay, ladies, I really want to see these guys hauled in here before they die of heatstroke, so let's get this show on the road a few minutes early. You know the rules. Bring home your man, and he's all yours for supper tonight and dinner tomorrow. Get on your mark!" the preacher yelled.

"Well…" Betsy nudged Leah.

"I'd hate to see you lose your money."

The preacher lowered his voice like he was telling a big secret. "They're out there hiding from you, so look under every rock, under the hanging limbs of every willow tree, and you might even check the river for signs of air tubes. These are some wily guys, ladies. You should keep your eyes wide open and search for signs. We don't care what condition you bring them back in, long as they're handcuffed to you. Get set!"

The gun blasted, and Leah followed the path exactly as they'd practiced. Rhett was supposed to be waiting in the barn, so she didn't have to hurry.

Rhett's feet hurt, but he was making good time when he heard the second shot and knew the women were on the way. He kept his eyes on the path in front of him, hoping to see Leah at any time, when suddenly someone ran up behind him and cuffed his hand to hers. Breathing a sigh of relief that she hadn't gotten into the dangerous area, he turned around and looked down into Betsy Gallagher's emerald-green eyes.

"Well, Rhett O'Donnell, looks like you belong to me for the ice cream supper and Sunday dinner tomorrow. I hear that you really like steak, so that's what we're having on Wild Horse Ranch tomorrow. The whole family will be there to meet you. Who knows? Maybe we'll show you a better life than Fiddle Creek." She smiled up at him. "Let's go on back now. I know a route that's gentle on the feet. Maybe I'll even get the prize for bringing in the first catch."

"And that would be?"

"The look on Leah's face when she comes in empty-handed. Or better yet, when Tanner catches her."

"You put those stickers in the path, didn't you?" he said.

"All is fair in wars, feuds, and the Sadie Hawkins race." She laughed. "Now come on, darlin', we're takin' a shortcut back to the store."

"But I've got to warn Leah," he said.

"Sweetheart"—Betsy smiled at him—"there won't be a single sticker on the path by the time she gets to that spot."

"You are mean," Rhett said.

"Like I said, all's fair." She laughed again.

Leah kept on the path in a slow, steady jog until she saw the barn. Then she slowed to a walk and shaded her eyes with her hands, but she couldn't see any sign of Rhett. That meant he was already there, waiting on her.

"Not giving up on me." She smiled.

He was everything she'd ever wanted in a man, and

if their relationship got her thrown off River Bend, well then, so be it. She wasn't going to live like her father had the past twenty-five years. No, sir, she'd found the right man, and he was a fine person.

Who are you trying to convince? Yourself or your family? the voice in her head asked, which reminded her of the Chris Young song about hearing voices all the time. Maybe Eve had always been there, waiting for the right time to give her the strength to get out of this damn feud.

She noticed a single wild daisy blooming beside the path and stopped long enough to pick it. She tucked it behind her ear as she covered the last hundred yards to the barn where Rhett waited for her. Would he be in the loft? Her skin went all tingly at that idea, and she started jogging again. The barn was dark and smelled like fresh hay. It was eerily quiet as she stood inside the shadows and let her eyes adjust to coming in out of the hot, broiling August sun.

"Rhett?" she whispered.

Nothing.

He should have been there, but maybe he'd had to alter his plans to outrun someone and was behind her. She turned around and looked out over the landscape. No Rhett, and the way her stomach had twisted up into a pretzel, her gut was telling her something was wrong. She went back inside and sat down on a hay bale to wait for him. If she couldn't have him, she damn sure didn't want anyone else, and the barn was a fine hiding place.

Someone slipped their hands over her eyes, and she smiled. After she kissed him, she fully intended to read him the riot act for scaring her.

"Keep your eyes shut." He whipped the cuffs out of her pocket, snapped them on his wrist, and then on hers.

"Can I open them now?" she whispered.

He sat down beside her, their hands brushing together. "You sure can, Leah."

She had already moistened her lips for the kiss, and her eyes were half-open when she realized that Tanner Gallagher was sitting beside her, his bare feet propped up on a bale in front of them.

"Congratulations, you caught me," he said.

She rubbed her eyes with her free hand. Surely she was seeing things. Maybe she'd even had a heatstroke.

She gasped. "You cheated."

"All is fair in the Sadie Hawkins race. Besides, if you yell that I cheated, who will believe you? Why in the hell would a Gallagher rope himself to a Brennan on purpose?"

"Tanner, please don't do this," she begged.

He held up his hand. "Too late. We're together until after dinner tomorrow. Are we going to River Bend?"

"Hell no! Granny would roll you in honey and cornflakes and feed you to her new hogs. I don't like you, but I don't want to see the hogs eat you."

"I've never heard you cuss, Leah Brennan."

"You don't know me," she said.

"Then I'll get to know you on the way back to the church for the ice cream supper."

"How did you know I'd come to the barn?"

"Nothing is a secret in Burnt Boot. Betsy overheard someone talking about having seen y'all driving this way and then walking around the end of the store. She figured your plan out and told me. I've got a confession."

"I'm not a priest," she smarted off.

"Betsy put stickers on the path, and she's already cuffed Rhett. And, darlin', I like this new Leah with the sass better than the old one. But that's not my real confession. It's that when this started, it really was all Granny's idea. She knows you're being groomed to run River Bend like Betsy has been raised up to do at Wild Creek. After that shit storm on both sides, she decided if she could steal you, it would hurt Mavis worse than anything she could do."

He stood up, and Leah had no choice but to follow him. "And?"

"It was a game until a few days ago, and I figured out that I really do like you. So say good-bye to Rhett. You're going to be mine when it's all said and done. I get what I want, and I want you." He chuckled.

"When pigs fly. I might let Granny at you yet," she said.

"No, you won't. You have a nice side that keeps you sweet and a wild side that I damn sure intend to enjoy," he said.

—⁂—

Leah and Tanner were one of the last couples to make it back to the trailer, and the preacher really made a big to-do about it. "Well, would you look at this, folks? I do believe this will go down in history as the first time a Brennan has ever chased down a Gallagher."

Tanner played into the whole thing like a movie star. He hung his head as if he was totally ashamed that a Brennan had caught him. "I'm so sorry, Granny. Don't shoot me and don't let Mavis hang me from the nearest old scrub oak tree."

Naomi yelled from the other side of the road, "Mavis, if you lay a hand on my grandson, you'll pay for it."

"If he sets a little toe on Wild Horse, he's as good as dead," Mavis yelled back. "What the hell were you thinkin', Leah?"

"We'll talk about it later," she answered.

"You are damn right we will."

"I expect we'd best take a picnic to the river tomorrow, since I'm not welcome on River Bend. Or maybe you'll let me take you to a nice restaurant," Tanner said.

"It's my job to provide dinner. I hope you like bologna sandwiches. We're having a tailgate picnic, but not at the river."

"I'll love anything you make, darlin', and I'd have dinner with you sitting on a barbed wire fence in hell." He grinned and held up the cuffs for everyone to see.

The crowd laughed at his joke and applause broke out. The preacher let it go on for a full minute before he said, "Crawl up here on the wagon with the rest of the couples. Ten more minutes and we'll give you all a ride to the church. I imagine your feet are sore from all the barefoot business. Make the best of the bad situation, boys. It's only for a supper today and for dinner tomorrow, then you can get on with your wild and woolly ways."

Leah caught Rhett's eye, and he mouthed, "Stickers."
She nodded.

Tanner cupped her chin in his hand and turned her face toward his. "Don't look at him. You belong to me."

She scooted away from him as far as the cuffs would allow. "I will never belong to you."

"For this ice cream supper and for our bologna

sandwiches tomorrow, you do." He moved close enough that their shoulders touched, and he ran a forefinger down her bare arm. "I can change your mind about me if you'll give me a chance."

It didn't produce sparks, but it did bring on a desire to spit in his eye. Maybe that's what this was all about: to show her once and for all that the childhood crush was just that and that there wasn't even a tiny part of her heart that belonged to Tanner.

"Sometimes it's too late for chances, Tanner. Let's simply get through this ice cream business and get these cuffs off," she said.

"I was thinking about asking the preacher to leave them on until tomorrow evening, say, at five o'clock. That way the ladies could have us for a full twenty-four hours."

"Showers? Bathroom? Sleeping?"

"I'm not bashful. And I've got scissors to cut off whatever clothing we can't remove." He grinned.

"Preacher wouldn't ever go for such immorality," she said.

"Everyone and everything has a price, Leah. We donated enough money to buy a youth director. You think we can't donate enough to make a new rule about the cuffs? The preacher was saying last week that the church needs a new piano."

"It's not happening. If he doesn't take them off, I promise I will take that little snub-nosed pistol out of my purse and shoot them off. I'm not an excellent shot, so you might think about how close your hand will be when I fire the gun," she said.

"There's that sassy side I like." He chuckled. "But,

Leah, darlin', please keep in mind that my granny will do anything to have her way. I told you how I feel about you, and it's above and beyond the feud. Don't think for a minute that something as small and insignificant as Rhett O'Donnell can't be made to disappear."

Her blood turned to ice water. "Are you threatening to hurt Rhett if I don't play along with this farce?"

"Now did I say that? I said that he could disappear. Everyone has a price."

"And if you couldn't buy him?"

Tanner flipped a strand of her blond hair back from her face and leaned closer to whisper in her ear. "Then, darlin', I expect that his body will go the way of others before him."

The ice water in her veins froze solid. "The feud hasn't had a killin' in decades."

Tanner kissed her on the earlobe and whispered, "That you know of."

"I do not appreciate any of this, Betsy," Rhett said.

"Like I told you, all is fair in love and war and feuds and Sadie Hawkins races."

"Especially in shit wars, right?"

"Ah, now, sweetheart." She batted her lashes at him. "You don't have to bring up unpleasant things because I got you. Leah is not your type, Rhett. She's lukewarm. You deserve someone with a little fire in their veins, and I can deliver that right to your bedroom."

"You know how I feel about Leah, and this thing is a distraction, nothing more." He held up the cuffs. "Nothing but a nuisance until it's over."

She leaned over and kissed him on the cheek. "Have you told her that you are in love with her?"

He stiffened, and she wiggled her cuffed hand against his. "You haven't told her, which means you aren't sure, which means I can change your mind in twenty-four hours. Besides, remember what Mavis said. If Leah doesn't break it off with you, she's lost her free five-star hotel. I wonder if she even knows how to do laundry or pick up her own clothes. She's been spoiled rotten her whole life."

"And you haven't?" Rhett asked.

"Darlin', I can work a ranch as hard and good as any man. My granny trained me from the ground up. I was cuttin' hogs and cattle when I was ten years old and brandin' them at eleven. I didn't get sick one time either. Listen to me. You need a woman like me, and I can offer you Wild Horse."

"I'll never be a kept man," Rhett said.

"Who said you'd be kept? Honey, we'd work side by side to make it even bigger and better than it is now."

"And if you don't like me once we got to really know each other?" he asked.

She scanned him from bare feet to eyes. "That's not even a possibility. Besides, my granny wants this to happen with Tanner and Leah. But if Leah isn't willing, there're always ways to take care of things so that Mavis still loses her."

"Is that a threat of some kind?" Rhett's heart stopped and then raced.

"It's stating facts. This new phase of the war has taken on the style of the old ways, and in those days, people disappeared."

"Naomi wouldn't hurt Leah, would she?"

"Not if Tanner wins her hand when it's all said and done."

Chapter 21

RHETT STOOD UNDER THE SHOWER FOR A VERY LONG time, washing away sweat and the feel of Betsy's hands from his arms, his face, even his thigh. Not even hot water could take away the feeling that he'd not only cheated on Leah but that he'd also disappointed her. He finally turned the water off and wrapped a towel around his hips. Leaving wet footprints across the floor on his way to his room, he heard his phone ringing.

He raced across the floor, grabbed the phone without looking, and said, "Leah?"

"No, this is Gladys. I think Polly had a heart attack, I called Jill, but she and Sawyer are in Gainesville at a movie with their phones turned off." Gladys's normally gravelly voice had a high pitch to it, her words coming out in breathless jumps and starts.

"I'll be right there. What do you need me to do?" Rhett flipped the towel onto the floor and opened a dresser drawer for a clean shirt.

"Would you drive me to the hospital? They won't let me ride with her in the ambulance, and I'm too shook up to drive," Gladys asked.

"Give me five minutes to get dressed," Rhett said.

"I can drive from here to the bunkhouse. I'll be waiting out front."

He was putting on his boots when he heard the gravel crunching beneath the truck tires. He shoved the bunkhouse keys, his phone, and his wallet into his pockets and crossed the living room in long strides with Dammit and the cats following him single file.

"Sorry, old boy. You can't go this time. You take care of the cats, and I'll be back soon as I can," he said as he rushed out the door.

Gladys was in the passenger's seat with a big black purse on her lap. She started talking before he even got the door shut. "I told her she was overdoing it, but she wouldn't listen to a damn thing."

"Maybe it's not a heart attack." He backed the truck out of the driveway and headed toward the main road.

"If it's not, then we're going to have a serious talk about retiring. We're past eighty years old. It's time for us to slow down," Gladys fussed.

His phone vibrated in his shirt pocket, and Gladys looked at him, wide-eyed with tears. It was written all over her face that she was hoping for the best but thinking the worst.

"I gave the EMTs your number because my cell phone was dead. I left a message on Jill's phone to meet us at the hospital."

He handed her the phone and pressed the gas pedal down harder.

She chuckled as she read the message.

"Good news?" he asked.

"Depends on who we're talking about. It's a message to you from Leah. She's sorry about the way things went to day and she wants you to call her."

"Call her, Miz Gladys. Tell her what's going on. I can't drive this fast and talk."

"You drive. I'll text her rather than calling. It might embarrass her if she thinks I read her message," Gladys said. "Just tell me the words."

"Polly on the way to the hospital. Taking Gladys that way. Talk to you later."

With the speed of a teenager, Gladys hit the keys with her thumbs and sent the message. In seconds, another one came back, and she read, "'Miss you. Call ASAP.'"

She handed him the phone, and he shoved it back into his shirt pocket. "What did the EMTs say about Polly when they got to the house? Did they think it was a heart attack?"

"They put her on oxygen and hooked her up to an IV, and believe me, she hates them, so she threw a hissy that raised her blood pressure even more when they stuck that needle in her arm," Gladys answered.

"How high was her blood pressure?"

"They wouldn't tell me. I asked, and they said it was high. They probably only had one stretcher and thought if they told me, it would shoot mine up and they'd have to stack me and Polly up like cordwood," she said. "Changing the subject to get my mind off Polly, how in the hell did Betsy catch you? I thought you and Leah had a plan."

"Betsy peppered the path to the barn with a handful of goat head stickers. I stepped on them really hard and she caught me."

"Damned feudin' people. So that's how you got caught. How'd they find out, anyway?"

"I have no idea unless someone happened to see us walkin' that way last night. We decided to do a trial run, but we didn't tell anyone our plan," Rhett answered.

"You should have come to me and Polly. We would have helped you hide in the store. Someone must've seen or overheard something one of you said or hell's bells, knowing the Gallagher's, they might have bugged your truck," Gladys said.

Rhett nodded. "Paybacks are a bitch, so they'd better be careful."

"Let it go. Get past the dinner tomorrow and forget it."

Rhett inhaled deeply and asked, "Do you think that they'd do something stupid, like kill Leah?"

Gladys whipped around in the seat, and the whites of her eyes were visible all around her dark eyes. "What makes you ask a fool question like that?"

"Betsy was probably pulling my chain, but she made a veiled threat that Leah could disappear if I didn't back off and let Tanner have her," Rhett answered.

"It's part of the war between Mavis and Naomi. If Tanner did wind up with her, it would be a revenge match, not a love one. But then again, this is the Gallaghers and the Brennans. There ain't no love there anyway. But to answer your question, there hasn't been a killing between them in decades."

"But this is the worst case of feudin' in a long time, right?"

Gladys nodded. "Only thing worse would be if a Gallagher and a Brennan really fell in love with each other and Mavis or Naomi neither one was behind it. Lord that would be a holy mess."

"But Tanner and Leah—" he started.

Gladys held up a palm. "That doesn't count because it's sanctioned by Naomi to get back at Mavis. I'm talking about a real, honest-to-God love."

"Like Betsy and Quaid or Honey and Declan?" he asked.

"Oh my Lord." She gasped. "Betsy, because she is Naomi's pride and joy, and Declan, who is Naomi's favorite grandson. Now that might bring on a killin'."

"Well, I hope it never happens because Leah wants the feud to end. We're here and would you look at that? We've got a wonderful parking space not far from the emergency room door," he said.

Gladys bailed out of the truck the moment Rhett stopped the engine, and she was halfway to the doors when he caught up to her. His phone rang, but he ignored it and followed her through the automatic doors, into the waiting room. She marched right up to the desk and said, "I'm here for Polly Cleary. Just hit the button and let me through those doors."

"Are you family?" the lady asked.

"Damn straight I am," Gladys said.

The doors opened, and Rhett followed her through them and to the next station, where the nurse pointed toward a curtained-off area. They found Polly sitting up in the middle of the bed, with oxygen tubes in her nostrils and an IV drip in her arm.

"Come on in and sit down. There're two chairs. One is for the doctor, but he's not here right now. I may never forgive you for this, Gladys Cleary. I told you it was heartburn, and look at this needle. I swear to God, it's as big as a tenpenny nail, and I'll have a bruise as big as a dollar bill tomorrow. Old women like us don't get rid of bruises like we did when we was kids."

"Will you shut up bitchin' and tell me what they've done?" Gladys asked. "We got here as fast as we could."

"They've run an EKG, and I'm waiting for the doctor to bring back the report on that, but they mixed up a thing that was green and tasted like shit. They made me drink it, and the pain eased up right away. I think they ground up bullfrogs, guts and all," she whispered.

Rhett chuckled. "Acid reflux?"

"That's the new fancy word for it. We called it heartburn when I was your age. They tell me it feels like a heart attack. I guess I shouldn't have eaten them hot tacos for dinner and supper both. Your phone is ringing. You'd better step on out of here and answer it. Never know what all them crazy currents might do to the machinery, and I'm not stayin' in this place all night because of heartburn." Polly pulled the oxygen tubes from her nose. "Let's retire and go on one of them senior cruises. You ready?"

"Hell yes," Gladys said.

"We'll take Verdie with us," Polly said.

"You ain't leavin' this place until they convince me it was tacos and not your heart, you crazy old fart," Gladys said.

Rhett's phone rang again, and he stepped outside the curtain to answer it. "Hello, it's been a crazy night."

"Is Polly all right?" Leah asked.

"Sounds like a bad case of acid reflux," he said.

"I know about the stickers," Leah said.

"I'd like to give them a taste of their own medicine. I hate this."

"I want to get it over with and get on with my plans. I'm packing. You want to help me move out?"

"Yes, I will. Want me to be in front of the ranch about six?"

"No, I'm hoping that you can be in front of Polly's house at seven tomorrow evening. You might not know it, but Polly has been living with Gladys for over a year now. I'm going to talk to them tomorrow about renting Polly's house. If she doesn't want me to do that, I'll stay in a hotel in Gainesville until I find a place," she said.

"Are you sure about this, Leah?" he asked.

"Yes, I am, and right now, I just wanted to hear your voice. Call me when y'all get home and let me know how Polly is?"

"I sure will. Here comes Jill and Sawyer."

"Go explain to them what's happening, and I'll talk to you later," she said.

‒‒‒‧ᴠᴠᴠ‒‒‒

It was after ten when Rhett drove Polly and Gladys home in the backseat of Gladys's truck. The arguing and fussing began the minute Gladys and Polly crawled into the backseat.

"I told you not to call that ambulance. If my insurance doesn't pay for it to come all the way to Burnt Boot and haul me to the hospital, I'm going to make you pay for it," Polly grumbled.

"Next time, I'll kick you out in the yard and let you die, because I don't want your stinkin', old body on my sofa," Gladys popped back at her.

"Lot of surprises at the festival today, right?" Rhett tried to steer the conversation away from the ambulance.

"I'm thinkin' about puttin' out a contract on Betsy Gallagher. I heard about the sticker trick. That was just downright evil," Polly fumed. "Tell me that we ain't goin' to lose you to Wild Horse, Rhett."

Rhett looked at them in the rearview mirror. "Hey, who says I'll go to either one? Maybe I'm happy at Fiddle Creek. Besides, I'd never be happy on a ranch that big or takin' orders from Mavis or from Naomi."

Polly nudged Gladys, who nodded. Now what was that all about? Had they given him a test, and if so, did he pass the damn thing?

"Leah! Come down here!" Mavis's voice echoed up the stairs, across the landing, and through her shut door.

Leah had been stretched out on her bed, replaying the horrible day, trying to figure out what she might have done different. Her feet hit the floor, and she made a dash for the door, leaving her cell phone behind on the pillow beside her.

She leaned over the railing and said, "What?"

"I've told you a thousand times not to answer me like that. It's disrespectful to say one word in that tone. Come down here."

"At this time of night?" Leah asked.

"I can't sleep, and I want to get this settled." Mavis wore a long, pink cotton robe and matching slippers. Her new short hair stuck up like she'd stuck her finger in an electrical socket and, in the harsh overhead lighting, every single wrinkle showed.

"Okay, Granny, but you might not like the outcome," Leah said.

"Right now! In my office."

Leah was halfway down the steps when her father came in the front door. He raised an eyebrow, and she nodded toward Mavis.

Mavis turned her glare to Russell. "Where have you been?"

"I'm pushing sixty, Mama. I don't reckon I have to tell you where I'm at every minute of the day or night," he said. "What's going on here?"

"We're going to draw up the lines. On one side, it will be white, on the other side, black. There will be no gray," Mavis said.

"She's upset over the fact that Tanner tricked me and I have to have dinner with him tomorrow," Leah said.

"Leah will be thirty this fall, Mama. She's proven time and time again that we can trust her judgment. She'll take a picnic to the church in the morning, have a sandwich with him, and be home by one o'clock. It will be over. You are letting Naomi get under your skin."

"It's not Tanner I'm worried about or Naomi. It's that Rhett O'Donnell."

Leah sat down on the bottom step. "I'll make it easy for you, Granny. Tomorrow I'll have my picnic with Tanner. Monday is my first day of school, and after the day is finished, I'll pack my things and move off of River Bend."

Russell sat down beside her and draped an arm around her shoulders. "That won't be necessary. This is your home and my ranch. You can date whoever you please."

Mavis crossed her arms over her chest. "It's not your ranch until I die, and I can change the will."

"But can you run this place without me?" Russell asked.

Mavis glared at him. "You've got brothers who can step up and take your place."

Leah threw up both hands, fingers splayed out, as she shook her head from side to side. "Stop it! You aren't going anywhere, Daddy. I am moving away, not because of Rhett, but because I want to. I need my own place."

"Then I'll build you a house anywhere you want on the ranch."

"That's it. I don't want a place on the ranch. I want outside of it so I can breathe. This place is smothering me to death. I'm going to talk to Polly tomorrow evening about renting her house. She's not living there, and if she won't rent to me, then I'll live in Gainesville and commute to work."

Mavis stomped her foot, but it didn't make much noise. "I forbid it. If you move away, you'll fall into bed with Rhett, and I won't have it."

Leah stood up and stretched. "Daddy, you will come see me often, won't you?"

"Yes, I will, and you know you can always come home if you change your mind," Russell said.

She dropped a kiss on top of his dark hair and hurried up the stairs to call Rhett.

Mavis called after her, "Leah, you better rethink this. It's a bad decision."

Leah's phone was ringing when she reached her bedroom, and she raced across the floor, grabbed it, and said, "Hello."

"Hey," Honey said. "What in the hell happened today? I want to hear your story about how in the devil Tanner caught you."

"Easy. He knew where I was meeting Rhett. Betsy caught him by putting goat head stickers on the pathway, and Tanner waited for me in the barn, stole my cuffs, and the next thing I knew, we were together," Leah said. "I told Granny I'm moving out on Monday. I'm going to see if Polly will rent her house to me."

"You can live with me, or with Kinsey and Quaid."

"I want to be totally away from River Bend," Leah said.

"Granny will fight you tooth, nail, hair, and eyeball. Get ready for it. She'll cut you off completely."

"I'll be okay, Honey. I've got a savings account from my teaching, and my first paycheck from the public school will come in September."

"It won't be pretty. You'd better think long and hard about it," Honey said seriously.

"Want to help me pack tomorrow afternoon?"

"Hell no! I'm not even going to sit beside you in church tomorrow or she might throw me off River Bend right behind you," Honey answered.

Leah shifted the phone to her other ear. "Some cousin and friend you are. I've got a beep. It might be Rhett. I'll talk to you later."

She switched over to the next caller to hear Kinsey's voice. "Granny called and she's hotter than she was when the Gallaghers blew up our school. I'm supposed to talk you out of what you're fixing to do. Come live with me until this blows over. You know you are welcome here."

"I want off the ranch, not in a different place on it," Leah said.

"Good luck, darlin'. She's going to roast you before this is over. Who would have thought you would be the one to cross her?"

"Daddy offered to build me a house of my own. He told me that he'd come see me if I did move away, and I don't think Declan will disown me. It's her loss if she wants to play hardball. Want to come help me pack tomorrow afternoon?"

"I'm not coming near the big house for a week, maybe a month. Besides, she says the only thing you get to take out of the house is your clothing and personal items. You don't even get to remove your bedroom furniture like I did," Kinsey said.

"She gave me that furniture for my sixteenth birthday."

"And she's takin' it back from what she says. Got to go. Honey is calling," Kinsey said.

Leah pushed end and dialed Rhett's number, but nothing happened. She checked the phone to see if she needed to recharge, but a message floated across the black screen saying that the service had been disconnected.

She tossed the phone on the bed and wondered how in the world her grandmother had managed that in so short a time. Her first thought was to tattle to her father, but she stopped on the landing. She was an adult. She'd handle this on her own, without any help. There was a landline in the kitchen, one in the living room, and one in the office.

Somehow, she wasn't surprised to see all three phones had been disconnected from the walls and removed. Her grandmother probably had them in bed with her to be sure that Leah couldn't make a phone call that night.

"There is more than one way to skin a cat," Leah mumbled as she took the steps two at a time. She grabbed her purse, stomped into the first pair of boots she found in her closet, and marched back down to the foyer. Planning to go over to Fiddle Creek even though it was midnight, she opened the garage door to find her truck gone.

Tears welled up in her eyes. Granny had given her that truck last year for her birthday. She'd driven her previous truck since she'd graduated from high school twelve years before, and her dad had declared that it had too many miles. This was beyond hardball. This was downright mean.

A paper fluttered on the otherwise spotless floor and she picked it up. A yellow sticky note informed her in Mavis's tight, little handwriting that the truck title said River Bend Ranch on it, and since Leah was determined not to be a part of River Bend, then she wouldn't be needing the truck.

Or your phone service, and you may no longer charge at the store, the note ended with a big *M* at the bottom. Not Granny but *M* for Mavis. She'd been disowned as an example to all the other grandchildren—don't cross Granny, or you'll be walking in Leah's shoes.

"Thank God I've got a job." Leah turned around and went upstairs to write a long letter to Rhett. She'd hand it off to him in church the next morning. She hadn't been driven to church since she got her driver's license at the age of sixteen, but hopefully her dad wouldn't mind some company. She had to see Rhett, give him a note, and explain why she hadn't called him that evening—or worse yet, why she hadn't answered when he'd called.

Chapter 22

RUSSELL WAS WAITING AT THE BOTTOM OF THE STAIRS as Leah started down them that Sunday morning. When she took that last step, he said, "Your truck is parked out front. Your cell phone service is back on for two weeks. That should give you enough time to get a plan of your own. And as soon as I can get to the tag agency in the morning, the truck title will be in your name."

She hugged him. "Are you a miracle worker?"

"No, but this isn't happening. I wish I'd never moved back to River Bend after your mother and I graduated from college. Even more, I wish I hadn't stayed here after she left me, so I fully understand how you feel right now. I know you're moving out, but that truck is yours and turning your phone off was childish. I swear if she gets any more cantankerous, I'm putting her in a nursing home."

Leah gasped. "Did you tell her that?"

Russell nodded seriously. "It wasn't the first time and it probably won't be the last, but she'd best be careful. The feud is one thing, but she's not turning on the family."

Leah slipped the keys into her purse and hugged her father. "Thanks, Daddy."

"Tread softly. She's on the warpath and she's in the kitchen. And, Leah, I meant it when I said you can come back to the ranch anytime. That's to talk to me, for Sunday dinner, to sit on the front porch, or to move back into your room. This is your home too, and your grandmother is going to have to realize that."

One tear rolled down her cheek, and she hugged him tighter. "I love you, Daddy. And it's not like I'm moving out of the state. I'll still live in Burnt Boot if Polly lets me rent her house."

"I want you to understand." Russell wiped the tear away with his forefinger. "Don't let the old gal see a drop of weakness or she'll devour you."

Leah managed a smile. "Yes, sir. Off to do battle with the dragon."

Russell kissed her on the forehead. "That's the spirit."

Mavis didn't even look up from her Sunday paper when Leah entered the room. She sighed a few times, but Leah didn't comment as she went about making sandwiches and loading a picnic basket that she brought in from the pantry.

"So," Mavis finally said in an icy tone, "you're going to have a picnic with Tanner Gallagher. I've never been so embarrassed in my life as when you came dragging him back to the flatbed truck."

"He caught me. I didn't catch him." Leah brought out a small cooler for a couple cans of soda pop and a few bottles of water. "Betsy wouldn't have caught Rhett, but she threw out stickers on the pathway where he was running."

"Shows how stupid he is. And you should have run faster. I heard that Betsy is taking Rhett to Wild Horse today for dinner. When he sees all that she has to offer, you might be out in the cold anyway. Man like him is out for all he can get."

A visual of Rhett's body tangled up with Betsy's hung in her mind, and no matter how many times she blinked, she couldn't get rid of it.

Your grandmother is right, the voice in her head said. *Rhett is better matched with Betsy than he is with you. Admit it and then if he sees something at Wild Horse that appeals to him, it won't hurt so badly.*

Mavis put the paper aside and pointed her finger at Leah. "I do not agree with Russell about your truck or that phone. If you leave River Bend, you should only be allowed to take your clothing."

"There is no if, Granny. I'm leaving before you throw me out."

"You can stay. You have to promise me that you won't see that hippie cowboy no more and that you won't get something started with Tanner today," Mavis said.

"Can't do it." Leah picked up the basket and the cooler, dropped a kiss on Mavis's head, and headed out to her truck.

"If you move out, you can't come back," Mavis yelled.

Leah kept right on walking. "See you in church, Granny. Save me a seat and I'll sit beside you this morning."

She parked in front of Gladys's house, checked her makeup and hair in the rearview mirror, and opened the truck door. The skirt of her bright-colored sundress swished against her bare legs as she made her way to the door and knocked. It was already hot at eight o'clock in the morning. Not so much that she should have been sweating, but then nerves did that and she was about to ask for a pretty big favor.

Gladys opened the door and then the screen door and motioned her inside. "What are you doin' out this early? Tryin' to get two old women to hide you on Fiddle Creek so you don't have to go to dinner with Tanner?"

Leah stepped into the cool house and caught a whiff of bacon. Her stomach growled and tightened up like a ball of yarn. "No, ma'am. He tricked me, and Betsy sure enough tricked Rhett, but I've got a picnic out there in the truck. Granny would skin me alive if I brought him to the ranch for dinner."

"You had breakfast?" Polly yelled from the kitchen.

"Way her stomach is carryin' on, I'd say that she hasn't. Throw another couple of eggs in the bowl and she can eat with us." Gladys took her arm and led her from the living room, through the dining area, and into the country-sized kitchen. "You really think a picnic is a smart idea?"

"Didn't know what else to do. The rules say I have to take him to dinner. I thought we'd eat on the church steps or have a tailgate party in my truck in the church parking lot."

Polly nodded. "That sounds safe enough. You could bring him here. We're putting a roast in the oven and there'd be plenty for two more."

"Thanks, but I think a tailgate party out in the open would be best, and besides, I don't want to drag y'all into this mess. Can I help with anything?"

"You can set the table," Gladys answered.

Leah washed her hands at the kitchen sink, dried them, and opened the cabinet door. "I need a place to live. Polly, would you rent your house to me?"

"So it's come down to that, has it?" Polly asked.

"I understand if you don't want to get in the middle of the feud, but this hasn't got anything to do with that," Leah said.

"Rhett?" Gladys asked.

"Yes, and Tanner. Granny says that if I don't break it off with Rhett or if I start something up with Tanner as a result of this dinner today, then I have to move out. I told Granny I was leaving tomorrow evening, as soon as I get home from the first day of school. So..." Leah paused.

"So you made the decision to move before Mavis made good on her word, right?" Polly asked.

"There's a spare room in the bunkhouse," Gladys said.

"That would complicate things too much," Polly said. "Me and Gladys been doin' some serious talkin' after that episode I had. This could be the first step in makin' some decisions, so, yes, you can rent my house. It's full of my stuff, but you can sleep in the guest room. When we get our plans all settled, I'll get it cleaned out, but right now it's livable and you can have it."

"How much?" Leah asked.

"Well, if you'd be willin' to help Rhett and Sawyer take care of the place, I reckon that would be payment enough. They're feeding my cows and takin' care of the ranch for me and..." It was Polly's turn to pause.

"Might as well go on and tell her the rest of the story, but make her promise to keep it a secret," Gladys said.

"I've got a buyer for the bar. She wants to take over the first of September. And I'm thinkin' about offering the ranch to Rhett and financing the sale myself, but I haven't talked to him about it yet, so don't let the cat out of the bag. He'd take possession the same time the new bar owner would."

Gladys pulled a pan of biscuits from the oven and carried them to the table. "And I'm going to give Fiddle Creek to Jill —all but this house and the acre it sits on, so me and Polly will have a permanent place to live. Then me and Polly and Verdie are going to do some traveling, starting with one of them senior cruises that takes two whole weeks, maybe in September if we can get it arranged that fast. We don't want to be away from Burnt Boot for Christmas, and Verdie has to be here in late January to help out when the new baby arrives."

"Sounds like y'all have given this a lot of thought," Leah said.

They both nodded at the same time.

"And"—Gladys patted her on the shoulder—"if Rhett buys Polly's ranch, and he wants to live in the house and y'all ain't comfortable bein' roommates, you can rent a room in the bunkhouse from Jill and Sawyer. You'll have a place to live, honey, so don't worry about it."

"Thank you." Leah smiled.

"I'll get you a key to the house after breakfast. Refrigerator is empty, but the freezer has about a quarter of a hog in it and half that much beef. Help yourself to any of it that you want." Polly picked up a platter of bacon and eggs and carried it to the table.

"And you can start a charge at the store. Just tell Jill to put it in your name and keep it separate from River Bend."

Leah's eyes misted for the second time that morning. "Y'all don't know how much I appreciate this."

"Ah, honey, it ain't nothin' but a simple breakfast. If

we'd have known you were comin', we would've made sausage gravy to go with it." Polly grinned.

Gladys patted her shoulder again. "It'll all work out. In a year, it'll only be a line in the history of your life."

"I hope so," Leah said.

―――⁓⁓⁓―――

Leah made arrangements for one of her cousins to teach her Sunday school class that morning and went to check out Polly's house, walking from room to room in the small two-bedroom house, and thinking that she'd like to have a home like it someday. All she really needed was a little place with a front porch big enough for lazy dogs and cats on a hot summer day and a yard for some roses and petunias.

If Rhett didn't want to buy the ranch, perhaps Polly would make her the same deal. She could hire one full-time foreman and a couple of part-time cowboys to help out, and in a couple of years, she'd be making a profit.

The guest room that was to be hers was only about half the size of her bedroom at the ranch, but it had a good-sized closet. Her heart was as empty as the closet right then, waiting for something to happen in her life that would prove to her that she'd made the right decision. She heard her phone ringing in her purse, rushed to the living room, and fished it out, hoping that it was Rhett.

Before she could answer, it vibrated in her hands letting her know someone had sent a text message. Honey was asking her where in the hell she was. They were at church, and it was starting in ten minutes. She was already in hot water with Granny, so she'd best get her ass in gear.

She sighed on her way out the door and was only five minutes late when she slid into the pew beside Honey.

"You are late," Honey whispered.

"Yes, I am, and I didn't go to Sunday school, but I made arrangements, so don't fuss at me."

"You still hell-bent on leaving River Bend?"

Leah nodded.

"Shhh." Quaid tapped her on the shoulder from the pew right behind them.

The song ended and the preacher took the podium. Leah glanced over to the other side of the church and met Betsy's gaze. Betsy's smile was smug. Movement on another pew farther back grabbed her attention, and Tanner blew a kiss from the tips of his finger across the church toward her.

The preacher's voice droned on for what felt like hours and hours instead of the usual thirty minutes. She kept her eyes glued ahead and wished the next two days were already over. The preacher made reference to a verse that talked about honoring your mother and father, and that set her mind on another loop, one that involved her mother, Eden. Now that she was divorcing River Bend, should she try to approach her again, or leave it alone and not reopen old wounds?

One thing at a time, she thought. *Get the tailgate picnic over with. Then call Rhett. Go home and pack. Sleep in the house you were born in one more night. Go to school. Move into Polly's house. Settle in, and then think about calling Eden.*

That's the way it lined up, and the first thing on the

list had to do with Tanner Gallagher, something that she dreaded worse than anything else on the list. She carefully snuck her phone out of her purse and sent Rhett a text message, asking him to call her as soon as he got home from dinner at Wild Horse with Betsy.

He sent one right back that said he would, then leaned back across the pews and smiled at her. She tucked her phone away and tried to pay attention to the end of the sermon, but it was useless. Finally, she played out a dozen scenarios about how she would handle Tanner when they were alone. The second that the last amen was said after the benediction, Betsy latched on to Rhett's arm and pulled him toward the door.

Leah stepped out into the aisle, and Tanner quickly crossed over to the Brennan side of the church, laced his fingers in hers, and squeezed. She pulled her hand free, so he slung an arm around her shoulders and escorted her outside into the hot, broiling August sun.

What was she thinking when she'd planned a tailgate picnic? Even parked under the only shade tree in the parking lot, the metal pickup bed would be hot. A nice, public restaurant would have been a much better choice. After all, it did not have to be a secret. The whole damn town knew she was having dinner with Tanner Gallagher.

"Where to, darlin'?" he asked.

She stopped beside her bright red truck. "It's a tailgate picnic right here."

"Too hot for that kind of thing, Leah. Let me take you out to dinner in a nice restaurant," Tanner said.

"Rules say that I have to produce dinner, so this is it. Now if you can't take the heat, then it's your prerogative to forfeit the dinner and then the whole Sadie Hawkins race will be done and finished," she said.

"No, ma'am, but I would like to go somewhere a little cooler."

"Right here," she said.

"Okay then, if that's the way it is, then that's the way it is." He grinned. He put the tailgate down and sat down on it. His boots came off first and then his socks.

She could feel her eyes trying to pop right out of her head. "What are you doing?"

"It's hot. I came dressed for church, not dinner in the broiling-hot sun. If it's going to be right here, then I'm shucking out of half of these clothes," he said. "You are free to do the same if you'd like."

The noise of engines starting, trucks, cars, and vans all leaving the lot, muffled the sound of a truck when it came to a stop right beside Leah's. Betsy rolled down the window and yelled, "Good grief, Tanner, you are still on church grounds. Don't take it all off."

The next truck to pull out of the lot left behind a long, sexy wolf whistle, and she turned back around to see Tanner swinging his long legs off the edge of the tailgate, waving at everyone like he was the newest model for romance novels. His jean legs were rolled up to below his knees, and his unsnapped shirt flapped in the hot wind, showing a bare chest and ripped abs.

Leah might be moving away from River Bend, but that didn't mean she was befriending the Gallaghers. Someday, she intended to yank every single red hair out of Betsy's scalp, a handful at a time, for today, if for no other reason. Leah's hands knotted into fists thinking about the joy of that fight.

"Ahh, a picnic basket and a cooler. Does that mean we have cold beers?" Tanner asked.

"It means you have cold soda pop and ice water," she said.

"Are you going to feed me from your fingertips?" he asked.

"The rules say I have to supply dinner. They do not say a word about feeding you or providing beer." She opened the tailgate and set the basket and small cooler on it. "It's help yourself from this point on, like at a buffet. And, Tanner, dinner does not mean the whole afternoon. One hour is what I've allowed, and then I'm going home to pack."

Shit! Why had she said that? And why was it that swearing came so quickly to her thoughts these days?

"I heard that your Granny was ready to kick you out, darlin'. We've got lots of room over on Wild Horse, and you are welcome. I even talked to my Granny about it, and she said you could have a room in the main house."

"And it's all part of the feud, so no thank you. I'm so sick of all this, I could cry," she said.

Tanner cocked his head to one side. "I'm not used to hearing you say bad words or that tone in your voice."

"Get used to it," she said.

The last vehicle pulling away from the parking lot was the preacher and his wife. He stuck a hand out the window and waved, then tooted his horn as he left. Did the fool think that this dinner would end the feud? Even the angels in heaven knew that this would only fuel it up hotter than ever.

Tanner waved and kept digging in the picnic basket,

bringing out two paper plates and plastic cutlery. He set a pretty nice little table right there between them, spreading out two napkins to use as a tablecloth. "Leah, all kidding aside, because now I'm going to talk serious. I know you like Rhett and that you think all of this with me is part of the feud. Ham or turkey?" He pulled two sandwiches from the basket.

"Turkey," she said.

"Rhett is a decent man, but he's a ranch foreman and that's all he'll ever be. I can offer you a lifestyle like you're used to," Tanner said.

She pulled out a bag of potato chips and one of Fritos and held them up. He pointed at the chips, so she laid the Fritos beside her plate. "Are you proposing to me, Tanner? We haven't even been on a proper date."

"This is a proper date and, no, I'm not proposing to you. But the more I get to know you, Leah Brennan, the better I like you. I would like to date you. I would like to spend time with you and to hell with the feud. Who knows? Maybe if we connected, it would end this damn thing once and for all," he said.

Now that was a novel idea. Ending the feud forever because of a Gallagher and a Brennan falling in love; she'd had a crush on Tanner for more than a decade, so maybe it wouldn't be difficult to rekindle her past feelings for him.

She looked up to see his face so close that he had four eyes instead of two and they were closing as his lips brushed across hers. The first kiss was sweet, and the next was clearly supposed to be filled with passion and heat, but it did nothing for Leah. There were no sparks, no bursting stars, not even a little sizzle.

"Give me a chance, Leah," he whispered seductively as his hand grazed her shoulder.

The feud could be over, her conscience whispered as softly.

"I'm moving away from River Bend because I want to figure out who I am. I'm almost thirty, and I have to get some things settled before I make a commitment to anyone for any kind of relationship," she said.

"I'll be right here in Burnt Boot waiting for you," Tanner said.

"Yeah, right!" She smiled. "Until the next woman comes along who catches your eye, and then you'll be hugged up to her on the dance floor?"

"Honey, if you'll dance with me, I give you my promise that I'll never dance with another woman," he said.

Leah didn't believe him for a minute, but still, the end of the feud? And what if the Gallaghers were serious about making Rhett disappear?

Chapter 23

RHETT HAD BEEN MISERABLE IN CHURCH THAT MORNING. Sitting in the middle section with Tanner on one side and Leah on the other was purely symbolic; especially after the night before, when he'd called and sent Leah text messages so often that he'd begun to feel like a stalker. He'd wanted to get off his cycle and beat the shit out of Tanner for sitting in the back of Leah's truck with his shirt opened and flapping like that.

Now he was miserable sitting between Betsy and her grandmother, Naomi, in a huge room of Gallaghers. He'd meant to steer clear of the feud when his cousins Sawyer and Finn told him about it, and now he was a pawn in the whole damn mess of things. He hated it and wished he could talk to Leah. He'd be willing to pawn his cycle and cut off his ponytail if he could get things straightened out with her.

"I understand Leah fixed up a cute little picnic for her and Tanner, and they're having it in the church parking lot." Naomi smiled.

Betsy tapped him on the arm. "She's had a secret crush on him since they were kids. This is a dream come true for her. And I think Tanner is finally ready to stop his womanizing and settle down."

"Never thought I'd say this, but I'm glad. Leah is a fine young woman who knows ranchin' and is such a good girl. I've been afraid he'd bring home a barroom hussy with dollar signs in her eyes. Even a Brennan is better than that," Naomi said. "But enough about this, Rhett. Tell me where you grew up."

"Same place as Finn and Sawyer—on a ranch down around Comfort, Texas. I have relatives over in Ringgold, not far from here," he said.

"Those O'Donnells? I've been thinking about putting my name on the list to buy one of their fine horses. Now I know that you're a relative, I'll have to give them a call this week." Naomi smiled.

"They do grow some good horses," he said.

Betsy's hand landed on his thigh and squeezed. "We'll get through this dinner and then we'll have a tour of the ranch."

"The rules of the race say that we only have to have dinner together," he said. "I've allowed an hour and a half for the dinner, and then I have a meeting with Gladys, Polly, Sawyer, and Jill planned. I have to be there at two o'clock."

"Well then"—her hand slid farther up his thigh—"I expect we'd best make the best of what time we have. How do you like what you see here on Wild Horse?"

"As in?" he asked.

"As in how would you like to be a part of what you see here?"

"Are you proposing to me, Betsy?"

Her smile was brilliant, but her eyes told a different story. This was all a game to Betsy and had nothing to do with love, ranches, or anything but the feud.

"Why, Rhett O'Donnell, I'm most certainly not proposing anything but asking you if you like what you see. If you do"—she squeezed his leg again—"I was thinking about making you one of those offers you can't refuse."

"Such as?"

"Such as jumping the fence from Fiddle Creek over to Wild Horse. I'll pay you double whatever Sawyer and Gladys are paying you, and there's all these wonderful benefits." Her fingers walked up his thigh, all the way up to his zipper.

He reached under the table and moved her hand to her own lap. "I like my job and I never was too good at jumping fences."

"Don't say no until you hear the benefits."

Naomi laid a hand on his arm. "We've got an empty two-bedroom house not far from where Betsy lives, and I'll throw in medical insurance with your salary and give you a two-week paid vacation after six months."

"Thanks for the offer, but no thanks. By the way, this steak is really good. What's your secret?"

"Good beef. I'll show you my secret in raising prime stock, but you have to take us up on the offer. This is a big place, Rhett. Even though Leah will wind up living here, there will be miles between you. Besides, she's not serious about a plain old hired hand. She's been flirting with you to bring Tanner to his knees," Naomi said.

"I figured you'd fight the idea of bringing a Brennan onto Wild Horse," Rhett told her.

"I would if it was any other woman from over on River Bend. But Leah, now that's special circumstances. I hope it causes Mavis's blood pressure to shoot up so high that she has a stroke and dies." Naomi's tone was icy cold.

"But the benefits I have to offer are a lot hotter,"

Betsy whispered in his other ear. "Think about long, hot nights with no commitments, dancing at the bar, fishing in the river, skinny-dipping after either or both. It's win-win. Leah gets to keep living in the style she's accustomed to. My granny wins a battle in the feud. Mavis drops dead. You get more money and lots more fun. No losses here, darlin'."

"Maybe I'm looking for a commitment," he said.

She kissed his earlobe. "Maybe you'll find one. And, honey, remember what I told you yesterday—there's more than one way to skin a cat. If I want you, and Leah is in the way, Granny can fix that little problem real quick."

Dinner dragged on forever, through course after course, served by waiters dressed in black slacks and white shirts. It wasn't the first time Rhett had been to a dinner like that, but they'd usually been at weddings or some other such celebration, not merely a family meal after church on Sunday. By the time they got to the dessert cart, which featured cheesecakes in about a dozen varieties, blackberry cobbler with or with ice cream, and pecan pie, it was one thirty.

Betsy chose a slice of turtle cheesecake and he nodded. He didn't care if he had sawdust with ice cream on top; he wanted to finish dinner and get the hell away from Wild Horse Ranch.

"I hate to eat and run, ladies," he said after he'd swallowed the last bite. "It's been a lovely dinner, and it was so nice to get to know you better, Naomi. But I have a meeting scheduled that I must get to, so I should be going. Y'all have a wonderful afternoon."

"I'll walk you out." Betsy laid her napkin down.

"Come back anytime, Rhett," Naomi said. "And

remember my offer. It's only good for twenty-four hours, so don't ponder on it too long."

"Yes, ma'am," he said.

Betsy looped her arm in his and led him through a maze of Gallaghers. When they were finally at his cycle, she looped her arms around his neck, rolled up onto her toes, and kissed him full on the mouth, tongue, and the whole nine yards. It wasn't a bad kiss, not bad at all, but it did nothing to excite Rhett like Leah's kisses did. There was no flashing sparks, no breathlessness, and no racing pulse.

"You take that home with you, cowboy, and remember, it can be yours if you move on over here to Wild Horse. And, Rhett, don't be thinking that Leah is in love with you. A girl never forgets her first love, not ever, and Tanner is hers. She's getting a once-in-a-lifetime chance right now to fill the hole in her heart. It's never been possible before and probably never will be again, that a Gallagher and a Brennan can get together," Betsy said.

"Who was your first love, Betsy?" Rhett asked.

"I haven't found him yet. You want to apply for the job?"

"Not today," he said as he got into his truck and started the engine.

"I'll give you a whole week to think about it and change your mind." She laughed and waved as he drove away.

He parked in front of Gladys's house beside Sawyer's truck and sat on the cycle a couple of minutes before going inside. Why was the whole family there, anyway? Surely they weren't going to fire him because of the dinner. That wasn't his fault, and even though he had mixed feelings about what was going on with Leah, he damn sure wasn't ready to walk away from Burnt Boot.

"Hey, get on in here, Rhett. It's hot out there, and we've got sweet tea and cookies," Polly called from the door.

"Sounds wonderful." He parked the cycle and headed toward the porch. They wouldn't be feeding him tea and cookies if they planned on kicking him off Fiddle Creek, now would they?

You could always take Naomi up on her offer, his conscience reminded him.

"Like hell," he muttered under his breath. "That ain't about to happen. I'm flat-out not interested in that shit. Me and Dammit will pack up and go back to Comfort before we consider that offer."

"So how did the dinner go?" Jill asked the minute he was in the house.

"They tried to steal me from Fiddle Creek and Betsy tried to seduce me," he said.

"And they told you how Leah would be so much better off if she broke it off with you and wound up with Tanner, right?" Gladys laughed.

Rhett nodded. "And like I told Gladys last night, they keep making threats about how they could make Leah disappear."

"Don't believe a word of that. Tanner Gallagher is a womanizer, and he will never settle down with one woman. It's all part of the feudin' game. If he did talk her into dating or even getting into what you kids call a relationship these days, it would only last long enough for Naomi to gloat like hell about it to Mavis. Then he'd drop her or go out with another woman so that she'd break it off with him," Polly said. "Come on in here and sit with us at the table. That's where deals are made in our part of the world."

"You think Tanner would do that?" Rhett pulled out a chair.

"Don't think so. Know so." Polly nodded. "We hadn't planned on doing this so quick, but Verdie reminded us that Finn and Callie are expecting their baby in October, so we can't put it off until then."

"I told them that I have to be in Burnt Boot when the baby comes, because Finn and Callie will need me." Verdie came from the direction of the restroom and sat down at with them.

"We're gettin' old, and we've always talked about doing some fun stuff when we retired, so we're going on a senior cruise in September. And we plan on doing lots more stuff after the new baby is here and Verdie is free," Gladys said.

Jill picked up a second cookie. "I think that's a wonderful idea. Y'all have worked your whole lives. We can hold down Fiddle Creek while you're gone."

"That's where the next step comes into play," Polly said. "The man I've had doing the work over on my place has given notice. September first is his last day unless I sell the ranch to him. I've got a relative up in Oklahoma who wants to buy the bar. Rosalie has run a couple of places like mine up there in the past. Sold out a few months ago and isn't happy staying at home. She wants to get back into the business. So I've sold the bar to her. She takes over on the first day of September."

"Wow!" Jill said.

"Then we only have night jobs for another couple of weeks?" Sawyer asked.

"No, I reckon you'll be burning some midnight oil, but it will be on Fiddle Creek because you'll have full control of the store too," Gladys answered.

"Yes, ma'am." Jill smiled.

"I've always told you that you'd inherit the bar and my place. Aren't you disappointed?" Polly asked.

Jill patted Polly on the arm. "Fiddle Creek is plenty for us to handle, Aunt Polly. Sell your ranch and use the money to have a good time while you feel up to it."

"I don't need the money. That bar and the ranch have made me a rich woman, but I don't want you to be disappointed in my decision," Polly said.

Jill sipped at her tea. "I'm not one bit disappointed."

"Good," Gladys said. "Because tomorrow morning, I'm getting in touch with my lawyer and the title to Fiddle Creek, minus this house and the one acre it sits on, is going to be put in joint tenancy for you and Sawyer. You can have this much while I'm living. You can have the last acre and the house when I'm dead. The only thing you have to promise me is that you will never let either the Brennans or the Gallaghers get their grubby little fingers on it."

"Gladys, are you sure about this?" Sawyer asked.

"Very sure. It's the way I want to do things. This last scare with Polly has taught all three of us—that would be us two and Verdie, who's been our lifelong friend—that it's time for us to get busy and do what we've dreamed about before one of us drops dead," Gladys answered.

"And it wouldn't be any fun if we couldn't all go together," Verdie said.

"Thank you," Sawyer said softly as he reached for Jill's hand. "Thank you so much, Gladys."

"And thank you, Aunt Polly, for selling the bar, so we can have more time to devote to Fiddle Creek and to the store," Jill said. "Pinch me, Rhett. I'm sure this is a dream."

He chuckled. "Just don't throw me off Fiddle Creek or I'll think it's a nightmare instead of a dream."

"That's where my next proposition comes into play," Polly said.

"Leah came by this morning before church, and Polly gave her permission to move into the guest room in her house," Gladys said. "Now go on, Polly. He needed to hear that first."

"I could have told him. I didn't have a damn stroke, so there ain't nothin' wrong with my brain or my ability to speak," Polly fussed.

"Get on with it, Polly, and quit your whining," Gladys said.

"Okay! Okay! I'm going to sell my ranch to you, Rhett, if you want to buy it. You can change the name and brand if you want to. It's been called Polly's Ranch for so long that most folks won't even remember the original name anyway, but it won't hurt my feelings one bit. I don't have any idea what you have in the bank, but we'll negotiate a down payment, and you can pay me the rest of it in yearly installments after you sell off the calf crop each fall," she said.

Rhett's hands went clammy. His heart thumped around so hard that it hurt his ribs and his pulse raced. He'd been saving for years while looking for a ranch the size of Polly's operation—a good solid start that would support a few hundred head of cattle.

"What's your asking price?" he whispered.

"I've got a section of land, six hundred and forty acres. Prime is selling for about three thousand an acre, but—"

"I'll take it," he said.

"Hey, barter with me a little here. I'm prepared to let you have it for two thousand an acre and throw in what cattle is on the land right now. That's three hundred head of Angus."

"I'm not arguing with that price. I can give you half down and pay you the rest out in ten years," he said. "I could pay for all of it, but I need working capital for the first two years."

"Smart man," Sawyer said.

"Whoa! Wait a minute! That means we're losing our foreman on Fiddle Creek in two weeks," Jill said.

Rhett grinned. "There's lots of O'Donnell cousins who'll jump at the chance to move up here and work for Sawyer."

Polly stuck out her hand. "Deal! I'll tell the lawyer to draw up the papers tomorrow when me and Gladys go to town. Now, this business with Leah—I told her this morning what I was offering you. If you got a problem with havin' her for a roommate, she can either live in one room of the house, or Jill can give her your old room until she can find a place to live."

"I don't have a problem, but if she does, then she can talk to Jill," Rhett said.

What if after today, she doesn't want to live in the same house with you? the voice in his head said.

Then I guess she'll have to find another place to live.

"Oh, and one more thing goes with that deal," Polly

was saying when his mind stopped arguing with his heart. "I'm not able to clean out the house, so that's up to you three to do for me. You can store it all in the barn down at the back of my ranch until I feel like going through it and having an auction."

"That's only what's in the house, right?" Rhett asked. "The equipment does come with the sale?"

"Lock, stock, and barrel. Just not the household things. Most of them are pretty sentimental," Polly answered.

"Then I'll be more than happy to move it all out."

"Good. All except whatever is in that guest room. That belongs to Leah now, and it never meant much to me anyway," Polly said, "You can have the house with all the appliances plus the freezer that's in the utility room and whatever is left in it. The rest goes to storage."

Leah threw herself onto her bed. There was work to do and lots of it. Her personal things had to be boxed up to move to the new house. Clothing could be taken downstairs on the hangers and piled in the backseat of her truck. Not a single person had stepped up to help her, so the job was all hers.

That plus what Tanner had said about ending the feud had put her into a terrible turmoil. All she wanted to do was run away, maybe back to the beach, alone this time, to think about this emotional roller coaster.

She sat up and reached for her purse and the letter she'd written to Rhett fell out on the floor.

"Dammit!" she exclaimed. "He doesn't have any idea that I didn't have access to a phone or a vehicle. I wonder what went on over at Betsy's. Dammit! I bet she tried to wow him with all that Wild Horse could offer him, right along with her body. I'd like to cover her with honey and stake her out on a fire ant bed."

"Hey, Sis." Declan knocked on the door and poked his head inside. "I hear you're leaving us tomorrow after your first day of school."

"I am."

He crossed the room and sat down on the edge of the bed. "You realize that means no one to clean your room, make your bed every day, and cook for you. It means taking care of yourself."

"Just like college, right?"

His dark blue eyes darted around the room. "This place is all either of us has ever known except for those four years at college, and then we came home every weekend."

She sat down and threw an arm around him. "I'll miss seeing you every day but, hey, I'm only a few miles away. Polly's house sits a quarter of a mile back behind the bar, as you well know, and you can come visit anytime you want."

"How was it today with Tanner?"

"I don't know, Declan. He says that the two of us could end this feud if we got together."

"He's lying. He'll leave you with a broken heart if you trust him. And, honey, it'll take more than you and Tanner to end this crap. It will take the deaths of our granny and Naomi."

Leah's eyes misted. "But if he's right, I could end it, and we'd all be free of this damned curse we were born into."

Declan wiped her tears away with his palm. "Would you be happy with him?"

More tears flowed down her cheeks. "Wouldn't we all be happier to get away from this constant war? One person's happiness seems so small compared to everyone being happy after more than a hundred years of fighting."

He pulled his sister over, so her head was on his shoulder. "Not if it's your happiness, Leah. You deserve your soul mate. Don't cry. If you're determined to move, I'll help you pack things up."

"You'll be in big trouble if you do." She managed a weak smile.

"You've got a house and I can always crash on your sofa."

Chapter 24

Kinsey, bless her heart, took Granny Mavis to Dallas on Monday to shop and kept her out until Leah's dad and brother loaded everything into her truck. The backseat was full of her clothing still on hangers and the bed of the truck was stacked from back to front with boxes.

Russell hugged her and pointed toward the southeast. "You'd best get going if you're going to get all this into your new place before that storm hits. It's going to be a toad strangler from what the weatherman says."

"We need the rain, so we're not complainin'." Declan opened the door for her. "You sure you don't want me to go with you and get all this inside?"

"No, Rhett promised he'd be there. Y'all come on over and see me regular. I'm going to miss seeing you every day," she said.

"Go, before you make me change my mind and chain you to the porch post," Russell teased.

She got into the truck and rolled down the window. "Thanks for making this…" Her voice cracked.

Declan popped the fender and said, "Move 'em out. Wagons, ho!"

She wiped away the single tear that had escaped and drove away. She thought she might have a panic moment when she pulled out onto the highway and turned north, leaving River Bend behind her. She inhaled deeply and got ready for her chest to tighten. After all, she'd left what she knew behind and was going forward to a shaky future. But all she felt was a sudden burst of pure joy.

Rhett was sitting on the porch with Dammit beside him when she parked in the driveway. He waved and stretched when he stood up, and he had a smile on his face. She hopped out of the truck and opened up the back doors to take out a load of clothing.

"You really did it." He smiled as he lowered the tailgate.

"And it wasn't nearly as hard as I thought it would be," she answered.

Suddenly his arms were around her waist and her back was against his chest. He buried his face in the hollow of her neck and held her for several seconds before he loosened his hold enough to turn her around. His eyelids fluttered shut and she stood on tiptoe at the same time he leaned toward her. His lips found hers in a scorching-hot kiss that left her knees weak. She tangled her hands in his dark hair that fell free that evening and pressed her body against his.

"I was afraid you'd change your mind," he whispered.

"I was afraid you wouldn't be here," she said.

He took a step back and took her hand in his. "Don't unload anything until you walk through the house. It could change your mind about living here."

"I don't think anything could change my mind," she said.

He led her onto the porch and swung open the door. Light poured in from the bare windows. Two lawn chairs sat beside a wooden crate with a mason jar full of wild flowers in the middle. The kitchen was bare except for a folding card table with four metal folding chairs around it.

She stopped in the middle of the hallway, almost afraid to open the guest bedroom door for fear she'd find it swept clean of everything too. But when Rhett swung the door open, the bed and dresser were still there. No sheets, pillows, or throw rugs, but at least she had a bed to sleep on that night.

"And now…" He swung open the door to the room across the hallway. She recognized the bed they'd shared in the bunkhouse and the dresser. Again, no sheets but the closet doors revealed his clothing and there were a few things on top of the dresser. "I bought this ranch and I've moved into this room. If that's going to be a problem, then Jill says you can live at the bunkhouse. And I will understand. No questions asked. I'll even go with you and help you move in. I officially take over duties on September first, but I wanted to get moved in now so the man who's been taking care of the place could show me around."

He sucked up a lungful of air like he was going to keep talking, but Leah put her fingers over his mouth. "I have no problem with you living across the hall from me, Rhett. And I love what you've done with the place. Thank you for the flowers in the living room. Anything else we should talk about?"

"Lots, but right now we have to get your things in the house before it rains. Then we have to go to Gainesville to buy groceries. We'll make a list on the way." He tipped her chin up for another kiss that glued her feet to the floor.

No, she didn't mind him living across the hall or sharing the one bathroom in the house with him, but were they roommates, lovers, or had she moved in with him on a much higher plane?

He stacked the boxes against the wall in the living room and helped her hang all her clothing in the closet in her new room. She'd organize the closet later and unpack the boxes when she had time. Today, they had to concentrate on basics because tomorrow, Rhett would be still working at Fiddle Creek while learning what he could about his new ranch. She would be at school all day. They needed to be able to eat and go to bed in that order. While he drove, she took a pad and pen from her purse and started a list.

"I've written down sheets and pillows for two beds," she said.

"Bath soap, towels, and a shower curtain, and maybe a rug to go in front of the tub," he said.

She wrote that down and said, "Laundry soap, fabric softener, and spray starch."

He nodded. "Ironing board and iron if you liked pressed clothes."

She finally looked up and asked, "What else?"

"Food," he said. "Do you know how to cook?"

"A little," she said. "This reminds me of the list I made when I went to college."

"Me too, only I like being thirty better than being eighteen. Besides, you're prettier than my roommate was back then. He was a nerd who kept losing his glasses and accusing me of stealing them," he said.

"Mine was a red-haired cheerleader who was seldom in our room. She liked to party and she liked the cowboys," Leah said. "Paper plates for now?"

Rhett nodded. "But I want a real coffee mug."

"Me too." She made a note on the pad and turned the page.

"Leah," he said seriously, "my eyes got opened really wide yesterday when I was on Wild Horse Ranch. I realized what you could have, what you deserve, and I don't ever want to stand in your way if you and Tanner really have something in the past you have to settle. I'm not saying I'll like it if the chips fall in his favor but hell, I'm not stupid. The Gallaghers are a force," he said.

"And so are the Brennans, which is why I want to be away from them both before they swallow me up in their feuding and bigness."

Rhett circled the parking lot in the small shopping plaza until he found a spot close to the barbecue place and snagged it. "I haven't had supper. Have you?"

"No, I have not, and I'm starving. Is this a date?" If he said yes, it was a third date, and by damn, she was going to find out the story behind the horns and the tat.

"It can be. Why? Does magic happen on a third date?" He opened the door and rushed around to help her out.

"You have to tell me about the tat and the horns on your cycle, which reminds me—I didn't see it or your new truck."

"I can't think of a better time for a third date than the night that we become roomies. The cycle is in the shed out back of our new place and the truck didn't arrive today. It should be here by the end of the week, but Gladys is still letting me use the old work truck from Fiddle Creek as long as I'm working for them." Rhett ushered her inside with his hand on the small of her back.

Since the dinner rush had already passed, they were

seated quickly. Rhett ordered a pulled pork sandwich and Leah followed his lead, ordering the same thing only changing her drink to a diet cola rather than sweet tea.

"Now about those horns," she said as they waited on their orders.

"I was going to be a bull rider. From the time I was too little to ride anything but an old tire hung from a tree on a rope, I was going to ride bulls. And I did, made a few dollars to sock away toward my ranch. Ever been to the Resistol Rodeo down near Dallas?"

She nodded. "Many times. Daddy and Declan love rodeos, and I got dragged along or tagged along, depending on my age and my mood."

"I was twenty-two that summer and fresh out of college, full of piss and vinegar, and ready to get right into my rodeo career. I was practicing my bull riding on some of my cousin's rodeo stock up at Ringgold. The bull I was on was a mean old devil, and I knew if I could stay on his back eight seconds, I was a shoo-in for the big tour that year. I climbed on his back, got the ropes right, and nodded for them to open the gate. He snorted and came out of the shoot like a bat out of hell. Three seconds in, he threw me into the dirt, came back around, caught me with those big horns, and threw me up in the air, then stomped me when I landed the second time," he said.

"Good grief, Rhett! It's a wonder you weren't killed."

"He busted me up pretty good, messed up my neck and several of my vertebrae, broke my wrist, and gave me a damn fine concussion. I was on the ground, unconscious, when he started at me again and my cousin Rye dropped him in his tracks."

"How?" Leah asked.

"A bullet right between the eyes. His horns are on my cycle and when I got out of the neck brace and got the cast off my wrist, I got the tat on my arm. It's to remind me every day to be thankful that I'm alive. To remember that when one door closes, another one opens, and not to take a damn thing that comes into my life for granted," he said.

"That's poetic and romantic," she said. "Why is it a third-date story?"

"I don't want a woman to go out with me a second time out of pity. I want to woo them with my charm."

She covered his hand with hers. "I don't think many women would pity you."

"Well, I'm not taking any chances," he said.

"I have a question," she said.

"About the horns."

"No, about the visit you had on Wild Horse yesterday."

"Ask away," he said.

"What happened?"

"I had dinner and escaped."

"Escaped?"

The waitress brought their food and drinks and asked, "Anything else?"

"Not right now," Rhett said.

She went on to take orders from a couple sitting at a table on the other side of the room, and Leah repeated the question. "Escaped?"

"That's what it felt like. I felt trapped at that place with Betsy on one side and Naomi on the other. Then there was the meeting with Polly and Gladys, and I didn't know if they were going to toss me off Fiddle Creek or what," he said.

Leah removed the top bun from her sandwich and poured barbecue sauce on the meat. "Is that when Polly offered to sell you her ranch? Are you going to change the name?"

"Yes and no. I like the name fine. Had no idea its real name was Double Shot Ranch, but I like it, and she's even going to let me keep the brand. We have to do some paperwork, but as of the first day of September, the ranch is mine."

"Did Betsy make a move on you?"

"No, she made several, and then she kissed me, and it did not create sparks like it does when you kiss me," he said.

Leah could feel anger and jealousy mixing in her veins, and it wasn't a pretty feeling. Just one time, fate could be kind enough to give her a chance to knock that redhead square on her ass. She was seething already when she looked up and there was Tanner Gallagher coming right at their table. He was dressed in his Sunday best. Starched and creased jeans, boots polished to a shine, belt buckle gleaming in the dim light, and a pale blue shirt with pearl snaps. Bad luck followed her around like a hungry puppy.

"Dammit! I swear he's stalking me."

"Who?" Rhett asked.

Tanner's eyes were glued on Leah, and his smile was wide, and it looked sincere and genuine—but then a wolf in sheep's clothing didn't look too dangerous either, now did it? He laid a hand on Leah's shoulder and said softly, "Leah, darlin', I thought that was your truck out there in the parking lot. I went to the bar, hoping you would be there. I overheard Honey talking about you moving away from River Bend. I was heartbroken that you didn't call me to help you. I drove out to Polly's, but you weren't there. Imagine my surprise to see your truck sitting right outside the very place I was coming in to have some supper."

Leah shrugged his hand away.

"We're having dinner here, Tanner," Rhett said.

Tanner barely glanced his way before dropping down on one knee. The red velvet box appeared in his hand as if it came from thin air. He popped it open to reveal a diamond half the size of Rhett's thumbnail that sparkled like a lit up crystal chandelier.

Lord, have mercy! That thing was the gaudiest damn ring she'd ever seen. Sure it was sparkly and glittered in the light, but a woman would be afraid of being mugged if she wore the thing. What was he trying to prove anyway, showing up with a ring like that?

"I'm tired of playing games, Leah. I want you to know how serious I am and how much I love you. Will you marry me? We can have a long engagement and get married next summer, after your school year is over. And I can help move you to Wild Horse tonight. You deserve so much more than that little house of Polly's," he said.

When she didn't answer, he went on. "We'll have a honeymoon on an island that caters to our style of life, since I know you like the beach. And I'll build you a proper home between now and then, that we can come home to after our honeymoon. Until then, Granny says you can have a room at the main house."

"Are you crazy?" Leah asked.

"Crazy in love with you, and I don't want you to make the mistake of your life with this hippie cowboy." Tanner continued to grin like he expected her to throw her arms around him and say that she would marry him. Well, it would snow a foot in hell when she did that, even if he proposed in a very private place with a ring the right size for a teacher.

"No. The answer is no," she said. "Now get up and go away."

Tanner snapped the box shut, the noise causing several people to look their way. When he stood up, he bent and kissed Leah on the forehead. "This is only the first proposal. I have lots more, and I will use them all. You've seen the ring, and you know I mean what I say. I will never give up."

"Tanner, the answer will never be yes," she said.

"It might be next week or next month. You'll get tired of slumming someday, but don't wait too long."

She wiped the kiss away with the back of her hand. "Forever doesn't have a deadline, and I'm not slumming. I'm living my life the way I want to live it."

"My forever has a deadline, and it's Halloween, darlin'," Tanner said.

"Why Halloween?" Rhett asked.

"That gives her a little more than two months to figure out that you can't begin to give her what I can. She'll get tired of living in poverty," Tanner said.

He swaggered out of the café and blew her a kiss as he went out the door.

"Rhett, I'm so sorry." Leah blushed.

"You have no reason to apologize. He's rattling your

cage and trying to keep the feud alive. Nothing much has happened in the past couple of weeks," Rhett said. "If he can entice you away from Double Shot Ranch with a ring, then it would start some more crap. I got to admit, that was one honkin' big-ass diamond."

Leah rolled her eyes toward the ceiling. "Someday we'll look back on this and think it's funny, but right now I'm so angry I can't even think about that day. I can't imagine why you aren't mad."

"I wish you would have told him yes." Rhett bit into his sandwich.

Leah slapped the table so hard that the salt and pepper shakers rattled together. "Why? So you'd be rid of me?"

"No, so I could watch that fool backpedal. He probably has that ring on a ninety-day deal. He's put up the money for it with the deal that if you don't say yes and he returns it, the jeweler will give him his money back. You are a pawn in the feud. I'm surprised that Mavis hasn't shoved Declan or Quaid at Betsy to show Naomi she can play the same game," Rhett said. "Hey, put beer on that list and maybe a bottle of Jack if we can hit a liquor store before they close."

Leave it to a man to think about beer at a time like this. She picked up her drink and downed half of it before she came up for air. "I don't want you to think that I'm measuring you or what you have by him and Wild Horse."

"I don't. I'm me and that's all I am or ever will be. And believe me, even if I could afford a ring like that, I wouldn't, because it's not you, Leah. You aren't a gaudy, flashy woman," he said.

"What kind of woman am I?" she asked.

"My kind." He grinned.

Chapter 25

THE WEEK WENT BY IN A BLUR. RHETT WAS UP AT FIVE every morning, let Dammit out, peeked in on Leah, and wished they had more time together. For the next three hours, he and Dammit were outside, learning where everything was located on Double Shot until eight, when he drove to Fiddle Creek and worked until the afternoon. Then he came home long enough to take a quick shower, change clothes, and kiss Leah as she graded papers at the card table and go to the bar. By the time he got home at near midnight, she was sleeping.

Tempers were running as hot as the temperature outside on Saturday night. It had been days since it had rained. The last threat of it they'd even seen had been on Monday, when Leah had moved into the house. That storm had moved around them, and they hadn't seen so much as a drop of rain. The thermometer didn't drop below ninety that week, not even at night, and the days were triple digits.

Then there was the fact that the Gallaghers had not retaliated for the last stunt the Brennans pulled, and they were getting nowhere with getting Leah to move onto Wild Horse. Tension in the air at the bar that night said there was something underfoot, and Rhett hoped it wasn't something to do with Leah.

"Hey," Jill said when they had a lull in business, "I want you and Leah to know that I fussed at Aunt Polly for leaving y'all with nothing in the house but your bed-room furniture."

"Know what she said?" Sawyer propped a hip on a tall stool beside the beer machine. "She said that y'all needed the experience of finding your own things, that it would make you closer and give you something to do and talk about. I told Jill we should go back to the bunkhouse and strip it down to nothing so we could do the same thing."

"And I told him that we didn't have time for that. I'm so glad this is our last barroom duty. Now we can concentrate on the ranch and store," Jill said.

"Is it really? I thought we had one more week, or at least Monday night since Rosalie isn't taking it until the first day in September," Rhett said.

"No, she says it won't be open Monday so she can take inventory, and then Tuesday night it's all hers. I hear she's got a daughter who'll be doing relief work for her," Sawyer said. "And I talked to our cousin Lawson, and he'll be here by Wednesday evening. We're going to miss you."

"Lawson will do you a good job." Rhett nodded.

"I know, but we're going to miss you and Dammit," Jill said. "The cats whined for the first three days he wasn't there."

"Get a dog." Rhett grinned.

"We've got ranch dogs already," Jill said.

"A ranch dog is different than a pet. They can be both, but you got to train them," Rhett told her.

"Hey, we need two pitchers of beer and four cheese-burger baskets," Tanner said.

Sawyer slapped four pieces of meat on the grill. Rhett

took two pitchers from under the bar and filled them. Jill took the money and made the change.

"I hear the bar will be closed Monday and when it opens on Tuesday, it'll have a new owner," Tanner said.

"That's right. And I hear that Rosalie is tougher than Polly ever was, so y'all best not start anything in here," Jill told him.

"Where's Leah tonight?" Tanner asked.

"That wouldn't be a bit of your business," Jill said.

Tanner picked up the two pitchers. "I'm going to marry her, so I expect it is my business."

"Can't marry someone that isn't willing," Rhett said.

"She'll be willin' real soon. Livin' in poverty isn't her style. She'll figure it out real soon, so get ready for a broken heart. I'll miss seeing you in here, Jill." Tanner nodded her way.

Leah finished up her papers and got her lesson plans ready for the next week. The first week of school was always the week from hell, but this one had been even worse, with Gallagher and Brennan kids leery of each other and the other kids not knowing which side to take.

She thought about going to the bar, but that would have required getting cleaned up and she was very comfortable in her faded chambray shirt and cutoff jean shorts. She was sitting on the porch with Dammit right beside her when she saw headlights coming done the lane. Her heart did one of those familiar leaps that said Rhett was nearby and her pulse quickened.

The big, black truck parked right behind her red one and sat there several minutes. The hair on Dammit's back stiffened, and he lowered his head. A low growl emitted from his throat, and his whole body quivered.

She looped an arm around his neck and said, "It's okay, boy. Remember he got the new truck a couple of days ago. You'll have to get used to him coming home in it rather than the old Fiddle Creek work truck."

The truck door opened, and the moonlight lit up a blond-haired cowboy, not a dark-haired one. Dammit growled again and stood at attention, ready to leap.

"Stay," she said softly. "I'll get rid of him, and if I can't, then I'll call you."

"Leah, darlin', when did you get a big dog like that?" Tanner asked.

His boots crunched on the gravel and Dammit growled again.

"It's okay, boy. He's made of hot air and belt buckles. Nothing to be afraid of with him," Leah whispered.

"Well?" Tanner asked.

"Dammit belongs to Rhett, but he and I are pretty good friends. He's telling me he'd like to tear your ears off and have them for a midnight snack, but I'm keeping him at bay long enough for you to get off Double Shot Ranch."

"I want to talk to you, Leah, and I'd like to do it without yelling."

What in the hell did she have to do to make him back off and leave her alone? She had enough on her plate without adding an extra cowboy. There was the adjustment of the new job, getting used to living in a very different house with Rhett and yet seeing him even less than she had before, and trying to decide what to do about her mother.

"Stay right here," she whispered to Dammit as she stood up.

She met Tanner halfway across the yard, both of them lit up by the headlights on his truck. "For the very last time, Tanner, I want you to leave me alone."

He reached out and laid a hand on her shoulder. "What about our history?"

She shrugged it off. "There is no history. I had a crush on you when we were only kids, but I'm over it, and this thing isn't going to happen. This is a game. You want me because you can't have me and women always fall at your feet when you pay them any kind of attention. But once you conquer them, you throw them in the ditch like trash."

"Not this time." He grabbed her by both shoulders and dragged her into his embrace, his lips bearing down on hers fiercely.

She wiggled, but he held on tighter, his mouth grinding against hers and his tongue forcing its way into her mouth. She kicked him in shins, but he hung on tighter, like a bulldog in a fighting ring. Finally, she landed a good right hook to his chin, and his head popped backwards.

"You'll change your mind after a couple of nights with me. And, Leah, don't you ever hit me again," Tanner growled as he grabbed for her again.

She ran back a few steps and yelled, "Dammit!"

Tanner laughed and went for her. "Never knew you to cuss."

"Dammit!" she said again.

The dog howled and bailed off the porch. By the time Tanner realized she wasn't cussing, he barely had time to make it to his truck and close the door. He rolled down the window and hollered, "Leah, this was your last chance. No more waiting until Halloween. It's over between us. And you will regret this, believe me, you will."

She whistled for Dammit to stop trying to jump inside the window and the dog returned to sit in front of her. "I hope it's over, Tanner. I really do."

He pulled a phone out of somewhere in the truck and she heard him say, "Do it right now."

Tanner sped away and Rhett parked in the place he'd been. Dammit whined and ran to greet him, tail wagging the whole way.

"What the hell happened? I saw Tanner kissing you and then Dammit chasing him to the truck." Rhett talked as he crossed the yard.

Leah put her head in her hands, dropped to her knees, and let all the frustrations out in a long weeping wail. "I'm so sorry you saw that, Rhett," she sobbed.

He gathered her up in his arms like a baby and carried her to the porch, where he sat down with her, tears wetting the front of his shirt. Poor old Dammit whined and licked her hands and cheek as Rhett rocked from side to side with her in his lap.

"His truck looks the same as your new one, so I thought you'd come home a little early and..." She hiccuped. "I made Dammit wait on the porch because I thought I could take care of it."

He hugged her tighter to his chest with one arm and rubbed her back with the other. "From what I saw, it looked like you gave him something to think about. How're your knuckles?"

She raised her hand and showed him. "If they bruise, it was worth it. I feel violated. I think he planned to kidnap me, but when I hollered at Dammit, he changed his mind."

"From now on, I'll be home in the evenings."

"I think it's over," she said.

He continued to rub her back. "Why?"

"Because he called someone on the phone and said something to them about doing it. He was so mad, and I think whatever is about to happen was the Gallaghers backup plan," she said.

"Think you should call your father?" he asked.

"In a minute. I want to sit right here until I get control of my voice. If Daddy finds out what Tanner did, there'll be blood and the feud will never stop," she answered.

Dammit whined and whipped his head around to the south. His nose shot up and he sniffed several times before he let out a lonesome howl. Leah stuck an arm out from the cocoon that Rhett had her wrapped up in and looped it around his neck.

"It's okay, boy. He's gone and he won't be back. You did good," she said.

"He is not getting away with this," Rhett said.

"Promise me you won't do anything. If we leave it alone and live our own lives right here on Double Shot, it'll quiet down." She wiped the tears from her cheeks.

Dammit sniffed the air again, whimpered, and shook free of Leah's hold. He ambled around to the end of the house, let out a howl, and took off like he was chasing down a coyote or a jackrabbit.

"What's gotten into him?" Leah asked at the same time the smell of smoke hit her nose. "Oh. My. God. They've set fire to our ranch."

Sirens sounded before she could unwind herself from Rhett's embrace and get to her feet. He grabbed her hand and followed Dammit's baying, taking them out to the road, where smoke billowed. The fire trucks were already there, putting out a long line of grass fires running parallel to the ranch fence line when Leah and Rhett arrived.

One of the firemen shouted from the road. "Y'all call this in?"

"No, we had no idea it was on fire. What caused it?" Rhett asked.

"Dry as it's been, could have been a lit cigarette thrown from a car window. Crazy thing is, it's running up and down the road, and the way the wind is blowing, if it had been from a cigarette, it would have traveled right onto your property. You're a lucky man tonight."

"Lucky, my ass," Rhett mumbled. "It was set and… hell's bells, Leah, this is a diversion. Call your dad right now."

"It's after midnight," she said.

"Call him and tell him the Gallaghers are about to do something tonight. Probably a fire since the fire trucks are out of water," he said.

"We got it all wet down. Call us if any hot spots fire back up. Took every drop of our water to put this one out because it was so long," the fireman said.

Leah yelled across the blackened earth. "Thank y'all for getting out here so fast."

"We got the call forty minutes ago."

"Here." Rhett handed Leah his phone. "Call your dad now. I haven't been home forty minutes. They made the call before the fire was even set."

Leah punched in her dad's cell phone, and it went to voice mail after the fifth ring. She didn't bother with a message but hit the numbers again. He picked up on the fourth ring that time.

"Daddy, listen to me. The Gallaghers are about to set fire to something. I don't know what but,.," She went on to tell him what had happened.

"It's probably a threat, but I'll get Declan up, and we'll check things out on this end. Why would they set fire to Rhett's ranch?"

"Because…" She told him what Tanner had done in the restaurant the previous Monday and about him showing up at the ranch that night.

"I'll kill the bastard with my bare hands," Russell said.

"Daddy, please forget that and go check out the ranch. The fire trucks are empty and on their way back to Gainesville," she said.

"I'm up and on my way. I'll call you later if anything is wrong. If I don't call, then you'll know it's okay. And, Leah, honey, thanks for the call."

"It's Rhett's idea. He thinks this fire was a diversion," she said.

"Then tell Rhett thank you."

Rhett took Leah's hand in his and headed back toward the house with Dammit right behind them. They made it to the porch before his phone rang. Leah knew before he even answered it that it was her father and something was burning on River Bend. It was one of those gut feelings that was never wrong, and her insides clinched up into pretzels as she waited to hear what was on fire.

"It's probably Sawyer wanting to know what's going

on over here or Polly if she and Gladys are up late watching television," he said.

Rhett sat down on the porch step and pulled her into his lap before he handed the phone off to her. "It's your father," he said.

"Daddy?" she said.

"It's the hay barn at the back of the property. We've called the fire department, and they said they'd come back to town but their trucks are empty and it's too far from a pond to pump water from it. It's already too far gone for them to do much good. We'll have to stand watch for a couple of days to make sure the hot spots don't fire back up and get carried to another part of the ranch with this wind. They will pay for this," Russell said.

"So Rhett was right. It was a diversion and a means to make sure the fire trucks were empty," Leah said flatly.

"Looks that way. And before you figure it out and go into hysterics, your old barn cat, Ella, put all five of her kittens in the back of my truck. The place was on fire when we got here, so I guess she'd moved them out before that. Want me to bring them over to you after church in the morning? She won't like it, but I can put her and the kittens in the carrier you used to take her to the vet," Russell asked.

"Daddy, I'm so sorry. This is my fault for not playing along with Tanner." She turned to tell Rhett what her father said about the cats and the barn.

Rhett kissed her on the cheek and said, "You don't get to blame yourself for what they did."

"Think Dammit will have trouble with cats?"

"You can bring whatever you want to the ranch and however many kittens you want into the house," he answered. "And Dammit loves cats. He thinks they're his toys."

———

Rhett finally got into bed at three o'clock in the morning, but he was still too wound up to sleep. The adrenaline rush hadn't settled down nearly enough for him to shut his eyes, so he laced his hands behind his head and tried to figure out exactly when he'd fallen in love with Leah.

It must've been the day he rode into town and met her in the store. *But*, he argued, *I do not believe in that love at first sight like my cousin did when he went all crazy in love with his wife*.

The door eased open, and he figured Dammit had pushed his way inside his bedroom so he kept his eyes on the ceiling. Then Leah slipped beneath the covers, and his arm went out to draw her close to his side.

"I can't sleep alone in that bed tonight. It might not be right to come in here like this, but right now I don't care. I want to feel you next to me," she said softly.

"I couldn't sleep either. I should've gone over to River Bend and helped your dad tonight, but I couldn't leave you alone, and I didn't want you to be around a fire that big." He pushed her hair back, tucking it behind her ear so he could see her face better. The moonlight filtering through the window lit up her light green eyes.

"You fit pretty good right here in my arms," he said.

She covered a yawn with her hand. "I like being here."

"Sleepy now?" he asked.

She nodded.

His own eyelids drew heavier and heavier until

finally he couldn't hold them open anymore. When he kissed Leah's lips, she didn't even stir, but one of her legs was suddenly over his and she snuggled down closer.

It was full daylight when he awakened and his first impulse was to jump out of bed, call Sawyer and apologize for not being at Fiddle Creek in time for morning chores, and rush around to get dressed. Then he realized it was Sunday morning. Not only was Sunday his day off but the day before had been his last day to work at Fiddle Creek or at the bar. From now on, he'd be responsible for his ranch seven days a week.

"And those damn Gallaghers best never step one foot on it or they'll find themselves in a war like they've never seen before," he mumbled.

"What?" One of Leah's eyes slid open. "Oh, I remember."

"Good mornin', gorgeous. How did you sleep? I slept like a baby with you by my side," he said.

"Best in a long time," she said. "Let's go back to sleep until noon."

"Oh no," Rhett said. "It's eight o'clock. We're making breakfast and then we're going to church."

"No!" she said.

"Yes, ma'am. Best way in the world to thwart any future crap from either the Gallaghers or from your grandmother is for us to walk right into that church and sit together in the middle section. Maybe we'll put a roast in the oven and invite your dad to have dinner with us when he brings your mama cat to the ranch."

She sat up in bed and wrapped her arms around her knees. "I'd like that, Rhett."

Rhett pulled her back down beside him. "Are you ready for a real kiss?"

"Why would you ask that?"

"Last night you said you felt as if you'd been violated, I don't want to pressure you until you are ready," he said.

She pulled his face down to hers and their lips met in a kiss so full of passion that his heart raced. Her hands slipped beneath the covers and circled his semi-erection, and in minutes he felt as if he couldn't breathe.

"I want you to make love to me. Sweet love without a lot of foreplay," she whispered.

"I believe I can do that," he said.

She rolled over on her back, pulled him on top of her, and guided him inside. They rocked together until they were both panting, and then she dug her fingernails into his back and gasped.

"Oh, oh," she said.

"Yes?" he asked as they reached the peak together.

"Let's skip church and do that all over again."

He smiled and shifted his weight to his elbows as he leaned in to look deeply into her eyes. "We might miss church a few times a year, but this is not one of them. This is the day we declare to the whole town that we are a couple and no one can mess with what we've got."

Chapter 26

Guilt and freedom mixed together produced an antsy feeling in the pit of Leah's insides when she and Rhett walked into the church hand in hand. He tapped Sawyer on the shoulder and the whole bunch of folks on the pew scooted down to make room for them. Jill leaned around Sawyer and smiled at her; Gladys winked and Polly gave her a thumbs-up.

"See, that wasn't so bad, was it?" Rhett whispered.

"Depends on whether the looks from Tanner and my grandmother burn me into nothing but a pile of ashes right here in the church. We should have brought Dammit with us," she answered.

"I'll protect you. If I didn't, Dammit would bite me. That dog loves you." He grinned.

He laid his arm on the back of the pew and patted her upper arm. That simple gesture gave her enough courage to glance over toward the Gallagher side. Tanner was sitting beside a tall brunette that looked at him like she'd already had him for breakfast and was contemplating a second serving of the same for dinner. Leah wondered if the new woman would get the big diamond ring or if he really would return it to the jeweler. Maybe it wasn't even real. Fake diamonds, like fake love, were hard to tell from the real thing.

She turned her head slightly and looked over toward the Brennan side of the church. Honey smiled and made a sign with her thumb and little finger that said to call her. Leah nodded slightly and noticed Kinsey tapping a message into her phone.

"Your phone is vibrating against my hip," Rhett whispered.

Leah dug it out of her purse and scrolled down to read what Kinsey had written: *Insurance will take care of the barn burning but it's your fault.*

She quickly wrote back: *Did she want me to marry Tanner Gallagher?*

She glanced toward Kinsey and got a wink as an answer.

The preacher took his place behind the podium, cleared his throat, and said, "I'm sorry to hear about the Brennans' hay barn burning to the ground last night. I understand there was also a grass fire over at Polly's ranch. Speaking of that, Rhett O'Donnell has bought Double Shot Ranch. He'll be putting permanent roots down here, and we want to welcome him to the town with open arms. My sermon this morning is on love. We're all familiar with the love chapter in Corinthians, but today I want to talk about another love affair. The one between Adam and Eve," he said.

Rhett leaned over and whispered, "Got an apple in your purse?"

Leah bit back a giggle and squeezed his thigh, letting her hand rest there afterward. If lightning bolts didn't come through the ceiling and zap her on the spot for sitting in the neutral section of the church, then touching a hippie cowboy's leg probably wouldn't get her fried into a pile of ashes.

The preacher talked about how that love didn't seek

revenge, but neither the Gallaghers nor the Brennans looked like they were in the forgiving mood that morning. Forgiveness?

Love?

No, sir! The Brennans were figuring out what they could do in retaliation for the barn burning, which was payback for the shit storm on Wild Horse, which was... And the list went backwards for a hundred years. And then the Gallaghers would huddle up and plan their next move.

But you are free from all that, Eve's voice said in her head.

I'll always be a Brennan. DNA and blood are permanent, she argued.

Well, at least you aren't living in the middle of it.

Leah nodded.

"Fighting or agreeing with Eve?" Rhett whispered.

"A little of both," she answered.

The sermon ended with a plea that everyone in Burnt Boot show love toward their neighbors, their friends, their spouses, and even their enemies. Leah figured most of it fell on deaf ears. Quaid gave the benediction, which was short and to the point, then everyone was on their feet and the noise level went from stone-cold quietness to whispered conversations.

"Fire hurt anything on your place last night?" Sawyer asked.

"Didn't get past the fence in most cases," Rhett answered. "Fire trucks got there before it got out of hand. They thought it was caused by a cigarette, but I reckon it was a diversion. One cigarette wouldn't have burned a quarter mile long and twenty feet deep."

"You're probably right." Sawyer nodded. "It had to be long enough to use up all the water in the trucks, right? More feudin'."

"That's what I thought from the beginning."

"You and Leah want to go to dinner with us? We're taking Polly and Gladys out for Italian and a matinee," Sawyer said.

"Thanks, but we've got a roast in the oven, and we're going to invite her dad and maybe Declan over to our place," Rhett said.

"Whew!" Sawyer wiped a hand across his brow dramatically. "You really are diving right into the deep water. Mavis will pitch a bitchin' hissy if he accepts."

"That's her problem."

Honey Brennan wasted no time getting to Leah and giving her a hug. "I might get disowned for this, but I understand you've got a big empty living room where I can throw down my sleeping bag. Do you realize you are the very first from either family to ever sit in the middle section? You've broken the ice for the rest of us."

"I guess I am. I didn't think of that. To tell the truth, I was so nervous this morning that if Rhett hadn't held my hand, I'm not sure I could have faced everyone. Does Granny really blame me for the fire last night?"

Honey's head bobbed up and down. "Oh, yes. It's your rebellion that caused us to lose our school, and I'm not sure, but you might have caused everything for the past year."

"Hey, Honey," Rhett said, "why don't you come have dinner with us? You can lay claim to which corner of the living room you want if you get thrown off River Bend."

"I'm not that brave yet," Honey said.

Betsy looped her arm through Rhett's and leaned against him. "The preacher said we should love our neighbor. I'd like to do that. You name the time and place."

"He also said you should love your enemy," Rhett said.

She backed away quickly. "That ain't happenin'. Not in a million years."

"So do you love Tanner?" Leah asked Rhett.

"Sure I do. I'd love to beat the shit out of him," Rhett said.

Leah slapped a hand over her mouth to keep the giggles from echoing off the church walls. Before she could get control, a little girl tapped her on the arm and she looked down at one of her students—Millie Gallagher.

"Hello. Are you having a good weekend?" Leah asked.

"No, I am not. I'm having a birthday party next weekend, and I want to invite my new friend, Carrie Brennan, and Mama says it ain't happenin'. But the preacher said we should show love to everyone, and I really like Carrie, and she's my new best friend at school."

Leah hugged the child to her side. "I'm so sorry, Millie. But Mama's rules are the law and teacher's rules can't override them."

"Can we have a party in the classroom?" Millie's eyes misted, and she sniffled.

"We'll see what we can do," Leah said. "No promises about a real party, but we will sing to you on your birthday."

"Thank you, Miz Leah." Millie waved at Carrie and skipped across the church to talk to her.

"And so it begins," Rhett said.

"What begins?"

"The end of the feud. It'll be baby steps, but we might see it done and finished in our lifetime," he answered.

"I hope so. There's my dad and Declan. Let's invite them both to dinner," she said. "Hey, Daddy," she called out and waved.

He and Declan stopped and waited for her and Rhett to catch up.

"How much hay did you lose?" Rhett asked when they were closer.

"Whole barn full of hay. Insurance will take care of it at today's market price, but we all know in the winter, when it gets scarce, the price goes up. I'm glad no one got hurt." Russell shook hands with Rhett and then hugged Leah. "Your mama cat is out in my truck in the carrier. She don't like to be penned up, so I reckon we'd best get on out there and transfer her over into your vehicle so you can take her to her new home."

"We'd like for you and Declan to come to Sunday dinner at our place. You'll be our first guests," Leah said.

"Yes," Declan said in a hurry.

"That didn't take long," Leah said.

"Granny is on the warpath. I'm the one who helped you pack and load up, so I'm in trouble too. I'd gladly eat a bologna sandwich in peace instead of listening to her bitch while I'm having turkey and dressing," he explained.

"I'd love to have dinner with y'all. We'll leave the cat and kittens in my truck and take them out when we get over to Rhett's place—seems strange to call it that after all these years of it being Polly's place," Russell said.

"Or to call it Double Shot instead of Polly's Place," Rhett said. "I like the name, so I'm leaving it as is."

"Glad to hear it. Some stuff needs to be changed, but that was the second ranch to get started here back when old man Cleary threw his boots in the fire. He built the general store and settled on Fiddle Creek. Then his brother relocated here and built the bar and named his ranch Double Shot. That was before they even had a post office," Russell said. "I'm going to catch up with Kinsey and tell her what our plans are, so they won't hold dinner for us on River Bend. Declan and I'll see you in a little bit."

"And thanks." Declan smiled.

"This is a special day," Leah said. "It's the first time I can ever remember that my father, my brother, and I will sit down to the table together."

"You don't eat together every Sunday?"

"We eat together as a family every day, but I can't ever remember a time when Granny wasn't there or when it was only the three of us," she said.

"I'll be there, Leah. It won't be just your immediate family."

She smiled up at him. "Darlin', you and Dammit are my family too."

Chapter 27

LEAH LOVED THE SIMPLICITY OF THE DINNER. POT roast with potatoes and carrots, salad, and a loaf of sourdough bread, sliced and toasted in the oven.

"This is taking it back to the basics," Declan said.

Russell wiped his mouth with the paper napkin and said, "Don't you love it? Food is great, Leah."

"Save room for ice cream. We've even got caramel topping and chopped pecans if you want to make it into a sundae."

"I really do love it," Declan said. "You are a lucky dog, Leah."

"Is that a polite way of calling me a bitch?" She grinned.

"No, ma'am. I'm not stupid. Anyone that would buck up against Granny has my respect enough that I'd never call her names."

"Would you look at that?" Rhett pointed to the corner of the kitchen.

They'd brought Leah's mama cat, Ella, into the house to get her acquainted with the place. Now Dammit was lying close enough to the carrier that the kittens were sticking their paws out to touch him. He licked every one that came out the slits in the sides.

"He's getting his scent on them so that Ella will trust him. Smart dog," Russell said.

"You think we could open the door?" Leah asked.

"If you're careful not to let her out for a day or two. She might try to bring a kitten at a time back to River Bend and wind up getting killed on the road," Declan answered.

Leah left the table and pulled the door open. Dammit didn't move, but Ella tiptoed out with her hair fluffed up, a low growl in her throat. She eyed Dammit and laid her ears back like she might be about to claw him into shreds. He wagged his tail and licked her from chin to ears. She sputtered and spewed and then ignored him completely. The kittens tumbled out one after another and attacked Dammit's moving tail, crawling over his body like he was a big throw pillow.

"I think they'll be friends," Rhett said.

Leah had it all—cats, a dog, and a man that she loved.

Whoa! Love was a pretty strong word right there in the middle of all the chaos surrounding her.

That is your grounding wire, Eve said in her head. *All the rest you can take care of a little at a time, but Rhett O'Donnell has been your solid ground since the day you met him. So yes, you love him. When do you plan on letting him know?*

After ice cream and coffee, Rhett really wanted a nap, but country manners said that he should ask Declan and Russell if they'd like a tour of the ranch. "I'm just now figuring out what is going on here. I've been a rancher my whole life, at least when I didn't have big dreams about being a bull rider or a Hell's Angel. But y'all know the land and the climate up here better than I do and I'd appreciate any advice you might give me."

Russell chuckled. "I was going to be a fireman or a science teacher."

"Really?" Leah asked.

"Of course. My first love was science. My second was ranching. But man, those firemen looked cool in all that gear," Russell said

"I wanted to grow up and be an astronaut. My advice is to stay away from the feud and put up lots of hay. And shoot any Gallaghers that set fire to your property," Declan said.

"We'd love to look at the ranch," Russell said. "Can't even remember the last time I was on this place."

"I've never seen the lay of the land," Declan said.

"Well, you cowboys go on and I'll clean up the kitchen," Leah said.

"Paper plates, paper napkins, and disposable cups," Declan laughed.

"That's cleanup around here, I'll stay behind to be sure my cats don't hurt Dammit."

The dog's ears popped up at the sound of his name, and he trotted over to her, five kittens chasing along behind him.

Rhett helped her carry all the paper goods to the trash can. "Dammit will want to go with us. He probably already knows places that I haven't seen. Maybe he'll take us on an adventure."

"Then my cats and I will have a nap," she told him.

Rhett dropped a kiss on her forehead. "Sounds good. If Honey shows up, tell her that Declan is already eye-balling the space in front of the fireplace."

The guys had barely gotten the back door shut when someone pounded on the front door. Dammit had gone with them, and a mama cat and five kittens wouldn't offer much help if it was Tanner again, so she peeked out the curtain.

"Honey?" she said aloud as she swung the door open.

"I got here as fast as I could. Granny is seething that Uncle Russell and Declan are here for dinner. She says that they're taking your side. I swear we may have a civil war in the Brennan family before this is all over. Is that roast I smell? I couldn't eat over there, and I'm starving. Got any leftovers?" She talked the whole way to the kitchen.

"It was a big roast. Get a paper plate out of the cabinet and help yourself." Leah poured two red plastic cups of sweet tea and carried them to the table, being careful not to step on a kitten on the way. "Salad is in a plastic container in the refrigerator. Bread is on the top of the cabinet beside the roast. We had ice cream for dessert."

"Cats in the house?" Honey picked her way to the table with a full plate of food.

"This is not River Bend."

"Enjoy it because if Uncle Russell overrides Granny, you'll probably be living back at River Bend by the end of next week," Honey said.

"Why?"

"You won't be able to afford to live outside of the ranch without a job and the Gallaghers are putting up a big stink with the school board. According to them, a fourth-grade schoolteacher should not be living with a man in sin," Honey said between bites.

"You are kiddin' me." Leah's eyes widened in shock.

Honey shook her head slowly. "Wish I were but I'm not. They've caused such a problem that there's going to be an emergency school board meeting on Thursday next week. Naomi is on the agenda and so is Granny."

"I wonder how much money will change hands between now and then." Leah sighed.

"Uncle Russell won't let you down. He'll let you come back to River Bend if they fire you," Honey said.

"I'm not going back there, Honey. I like it here. Maybe Rosalie will give me a job at the bar at night and I can always pick up substitute work in Gainesville until next year," Leah declared.

"God, I wish I had your nerve and determination," Honey said.

"I wish I'd had it a long time ago," Leah whispered. A picture of her little student, Millie Gallagher, flashed through her mind. If they fired her, it wouldn't be until Friday morning, so that sweet little girl would damn sure have a party on Thursday, complete with cupcakes and party hats and games.

Chapter 28

RHETT FOUND LEAH IN THE UTILITY ROOM SITTING ON the floor with a lap full of sleeping kittens. Her mama cat was in the carrier, purring loudly. Before the scene could, change he took his phone from his pocket and snapped a picture when she looked up.

"I'm sending this to my sister, Katie. She loves cats too." He sat down close enough that their hips touched. "Did you name them yet?"

"Sure I did. That's the fun of kittens. You can name them all kinds of silly names."

"Your mama cat doesn't have a silly name," he said.

Leah laid her head on his shoulder. "Yes, she does. I named her Cinderella because she has gold hair, but she was so wild that her middle name is Deville. Ella is her nickname."

Rhett chuckled. "And do each of those critters have two names?"

"No, they are all boys but one, which is unusual. The girl is Rose." She pointed at the yellow kitten. "The boys are Jack, Jim, and Jameson, and the runt here is Johnny."

He reached out and rubbed each one on the head with his forefinger. "I like it. Think they'll grow up to be outlaws and be known as the Whiskey Kids?"

"You never know what a kid is going to grow up to be," she said.

"Are we still talking about cats?"

"Probably not."

Dammit flopped down beside the carrier and whined. Ella hissed at him once, then went back to purring.

"I believe they'll be friends. No one can resist Dammit's charm, not even a cat," Rhett said.

"He's like you. Not many people can resist your charms either," Leah said. "Daddy and Declan like you."

"Feeling is mutual. We're going to win this Brennan war a relative at a time. Your dad had some good advice to pass on to me about the cattle. We agreed on almost every one that needed to be culled out and replaced with new blood this fall. He even said that he'd give me first chance to buy a couple of new bulls from the River Bend sale in October."

"He must like you, but I don't think six weeks is enough time for Granny to let you set a foot back on River Bend," she said.

"Maybe we need a miracle," Rhett said.

"It would take more than a simple little miracle. Hell would have to freeze over and the angels in heaven would have to be willing to ice skate on it." She sighed.

"Are we still talking about buying two new bulls?"

She shook her head.

"What's on your mind, Leah?" Rhett cocked his head to one side to see her face better.

"They've called a special school board meeting, Rhett. The Gallaghers want me fired for living with you," she blurted out.

His first thought was that he was going to beat the hell out of Tanner Gallagher. The egotistical fool had begged for it, and Rhett had kept his temper on ice, but this was going too far. It might not help matters, but it would damn sure make Rhett feel better.

The next thought was far more rational and would probably produce more results than a black eye and busted knuckles. They'd take a lawyer with them to the school board meeting and threaten to file a suit against the Gallaghers. That might back Naomi up a step or two.

"Who's on the school board?" he asked.

"Not Gallaghers or Brennans because it's an elected position and the next election isn't until spring. But the Gallaghers have deep pockets. Think about it—they already donated enough to the church to pay a youth director's salary for three years."

He tipped her chin up with his knuckles and traced her lips with his forefinger. By the slight shiver, he could tell that merely a touch affected her as much as it did him. Her tongue flicked out and moistened her lips and her eyelids fluttered shut. When his lips claimed hers, there was no more thought about ranches, school board meetings, or even the kittens.

He broke the kiss and together they gave Ella back her babies while Dammit watched protectively. Then Rhett stood up and extended a hand. She put hers in it and he scooped her up with one arm under her legs and the other around her shoulders. Her head, resting on his chest, felt so right that he could not imagine life without her.

In his bedroom, he shut the door with his boot heel, laid her down gently on his bed, and stretched out beside her. She rolled toward him and wrapped her arms around his neck, tangling her fingers in his hair and bringing his lips back to hers.

"Nothing outside this room matters when I'm in your arms," she whispered between hot and heavy kisses.

"I know," he said as he slowly untied the strings of her sundress and trailed kisses down the curve of her bare shoulder, her arm, and to each fingertip. "We're in our own world where no one else is allowed entrance."

Her phone rang but she ignored it. "Not even telephones."

"What telephone?" He grinned.

Her body was familiar, but every time he touched her, it was a brand-new experience, one that dug deeper into his heart and hollowed out a place for more memories and more emotions. Leah had damn sure brought out a side that he'd never realized he had.

The sex was utterly fantastic like always. She'd completely lost herself in it, and the afterglow was as spectacular as it had always been. In that moment, she realized that Rhett completed her soul. When she couldn't breathe for panting and sweat covered her whole body, when her pulse was still thumping against her wrist with such force that she feared it would blow a gasket any minute, she looked up to find Rhett staring down at her.

At the same time, without a moment's hesitation, they both said, "I love you," in perfect unison. She pulled his face to hers in the sweetest yet most passionate kiss they'd ever shared.

"When did you figure this out?" he asked.

"I think I always knew, but it took a while for me to admit it, even to myself," she answered.

"Me too. I fell in love with you in the store that first day."

"Now what?" she asked.

"Now we lie here and be in love for the rest of the afternoon," he said. "This is our last free Sunday. Next week, Double Shot will belong to me, and I'll have to work seven days a week until I get on my feet to hire someone." He rolled over on his back and took her hand in his, bringing it to his lips to kiss the palm before he tucked it inside his.

"I might have to apply for that job," she said.

"You like to teach better than you like to plow and fix fence, right?"

"I love teaching, Rhett, but I can do anything on a ranch."

"You should do what you love to do. That's what makes a person a success, whether he's a ditchdigger or a bull rider. The way I see it, you've got three choices. You can move out of here so you aren't living in sin, and get your own place somewhere else. I'm sure that Jill will let you have a room at Fiddle Creek until you can find something else. Or you can go back to River Bend. I have no doubt your dad will stand up to Mavis and will give you a place to live, but your granny will treat you like shit because she won't."

She propped up on an elbow and with the other hand, brushed a strand of his dark hair from his forehead. "I don't like either of those options. Tell me the third one."

"Marry me and then we won't be living in sin. They won't have a leg to stand on and you will keep your job," he said.

"Rhett, we've known each other less than a month," she said.

"My heart has known you my whole life, Leah Brennan. I've been waiting for you to show up in person," he answered. "You don't have to answer me right now, darlin'. We've got until Thursday."

"I love you. I trust you. The answer is yes, I will marry you. But, Rhett, that gives us four days to plan a wedding."

"What all do you need? A dress, a bouquet, and what else?"

"A wedding band and a marriage license," she answered.

"I'll get the license, the ring, and the bouquet. You can get the dress and meet me at the courthouse one evening this week."

"How about Thursday, right after school?" she asked.

"And then we'll attend the school board meeting together, right?" he asked.

"You are reading my mind, Rhett O'Donnell."

Chapter 29

Leah appreciated the cool air in Rhett's truck when he picked her up in front of the school that afternoon. "It still smells like a new truck," she said.

"Dammit's been doing his best to give it some dog aroma by riding inside when I let him. You ready to do this?"

"I am ready. Courthouse first?"

"Yes, I called and the judge is there," he said.

"I've been thinking about that Rhett. I want to be married in the church, not in a courthouse. I called our preacher, and he said he could do the ceremony right after school on Thursday, but we'd have to bring two witnesses."

"I think we can find a couple of those, don't you?"

"I believe so. Gladys and Polly?"

"And Verdie."

"We only need two, but Verdie would have her feelings hurt, wouldn't she? So how do we get them to the church?"

"Tell them we want to talk to them about the school board meeting."

Rhett drove with one hand and held her hand with the other one. "I had a plan and it's working out."

"And that is?"

"I didn't want to get married until I owned a ranch of my own, and tomorrow, it becomes officially mine."

"I didn't want to get married until I found my soul mate," she said.

"Well, that was the center of my plan the whole time, and I did. Want to go to the church on the cycle on Thursday?"

"I'd love to." She smiled.

On Tuesday night, Leah came into the house looking like the last rose of summer that a puppy had hoisted his leg on. She tossed her tote bag on one of the chairs in the living room and melted into a kitchen chair. "I graded all the papers before I left school so I would calm down and not absolutely come in here bitchin'," she said.

Rhett left the kitchen where he'd been cooking supper and massaged her shoulders. "You muscles are so knotted up. Come into the bedroom, stretch out on the bed, and let me work on those shoulders."

"Yes, sir. I will gladly obey. This has been the day from hell. Millie cried and Carrie cried, and that made all the other little girls weepy eyed most of the day. The Brennan girls can't go to the Gallagher party, and they were so dramatic about it that we should put them on a reality show."

"Clothing off except for underwear and then lie on your stomach," he said.

She stripped out of a flowing gauze skirt in vibrant colors and a lime green knit shirt so fast that it was a blur. When she was lying facedown, he kicked off his boots and started to work on her toes first.

"Is that all that got you twisted up?" he asked.

"Oh, no. That's barely the tip of the iceberg.

Damian Gallagher doubled up his fist and threatened Lester Brennan, and believe me, that started a war as big as the shit war and the pig war combined. Brennan boys and Gallagher boys took sides and started one of those ultimate fight things right there in my classroom. I'd pull one off and tell him to go stand beside the bookcase, and before I could man-handle another one, the first one would already be back in the battle."

Rhett chuckled as he moved up to her calves. "I'd like to have seen that one. My advice would have been to let them fight until they got tired and then punish the whole lot of them."

"Oh, I punished them. Every one of them that were in the fight has to write one hundred sentences before class tomorrow. I imagine the Gallaghers and the Brennans both will bring that to the school board to add to my sin charges."

Rhett brushed her hair away from her neck and blew on it to cool her down.

"God Almighty, Rhett. That is heating me up from the core, making me think about sex."

He kissed her between the shoulder blades and unfastened her bra. "And that takes your mind off everything, right?"

"But I'm not through bitchin'," she said.

"Bitch away, sweetheart," he said.

"The sentence they have to write a hundred times is: I will not punch another child in the face, no matter what the reason, ever again at the Burnt Boot Public School, and I will talk to my teacher when I am angry instead of hitting another kid."

"Good grief." He laughed. "That's a paragraph, not a sentence."

"I tried to get more words into it but I was too mad to think," she said.

"Is that all that happened?"

She sighed. "Wanda called me into her office to tell me about the school board meeting. She says that of the five members, three have been approached by the Gallaghers. I didn't tell her we were solving the problem ourselves. I want Betsy Gallagher to be totally surprised."

"The end?" he asked.

"Oh, no. We're only about halfway through the iceberg. My mama sent me a message. She said that she heard I'd moved off River Bend, and when I was ready to talk, she'd meet me somewhere."

His thumbs worked the knots from her shoulders and neck as he thought about that for a few seconds. "And how do you feel about that?"

"I want to talk to her. I really do, and I will, but not this week—maybe not even next week. This week, I'm planning a birthday party for Millie at school on Thursday and then I'm going straight to the church to put on my pretty dress and marry my soul mate. After that, I'll talk to my mama."

"Whatever you decide, I'll support you, Leah." He stopped massaging and took a T-shirt from one of his dresser drawers. "Supper is ready. Put this on and we'll eat."

"A man who cooks and massages. I'm one lucky woman."

"Not as lucky as I am to have found you," he said.

—*∿∿*—

Thursday lasted three days past eternity. The boys turned in their papers with all their sentences, along with a few notes from Brennan parents saying that this was excessive punishment for fighting. The Gallaghers notes were much more colorful and promised that she'd be fired at the end of the year for picking on their children.

There is nothing like cupcakes and juice packs to make a kid forget all about fighting and punishments, and Millie beamed when everyone in the classroom sang happy birthday to her. Carrie stood beside her and sang the loudest of anyone, which gave Leah a ray of hope that someday the feud would end.

The minute the last bell rang and the last child was out of her classroom, she pulled the blinds in her classroom and locked the door. She peeled out of her slacks, removed her shirt, set her blond ponytail loose, and reapplied makeup. Then she pulled the white eyelet dress from the box under her desk and stepped into it.

She'd always thought she'd get married at River Bend and come down the big staircase on her father's arm. But in that dream, she hadn't felt the excitement that she did right then. Today, in less than an hour she was going to marry Rhett O'Donnell. She would no longer be a Brennan, and tomorrow she could tell the kids to call her Mrs. O'Donnell instead of Miz Leah. She pulled on a pair of new, white cowboy boots with lace insets and tucked all of her other things into the box, leaving it under her desk.

He picked her up at the school on the cycle, and that day he wore a white pearl-snap shirt, a string tie, and

black jeans that hugged his body like a glove. His ponytail had been set free, and he smelled like pure heaven.
Whatever that shaving lotion was, it was intoxicating
as hell.

"You look gorgeous," he said.

"You look sexy," she whispered.

"Oh, honey, this old cowboy could never be as sexy
as you are." He bent to kiss her, but she turned away.

"Not until the preacher says it's okay for you to kiss
the bride." She grinned.

"Then it had better be a short ceremony." He handed
her a bouquet of mimosa, baby's breath, and greenery
tied up with a sage-green ribbon. "The ribbon is the
color of your eyes."

"You are a romantic," she said.

"Only with you."

"We've got about twenty minutes to get this done and
get to the school board meeting," Gladys called from the
front pew.

"Yes, ma'am." Rhett crooked his arm and Leah put
hers though it. Polly played the traditional music on
the church piano as they strolled up the aisle together
toward the pulpit.

"Dearly beloved, we are gathered here this fine
September day to join Leah Christina Brennan and Rhett
Jonathan O'Donnell in holy matrimony." The preacher's
voice echoed off the walls of the nearly empty church.

Leah handed her bouquet to Gladys and slipped both
of her hands into Rhett's. His touch gave her the courage
to take the leap of faith even though they'd only known
each other a few weeks. "I love you," she mouthed.

"I love you," he mouthed back.

Ten minutes later, the preacher finished the ceremony with a prayer and then said, "Rhett, you may
kiss your bride."

He bent her backwards in a true Hollywood kiss that
made her knees go weak. As he was lifting her up, she
got a little vision of what life would be like with him and
every single moment was wonderful.

"And now, I believe we all have a school board meeting to attend," Polly said.

Gladys shook her head. "Not until all three of us sign
that paper. Then we'll go to the meeting."

Leah rode on the back of the motorcycle back to
the school, dress hiked up to her knees, hair blowing behind her, and the bouquet in her hands that
were wrapped around Rhett's chest. A few sprigs of
baby's breath blew past her arm, but she only wanted
a small piece of mimosa to press as a keepsake, so
that didn't matter.

He parked, helped her dismount, and waited for her
to choose the prettiest bit of mimosa. Then he snipped
a bit of the ribbon away with his pocketknife for her to
tuck away in the saddlebag.

"I'm going to throw this right at Honey," she explained.

"Too bad I don't have a garter to toss." He smiled.

She jerked her dress's hem up, and there was a blue
satin garter up high on her thigh. "I had to have something
blue. Take it off and throw it, but not toward Tanner."

Rhett kissed her on the thigh as he pulled the garter
down and over her boot.

The dull sound of lots of people talking at once filled
the cafeteria, but everything went totally quiet when
Leah and Rhett made their entrance. If a dust bunny had

scooted across the floor, it would have sounded like a mountain lion plodding across a tin roof.

"You ready for this part?" Rhett asked.

"I'm ready to get it over with and go home to Double Shot to be your wife for the rest of our lives."

The president of the school board tapped a gavel on the wooden table. "The meeting is called to order and the first thing on the agenda is a petition from the Gallaghers to have Leah Brennan removed from the classroom because she is cohabiting with Rhett O'Donnell. Naomi, you may have three minutes to state your cause."

The preacher maneuvered his way through the people and laid the marriage license out in front of the five-member school board panel sitting at the front of the room. "Excuse me, sir. I'm not on the agenda, but I do have pertinent information that may have a bearing on this part of the school board meeting."

"Is this what I think it is?" the president asked.

"It is a marriage license stating that Leah and Rhett are married. I have the three witnesses who signed it right here with me, and I'm the one who performed the ceremony," he said.

"Well then, I believe that satisfies this school board and settles the issue. That's all we were going to discuss at this emergency meeting so I declare the meeting adjourned," he said.

"We will have this annulled tomorrow morning!" Mavis yelled across the room at Leah.

"I don't think so, Granny. You don't have the power or enough money to do that," Leah answered. "Hey, Honey, catch this." She threw the bouquet right at her cousin, but it went over her head and landed in Betsy Gallagher's lap.

"Some eligible bachelor needs to catch this!" Rhett yelled.

He popped the garter out across the room and it hung on Declan Brennan's ear.

"Well, how about that?" Leah said.

"I'm not even sure God could make that come true." Gladys giggled.

Rhett carried Leah over the threshold with Dammit right behind them. "Welcome home, Mrs. O'Donnell. I do like the way that rolls off my tongue."

"Tastes like a double shot of Jack, doesn't it?" She smiled.

"Better. Much better. Supper awaits in our room, with the door shut to the dog and the cats," he said.

"Dessert first or after?"

"Your choice." He grinned. "Now wouldn't it be something if we sealed your brother's fate with Betsy Gallagher's, since they caught the garter belt and bouquet?"

"I'll shoot him before I let him get tangled up with that hussy. Now carry me on into the bedroom. I'm thinking I want dessert first."

"Yes, ma'am," he said.

Read on for a peek at *What Happens in Texas* (previously released as *The Blue-Ribbon Jalapeño Society Jubilee*), coming soon in mass market format

IF PRISSY PARNELL HADN'T MARRIED BUSTER JONES AND left Cadillac, Texas, for Pasadena, California, Marty wouldn't have gotten the speeding ticket. It was all Prissy's damn fault that Marty was in such a hurry to get to the Blue-Ribbon Jalapeño Society monthly meeting that night, so Prissy ought to have to shell out the almost two hundred dollars for that ticket.

They were already passing around the crystal bowl to take up the voting ballots when Marty slung open the door to Violet Prescott's sunroom and yelled, "Don't count 'em without my vote."

Twenty faces turned to look at her and not a one of them, not even her twin sister, Cathy, was smiling. Hell's bells, who had done pissed on their cucumber sandwiches before she got there, anyway? A person didn't drop dead from lack of punctuality, did they?

One wall of the sunroom was glass and looked out over lush green lawns and flower gardens. The other three were covered with shadowboxes housing the blue ribbons that the members had won at the Texas State Fair for their jalapeño pepper entries. More than forty shadowboxes all reminding the members of their history and their responsibility for the upcoming year.

"It appears that Martha has decided to grace us with

her presence once again when it is time to vote for someone to take our dear Prissy's place in the Blue-Ribbon Jalapeño Society. We really should amend our charter to state that a member has to attend more than one meeting every two years. You could appreciate the fact that we did amend it once to include you in the membership with your sister, who, by the way, has a spotless attendance record," Violet said.

Violet, the queen of the club, as most of the members called it, was up near eighty years old, built like SpongeBob SquarePants, and had stovepipe jet-black hair right out of the bottle. Few people had the balls or the nerve to cross her, and those who did were put on her shit list right under Martha, a.k.a. Marty, Andrews's name, which was always on the top.

Marty hated it when people called her Martha. It sounded like an old woman's name. What was her mother thinking anyway when she looked down at two little identical twin baby daughters and named them after her mother and aunt—Martha and Catherine? Thank God she'd at least shortened their names to Marty and Cathy.

Marty shrugged, and Violet snorted. Hell, if they wanted to write forty amendments to the charter, Marty would still do only the bare necessities to keep her in voting standing. She hadn't even wanted to be in the damned club and had only done it because if she didn't, then Cathy couldn't.

Marty slid into a seat beside her sister and held up her ballot.

Beulah had the bowl in hand and was ready to hand it off to Violet to read off the votes. But she passed it to the lady on the other side of her and it went back around the circle to Marty, who tossed in her folded piece of paper. If she'd done her homework and gotten the numbers right, that one vote should swing the favor for Anna Ruth to be the new member of the club. She didn't like Anna Ruth, especially since she'd broken up her best friend's marriage. But hey, Marty had made a deathbed promise to her mamma, and that carried more weight than the name of a hussy on a piece of paper.

The bowl went back to Violet and she put it in her lap like the coveted jeweled crown of a reigning queen. "Our amended charter states that only twenty-one women can belong to the Blue-Ribbon Jalapeño Society at any one time, and the only time we vote a new member in is when someone moves or dies. Since Prissy Parnell got married this past week and moved away from Grayson County, we are open for one new member. The four names on the ballet are: Agnes Flynn, Trixie Matthews, Anna Ruth Williams, and Gloria Rawlings."

Even though it wasn't in the fine print, everyone knew that when attending a meeting, the members should dress for the occasion, which meant panty hose and heels. Marty could feel nineteen pairs of eyes on her. It would have been twenty, but Violet was busy fishing the first ballot from the fancy bowl.

Marty threw one long leg over the other and let the bright red three-inch high-heeled shoe dangle on her toe. They could frown all they wanted. She was wearing a dress, even if it only reached midthigh, and had black spandex leggings under it. If they wanted her to wear panty hose, they'd better put a second amendment on that charter and make it in big print.

God Almighty, but she'd be glad when her great-aunt died and she could quit the club. But it looked like Agnes was going to last forever, which was no surprise. God sure didn't want her in heaven, and the devil wouldn't have her in hell.

"One vote for Agnes," Violet said aloud.

Beulah marked that down on the minutes and waited.

Violet enjoyed her role as president of the club and took her own sweet time with each ballot. Too bad she hadn't dropped dead or at least moved to California so Cathy could be president. Marty would bet her sister would get those votes counted a hell of a lot faster.

There was one piece of paper in the candy dish when Beulah held up a hand. "We've got six each for Agnes, Trixie, Anna Ruth, and two for Gloria. Unless this last vote is for Agnes, Trixie, or Anna Ruth, we have a tie, and we'll have to have a runoff election."

"Shit!" Marty mumbled.

Cathy shot her a dirty look.

"Anna Ruth," Violet said and let out a whoosh of air.

A smile tickled the corner of Marty's mouth.

Saved, by damn!

Agnes was saved from prison.

Violet was saved from attending her own funeral.

The speeding ticket was worth every penny.

Trixie poked the black button beside the nursing home door and kicked yellow and orange leaves away as she reached for the handle. She heard the familiar click as the lock let go and then heard someone yell her name.

"Hey, Trixie. Don't shut it. We are here," Cathy called out.

Trixie waved at her two best friends: Cathy and Marty Andrews. Attitude and hair color kept them from being identical. They were five feet ten inches tall and slim built, but Cathy kept blond highlights in her brown hair and Marty's was natural. In attitude, they were as different as vanilla and chocolate. Cathy was the sweet twin who loved everyone and had trouble speaking her mind. Marty was the extrovert who called the shots like she saw them. Cathy was engaged, and Marty said there were too many cowboys she hadn't taken to bed to get herself tied down to one man.

Marty threw an arm around Trixie's shoulder as they marched down the wide hall. Trixie's mother, Janie Matthews, had checked herself into the nursing home four years before when her Alzheimer's had gotten so bad that she didn't know Trixie one day. Trixie had tried to talk her mother into living with her, but Janie was lucid enough to declare that she couldn't live alone and her daughter had to work.

"Congratulations, darlin', you did not make it into the club tonight. Your life has been spared until someone dies or moves away and Cathy nominates you again," Marty said.

"Well, praise the Lord," Trixie said.

"I know. Let's string Cathy up by her toenails and force-feed her fried potatoes until her wedding dress won't fit for even putting your name in the pot." Marty laughed.

"Trixie would be a wonderful addition to the club. She wouldn't let Violet run her around like a windup toy. That's why I keep nominating her every chance

I get," Cathy said. "Anna Ruth is going to be a brand new puppet in Violet's hands. Every bit as bad as Gloria would have been."

Trixie stopped so fast that Marty's hand slipped off her shoulder. "Anna Ruth?"

"Sorry." Cathy shrugged. "I'm surprised that she won and she only did by one vote."

Trixie did a head wiggle. "Don't the world turn around? My mamma wasn't fit for the club because she had me out of wedlock. And now Anna Ruth is living with my husband without a marriage certificate and she gets inducted. If she has a baby before they marry, do they have a big divorce ceremony and kick her out?"

"I never thought she'd get it," Cathy said. "I don't know how in the world I'm going to put up with her in club, knowing that she's the one that broke up your marriage."

Trixie paled. "Who's going to tell Agnes that she didn't get it again? Lord, she's going to be an old bear all week."

"That's Beulah's job. She nominated her. I'm just damn glad I have a class tonight. Maybe the storm will be over before I get home," Marty said.

Cathy smiled weakly. "And I've got dinner with Ethan back at Violet's in an hour."

"I'm not even turning on the lights when I get home. Maybe she'll think I've died." Trixie started walking again.

"You okay with the Anna Ruth thing?" Marty asked.

Trixie nodded. "Can't think of a better thing to happen to y'all's club."

"It's not my club," Marty said. "I'm just there so Cathy can be in it. I'm not sure Violet would let her

precious son marry a woman who wasn't in the al-
damn-mighty Blue-Ribbon Jalapeño Society. I still can't
believe that Violet is okay with her precious son marrying one of the Andrews twins."

Cathy pointed a long slender finger at her sister. "Don't
you start with me! And I'm not the feisty twin. You are. I
can't see Violet letting Ethan marry you for sure."

"Touchy, are we? Well, darlin' sister, I wouldn't
have that man, mostly because I'd have to put up with
Violet." Marty giggled.

"Shhh, no fighting. It'll upset Mamma." Trixie
rapped gently on the frame of the open door and poked
her head inside a room. "Anyone at home?"

Janie Matthews clapped her hands and her eyes lit up.
She and Trixie were mirror images of each other – short,
slim built, light brown hair, milk-chocolate-colored eyes,
and delicate features. Trixie wore her hair in a chin-length
bob, and Janie's was long, braided, and wrapped around
her head in a crown. Other than that and a few wrinkles
around Janie's eyes, they looked more like sisters than
mother and daughter.

"Why, Clawdy Burton, you've come to visit. Sit down,
darlin', and let's talk. You aren't still mad at me, are you?"

Marty crossed the room and sat down beside Janie
on the bed, leaving the two chairs in the room for Cathy
and Trixie. It wasn't the first time Janie had mistaken
her for Claudia, the twins' mother, or the first time that
she'd remembered Claudia by her maiden name, either.

"I brought some friends," Marty said.

"Any friend of Clawdy's is a friend of mine. Come
right in here. You look familiar. Did you go to school
with me and Clawdy?" Janie looked right at her daughter.

"I did," Trixie said.

Janie's brow furrowed. "I can't put a name with your face."

"I'm Trixie."

Janie shook her head. "Sorry, honey, I don't remember you. And you?" She looked into Cathy's eyes.

"She's my sister, Cathy, remember?" Marty asked.

"Well, ain't that funny. I never knew Clawdy to have a sister. You must be older than we are, but I can see the resemblance."

"Yes, ma'am, I didn't know you as well as"—Cathy paused—"my little sister did, but I remember coming to your house."

"Did Mamma make fried chicken for you?"

"Oh, honey, I've eaten fried chicken more than once at your house," Cathy said.

"Good. Mamma makes the best fried chicken in the whole world. She and Clawdy's mamma know how to do it just right. Now, Clawdy, tell me you aren't mad at me. I made a mistake runnin' off with Rusty like that, but we can be friends now, can't we?"

Marty patted her on the arm. "You know I could never stay mad at you."

"I'm just so glad you got my letter and came to visit." Janie looked at Trixie and drew her eyes down. "You look just like a girl I used to know. It's right there on the edge of my mind, but I've got this remembering disease. That's why I'm in here, so they can help me." She turned her attention back to Marty. "You really aren't mad at me anymore?"

"Of course not. You were in love with Rusty or you wouldn't have run off with him," Marty said.

They had this conversation often so she knew exactly what to say.

"I did love him, but he found someone new, so I had to bring my baby girl and come on back home. How are your girls?" She jumped at least five years from thinking she and Claudia were in school to the time when they were new mothers.

"They're fine. Let's talk about you," Marty said.

Janie yawned. "Clawdy, darlin', I'm so sorry, but I can't keep my eyes open anymore."

It was always the same. On Wednesday nights, Trixie visited with Janie. Sometimes, when they had time between closing the café and their other Wednesday evening plans, Marty and Cathy went with her. And always after fifteen or twenty minutes, on a good night, she was sleepy.

"That's okay, Janie. We'll come see you again soon," Marty said.

Trixie stopped at the doorway and waved.

Janie frowned. "I'm sorry I can't remember you. You remind me of someone I knew a long time ago, but I can't recall your name. Were you the Jalapeño Jubilee queen this year? Maybe that's where I saw you."

"No, ma'am. They don't crown queens anymore. But it's okay. I remember you real well," Trixie said.

Less than half an hour later, Trixie parked beside a big two-story house sitting on the corner of Main and Fourth in Cadillac, Texas. The sign outside the house said *Miss Clawdy's Café* in fancy lettering. Above it were the words: *Red Beans and Turnip Greens*.

It had started as a joke after Cathy and Marty's mamma, Claudia, died and the three of them were going through her recipes. They'd actually been searching for "the secret," but evidently Claudia took it to the grave with her.

More than forty years ago, Grayson County and Fannin County women were having a heated argument over who could grow the hottest jalapeños in North Texas. Idalou Thomas, over in Fannin County, had won the contest for her jalapeño corn bread and her jalapeño pepper jelly so many years that most people dropped plumb out of the running. But that year, Claudia's mamma decided to try a little something different, and she watered her pepper plants with the water she used to rinse out her unmentionables. That was the very year that Fannin County lost their title in all of the jalapeño categories to Grayson County at the Texas State Fair. They brought home a blue ribbon in every category that had anything to do with growing or cooking with jalapeño peppers. That was also the year that Violet Prescott and several other women formed the Blue-Ribbon Jalapeño Society. The next fall, they held their First Annual Blue-Ribbon Jalapeño Society Jubilee in Cadillac, Texas.

The Jubilee got bigger and bigger with each passing year. They added vendors and a kiddy carnival with rides and a Ferris wheel, and people started marking it on their calendar a year in advance. It was talked about all year, and folks planned their vacation time around the Jalapeño Jubilee. Idalou died right after the first Jubilee, and folks in Fannin County almost brought murder charges against Claudia's mamma for breaking poor old

Idalou's heart. Decades went by before Claudia figured out how her mother grew such red-hot peppers, and when her mamma passed, she carried on the tradition.

But she never did write down the secret for fear that one of the Fannin County women would find a way to steal it. The one thing she did was dry a good supply of seeds from the last crop of jalapeños just in case she died that year. It wasn't likely that Fannin County would be getting the blue ribbon back as long as one of her daughters grew peppers from the original stock and saved seeds back each year.

"If we had a lick of sense, we'd all quit our jobs and put a café in this big old barn of a house," Cathy had said.

"Count me in," Marty had agreed.

Then they found the old LP albums in Claudia's bedroom, and Cathy had picked up an Elvis record and put it on the turntable. When she set the needle down, "Lawdy, Miss Clawdy" had played.

"Daddy called her that, remember? He'd come in from working all day and holler for Miss Clawdy to come give him a kiss," Marty had said.

Trixie had said, "That's the name of y'all's café—Miss Clawdy's Café. It can be a place where you fix up this buffet bar of southern food for lunch. Like fried chicken, fried catfish, breaded and fried pork chops, and always have beans and greens on it seasoned up with lots of bacon drippings. You know, like your mamma always cooked. Then you can serve her pecan cobbler, peach cobbler, and maybe her black forest cake for dessert."

"You are making me hungry right now just talkin' about beans and greens. I can't remember the last time I had that kind of food," Marty had said.

Trixie went on, "I bet there's lots of folks around here who can't remember when they had it either with the fast-food trend. Folks would come from miles and miles to get at a buffet where they could eat all they wanted of good old southern fried and seasoned food. And you can frame up a bunch of those old LP covers and use them to decorate the walls. It would make a mint, I swear it would."

That started the idea that blossomed into a café on the ground floor of the big two-story house. The front door opened into the foyer where they set up a counter with a cash register. To the left was the bigger dining area, which had been the living room. To the right was the smaller one, which had been the dining room. What had been their mother's sitting room now seated sixteen people and was used for special lunch reservations. Their dad's office was now a storage pantry for supplies.

Six months later and a week before Miss Clawdy's Café had its grand opening, Trixie caught Andy cheating on her, and she quit her job at the bank to join the partnership. That was a year ago, and even though it was a lot of work, the café really was making money hand over fist.

"Hey, good lookin'," a deep voice said from the shadows when she stepped up on the back porch.

"I didn't know if you'd wait or not," Trixie said.

Andy ran the back of his hand down her jawline. "It's Wednesday, darlin'. Until it turns into Thursday, I would wait. Besides, it's a pleasant night. Be a fine night for the high school football game on Friday."

Trixie was still pissed at Andy and still had dreams about strangling Anna Ruth, but sex was sex, and she was just paying Anna Ruth back. She opened the back door, and together they crossed the kitchen. He followed her up the stairs to the second floor, where there were three bedrooms and a single bathroom. She opened her bedroom door, and once he was inside, she slammed it shut and wrapped her arms around his neck.

"I miss you," he said

She unbuttoned his shirt and walked him backward to the bed. "You should have thought about that."

"What if I break it off with Anna Ruth?"

"We've had this conversation before." Trixie flipped a couple of switches, and those fancy no-fire candles were suddenly burning beside the bed.

He pulled her close and kissed her. "You are still beautiful."

She pushed him back on the bed. "You are still a lyin', cheatin' son-of-a-bitch."

He sat up and peeled out of his clothes. "Why do you go to bed with me if I'm that bad?"

"Because I like sex."

"I wish you liked housework," Andy mumbled.

"If I had, we might not be divorced. If my messy room offends you, then put your britches back on and go home to Anna Ruth and her sterile house," Trixie said.

"Shut up and kiss me." He grinned.

She shucked out of her jeans and T-shirt and jumped on the bed with him. They'd barely gotten into the fore-play when a hard knock on the bedroom door stopped the process as quickly as if someone had thrown a pitcher of icy water into the bed with them. Trixie grabbed for the sheet and covered her naked body; Andy strategically put a pillow in his lap.

"I thought they were all out like usual," he whispered. "If that's Marty, we are both dead."

"Maybe they called off her class for tonight," Trixie said.

"Cadillac police. Open this door right now, or I'm coming in shooting."

Trixie groaned. "Agnes?"

Andy groaned and fell back on the pillows. "Dear God!"

And that's when flashing red, white, and blue lights and the mixed wails of police cars, sirens, and an ambulance all screeched to a halt in front of Miss Clawdy's.

Trixie grabbed her old blue chenille robe from the back of a rocking chair and belted it around her waist. "Agnes, is that you?"

"It's the Cadillac police, I tell you, and I'll come in there shooting if that man who's molesting you doesn't let you go right this minute." Agnes tried to deepen her voice, but there was just so much a seventy-eight-year-old woman could do. She sounded like a prepubescent boy with laryngitis.

"I'm coming right out. Don't shoot."

She eased out the door, and sure enough, there was Agnes, standing in the hallway with a sawed-off shotgun trained on Trixie's belly button.

The old girl had donned her late husband's pleated trousers and a white shirt and smelled like a mothball factory. Her dyed red hair, worn in a ratted hairdo reminiscent of the sixties, was crammed up under a fedora.

Trixie shut her bedroom door behind her and blocked it as best she could. "There's no one in my bedroom, Agnes. Let's go downstairs and have a late-night snack. I think there are hot rolls left and half of a peach cobbler."

"The hell there ain't nobody in there! I saw the bastard. Stand to one side, and I'll blow his ass to hell." Agnes raised the shotgun.

"You were seeing me do my exercises before I went to bed."

Agnes narrowed her eyes and shook her head. "He's in there. I can smell him." She sniffed the air. "Where is the sorry son of a bitch? I could see him in there throwing you on the bed and having his way with you. Sorry bastard, he won't get away. Woman ain't safe in her own house."

Trixie moved closer to her. "Look at me, Agnes. I'm not hurt. It was just shadows, and what you smell is mothballs. Shit, woman, where'd you get that getup, anyway?"

Agnes shook her head. "He told you to say that or he'd kill you. He don't scare me." She raised the barrel of the gun and pulled the trigger. The kickback knocked her square on her butt on the floor, and the gun went scooting down the hallway.

"Next one is for you, buster," she yelled as plaster, insulation, and paint chips rained down upon her and Trixie.

Trixie grabbed both ears. "God Almighty, Agnes!"

"Bet that showed him who is boss around here, and if you don't quit usin' them damn cussin' words, takin' God's name in vain, I might aim the gun at you next time. And I don't have to tell a smart-ass like you where I got my getup, but I was tryin' to save your sorry ass so I dressed up like a detective," Agnes said.

Trixie grabbed Agnes's arm, pulled her up, and kept her moving toward the stairs. "Well, you look more like a homeless bum."

Agnes pulled free and stood her ground, arms crossed

over her chest, the smell of mothballs filling up the whole landing area.

"We've got to get out of here in a hurry," Trixie tried to whisper, but it came out more like a squeal.

"He said he'd kill you, didn't he?" Agnes finally let herself be led away. "I knew it, but I betcha I scared the shit out of him. He'll be crawling out the window and the police will catch him."

They met four policemen, guns drawn, serious expressions etched into their faces, in the kitchen. Every gun shot up and pointed straight at Agnes and Trixie.

Trixie threw up her hands, but Agnes just glared at them.

"Jack, it's me and Agnes. This is just a big misunderstanding."

Living right next door to the Andrewses' house his whole life, Jack Landry had tagged along with Trixie, Marty, and Cathy their whole growing-up years. He lowered his gun and raised an eyebrow.

"Nothing going on upstairs, I assure you," Trixie said, and she wasn't lying. Agnes had put a stop to what was about to happen for damn sure.

Trixie hoped the old girl had an asthma attack from the mothballs as payment for ruining her Wednesday night.

"We heard a gunshot," Jack said.

"That would be my shotgun. It's up there on the floor. Knocked me right on my ass. I forgot that it had a kick. Loud sumbitch messed up my hearing," Agnes hollered and reached up to touch her kinky red hair. "I lost my hat when I fell down. I've got to go get it."

Trixie saw the hat come floating down the stairs and

tackled it on the bottom step. "Here it is You dropped it while we were running away."

Agnes screamed at her. "You lied! You said we had to get away from him before he killed us, and I ran down the stairs, and I'm liable to have a heart attack, and it's your fault. I told Cathy and Marty not to bring the likes of you in this house. It's an abomination, I tell you. Divorced woman like you hasn't got no business in the house with a couple of maiden ladies."

"Miz Agnes, one of my officers will help you across the street." Jack pushed a button on his radio and said, "False alarm at Miss Clawdy's."

A young officer was instantly at Agnes's side.

Agnes eyed the fresh-faced fellow. "You lay a hand on me, and I'll go back up there and get my gun. I know what you rascals have on your mind all the time, and you ain't goin' to skinny up next to me. I can still go get my gun. I got more shells right here in my britches' pockets"

"Yes, ma'am. I mean, no, ma'am. I'm just going to make sure you get across the street and into your house safely," he said.

Trixie could hear the laughter behind his tone, but not a damn bit of it was funny. Andy was upstairs. The kitchen was full of men who worked for him, and if Cathy and Marty heard there were problems at Clawdy's, they could come rushing in at any time.

"Maiden ladies my ass," Trixie mumbled. "I'm only thirty-four."

———∿∿∿———

Darla Jean had finished evening prayers and was on her way back down the hallway from the sanctuary to her apartment. Her tiny one-bedroom apartment was located in the back of the old convenience store and gas station combination. Set on the corner lot facing Main Street, it had served the area well until the super Walmart went in up in Sherman. Five years before when business got too bad to stay open, her uncle shut the doors. Then he died and left her the property at a time when she was ready to retire from her "escort" business. She had been worrying about what to listen to: her heart or her brain. The heart said she should give up her previous lifestyle and start to preach like her mamma wanted her to do back when she was just a teenager. Her brain said that she'd made a good living in the "escort" business and she would be a damn fine madam.

The gas station didn't look much like a brothel, but she could see lots of possibilities for a church. It seemed like an omen, so she turned it into the Christian Nondenominational Church and started preaching the word of God. Straight across from the church was Miss Clawdy's Café.

She hadn't even made it to her apartment door when the noisy sirens sounded like they were driving right through the doors of her church sanctuary. She stopped and said a quick prayer in case it was the Rapture and God had decided to send Jesus back to Earth with all the fanfare of police cars and flashing lights. The Good Book didn't say just how he'd return, and Darla Jean had an open mind about it. If he could be born in a stable the first time around, then he could return in a blaze of flashing red, white, and blue lights the second time.

She pulled back the miniblinds in her living room. The police were across the street at Miss Clawdy's. At least Jesus wasn't coming to whisk her away that night. There was only one car in the parking lot, like most Wednesday nights, and she knew who drove that car. Hopefully, the hullabaloo over there was because Trixie had finally taken her advice and thrown the man out.

God didn't take too kindly to a woman screwing around with another woman's man. Not even if the woman had been married to him and the "other woman" wasn't married to him yet. Maybe it was a good thing that Jesus wasn't riding in a patrol car that night. She'd hate for her friend Trixie to be one of those left behind folks.

"Got to be a Bible verse somewhere to support that. Maybe I could find something in David's history of many wives that would help me get through to her," she muttered as she hurried out a side door and across Fourth Street toward the café.

"Holy Mother of Jesus, has Marty come home early and caught Andy over there and murdered him?" Darla Jean mumbled.

Had the cops arrived in all the noisy fanfare to take her away in handcuffs?

Then she saw a policeman leading Agnes across the street. So it hadn't been Marty but Agnes who'd done the killing. That meant Trixie was dead. Agnes had never liked her, and she'd threatened to kill her on more than one occasion. Lord, have mercy! The twins were going to faint when they found out.

About the Author

Carolyn Brown is a *New York Times* and *USA Today* bestselling author with more than seventy books published. Her bestselling cowboy romance series include the Lucky trilogy, the Honky Tonk series, Spikes & Spurs, Cowboys & Brides, and the new Burnt Boot, Texas, series. She launched into women's fiction with a Texas twang. Born in Texas and raised in southern Oklahoma, Carolyn and her husband make their home in the town of Davis, Oklahoma, where she credits her eclectic family for her humor and writing ideas.